WRETCHED

A LAST HERO NOVEL

CARA CRESCENT

CRESCENT BOOKS, LLC

For Gabriel
Who announced at the ripe old age of 7 that he *must've* gotten
switched with another child at the hospital when he was born
because he couldn't *possibly* belong with the rest of us (he *so* does).
And who, every time I'm ready to wring his neck, somehow makes
me laugh instead. You are a constant reminder to me that a person
can accomplish many wonderful things while still having fun.
Thank you for making me laugh. Love you, dude.

—·—

1

2268 AD
Royal Palace, Grand Helo Province, Troon
Antlia Wall, Hydra Supercluster
406 light years from Earth

Their captors were returning.

Somewhere down the hall, keys clattered against steel bars, echoing through the corridor outside their cell. Donovan Reese winced as the old, rusty hinges on the exterior gate screamed.

"Don't show any weakness."

Donovan groaned, turning his head to glare at Macie. His big, badass business partner had spouted that bit of wisdom from where he lay in a broken heap on the floor next to him.

If it wouldn't have hurt so much, Donovan would've laughed in his face.

Macie stared back through blackened, swollen eyes. Blood matted his blond hair and his lip was split in two places. The rest of him looked worse. He was, as they used to say in the Air Force, FUBAR—fucked up beyond all recognition. The vladsets had gone easy on Macie.

"Are you trying to tell me I need to get off my ass?"

Donovan wasn't particularly keen on moving. The floor of their cell might be hard and dirty, but the rough stone acted like a makeshift icepack against his swollen, overheated body.

Macie half-chuckled, half-moaned. "Come on. I'll help you up, if you help me."

Donovan snorted, rolled to his side, and pushed himself to his left hand and right knee, pausing to give his protesting muscles time to adjust. "You figure out what they want yet?"

The echoes of booted feet in the corridor grew louder. Closer. The vladsets were coming.

Macie shook his head. "Don't recognize the dialect. I'm catching bits and pieces. This last go-round, one of them referred to what they've been doing to us as hazing trials."

"Yeah? Back on Earth it's called torture."

Donovan put the heel of his swollen hand on the wall and leveraged himself to his feet. When he put weight on his left leg, pain shot through his knee, fierce and instantaneous. Neither of them could take much more vladset hospitality.

Macie coughed, turned his face away, and spit a bloody wad on the floor. "I caught something about proving we're strong enough to protect their treasure."

Donovan snorted. "Yeah, well, I don't want their fucking treasure."

"Don't tell them that. Take whatever they want to give you with humble gratitude. Don't let them see weakness."

The steady thud of boots grew louder. His heart picked up pace, doing double time to the tempo.

"Come on, Professor." Donovan held out his hand and hauled Macie upright. "Anything broken?"

Macie smoothed his leather vest and patted the dust from his jeans. "My nose. Couple ribs, I think. You?"

"Hand. Something's wrong with my knee."

He winced as he straightened. Maybe some bruised ribs, too. He glanced at his bare chest and, sure enough, he sported a dark purple blotch on his ribcage under his right arm. The first thing they'd done to him was strip him down to his skivvies to inspect him. Why the hell Macie got to keep his clothes, he didn't understand, but the vladsets had made one thing clear—their interest lay with him. The chief.

Macie touched his jaw and grunted. "At least they left your face alone."

"Probably figured I was ugly enough." People tended to avoid looking at his face due to a plethora of deep, webbed scars cutting across the left side and bisecting his eye.

"Sorry 'bout this." Macie sighed and the hardcore badass deflated right out of him. "Seems like I'm always getting you in shit."

Yeah, Macie had been heaping trouble on their collective shoulders for the last three years. He was hell bent on running from whatever demons were chasing him and his risky behavior had damned near gotten them killed on more than one occasion.

Donovan shook his head. "Don't start. I'll kick your ass later." *If we live.* "For now, don't think about it." It was his own damned fault those demons were chasing Macie in the first place. Least he could do was weather the resulting shit storm with some degree of grace. Besides, it might all be over for them both soon.

It'd been a bad month. They'd traveled into the Hydra Supercluster on a bounty-hunting mission. It was a two-week trip using both lightspeed and a series of wormholes, so to make the most out of the trip, they'd scheduled-in some cargo stops to pick up goods for the folks back home. And while they had picked up all the cargo, they'd had no luck hunting. Oh, they'd found their marks. Problem was, they were dead by the time they'd located them. The cargo would bring in some money, but without the bounty fees . . . .

Damn it, they needed that money.

They'd been headed home when Macie caught sight of another mark's ship. He'd followed Jerrod Williams straight into a restricted sector deep in the Antlia Cluster. A bad idea. Obviously.

When the vladsets' ship had overtaken their freighter, he'd assumed they were done for. The vladsets didn't tolerate other species in their sector. But, instead of killing them, they'd brought them to their home planet, Troon, and so far, seemed much more interested in beating them than ending them.

As the heavy footsteps neared, they both took a deep, bracing breath and donned an air of false bravado that bordered on annoyed impatience. Macie folded his thick, tattooed arms over his chest, which must have hurt like hell if he had broken ribs. Donovan braced his hands on his hips, struggling to ignore the shooting pain that ran from his busted hand to his elbow.

He instilled as much venom as he could muster into his tone when the vladsets came into view. "What the fuck do you want now?"

The guards stood well over seven feet tall, and while humanoid, their bluish-gray hides and overstated musculature made them seem unaccountably alien. Boney, black spikes ran up their spines and across their shoulders. Their bald heads gleamed in the dim light and their eyes blazed a deep red. They all, even the females, had muscular, robust bodies, and their physique wasn't just for show. He and Macie had the bruises and broken bones to prove it.

The guards had someone new with them. This vladset was slimmer, his face lined with deep wrinkles. "I'm Quimet, Queen Vessa's chamberlain."

Donovan narrowed his eyes. This vladset spoke Standard. None of the others had. And chamberlain? He glanced at Macie, who widened his eyes, tipped his head to the side, and blew out his cheeks.

In other words, this Quimet asshole had some clout.

"You'll give me the answers I seek." Quimet's lips pressed together, giving the impression he didn't appreciate having to lower himself to speak with humans.

"You'll tell me if you've ever mistreated a female."

Vladsets didn't seem to *ask* much of anything, they stated everything as "You will," never "Will you?"

They both answered, "No."

Briefly, dismissively, Quimet's red gaze flicked to Macie. "You'll tell me, *Chief*, if you are mated."

Donovan's stomach bottomed out. This line of questioning couldn't go anywhere good. He wasn't mated. Wasn't married. Didn't want to be. "No."

"You'll tell me if you function properly."

He glanced at Macie. "What is he asking?"

The corner of Macie's lips lifted. "He wants to know if your pecker works."

Oh, hell, no. "Look, I'm not fucking—"

Macie spoke over him, "Seemed to work fine at our last stop. The ladies certainly didn't complain."

Donovan glared at Macie for the outright lie. His face had gotten rearranged when the U.N. fragged Luke Air Force Base back on Earth. He'd survived because he'd been out near the front security checkpoint in body armor. Well, everything but his helmet. Since then, he avoided women like the plague—the last thing he needed was a pity fuck.

Macie turned his back on the vladsets and leaned toward Donovan. "Trying to keep us alive here."

"Chief, you'll wear this." Quimet set a small device no larger than a hearing aid on the rail between the bars.

A translator. Where had they gotten that? Vladsets were sanctioned from possessing off-planet tech. Donovan picked it up and tucked the device into his ear.

"Bring the chief." Quimet strode away.

"You." The guard pointed to Donovan. "Present your wrists. And you." He pointed at Macie. "Against the back wall." Though they spoke in Vladnese, the device in his ear translated their words to Standard.

Macie backed to the far wall, his swollen features pinched with worry. Donovan faced the bars and stuck his hands through a small opening to be cuffed. He wasn't sure he'd survive another round in the arena. There wasn't anywhere on his body that didn't ache.

A shudder wracked through him as the curved metal tightened over his broken wrist. He was still schooling his features when the door opened. They hustled him out of the cell and down the corridor, half dragging him when his bad knee refused to hold his weight.

So far, the guards had only taken him in the other direction—toward the arena—where vladset warriors watched him fight in unarmed challenges with other warriors. While he was glad to be going in the opposite direction from that hell, he hated not knowing where they were taking him or what might happen to Macie during his absence.

Most of the cells they passed were empty, but toward the end of the hall, there was one encased in glass, as well as bars. A lone figure huddled toward the back of the cell, everything but long white hair ensconced in shadows. A human?

One of the guards shoved him. "Keep moving."

The vladsets towered over him, and that said something. Earthers considered both him and Macie pretty damn big at six-five and six-six.

Here, he was a shrimp.

At the end of the hall, the guards shoved him toward a staircase. Everything was monster-sized, even the stairs. Each one was the size of two on Earth. He led with his good leg, leaning his shoulder against the wall, dragging the bad leg behind him. By the time they reached the top, sweat covered his brow, his legs shook, and he was breathing like an overheated coyote which hurt like hell because the muscles around his ribs seized if he tried to breathe too deeply.

The guards pushed open the door at the top, the rusty hinges whining. He entered the open-air palace, a frigid breeze lifting gooseflesh on his bare skin.

Ostentatious as palaces on Earth, everything here was decorated in bright reds, oranges, and yellows—colors of passion and strength to the vladsets. Richly appointed, over-sized furniture lined the hallway. Everything had rounded edges, even the walls. Murals of bloody battles and kings and queens past sprawled over the curved walls and ceilings.

"Where are we going?"

A guard shoved him forward. "Keep walking, whelp."

They maneuvered him into a domed room large enough to land a small ship inside. The walls and ceiling glittered as if painted in gold and their boots echoed off the polished red floors. A few scantily clad females lounged on backless couches, tittering behind their hands. Donovan dismissed them, zeroing in on the raised dais that dominated the room.

Quimet stood next to a vladset woman sitting on a throne. She rose to her feet, staring at Donovan. Like the other females, she was barely covered. The gown—if one could call it that—was little more than two bands of inch-wide red cloth stretched from shoulders, over the center of each of her voluptuous breasts, to converge at the v between her legs. The only thing fully covered was her ass—a long piece of golden material gathered at the bands crossing the small of her back trailed behind her down to the floor. She'd left the rest of her body on full display, leaving only the color of her nipples and pubic hair to the imagination. A crown rode low on her shiny, bald head and her deep red eyes held not a trace of warmth despite their fiery hue. She must be Vessa, the vladset Queen.

Hell, he'd never been known for his diplomacy. He wished Macie was here to tell him what was expected.

She waved them forward. "Bring the chief."

The guards jerked him into motion, forcing weight on his bad knee. He stumbled, struggled, and broke free. "I can walk on my own, goddamn you." If the guards kept manhandling him, he'd end up flat on his face and she'd see that as a sign of weakness. Game over.

Donovan growled as the guard reached for him again. "You'll be pulling back a stump, Stretch."

"Let him approach." The queen beckoned him forward.

One small battle won. He limped to the dais, wishing his hands were free. Wishing he wasn't half-naked. Each step sent bolts of agony shooting up his leg, but he did his best to keep his expression blank. He couldn't keep up this whole I'm-a-badass-who-feels-no-pain façade much longer. He stopped at the base of the stairs, putting all his weight on his good leg, and glared at the queen.

One of the guards kicked the back of his knees. He dropped to the floor. Pain shot up his leg as his kneecap slammed into the marble. *Fuck.* He took some slow, shallow breaths until he quit seeing stars, blinked the moisture from his eyes, and composed himself before turning his glare back on the queen.

She harrumphed. "I'm told you are a great chief among your people."

More of Macie's bullshit. He had been a Chief Master Sergeant in the US Air Force, back when there *had* been an Air Force. Back when there had been a United States. Then, after the UN had taken over as a global governing body, he'd become a Chief Master Sergeant in the rebellion against them.

Nowadays, he was pretty much nothing.

"I've also been told you survived full Trial Hazings."

Survived? Barely. The vladset warriors he'd been forced to fight were bigger and far more muscular than him. Hell, he'd admit it: He'd been fighting for his life; they'd been toying with him.

He cocked his brow. "I'm here, right?"

"You don't look like much." She approached, waving her arm up.

The guards pulled him to his feet and he moved his weight to his good leg.

The bands of her outfit shifted, each step threatening views of far more than he wanted to see. This woman might be beautiful by vladset standards, but he'd never be able to see beyond her cruelty.

"You'll tell me if all your people are so scrawny and pale."

He bared his teeth. "Even little dogs can have a big bite."

The corner of her full lips kicked up. "I've seen enough. Bring Celeka and the shaman." The queen sauntered around him, eyeballing him from top to bottom. She paused at his front and cupped his underwhelmed cock in her hand. Her gaze shot to Quimet. "You said he's functioning."

Quimet strode forward. "He is."

Her red eyes flared brighter. "I can't have any accusations of conspiracy."

"Of course not, my queen."

"He's not reacting to me."

Donovan grinned. "Don't see anything I like."

Retribution was quick—she back-handed him, sending him halfway across the chamber—and was quite efficient in shutting him up.

The air slammed out of his lungs. His skin burned from skidding across the polished floor. Everything hurt. He tried to inhale, but the angry muscles around his wounded ribs spasmed. *Shallow breaths. Breathe slow.*

And no more stupid remarks.

The guards had him on his feet and back in front of the dais before the room stopped spinning. He blinked, trying to bring everything back into focus.

The queen returned to her throne and sat, her gaze full of malice. She said something . . . nothing translated.

He shook his head. Lifted his cuffed hands to his ear. "Lost the translator."

She stood. Shouted to the guards, who ran back and searched the floor for the device. The shorter of the two held it up and shook his head.

Must've broke.

"I'll speak Standard."

His eyes widened. Vladsets weren't even part of the Intergalactic Alliance, the IgA. Both Earth and Troon had applied for membership at the same time, but while Earth had become the IgA's 242nd planetary member, Troon, due to its warring and pillaging, had been put on probation. There were over three-hundred cumulative planets that made up the IgA now, but Troon was *still* on probation. He hadn't expected any of them to speak Standard.

"I've decided to give you a great gift, Chief. The IgA will see my generosity and good will."

Ah. Things were beginning to make sense. "If you want to impress the IgA, then keep your people from scamming and scaring everyone who tries to interact with your people."

Her lips pressed together. "This is how it has always been. We had no problems with the IgA until you Earthers showed up. You'll accept my gift."

"My second-in-command and my ship would be a great gift. Just show us to the air-pad and we'll be off."

"You'll mate my daughter."

His heart stalled in his chest while Macie's advice echoed in his mind. *Accept whatever they want to give you with humble gratitude.*

Well, shit. The last thing he wanted was a wife. Especially a vladset wife.

Why the hell would she want to give him her daughter? The disdain vladsets showed for humans was overwhelming and not only was he human, he was *scarred*. Why didn't she marry her precious daughter to a vladset chief?

"I don't see how this will get you back in IgA's good graces. Forced arrangements between races is forbidden."

"I don't force." Her forehead furrowed. "You have a choice: mate her or die."

Fucking vladsets. No wonder they had such a bad rep.

Quimet leaned toward Vessa. "Celeka has arrived."

She stood, edging behind Quimet, a flash of something like fear crossing her features. "Translate for us."

The whole thing was very subtle, if he hadn't been watching, he would've missed her reaction to her own daughter and thought she'd stepped back to give Quimet the floor. This bitch feared this Celeka woman and he was supposed to marry her?

It wasn't just her, either. The guards on either side of the dais moved back. The females tittering in the corner fled.

With visions of towering, bald, muscular women with vicious tempers dancing in his head, he turned and blanched.

Celeka—if that's who this was—stood much shorter than the guards, the top of her head lower than their bared pecs. Hell, she might even be shorter than him. She wore thick black bands that wrapped her from head to toe and every square inch between. Not even her eyes were bared and, for good measure, a stiff black veil fell to her waist, obstructing the shape of her head and torso.

Holy hell. That wasn't normal. He'd been all over the known worlds, seen many an alien species, and *nowhere* was *that* normal.

Was she diseased? Malformed? Vladsets weren't exactly a demure bunch. They walked around half-naked despite the freezing temperatures, yet Celeka didn't show a speck of skin. Why? What was under all that black cloth that even the Amazon-queen-bitch feared?

Celeka came and stood next to Donovan. Something moved under her veil.

What the hell?

A closer look revealed a small creature hiding under there. It almost looked like a mouse-sized monkey. For the most part, the thing's black fur blended with her clothing, but the light-gray fur surrounding its bright yellow eyes gave it a perpetually surprised expression.

The top of Celeka's head barely reached Donovan's shoulders and considering her size, her slender frame, and her tiny pet, he had the sinking suspicion they wanted him to mate a youth.

"I'm not mating a child. Doing so goes against the laws of my planet." Not to mention the universal laws of decency.

Vessa brushed off his concern. "She's full grown. She's . . . ." She waved her hand. "What do you say . . .?"

"A runt, my Queen." Quimet descended the stairs and stood next to Celeka. He seemed to be the only one not afraid of her. "Your maman and queen found a chief willing to mate you."

The way he softened his voice gave the impression again, that the being under the black wraps was young . . . or simple.

Celeka's head swiveled to the side and tipped back. Despite the cloth obstructing her face, her cool regard made him shiver.

He shifted his weight, heart racing in his chest. This was something straight out of some grim tale of horror—*The Shrouded Bride*, they'd call it. A cautionary tale of interspecies mating where the husband is eaten alive by his terrible mate. "Why are you dressed like that?"

Her head snapped back to regard her mother, but she spoke to Quimet. "Maman hasn't been truthful with this chief." Her voice was mature, with a husky lilt, putting his fears about her age to rest. She folded her hands in front of her, squeezing them together while Quimet repeated her accusation.

When Vessa said she wanted a translator, he'd assumed Celeka didn't speak Standard. But she did.

Vessa frowned. "We'll lay it out, then."

Quimet was still repeating her comment to Celeka as the queen continued. "My daughter shames me. She is disgusting, deformed." Her voice echoed in the throne room.

Donovan stared. Vladsets were a harsh bunch, but *damn*.

"I cannot degrade our chieftains by asking them to take her to mate. But you will. You'll mate her and honor her as befitting her station, or you'll die." Quimet echoed every harsh word to Celeka as if the poor female hadn't heard every bit of venom in her mother's voice. The queen's attention settled on Quimet. "If Celeka doesn't obey my dictates, if she disgraces me further, I'll hunt her down and kill her—all of her—myself."

All of her? What the hell did that mean?

Despite his fear of what the black cloth hid, his protective instincts rose. He knew how it felt, being despised for the way he looked. After being scarred, his fiancée had refused to look at him. Couldn't even be in the same room long enough to tell him she didn't want him anymore. Her father had given him the humiliating news.

"Don't speak to her like that." His voice echoed in the sudden silence.

Everyone turned to stare. Even Celeka. They were all speechless. Truth be told, he'd stunned himself a little. He didn't want a bride, but he refused to leave this woman here with her abusive mother.

Celeka turned to Quimet. "Tell the chief—"

For Christ's sake, he'd had enough of this. "If you want to say something to me, speak to *me*."

She turned to Quimet, to the queen, and when she got no comment from either, faced him. Her husky voice dropped to the barest of whispers. "Thank you, my Chief."

Those must've been magic words because everything became a blur. The shaman conducted a brief ceremony spoken in Vladnese for the benefit of the clans watching via vid-screen. The whole thing was over and done in a matter of ten minutes and he was certain the only thing he'd remember tomorrow was how her tiny pet had scampered around his bride's throat, shooting stink-eye at the queen. There was no exchange of rings, no signing of papers, and no kiss—not that he was certain he could find her lips under all that black cloth. Occasionally, Quimet would say, "The chief will say yes now" and that was the extent of Donovan's participation in his own wedding.

Celeka didn't engage in the activities much more than he had and, with every glare from her mother, her shoulders sagged until he was sure his bride had shrunk a full inch.

He wasn't happy about this, but he was relieved Celeka wouldn't remain here. No one should be humiliated and scorned in their own home, especially by family.

Once the ceremony finished, Celeka turned to Quimet. "I'll gather my belongings."

Quimet was still repeating Celeka's statement when Vessa's swift reply interrupted him. "She'll take nothing. Her chief may take his man, his ship, and his supplies. Celeka will only take the clothes on her back."

The black-shrouded figure went still except for the tremors putting a shimmy in her veil and he had an urge to pull her into his arms.

Vessa wasn't finished. "She'll leave the creature."

Celeka whipped around, a rush of Vladnese pouring out of her, but Quimet came and removed the creature from her shoulder just the same.

Vessa's gaze bore into Donovan's. "You'll leave now or you'll not leave at all."

He hesitated the barest of seconds. As banged up as he was, he didn't stand a chance in hell of fighting all these guards to get the creature back nor to confront the bitch for her mistreatment of her daughter. He grabbed hold of Celeka and backed from the room.

"Come on, you won't have to put up with her shit anymore." He put his arm over his bride's narrow shoulders and they turned to leave. "We'll find you a new—"

The creature screamed. A sickening crack echoed in the sudden silence.

Donovan froze. Celeka emitted a low moan. A shudder ran through her.

The fucking bitch had killed her pet.

Don't show weakness.

"Don't cry," he whispered. "Not until we're out of here." His grip tightened on her shoulders as his heart slammed out a panicked warning against his ribs. They had to get out of here before everything went tits up. He set them in motion again, increasing his pace, leaning on her to help support his bad knee. "We have to get Macie. He's down in the prison."

She sniffed. "He'll be in your ship. This way." She guided him through a side door leading onto an airpad.

Frigid air rolled over them, increasing the shaking that had already taken hold of him. Macie waved from the cockpit of the *Red Slag* and fired up the engines. All the way across the airpad, Donovan searched the area for a threat. Would the vladsets shoot them in the back? Would they blow the ship as they climbed aboard?

The airpad remained deserted. There was no movement at all. Just the tips of massive, snow-capped trees swaying in the wind around the raised airpad.

They hurried up the cargo ramp and the hatch closed, ensconcing him and Macie inside with Celeka.

He couldn't let it go. The vladsets never freed their captives. So why had they allowed them to leave? Why had Queen Vessa been so desperate to get rid of her daughter?

He shot a sidelong glance at his new wife.

Hell, what if the threat he was searching for was hidden under all those wraps?

— · —

2

One problem solved.

Vessa handed the dead creature to the nearest guard. Usually, destroying something protected by another signaled war. Unfortunately, she couldn't war with the chief or her daughter. Not directly. Not yet. Instead, she'd killed the pet as a warning. If Celeka didn't behave, her sister would be next.

Years ago, she'd exiled Celeka to Erra—one of Troon's icy, barren, inhospitable moons. Living there among Troon's exiled should have broken Celeka's spirit. Living on the frigid moon should have weakened her flame. Vessa had expected Celeka to be thankful when she'd finally brought her home. Grateful to be given tasks and a purpose.

Instead, the girl questioned everything. Challenged her at every turn. It was only a matter of time before Celeka realized her own power and challenged her for the throne.

Many a time she'd considered killing Celeka, but some of the clans revered her and her sister. Those wretched girls were the only reason those clans didn't revolt and oust her from her throne. The dynamics kept her in an awkward position. The very beings she loathed were the only things keeping her from exile herself.

She let her lips curve into a smile. No longer, though. She didn't need the girls. With both of them married off, she could take her consort to mate and turn her attention to conceiving a true vladset heir—one way or another. And once she went public with her discovery, the clans would give her their full support and she'd go down in history as an untouchable queen.

Her discovery of sempisim would make Troon a sought-after trading partner in the galaxy. The locals of the planet Senna, the world where she discovered the sempisim, used the metal for building everything: houses, vehicles, jewelry, and weapons. The metal was soft and pliable when mined but became hard as diamond after being exposed to intense heat. That alone was valuable. There had been rumors, though. Rumors about it exploding under certain circumstances. She'd known at once that having possession of such a resource would give Troon unequivocal power within the known systems.

Which brought her to the second problem.

"Bring me Jerrod Williams."

The guards left to do her bidding.

She'd demanded a meeting with Larkin Astor, the CEO of Earth. Instead, he'd sent a common lackey, Jerrod Williams. One who was far too brazen for his own good. The fool had led Chief Reese straight to Troon; it was her warriors who'd rescued him from that capture, yet he'd done nothing but threaten and make demands since. Such behavior had to be discouraged so she'd thrown him to the guards, and after spending a week with them for company, he should be a much more malleable opponent. Which was good. She still needed help from the Earther corporation CorTech.

She'd tried to discover the secret of the sempisim, to duplicate the circumstances to make the mineral explode, but had been unsuccessful. Frustrated, she'd put out a call on the black market, looking for scientists to assist. CorTech, a research and development corporation on Earth, had answered that call. Their partnership was the perfect solution.

At first. Until they'd overstepped.

A cacophony preceded Jerrod Williams into the throne room. The human male stumbled in ahead of two smirking guards, wailing like a newborn whelp. The skin around his eyes was blackened and swollen and he favored his left side.

She wrinkled her nose. These humans were frail with their thin skin, they even bled beneath their flesh. They were almost as disgusting as Celeka.

"I'll report you to the IgA for your mistreatment." Williams struggled to his feet. "This goes against all alliance rules."

Vessa wanted to scoff, but this weak male could bring the full wrath of the IgA down on her. Not because he was powerful, but because the IgA seemed to take great pride in singling her out for punishment.

Then again, dead men couldn't tell tales.

First, she needed to see if he had any power to right the wrongs CorTech had committed.

"Did you hear me?"

His tone set her teeth on edge. What right did he have to speak to her that way? CorTech was in the wrong, not her.

"Keeping me here against my will breaks the terms of an IgA alliance—"

"So does breaking the terms of an interplanetary business contract." CorTech was stealing her discovery. Her guards had seen their freighters sneaking past her planet to reach Senna. They were mining her product behind her back. Traitors.

Not that she expected the IgA to side with her. "The terms specified that I would pay CorTech an outrageous fee and they'd discover all possible uses for the sempisim. Nowhere does that contract suggest their people have any ownership of my discovery." However, once they discovered they could weaponize the sempisim, the humans had decided to take their chances.

He stopped as if just realizing his peril. The guards shoved him forward. "I don't know what you're talking about. I came in good faith. Mr. Astor said you were demanding an audience."

Typical of a human, trying to brazen through his dishonor instead of addressing his crimes directly. "Yes, and CorTech vowed confidentiality. CorTech vowed no competition. No stealing or selling of my product. Larkin Astor must bring CorTech to heel."

He swallowed so hard, the wet gulp carried halfway across the room. His expression turned cagey. He glanced around as if seeking the exits. The guards wouldn't allow him more than a step or two in any direction.

"Had your employees not been stealing—"

He held up his hands. "They're not *my* employees."

"—the sempisim would still be secret. The IgA wouldn't have started an investigation."

"That bastard." He pulled at the neck opening of his shirt. "He knew, right? He sent me here because he knew you'd found out."

"The IgA has issued bounties worth tens of thousands of credits on most of the pilots and scientists CorTech sent me." According to the contracts, the IgA wanted those men and women alive to question them. If that happened, the IgA would know exactly how many sanctions she'd overstepped in the last few months. They'd take her discovery of the planet Senna as their own. They'd take the sempisim. They'd put more sanctions on her world. Her people would rebel. She'd lose everything.

His eyes widened. "It's you, isn't it?" He retreated a step. "You're the one killing CorTech employees."

As if she would allow them to live. They'd tell the IgA everything to save their own skin, which would put her in an uncomfortable position—her clans would never understand why she risked everything to partner with the humans, nor why she broke the IgA's sanctions. "I told you before, if you betrayed me, I'd destroy you and everything you hold dear."

"Not me. I wasn't part of those negotiations, Larkin Astor was." He wet his lips. "There was a ship following me—two guys, Reese and Macie. Are they still here? Can I talk to them?"

She bared her teeth. "From the data I discovered on their ship, they were following *you*, trying to capture *you* so they could question you about the marks on their contracts. They suspect CorTech's involvement. If they can punish Astor, that means they're more powerful than your CEO." She nodded. "I married my daughter to the chief, therefore, he can't touch me, but he will fight twice as hard against you."

With a tribal alliance firmly in place, the chief was honor-bound to attack anyone who opposed her. "If you're a smart man, you'll advise the CEO of Earth to force CorTech to return the sempisim and provide me with the frequencies now."

His lips parted and his head tipped to the side. "The CEO of Earth?"

"Your boss, Larkin Astor."

His brows furrowed. "The CEO of . . . ." he sputtered. Huffed. "Look, you and me, we've both been played. How 'bout I help you out by giving you a lesson in Earth history and you help me out by letting me live? I just need my Saph-link. I can show you pictures. It'll help you understand."

She turned her narrowed gaze on Quimet.

"My Queen, due to the sanctions, there are no satellites nearby which he would need to send messages."

She smirked. No, they didn't have satellites—they were too easy for the IgA inspectors to spot, but they had other, less obvious ways to communicate with their ships off-planet. Quimet had told her what she needed to know, though—Williams couldn't use their technology.

Williams shook his head. "No. No messages. I have data downloaded to the device, that's all. Please."

"Guards! Return his device and leave the room." She waited until they obeyed. As all good leaders knew, knowledge was power and she didn't like to share. She sat on her throne and crossed her legs. "I make no promises. If the information you provide is worth your life, I'll spare you. If it is not . . . ." She lifted her shoulder.

Williams unfolded the Saph-link, flipping each edge open until it resembled four rectangles held together by the one in the center. "Show Earth."

A hologram of a blue-and-white world appeared above the device. Earth. So far, he wasn't showing her anything new. "Larkin Astor rules this world."

"In his dreams," Williams scoffed. "He rules CorTech and those who work for him, nothing more."

"Show me."

"Let's start five years ago."

She didn't need history. "I want to know what's happening now. Who's in charge? Who can help me?"

"It'll help give you a fuller picture."

"Fine."

He held the device to his mouth. "Show map of nations from five years ago." The globe turned, showing bright-colored splotches on the landmasses. "Up until five years ago, there were two-hundred and two nations, each with its own leader."

She stilled. There weren't even that many clans on her planet. Her gaze shifted to the colorful orb. Perhaps Earth was larger than it appeared.

"We also had an organization called the United Nations. They were kind of like the IgA, only instead of mediating and assuring the balance of power between planets, they did the same for the nations."

Her lips pressed together. "I assume the United Nations, like the IgA, didn't allow *all* nations to participate."

He shrugged. "Yeah, well, they had to follow the rules if they wanted in."

She scoffed. Rules always benefited one over another.

"Anyway, all the nations were fighting. Our populations had grown too much. Our resources were depleted. Each nation thought themselves, and their people, more important than the others. We were all just fighting to survive, but it made things worse. Too many bodies. Too much disease. Too much money spent on wars with no end in sight. The nations were bankrupt. Their people dying by the thousands. When Alfred Parnell took over as the UN Prime Minister, he offered a solution—uniting all nations under one government. Sold everyone on the ideal of a perfect utopia, where resources would be shared."

These humans must be dull to believe such things. "Lies."

"No. He did it." Williams spoke to the device, "Show Earth three years ago." The map changed, the colorful blobs disappearing one by one until all the land masses turned completely green. Everything but a few tiny red dots. "The nations ceded to the UN. The militaries disbanded. Well, aside from these military bases. He pointed to the dots. "And the soldiers became Blue Helmets—members of the UN's army. Not everyone appreciated the way Parnell made that perfect utopia. He started by exiling prisoners off-planet to Asteria."

Asteria was a planet only three-days travel from Troon. It should've been part of *her* kingdom, but the humans had claimed it as theirs and the IgA had backed them.

"Then the mentally ill. The infirm. The poor. Those who challenged his campaign. And in the end, when almost no one was left to oppose him, Alfred Parnell had his Blue Helmets bomb the remaining military bases."

Decisive. Swift action. She nodded. Parnell was a good leader.

"Unfortunately, some of the old soldiers survived—like Chief Reese. Most went into hiding or were too injured to do anything but lick their wounds. But one—a Marine, Chief Payne—went to a globally broadcast speech Alfred Parnell was giving and shot him dead. That's what started the rebellion. Alfred's brother, Randolph, took over the UN and had Chief Payne exiled to Asteria, but Donovan Reese picked up where he left off. Reese found all the surviving military, mobilized them, and led a coup against the UN. He won."

Nonsense. "One man did all that?"

"Yeah. I mean, Chief Payne killed both the Parnells, but Reese led the rebellion. No one knows how. Some speculate that because he was high up in the ranks of the Air Force he had access to technology that allowed him to track the surviving soldiers' chips."

Ah. The humans all seemed to put tracking chips in themselves. CorTech chipped their employees. She'd had to have her guards remove the employees she'd killed from her planet so it would seem they'd left here in one piece and died elsewhere.

Williams paced while he outlined the rumors. "Others say a rebellion was already brewing before the UN fragged the bases and the rebels met at a pre-ordained place, on a pre-agreed-upon date. That they already had a stash of weapons. Doesn't really matter." He stopped and faced Vessa. "What matters is, there's no longer a leader of Earth."

She gave Williams her full attention. Larkin Astor claimed to be the CEO of Earth. "Explain. Show me what Astor rules."

"Show North America." The hologram focused in on one large continent out of many on the planet. "Show Arizona."

Again, the hologram narrowed, showing an irregular rectangle of land. Her belly twisted. Astor Larkin wasn't anywhere near as powerful as he'd claimed. "He rules—"

"Show Glendale."

To her horror, a dot appeared near the center of Arizona and the hologram zeroed in until a cluster of buildings appeared.

"This whole area is Glendale, Arizona." With his finger, Williams circled five tall, gray-and-glass buildings with the CorTech logo on them. "He rules that. CorTech."

Her mind spun. Larkin Astor had tricked her. "Explain what the rebellion has to do with CorTech."

"The rebels staged a successful coup, but they didn't name a leader. Reese took a large platoon and went off to rescue Chief Payne and the others who were exiled on Asteria. While he was gone, anarchy reigned on Earth. By the time he returned, corporations had taken over the cities where they were located. For example, CorTech pretty much rules Glendale, Arizona. The corporation provides infrastructure—power, water, fuel, jobs, protection from outsiders and in return, the people who live there pay rent to CorTech. They work for CorTech, or they provide support services for them—sort of a symbiotic relationship."

Symbiotic. She huffed. No doubt Larkin Astor profited more than anyone else. "And Chief Reese lives there, so he works for Astor."

"Well, no." He held up the Saph-link again. "Show aerial view of Glendale." The view shifted as if she were staring down at the town from above. The CorTech buildings were nothing but five small rectangles surrounded by other rectangles and squares, separated by straight gray lines like on a grid. An irregular walled area sat just left of CorTech. Williams pointed to it. "Chief Reese lives here with the rebels in what's left of Luke Air Force Base. They call themselves Command Division Zero."

It was nothing but a walled-off crater. Demolished buildings and aircraft sat in jumbled heaps. Some areas had been cleared off and lined with makeshift shelters. Only two buildings stood in an area that rivaled the size of Glendale, Arizona.

"They're trying to find a leader, someone they can put in charge of a global government and when they do, war will break out again—this time between the corporations and the rebels. Before that happens, Astor . . . and probably all the other CEOs on Earth, are looking for ways to keep their power. To take over the other corporations and get more power."

Which is why Astor Larkin had risked her wrath to steal her discovery. He was a small man, ruling a small swatch of dirt, who wanted more.

He'd made her look like a fool. She'd believed Larkin Astor was the ruler of Earth. She'd believed that since the data they'd retrieved from Chief Reese's ship indicated he had some authority over Larkin Astor, that he was an important, rich chief. Both assumptions had been wrong. Chief Reese lived in a bombed-out crater and . . . . "Larkin Astor is only the leader of one corporation out of many."

He nodded. "Thousands of corporations. He doesn't have any more power than the rest of them."

Nothing. Larkin Astor was nothing.

"But Chief Reese—"

He shook his head. "We've allowed him to stay within our boundaries to keep tabs on him, but now, because of his relationship with the IgA . . . we're already working on plans to kick Command Division Zero out of the Air Force base and get rid of Reese permanently. He's too much of a liability now that he's focused on CorTech."

Chief Reese was poor. He wasn't even a chief the way she thought of chiefs. But he was a dangerous enemy if what Williams said was true. Praise the gods he was now her ally. "Chief Reese is my clan now. That supersedes all else."

Williams snorted. "You think Reese will continue going after CorTech, but leave you alone since he's married to your daughter?"

"It is the honorable thing." All species married to better their alliances and improve their bloodlines. It was common sense. "He's part of my clan now. He may live on your land, but he will fight for my interests."

He shook his head. "You obviously don't know Reese. He's a fucking Boy Scout, understand? If he sees something he thinks is wrong, he's gonna fight balls to the wall, until he wins or he's dead."

He'd fight for what "he thought was right"? These Earthers had no control. On Troon, the people accepted *her way* was the right way or they died for their treason. They fought for *her* or they died for treason. She didn't understand the Earthers.

"Add that to the fact that he's good friends with the Earth Ambassador at the IgA—they say she saved his life once—and . . . ."

She understood that. The Earther IgA representative had a blood bond with Chief Reese.

Vessa stood and began to pace.

She was in trouble. Big trouble. A blood bond would always trump everything else. Even clan.

This. This was all the IgA's fault. If they hadn't sanctioned Troon from outside communication, she'd have known the politics of Earth. She wouldn't have fallen for Larkin Astor's lies. She wouldn't have married Celeka to Chief Reese.

She needed to change her plans. Gods help her, she needed Celeka back. "Quimet, you will tell me if they've left."

"Yes, my Queen."

Of course they had. She'd told them to leave or die. She turned to Quimet. "Once we're finished here, take Williams' ship, a platoon, and follow the chief."

Williams sputtered. "That's outright theft."

Quimet bowed. "Yes, my Queen. According to the ship's data logs, their next scheduled stop is Asteria, but I put a tracking device on their ship in case they change course. We'll find them."

She smirked. She hadn't thought of that, but she had ordered the guards to weld a large piece of sempisim to the under-belly of the ship as insurance.

"You can't take my ship!" Williams stormed toward the dais.

Vessa faced him head on, grabbing him and slamming his body down onto the redstone floor. She put one knee in the center of his back, and leaned down to whisper in his ear. "Or what?"

"Please, please, please. I'm helping you. I'm helping."

This Jerrod Williams was a weak male. Pathetic.

"You'll tell me the light frequency that makes the sempisim explode."

He sniffled. "I'm not a scientist. I don't know. I'm just Astor's assistant. I don't know."

As much as these humans lied, she didn't trust him. She stood, pulling him up by his hair.

The fool was crying. She ripped his shirt and lifted the edge to wipe the spit and snot from his face. Gripped his chin in her hand and pressed her mouth to his.

He tried to resist but, as in all things, Jerrod Williams was weak. She felt the exact moment her pheromones overwhelmed his. The moment he quit struggling and began pressing his hardened sex against her thigh.

She pulled back with a smile. The soul-merge had taken effect. Soon he'd become aggressive. Be willing to harm himself trying to fight other males in the vicinity, trying to break free to come to her. Soon, he'd do or say anything to mate with her. Only her. Already his cock was hard, straining against his clothing.

She stepped away from him. "Guards!" If he was lying, he'd change his mind about telling her the frequencies.

The guards flanked Williams.

"Return him to his cell."

Jerrod Williams could suffer for a time. When he was out of his mind with need, then they'd talk again. If he knew the frequencies, he'd cooperate.

Either way, he'd die.

She turned her attention to Quimet. "We need Celeka back."

"I agree, my Queen."

"She'll need to go to Earth and deal with Larkin Astor. We need those frequencies. Go."

Quimet left the room.

Yes, she needed those frequencies. She needed Chief Reese dead before he compared notes with Celeka and discovered the truth.

This was what came from having governing bodies like the IgA. They'd forced her to remain ignorant. They'd forced her hand in breaking the sanctions to survive.

Yes. She needed the chief dead. She needed Celeka to get the frequencies. Then she could use the sempisim as a weapon against the IgA. Without their interference, she'd be free to trade, travel, and war however she saw fit.

—·—

3

Maman wanted her dead.

Once they'd boarded, the chief had left Celeka alone to go help someone named Macie get "this old girl" into space. She'd assumed Macie was his second-in-command and "this old girl" referred to his ship.

When Maman summoned her to the palace, she'd thought she'd make good on her promise to release her and her sister, Mujara.

She'd finished the last assignment . . . and the four others before. Always, Maman promised *this* assignment was the *last*. Promised to set them free. Let them marry and live out their lives in peace.

When Quimet told her she was to mate the human chief, she'd thought that was the end of the assignments. Of the traveling and killing. She'd thought she was free. That Maman had finally been brought to heel by the IgA's sanctions and had chosen to do right by both clan and IgA by mating her to a human chief. An alliance was the only way to do so.

All the way to the door, she couldn't believe her good fortune.

Right up until Maman killed Limic. Doing so had been an act of war. Only she wasn't sure who the declaration had been directed to, the IgA, Earth, the chief and his clan, or her. Still, the message was clear: the alliance was for show only. Maman planned to wage war.

A narrow bench lined the wall across from the loading ramp. Celeka sat and sent up a short prayer to Dedia for her pet's safe travel to the Beyond. Her little comrade was dead. Her entire life had changed. While she saw how this benefitted Maman, she couldn't see any benefit to her.

Now that she was mated to an acceptable chief, Maman could take her consort to mate. Maman could breed and ensure her offspring took the throne. She was no longer Maman's concern.

Now the human chief would have to deal with her. He had an air of meanness about him, with his dark scowls. Yet the shape of his face was pleasing—he had strong, symmetrical features. His honor marks showed strength of character. While smaller than vladsets, he was much larger than her and the fact that he walked out of the vladset palace after the hazing trials spoke volumes for his ability to endure and overcome hardship. He'd even given her the honor of speaking directly to him. She wished she could see him without the black haze of her cooling cloths and veil obscuring her vision.

The chief was obviously a male of great worth and now he was stuck with her. He'd be furious when he discovered what she was. Being human, he might not find her disgusting, though he'd find her coloring odd even by Earther standards. The things she could do, though, would terrify him. Maman once told her Earthers killed beings like her.

Was that why Maman chose the Earther chief? No, her life hadn't changed, she'd simply traded one threat—Maman—for another: The chief. Perhaps that was the goal. If the chief killed her, Maman would have the right to wage war.

No. If she was careful, she'd get through this.

If she wore her cooling cloths, all would be well. She'd be the epitome of a good and gracious mate. Her chief would never need to complain. Never need to punish her.

The Earthers never needed to know what she was.

With her plan decided, she made her way toward the front of the craft. From the loading bay, a narrow hallway led into an open room. A small galley with a table and attached benches sat on one side. Nothing lay out on the counter, but there were plenty of cabinets to stow all the comforts of modern living. A recreation area sprawled on the other side of the room. A large vid-screen was mounted to the wall in front of an overstuffed chair and an L-shaped sofa.

An open door at the far end of the room led into the cockpit. The chief's deep baritone shot off rapid-fire questions to his co-pilot in Standard. "Why the hell is she wrapped up like a mummy? I mean *fuck*. What the hell have I taken on?" His voice crept up into a sarcastic mimicry of a female. "Take whatever they offer you with humble gratitude. Show no weakness."

She'd thought she had a good grasp of Standard, but she was still learning and didn't understand some of the words.

Another deep baritone chuckled. "I don't sound like that."

That must be Macie, the second-in-command.

The chief cursed again. "I can't think of many reasons for her to be wrapped up like that and none of them are good."

"So divorce her. Or, hell, get an annulment."

Divorce? Annulment? She wished she had a translator.

"I can't."

"What do you mean you can't?"

"You didn't hear the way her mother carried on. I-I felt sorry for her."

Her whole body heated with shame.

"Oh, come on. Don't tell me she's become one of your strays."

Celeka narrowed her eyes. Not everything they said was in Standard. Some of the words they spoke must be some other language. What was a stray? Nothing good, based on his tone.

"I'm not saying that." The chief sighed. "She needs time. She's probably as upset about this as I am. When she's ready, she'll want to go off on her own."

"She's another stray."

"She's not . . . ." The chief hit something. "You know *why* I can't do it."

"Well, we can't have her on the fucking ship. What if she's carrying a disease or infection? What if—?"

"We wouldn't even be having this conversation if someone hadn't taken a fucking potshot at the vladsets."

The cockpit went silent. She shouldn't eavesdrop. The chief was angry; he'd be irate if he noticed her. She turned to leave.

"Breathe, chief." Macie's tone softened. "You're not looking so good. How's your knee?"

"Fucked. Just like everything else. We're four days late—"

Oh, no! This was a poor start to being a gracious wife. She hurried to the cockpit. "Pardon."

Both men jumped. Their cheeks flushed red. How odd.

"You'll tell me where your med bay is and I'll prepare for you." She glanced at the other male and blanched. He was helping pilot the ship and she wasn't sure he could see through his swollen eyes. "Both of you." Her people were vicious and by the look of things they'd showed no mercy to either of them.

"Back of the ship." His wary gaze searched her covered face. "Second door past the loading bay. We'll come back in a few minutes."

"Gotta set our coordinates first." Macie studied her as hard as the chief had.

Celeka followed his directions to the med bay and searched for supplies. She found only a handful of med wands. Hopefully, they'd be enough to heal their internal injuries. She laid out the thin, silver wands on the counter and continued her search, finding a needle and thread, antiseptic, and two syringes with antibiotics. When they appeared in the doorway, she froze.

Be a gracious mate.

Her chief hadn't had time yet to clean up or dress and, standing there in nothing but those short, tight pants, he stole the air from her lungs.

He nodded to his second. "This is my business partner, Theodore Mason, everybody calls him Macie. Macie, this is Celeka."

Macie was a hair's-breath taller than the chief and had thick, muscular arms decorated with brightly colored murals etched into his skin. She'd never seen anything like them and again had the urge to remove the cooling cloths from her eyes and lift her veil to get a clearer view. He held out his hand.

"Your hand is fine."

A broad smile broke over his face, making him wince. He took one of her wrapped hands in his and pumped their arms up and down. "Humans shake in greeting."

How odd.

"Quit touching her." The chief scowled.

Celeka snatched her hand back.

Macie lifted his other hand, which contained three translators. "Thought these might make things easier."

Praise Dedia. She understood Standard better than she could speak it. "Thank you." She put a device in her ear as they did the same.

Her chief motioned to the instruments. "Take care of Macie first, he's got galley duty."

She hesitated. "But I'll have to touch him."

A low rumble erupted out of Macie—a sort of barking she had no clue how to interpret. "She's got you there, Chief."

"Then touch him." His eyes narrowed on Macie. "Stop calling me chief. That's what got us into this mess."

She guided Macie to a chair and waited until he sat so she could reach his face with ease. "Aside from your nose, is anything else broken?"

He shrugged, which made him wince. "Maybe a couple ribs. Right side."

She worked quickly, touching Macie as little as possible while treating his wounds. She realigned his nose, cringing right along with him as the cartilage cracked back into place, then used med-wands on both his nose and his ribs. The light from the wand forced a rapid regrowth of cartilage and bone to heal the breaks. She put a couple stitches in the larger of two cuts on his full lower lip . . . all under the watchful, intimidating gaze of her scowling chief. By the time she reached for the syringe of antibiotics she shook too much to administer the drug.

"I got it." Macie injected the medicine into his arm. He handed the empty syringe back. "Thanks, Celeka." He stood and headed out of the room. "I'll start dinner."

She stared at the floor, her heart pumping hard. "I won't touch him again."

"What?"

"You're angry, but I only did what you asked. I won't touch him again."

"Sorry. I'm not angry, I'm sore."

She snuck a glance to discover his features had relaxed and released a shaky breath. "I'll need time to learn your expressions."

"Mm." His gaze searched her covered face. "You wanna take those off now?"

"No." She pulled him toward the seat Macie vacated. "I wouldn't shame you so."

Choosing another med-wand, she flicked the device on and scanned over his ribs with the blue laser. After several seconds, a beep signaled a completed diagnosis. She smiled. "They're only bruised."

He gave a short nod.

She calibrated the wand and scanned over his injuries, this time the light from the wand strengthening the weakened bone.

Her gaze roamed his bared chest, searching for bruises that indicated internal injuries among a plethora of smaller cuts and abrasions. He was a beautiful male, muscular without being brutishly large. He didn't have an ounce of fat and tawny hair dusted his chest. She had the distinct urge to reach out and pet him, letting her hand run from his collarbone down to the dusting of hair leading below the short, tight pants he wore. Even his legs were covered in the tawny stuff. And his head. He had lots of thick hair on his head that promised to be as soft as Limic's fur. "You'll tell me if all humans have body hair."

His lips parted on a strangled sound. "Adults, yeah. Some more than others."

She couldn't quite picture what the rest of him might look like. Did the dusting of hair grow wider beneath his short pants or disappear again?

The wand beeped, drawing her from her musings. Her gaze searched the rest of his body, coming to rest on his knee. The skin had blackened and the joint tilted off to the side instead of straight ahead. She'd have to reset it. "Hold on to something, Chief."

Placing one hand around his kneecap and the other over his muscular thigh, she pushed the joint back into place.

He didn't make a sound, though his face screwed up into a pain-filled expression and his breath whooshed out of his lungs. She rubbed her covered hand over his thigh. What would that fine sprinkle of hair feel like against her skin? She looked up to find him staring back. "The wands will take care of the rest." She grabbed another wand and set to work.

She was killing him.

Slowly.

Her gaze moved over every inch of his exposed skin and the only things keeping his body under control were the pain and not knowing what was under all those black wraps.

He was surprised he hadn't blacked out when she reset his knee. Pride was surely the only thing keeping him conscious and, while he was sucking air like a wounded buffalo, his voice remained clear. "Don't vladsets have body hair?" They were bald, sure, but he'd assumed they had hair in other places. He couldn't say why he continued the outrageous topic other than he was curious as hell about her.

"No."

"Oh." Visions of exactly what she meant brought his body to life. He cleared his throat and sat up a little, trying to hide the fact his dick had just gone from "could care less" to "what are we discussing?" She wasn't human. He'd be wise to remember that.

"You'll tell me what it's for."

His brows drew together. "Hair?" At her nod, he shrugged. "Leftover from earlier versions of humans, I guess."

"All the different intricacies of each species are interesting, don't you think?"

He nodded. She had the sexiest voice—both smoky and lyrical—he'd ever had the pleasure to hear. He didn't care what they talked about, but he wanted to keep her talking. "You have a pretty name, Celeka. What's it mean?"

"In my language?"

"Mm."

She cleared her throat. "Wretched." She straightened and busied herself at the counter.

He felt like an ass for asking. He should've known—her mother was the most hateful female he'd ever come across. "I'm sorry. I shouldn't hav—"

She faced him. "What, tried to make pleasant conversation?"

"You don't talk like your people."

Her whole body stilled. "I was raised off-planet." She returned with gauze in her hand. "I'll clean out these wounds by hand. You only have a couple med-wands left and I still need to take care of your hand."

She was nice. He hadn't expected her to give him a reprieve before working on his hand. He couldn't imagine many vladsets who would.

She cupped the back of his head and tipped his head toward the light. Her trim frame pressed up against his side and he could almost see through the material—just the edge of a pert nose—where the cloth pulled away from her skin between her nose and cheek. "You see through that stuff pretty good, huh?"

"I'm used to them, I've worn cooling cloths since I was little."

"Cooling cloths?"

For the barest of seconds, she hesitated. "The name of the material."

"Why do you wear them?"

"Maman didn't want anyone to see me or discover I was a late bloomer." She shrugged. "Later, she didn't want anyone to know I never bloomed."

Never bloomed? With her pressed to his side, he couldn't help but notice the soft curves of her breasts against his arm. "What do you look like?"

"My skin is thinner than yours and . . . different. See-through."

An image popped into his mind of a geko and the way he could see the creatures' organs through their gelatin-like skin.

"My hair and eye coloring would disturb you. I'm ugly. Even Maman fears me. She says my face gives her nightmares. She can't stand the sound of my voice because it reminds her of . . . what I am."

He had no idea what to say. She spoke so matter-of-factly about herself, he was afraid to offend her by offering comfort. He didn't want to insult her further and say he didn't care about her appearance when he might not find her attractive. He didn't know her enough to say she had a winning personality or a great sense of humor. After the horrors he'd seen in war, he knew all too well how gruesome a living person's face could become.

He hated himself a little for being superficial, especially after being on the receiving end of unfair treatment from a loved one because of his scars. He did his best to treat everyone with respect. Still, he avoided uncomfortable situations when possible.

"It's better to leave well enough alone. I promise, I'll never shame you by letting your clan see what you mated."

With every breath, he inhaled her perfume, an intoxicating combination of floral and musk. "Celeka—" The meaning of her name flashed through his mind. "I can't call you that. You have to pick another name."

"No one else cares. Even Maman—"

"I'm not your Maman." Did she harbor the false impression Vessa might hold some tender feelings for her? "I won't call you that name, so either pick another or I will."

She swallowed hard. Her hand paused on his skin. "There's no need to become irate."

"Don't you get angry? I'm demanding you change your name. Aren't you going to argue?"

"No." She cleaned the cut above his eye, her hands gentle on his face. She couldn't be a vladset. They argued and fought over every little thing and she . . . wouldn't. "I don't like your Maman."

"I noticed."

He sighed in defeat. "What will you argue about?"

"Allowing your passions to rule is unwise. I spent most of my growing years learning that lesson and I think I've learned it well. You'll not rile me into an argument. Now, what were you saying before you got off on this strange tangent?"

What was he . . .? Oh, that's right. "I don't expect you to hide yourself from anyone, including me. Personally, I think you'll draw attention to yourself wearing that get-up."

"Yet, less attention than I otherwise might."

Jesus, how ugly was she? "You don't need to tiptoe around me. I'm not your Maman. I'm not vladset. I won't treat you like shit no matter how you look." Christ, she smelled good. His voice still held a touch of anger when he demanded, "You wearing perfume?"

"No."

He shut his eyes. Ah, God help him—she was aroused. The scent a combination of her skin, her soap, and her desire.

Her attention moved to his mouth and his lips tingled under her covered hands. They were really starting to bother him, those cooling cloths. He wanted them off so he could read her expressions. "Isn't the alcohol going to bleach your wraps?"

"No."

Damn it.

She finished with his face. The hand holding the back of his head stroked down his neck and shoulder. He'd much prefer she do that with her bare skin than those damn cloths.

Good God, what was wrong with him? She'd just told him she was so ugly she frightened her own mother, but he'd be damned if his cock wasn't standing at attention. He needed something to take his mind of her nearness. Her scent.

"Why don't you take care of my hand? Dinner should be ready." If she doted on him anymore, he wouldn't be able to hide the tent in his boxers.

"Are you sure you're ready?" She smoothed her hand down his cheek, tracing one of the deeper scars marring his face.

"What are you doing?"

"I shouldn't take liberties. I wanted to touch your honor marks. Forgive me."

He had no idea what the hell to make of her. Maybe if he could see her expression he could tell if she was fucking with him or not. Had anyone else said that, he'd have walked away. Or knocked them out cold.

But she was worse off than him.

So, he tried to be nonchalant. "You can touch me. We're married." Part of him hoped she would because he was starting to want to touch her.

She set aside the gauze and stood between his outstretched legs, her rapid-fire breath the only sound in the room. Almost hesitantly, she put her hands on his face, her covered thumbs stroking over the deep lines crisscrossing his features and bisecting his brow.

He felt naked. He didn't like people staring at his odd-shaped lid or the way his iris bled into the white of his eye. The rest of the scars webbed and pitted his cheek and jaw, pulling the side of his mouth into a constant sneer.

"You are a very beautiful male. In my culture, such marks are sought in battle."

He scoffed. "In my culture, they're pitied."

"I cannot believe such stupidity exists. You'll tell me why someone would be pitied for bravery, for doing what others could not or would not?" The whole room seemed to grow warmer with her wrath. "That's *their* shame, not yours. *They* should be pitied for their poor logic. *They* should—"

"Shush." Finally, he'd riled her. He put his good hand on her hip and gave her a little squeeze. "Hush, now."

Her whole body shook, and, unsure if he comforted her or himself he leaned in and wrapped his arms around her waist. Her scent surrounded him and he drew in a deep breath.

"Forgive me." She threaded her fingers through his hair. "I didn't mean to become upset."

He smiled against her flat belly, surprised to find he liked the shape of her. Her trim body had an athletic build with tight compact muscles and sleek curves. She didn't *feel* different from a human woman. "You can speak your mind. You certainly don't need to apologize for what you said."

"You're not what I expected, Chief."

Neither was she. Except, of course, he still didn't know what he'd gotten in this forced arrangement. "Hey, how 'bout you call me by my name—Donovan, or, if you prefer, you can call me by my surname, Reese."

"You'll tell me what your name means."

He wasn't going to answer. He may as well have, though, because Macie stood in the doorway. "'Brown-haired chieftain of fire.' So even if you use his birth name, you're still calling him chief." Macie flashed a grin. "Dinner's ready . . . Chief."

— • —

4

Celeka found both males fascinating.

Especially the chief.

They joked and teased each other, but never came to blows. They sent curious and cautious glances her way, but they weren't cruel.

When they brought dinner to the table on three small, covered platters and set one in front of her, she froze. The meal smelled strange. What if she went about eating in a different way from them? What if they didn't serve anything she liked? She'd heard of some of the food other races enjoyed but had no idea what humans liked. Silver tools sat next to a cloth on the table by a glass filled with a white substance she didn't recognize. Instead of lifting the lid from her platter she folded her hands together. "How did you come to be on Troon?"

Donovan rolled his eyes and pushed Macie as they took their seats. "Yeah, Macie, how did we end up on Troon?"

Macie ignored him. He lifted the lid off his platter, picked up the pronged tool, stabbed an orange stick, and popped it into his mouth. Interesting. They avoided touching their food.

"My wise business partner over there"—Donovan jerked his head toward Macie— "decided to follow our mark—"

"You will explain this mark."

He glanced at Macie. "The IgA hires us to find some of the more slippery individuals they'd like a face-to-face with." He shrugged. "Anyway, he followed our mark into vladset airspace." He took the lid off his platter, too, placing it upside down inside Macie's.

"You were asleep." Macie cut up the dark slab on his plate into cubes. It looked dry. Tough.

"Next time Macie has to make a decision involving breaking inter-sector treaties, he's gonna . . . ."

Macie's gaze shot to the ceiling and he spoke through his teeth. "Wake your lazy ass up."

Donovan leaned his forearms on the table, a utensil in each hand. "And next time an unidentified ship approaches while he's breaking an inter-sector treaty . . . ."

"I'm gonna wake your lazy ass up."

Donovan leveled a droll stare across the table. "Numb-nuts here decided to fire a warning shot."

She gasped. "That's a declaration of war."

Macie set his tools down with a clatter. "Yeah, well, if the fucking ship had been properly marked I wouldn't have done it. I thought they were pirates."

She blinked. "In a vladset sector?" No one flew in the vladset's sector. Not unless they were invited.

He shrugged. "We were there."

"Macie's a pro at knowing the ins and outs of alien cultures and learning languages, but he's never been too good at recognizing the makes and models of ships or remembering IgA laws." Donovan uncovered her plate, putting her lid with the others. He pointed to each item with his pronged instrument. "Roast beef is meat—animals. Carrots, potatoes, and baked beans are all vegetables—plants. Everything is cooked."

They might think her rude if she didn't eat. She braced herself—at least dinner wasn't moving. She'd never developed a taste for Troon's delicacies. "Thank you." She lifted her veil, folding it back over her head so a double fold of material hung down to cover her face to her chin.

Both males stopped chewing and stared.

If she was careful, the double fold should prevent them from seeing more than they wished. The extra layer certainly obscured their faces. Ducking her head, she spread two of the cooling cloths to uncover her lips, making sure nothing else showed through. "The food looks nice. Thank you for sharing." They continued to stare. Could they see her lips? Make out her coloring? Could they not eat now? "Is everything fine?"

"Yes." Donovan smiled, glanced at Macie, then back at her. "Where did you learn to speak Standard so well?"

Her lips twitched. "I'm not." She tapped her ear with her finger.

His eyes widened and he shook his head. "I forgot I put on a new translator."

Maybe he was as nervous as she. Although at least he had Macie for support and was in familiar surroundings. "I do speak Standard, though not everything I wish to express has words."

They both stared without replying so she stabbed one of the brown gooey bits on her plate and, despite her misgivings, tried it. Mushy. A little slimy. But sweet. Not bad. She eyed her plate with renewed interest.

"Do you mean not all the words in your language translate into Standard?" Macie asked.

"Yes."

"The same is true for us. We use a lot of slang and certain words and sayings in English don't translate quite right," Macie agreed.

"So when did you learn?"

The chief was persistent. "On Erra." She held her veil out of the way with one hand and took another bite.

Donovan paused, mid-bite. "Erra is habitable?" He glanced at Macie. "I thought it was a frozen moon."

She and Macie spoke at the same time. "It is."

"Why were you there?"

"Maman sent me." The meat, she wasn't sure about. She poked at the brown substance and pulled a small stringy piece off. This was meat? She wrinkled her nose. Maybe. Dead and burnt meat. She scraped the bit on her fork onto the side of the plate and speared an orange bit, instead. Mm. The vegetables were good. "I learned Standard while I was there."

"You know"—Macie's lips spread into a smile that didn't quite reach his eyes— "I'm not sure why, but I thought Erra was a prison moon."

Donovan's eyebrows rose.

They were interrogating her. Nicely. Peacefully. But this was an interrogation nevertheless. Erra was a prison planet, filled with both vladsets and a variety of aliens from other planets that Maman considered enemies. "Perhaps like your own Asteria."

They both had the grace to look abashed. She didn't know much about humans, but she'd heard about Asteria from the IgA Inspector who sometimes visited. Asteria was only three days from Troon. Had the IgA not sanctioned her people from warring, that planet would've been theirs. Instead, the humans claimed it as their discovery—yet another reason Maman hated them.

Once the humans realized the indigenous creatures of Asteria were less than hospitable, they'd turned Asteria into a prison planet, exiling the undesirables from their population there.

"What I want to know"—Macie leaned his elbows on the table and smiled—"is how the vladsets managed to raise such a sweet-tempered female."

Her gaze narrowed. She hadn't been with them long enough for them to judge her temperament. He spoke false words. Was he trying to put her at ease or insult her? "You'll tell me if this is favored, sweet-tempered."

They both nodded. They must want to know why she was different from her people. She didn't know them well enough to share her story, though. "I never had much in common with my people. They left me alone." She took a bite, hoping to end that line of questioning. Since she'd parted the cooling cloths to expose her mouth, neither had taken their eyes off her even though her veil covered her features. "I've heard that your planet is more peaceful and tolerant than mine." What she wanted to ask was if she might be accepted there. Find friends. A purpose. Love.

Donovan snorted. "Peaceful is a bit of a stretch."

Macie shot him a droll stare. "Tolerant isn't?" He tipped his chair back and rubbed his palm over his tattooed arm. "As individuals, some humans would be considered peaceful and tolerant, but as a society? Depends on what you're asking them to accept."

"She's probably talking about when the UN was in control." Donovan turned the full force of his attention on her, which was a bit disconcerting. "Earth went through almost a century of severe war. Everybody was fighting with everybody over religion, depleted resources, and politics. Then, a few years back we had one government under the United Nations and they were messaging this whole 'united planet' idea. The whole while *that* government was selling its ideal of a perfect utopia, it was shipping every man, woman, and child who might challenge it by action, word, or even by their presence, off-planet to Asteria. That's why it has a reputation as a prison planet. It was, once."

She swallowed. Earth sounded like Troon. "You'll tell me how someone's mere presence could challenge this ideal?"

He rested his forearms on the edge of the table. "Well, in the Parnells'—they were the leaders of the UN—vision, there would be no crime in their utopia. So, anyone who was high risk for committing crime had to go—convicts, the poor, the mentally ill. And everybody should be equal in a utopia, right? So, there went everyone who had a disability or visible deformity." He motioned to his own face.

Did he consider his honor marks a deformity? A disability? Did Earthers?

"And, well, religion was all right, but fundamentalists might cause a problem with their ideas or actions, so off they went. The last to go was the military. Those of us who wouldn't join the UN, anyway. The top brass at the UN ordered all our bases bombed all over the world—messaged the whole event to the people in their new utopia as a 'controlled munitions destruction.'"

Even on Earth someone like her wouldn't be accepted. Would she never find a place to fit in? "You'll tell me if these Parnells are still in control."

"Hell, no," both men answered at the same time.

Macie clapped Donovan on the back. "A couple years back, big man here coordinated a global attack on the UN. The whole organization collapsed."

Donovan ducked his head. "It was just a matter of tracking down the military survivors and convincing them to help. They all wanted revenge after the UN fragged their bases. Those whose families had been shipped to Asteria wanted them back. Convincing them to join a coup wasn't a hard task."

Red bloomed on Donovan's cheeks. She was fascinated by how humans changed color. "You'll tell me what this means when you turn pink."

Macie emitted a booming sound. "Oh, that's rich. Big badass is blushing like a schoolgirl."

She watched in awe as Donovan's face flared a brighter shade.

"All I did was set a date and time for everyone to attack. There were military survivors all over the world. Each group focused on taking out the Blue Helmet base closest to them."

"What are Blue Helmets?"

"They were the UN's army—they wear light-blue uniforms. Now they're mercenaries—an army for hire."

Macie rolled his eyes. "Yeah, no biggie what you did. You just happened to pick a date and time where all the bases were at lower-than-normal capacity." Macie winked at Celeka. "It was a UN holiday, so the bases were working with skeleton crews. And then you helped them find munitions repositories that were near them. And—"

Donovan dragged his hand over his face as if trying to rub the stains off his cheeks. "Chief Payne shot Alfred Parnell and later his woman took down Randolph Parnell. If anyone deserves praise, it's them."

"Bullshit. Without you coordinating the surviving military, another asshole would've risen in the Parnells' place. They might have taken out the leaders, but you're the reason the UN collapsed for good. Even if the Parnells had survived, they wouldn't have had anyone to do their dirty work because of you."

"You'll tell me if you're very important in your world." Her hopes of fading into the background of a peaceful, tolerant society were quickly evaporating.

"Oh, yeah." Macie let out a loud sigh. "People recognize the chief everywhere we go."

Donovan ducked his head. "Jesus, Macie. Let it alone."

Celeka moistened her lips. "You lead many men." She finished off the remainder of the vegetables on her plate.

"I'm retired."

Macie snorted. "Yeah, you keep saying that."

"You'll tell me what it means, this retired." She set down her tools and lowered her veil again.

Donovan grimaced. "Earthers ask questions like this: 'What does retired mean?'"

After several seconds of silence, she realized he wanted her to ask the question again. "W-what does retired mean?"

"Good." He winked, and her skin grew warm. "Retired means I don't fight anymore." He stood, picked up his plate and hers, and walked to the galley.

How odd. "On my planet, warriors never stop protecting themselves or those they are responsible for." She sighed. This might be harder than she thought. She supposed she couldn't leave him if he was unable to protect himself from the vladsets. "Don't worry. I'll protect our clan."

Macie made a rumbling sound that filled the common room. "He doesn't mean he won't fight if he needs to. He means he doesn't kill anyone at another's command anymore." Macie picked up his plate and plopped it into a built-in tub where Donovan was running water.

"You'll tell . . . ." She paused, rearranging the words in her mind. "Why do you make that noise? That . . . barking."

They stopped and stared. "What, laughing?"

"Do it again and I'll tell you." Her request was reasonable, but they looked at each other instead of complying.

Donovan shut off the water and sighed. "You can't just laugh. You laugh when something strikes you funny. You know, like—"

Macie poked the chief in the ribs . . . and he made the noise.

"Yes!" She stood and came around the table. "So *that* is funny?"

He turned a dark expression on Macie.

"What?" Macie grinned. "She wanted to hear a laugh."

Celeka's gaze narrowed on the spot Macie had poked. She reached out, and—

The chief backed up. "What are you doing?"

Macie shook his head. "More like this."

The chief laughed and side-stepped, turning serious again in a blink. "Damn it."

She giggled. Froze. Covered her mouth.

"See." Macie eyes twinkled. "There you go."

The chief's gaze narrowed. "You think that's funny?" He stalked closer.

Had she angered him, already? "I didn't mean to off—"

He lunged. His hands wrapped around her sides, his fingers wriggling. Another burst of sound escaped her and she twisted away. Except he held on and she ended up with her back pressed to his front while he continued to make her laugh. She writhed and twisted and laughed and when she finally got away, her hair came tumbling down from her wraps, slithering over her shoulder to flop right down to her waist.

Everyone froze.

She gasped. "I—I'm sorry."

"You said vladsets don't have hair." The chief's wide-eyed stare didn't move from her hair.

"Most don't. I do . . . just not . . . ." She motioned to his body. "Everywhere."

Macie emitted a strangled sound. When she looked his way, he cleared his throat. "It's white."

This was worse than if her hair had escaped at home. Maman would have yelled. Had her removed from her presence. These two males kept staring, their expressions . . . far different from the grins and laughter of a moment ago.

She flipped her hair over her shoulder and began re-winding the locks into a bun at the base of her neck. An alarm went off—a low, steady electronic beep. The screen on the wall near the sitting area turned red, a logo with six planets orbiting a sun appeared. The IgA logo. "What's wrong?"

Donovan pulled her behind him. "Hush now."

Macie moved so they stood shoulder-to-shoulder, blocking her from view. "*Red Slag*, answer call."

She secured her bun under her wraps at the base of her neck.

5

Donovan pressed his shoulder to Macie's, blocking Celeka from view.

The screen changed to show Earth's Ambassador at the IgA scowling at them from the communications room on the IgA's space station. Linda Salcedo was tall and muscular, her black hair shorn tight to her scalp. She leaned in so close her face took up almost the entire screen. "What the hell happened?"

Somehow, he had the feeling she already knew what had happened. He wasn't afraid of Salcedo, the two of them went way back. They'd fought together many a time before she'd taken this position at IgA. They'd shed blood for each other. Saved each other's lives. Still, she could be damned mean when provoked.

"We followed Jerrod Williams, as requested."

"Into the vladset's sector?" Her full lips thinned. "I don't remember that being part of the contract."

Macie cleared his throat. "No, ma'am."

"I seem to remember you two coming to me with wild tales that all the contracts we've issued related to the unknown resource were all CorTech employees."

Donovan glanced at Macie. "Yes, ma'am."

"I remember you promising that if I gave you exclusive rights to those contracts you'd prove your claims, as well as capture the people named in those contracts, within six months."

They'd recognized several of the faces on those contracts as CorTech employees. Had even gone to CorTech looking for them. Unfortunately, when they raided CorTech, they'd found nothing. Couldn't even find proof they'd worked for CorTech in the past. It was as if all record of them had been erased. Macie had a theory that the reason they couldn't find anything was because they were now under-the-table employees. Contractors, maybe. The kind of shadow employees who took care of the shadier jobs. Of course both Jerrod Williams and Larkin Astor had denied that during the raid.

Macie elbowed him, bringing him back to the present. "Yes, ma'am, we did promise that."

"I also remember telling you that this had to stay off the books. You know what off-the-books means, right?"

They both nodded.

"It means you don't get caught in vladset airspace and allow them to broadcast your presence to everyone in God's grand universe."

Donovan closed his eyes. Shit. What had they broadcast? The wedding? The hazing trials?

Salcedo leaned in even more. "Explain to me why I should trust you to continue this mission. For all I know, you've been compromised."

"Compromised?" Donovan arched his brow. "No, ma'am."

"We're solid." Macie thumped his fist on his chest.

"You two just happen to be the first non-vladsets to leave the vladset's sector in one piece? You sure they didn't cut you a deal? Didn't ask any favors?"

Donovan cleared his throat. "They wanted an alliance."

She straightened. "So, it's true. You married the princess."

That wasn't a question. "They broadcast the wedding?"

"I may as well have had a front row seat!" She slammed her hand on the table, which made her image wobble. "You'll have to find a way out of this as quickly as possible. Where is the brute, anyway? They did an outstanding job of keeping her just out of the screen shot."

Celeka stepped out from behind them. "Good evening."

Salcedo's eyes widened, her lips parted, and she stepped back.

Donovan waved his hand toward Celeka. "My wife. Celeka, this is Linda Salcedo. She's Earth's ambassador to the IgA and Inspector for the planet Bwaran."

"It's an honor, Ambassador Salcedo." Celeka dipped her head.

No doubt as a vladset she feared the ambassadors. As a sort of check-and-balance, each ambassador was also an inspector for another planet, ensuring they remained in compliance with IgA treaties. Whoever Troon's inspector was, had imposed a laundry list of sanctions on the planet.

"Yes." Salcedo snapped out of her stupor and bowed at the waist. "We're honored you chose Chief Reese as your husband. I'm sure you'll find Earth—" She glanced to her side. Straightened. "Prax." Her gaze shifted to Donovan and panic flashed in her eyes. "I'm congratulating Reese on his nuptials."

Ambassador Wilit Prax of Ixtil waddled on screen. Short and rotund, his grayish skin gleamed under the harsh lighting. Each ambassador issued and managed bounty contracts for their own world, so Donovan had worked with Prax before. He'd always seemed fair and level-headed. He had no idea why Salcedo was upset about him joining the conversation. Prax's black eyes fixed on the screen. "This is a happy occasion." Prax bowed. "Princess Celeka, it is the greatest of honors to see you again."

Celeka tipped her veiled head toward Prax.

Prax's gaze settled on Donovan. "I've just come from the assembly hall where the ambassadors were discussing recent events." He turned to Salcedo. "We missed you in the discussions."

She appeared startled. "I didn't know . . . I only just got news of the situation. No one informed me of—"

Prax folded his webbed hands together. "It's of no matter, the ambassadors have discussed the situation and we've decided this union is to our benefit—"

Salcedo looked as horrified as he felt. Why had they left Salcedo out of the discussion? Did they even have all the facts?

Donovan cleared his throat. "With all due respect, Queen Vessa forced us to get married. Celeka didn't have any more say in the whole ordeal than I did. Once she's adjusted to life on Earth—"

"You'll both be very happy together," Prax said.

"I was going to say, she'll have her choice." Once on Earth, she'd discover Vessa had short-changed her. There was no way in hell he and Celeka were remaining married.

Prax lifted a webbed hand and touched the screen. The sound went off but the vid-cam continued. Prax turned to Salcedo, speaking rapid-fire. Her expression darkened. She nodded. Her gaze flicked to the screen as Prax continued to speak.

Macie leaned in, and whispered, "That's not good."

No, it wasn't. Prax was no more powerful than Salcedo, but he apparently had the weight of the full council behind him in this matter.

Prax touched his screen again and the sound returned. "Chief Reese, you may have heard rumors that the IgA has had difficulty attempting to make Queen Vessa understand the negative repercussions of warring indiscriminately with other civilizations."

"If that's a pretty way of saying you all have had no luck controlling the vladsets, yeah, I've heard rumors to that effect."

Celeka stepped forward. "Ambassador, the people of Troon don't understand the sanctions, nor why they were placed. They don't understand that the rest of the known worlds do not conduct themselves as vladsets do. Maman hasn't ever explained—"

Prax smiled. Bowed. "I understand the politics we're facing, Princess. That's why we're so pleased by this wedding."

Donovan glanced at Celeka. Macie. Then Prax. "Can someone explain it to me, because I'm lost."

Celeka leaned closer. "I think Ambassador Prax believes Maman's own laws will prevent her from warring with Earth or the IgA."

"Yes. In an effort to ensure Vessa's family couldn't oust her, she enacted a law stating that family cannot war against family unless a grave injustice has been committed," Prax agreed.

"So she can't war against me," Donovan clarified.

Macie chuckled. "Yes, but vladsets don't think in terms of individuals. They think in terms of clans. She believes you are a great chief on Earth and that Earth is part of the IgA's clan."

He shook his head. "But that's not how it works."

"Eventually, she'll learn." Prax shrugged. "In the meantime, we have a reprieve. An opportunity of peace to educate the people of Troon so they understand how Vessa has incurred sanctions from us."

"You'll go to Troon?" Celeka asked.

Prax nodded. "Soon. Until then, you're allied with us. If she attacks any of your ally's ships, the vladset people will view it as an act of war against her own daughter." His gaze shifted to Donovan. "The princess is revered; the clans will revolt."

Donovan's gaze shot to Celeka. Her spine had gone ramrod straight, her chin up. He hadn't witnessed any sign of reverence toward her. From what he'd seen, they feared and loathed her. "You're counting on a misperception on the queen's part to offer peace between us and the vladsets. So why can't we divorce and allow her to believe we're still married? Queen Vessa doesn't need to be notified of Celeka's actions. She's no longer dependent on her mother."

"What you need to understand, Chief Reese, is there's no spousal abuse, infidelity, or divorce on Troon. If Vessa found out, she'd count that as a grave injustice and the clans would back her if she went to war." Prax motioned to Celeka. "Princess, why don't you explain?"

Celeka stared at his shirt. "Vladset laws are explicit and unwavering. If a vladset female dishonors her mate, his family takes her captive and forces her to watch as he destroys everything she holds dear—family, home, clan, possessions. If a vladset male dishonors his mate, her family holds him captive and makes him watch while she destroys everything he holds dear."

Holy shit, they were a harsh species. "We'll be light years from Troon. Things are different on Earth." If they both agreed to separate, there wouldn't be any dishonor.

"She has—"

Prax spoke at the same time as Celeka, "—spies everywhere."

Salcedo finally spoke up. "This is the second time you tangled with the vladsets and lost, Reese. I wouldn't risk a third."

President Hobbs. The only mission he'd ever failed in the military. At the time, they'd suspected the vladsets had kidnapped Hobbs and his envoy and stolen their ship because they were so close to the vladset's sector, but they couldn't prove it. He sighed. Had they proved vladsets were behind it, the IgA could've brought Vessa up on charges of interstellar piracy and kidnapping and he wouldn't be dealing with this shit now.

"IgA rules state a choice must be given to both parties. Our choice was death or marriage, which wasn't a choice at all."

Salcedo folded her arms over her chest. "It is by vladset standards."

"A generous one." Prax shifted his weight. "Chief Reese, please kiss your wife."

Salcedo shot Prax a side-long glance.

Had he stepped into some alternate reality? "Why?"

Salcedo reached across Prax and slammed her hand against the screen. The volume blanked out again and Salcedo and Prax argued.

He looked at Macie who shook his head and shrugged. "No clue, man."

When the sound returned, Salcedo, looking decidedly uncomfortable, cleared her throat. "You're already on thin ice, Reese. You never should've risked flying into the vladset's restricted sector."

So, it was like that, was it? First Salcedo demands to know if they'd been compromised and now Prax thought he could force him to kiss the wife he had no intention of keeping? He didn't need this shit.

His ire must've shown, because Salcedo added, "How are the Zeros?"

All the air whooshed out of his lungs as if he'd been sucker-punched in the gut. That was low. Salcedo knew he needed exclusive rights to the IgA's CorTech contracts to support Division Command Zero—DCZ.

He had a whole platoon—the Zeros—who worked under his command, who ran cargo and took bounty hunting contracts to support DCZ. Still, it wasn't quite enough. Without the money he and Macie could earn from this exclusive contract, DCZ wouldn't last the month. Not at the rate CorTech was raising the rents back home. *Bastards*. He shook his head. "They're gonna be just fine, Salcedo."

He turned to Celeka and lifted her veil. If they wanted a damn kiss, they'd get a kiss. God knew he'd done worse things for money.

She backed up a step. "You'll tell me what you are doing."

"Don't worry." He took hold of her wrapped hands to keep her from drawing the veil back down. "I'll make this is quick. Part those wrap things like you did at dinner."

"No." She backed away.

"Princess, this is an Earth custom." Prax bowed his head in deference, but his tone brooked no disobedience. "You'll kiss your chief or the IgA will dissolve the marriage, send a patrol to pick you up, and return you to Troon."

The wraps over her mouth drew inward with the hard breath she sucked in.

There was his out. He could walk away now. Except he'd be sending Celeka back to that bitch. The same one who'd promised to kill her—all of her—if she failed to make this work. *Shit.* She hadn't even known what laughter was. No way was he that much of a bastard. He closed his eyes. A kiss. No big deal. Could be worse. At least they didn't demand he consummate the marriage in front of them like in the Middle Ages. "It's just a kiss."

She backed away. "Explain a kiss."

Wonderful. "Humans touch lips at the end of a wedding to make it official." What a bland, boring description. A good kiss was damned near everything. He just couldn't quite make himself explain when he didn't think he could bring himself to do more than give her a peck on the lips.

"A soul-merge?" She shook her head. "We can't. It's not wise."

He couldn't agree more. A glance at the vid-screen showed Salcedo and Prax were waiting. He lifted the edge of the band crossing over her mouth and revealed her lips. Out of the shadow of her veil, they weren't black, but blue. Midnight-blue. Was it make-up, lighting, or nature?

Celeka shook her head. "You don't understand. Once we soul-merge you won't want to leave me."

The corner of his mouth curved. Somehow, he didn't think that would be a problem. His mind had conjured all kinds of grotesque deformities hiding under those black bands. Once she was comfortable with being on her own and had a plan, he'd file for divorce. They'd both be better off. "Do you want to go back to Troon?"

"Maman would kill me."

Better to get this over with. He ducked his head and pressed his lips to hers in a chaste kiss. Started to pull away and . . . damn, she tasted good. Smelled good. As the edges of his vision started to blur, he touched his thumb to the corner of her mouth. She was soft. Warm. He pulled her closer. Parted his lips. When she mimicked him, parting hers, he slanted his mouth to taste her fully. Shivers zipped down his spine to collect at the small of his back. His dick turned granite hard.

"There," Prax said. "It's done. There will be no more talk of divorce."

The conversation had started again and he was still kissing his wife. One hand clenched around the curve of her hip. The other trailed down the ladder of her spine. She was thin. Almost fragile. He nipped her full bottom lip.

She gasped.

What the hell was he doing?

He took a full step back but couldn't quite drag his gaze away. Light shone from behind her and, despite the veil hanging down to her waist, it highlighted her shape, the sharp angle of her torso leading to a gentle slope of her hips. Heat washed over him. He blinked and shook his head. This wasn't right.

Something had happened there. Something . . . all he wanted to do was kiss her again. Hell, he wanted a lot more than a kiss, which was absurd under the circumstances. He didn't know her well enough. Had no idea what she looked like. He forced his gaze to the screen with effort. "What happened?"

Celeka edged away. He snagged her hand and pulled her back to his side. "You stay put."

Salcedo pointed. "You knew there were risks going into this mission."

Risks. Sure. The risk of imprisonment. Injury. Death. Nowhere in his mind had "married to an alien mummy with lethal lips" entered the list. They could kiss his ass if they thought he'd allow them to control him. He glanced at Celeka. *Any of them.*

Macie stepped in front of him, blocking him from their view. "Well, we have some celebrating to do, so you'll excuse us, right?" He yammered on a few minutes longer. Something about payments. The cargo they needed to drop at Asteria. Profiles on new contracts that had been posted.

What the fuck? He couldn't concentrate on the conversation. Everything took on a slight haze. His gaze kept straying to Celeka. His body swaying closer as if she were the center of gravity. He couldn't decide if he wanted to yell accusations at her or kiss her again.

She re-covered her mouth and lowered her veil. Held her hands together in front of her in a death grip but she didn't try to move away from him again.

What the fuck happened? He'd intended to give her a peck. A quick, let's-be-friends-not-lover's kiss. A dry, formal, nothing of a kiss.

Somehow, someway he was getting played. Was Celeka in on it, too? She hadn't wanted to kiss him . . . . What had she called it? A soul-merge? Part of him wanted to ask, but he didn't trust her. Not now. Didn't want anything from her, not even words.

So why was he hard? He shifted his weight and untucked his shirt to help hide the evidence.

Whatever this was had her frightened. She was shaking. Giving him side-long glances as if waiting for him to jump her. And damn it, he wanted to. Wanted to haul her over his shoulder, carry her to his quarters, and *claim* her.

Shit.

Any minute now, he'd attack. He'd hurt her. And then she'd lose control. Soul-merging was rare for vladsets to perform. The chief's gaze clouded. He untucked his shirt.

Oh, Dedia, not in front of Macie. She stepped back.

"I, uh . . . ." His lips thinned and his jaw flexed. "It's getting late. I'll show you to your room."

Her room? She wouldn't sleep with him? They were mated now and should sleep together. Then again, she didn't *want* to stay with him, not while he was under the influence of the soul-merge.

Though his tone was abrupt, the chief's expression didn't hint at any malice. He lifted his hand and rubbed the back of his neck. "You tired?"

Macie was still talking to Prax and Salcedo. She didn't want to be alone with the chief, but if she stayed here and he succumbed to the soul-merge her circumstances might get a thousand times worse. "Yes. Thank you."

"Come on." He placed his hand at the small of her back and his heat seemed to sear right through her cooling cloths. "There're clothes in the dresser. They'll be huge on you, but you're welcome to them."

"Thank you." They turned a corner and out of Macie's sight. Her heart hammered in her rib cage. *Don't hurt him. Breathe. Center. Find the quiet place.*

"We'll get you clothes soon."

"That's not necessary. I wouldn't shame you by removing my wraps in front of anyone."

He paused, turned, and stepped in front of her. When he scowled the scars on his face pulled taut, tugging at the corner of his eye. Why had she argued? Males under the throes of a soul-merge tended to be violent. Desperate.

And she couldn't risk losing her temper.

A bead of sweat trickled down her back. *Find the quiet place. The cool place with powder-blue ice floating in the water.*

The way he searched her face, he seemed to be trying to see through her wraps. "Is that why you wear them?"

She wore them so if she lost control, they might contain her flame. She bowed her head and swallowed past the sudden lump in her throat. "I promise I'll do my best not to shame you. I'll work hard. I won't cause more trouble for the rest of our marriage."

"But you have caused trouble, haven't you?" His brows drew together and he touched her face. Well, not her face exactly, but her cloths. Still, she flinched away.

"Why don't we get to know each other before we decide on forever? You might find you'd prefer someone else once we reach Earth."

Her gaze shot up and before she could make any comment on his outrageous statement, he turned and led her farther along the hall. He stopped at an oval hatch, pushed the door to the side, and offered a clipped, "Good night."

Good night? "May your flame never—" *Flicker.* He disappeared around the corner. She slipped into the room before he changed his mind.

Celeka closed the door. She studied the locking mechanism for several erratic heartbeats. Tried pulling the lever up and when it refused to budge, pushed down. A click echoed inside the door. Locked. Excellent.

Every time she'd flown on a ship, the guards had locked her in her room. Odd now that she had freedom, she wanted the door locked.

The chief hadn't attacked. He'd remained calm. Were humans immune to the soul-merge? She'd never heard of such a thing, but maybe her mate was? Or maybe his disgust for her overrode his need to mate?

The reason shouldn't matter. What mattered was she had a barrier between them.

Maman would be ashamed. Horrified she was hiding instead of facing her fate like a warrior. But she'd seen a soul-merge in action and the violence it ended in. She didn't want him to harm her, nor did she want to have to kill him.

Except, the chief hadn't attacked. Even under the influence, he hadn't wanted her.

You can't have it both ways. You can't have him want you and *avoid the violence of full mating.*

She didn't even want to think about full mating.

The room was bigger than what she had at home and much finer. There was even a window looking out at the distant stars. The edges of a blast shield hung down from the top, which they would lower if the ship were under attack or during planetary decent. A huge bed took up most of the space, with deep-blue silk sheets and a thick comforter. A vid-screen hung on the wall across from the bed right over a dresser, and a chair sat in the corner, a strap securing it to the wall. She removed the translator from her ear and set it on the dresser. She opened several drawers and found the clothes. All men's clothing. In the bottom drawer, she found a shirt made of thick, sturdy material with gray and blue splotches. Over a pocket on the left side a small patch read: D. Reese.

He'd given her his room.

Why that pleased her, she couldn't say because he must have a key. He might come back.

She pulled the shirt out and laid it on the bed, and while she unwound her cooling cloths, she explored his quarters. There were two other doors. One led to a bathing chamber complete with a deep tub. Did they have enough water on board to indulge in such luxuries? Considering how large these quarters were, they might. A wall-to-wall mirror hung over the sink and counter. She supposed if she had the chief's face, she might not mind such a thing.

The other door was locked.

She went back into the bathroom and opened a couple drawers, glancing through the odd conglomeration of items. She found a silver pinching tool with a thin, flat, rough arm that swung out to the side. Perfect. She slid it between the door and the jamb and finagled the locking mechanism. The door slid across to reveal a narrow room full of weapons. A variety of guns and knives were secured to the wall along with boxes of weapons' chargers, sheaths, and scopes. She stepped inside, looked to the left, and gasped. On the far end of the space, a gray-and-black body armor suit and helmet hung from a hook. A blackened handprint had been burned into the material on the right shoulder.

She knew the chief.

Not knew him like they'd shared a meal before, but she'd fought him once. Had seen him several times, in fact. They always seemed to be after the same marks.

She closed her eyes. If Gray Shield—that's what she'd come to call him—was the chief, Green Shield must be Macie.

Perhaps it was good that Maman refused to allow her to bring her personal effects. They'd never recognize *her*, but they *would* recognize her body armor. Her armor covered her from head to toe—except for the palms of her hands—but the mask was unmistakable—shaped like the skull of Malikat, a sneering, fanged creature native to Troon. She always felt strong in her body armor. The tight material conducted heat instead of retarding it like her cooling cloths. She didn't have to be careful of how she moved, the body armor was all one piece and never unraveled like the cooling cloths. Someday, once she was on her own, she'd commission another set made.

Yes, it was best he never found out. She didn't know the chief well enough to predict whether he'd congratulate her as a worthy opponent or become furious she'd beaten him. She'd stolen his marks right out from under his nose. They'd all been high-profile hits worth a lot of money. Maman had been thrilled to earn the bounties from the IgA.

Oh, Dedia. Was that why Maman had married her to the chief? Did she expect he would also work for her? Hand over money from his marks to her? Somehow, she didn't think he'd like that.

She took one of the smaller guns off the wall and studied it. The weapon was different from vladset guns. More compact. More moving parts. She found a charging-clip the right size and loaded it. She slid the closet closed and put the tool back in the bathing chamber. Hopefully, he couldn't get through the locked door . . . but if he did . . . . If he did, what? She'd scare him with his own gun? She had no desire to kill him. He was interesting. Handsome.

A small flesh wound might cool his ardor, though. She stuck the weapon under her pillow and finished unwinding her wraps.

The problem was the soul-merge. She liked the chief. He had a strong flame. Even when scowling, he radiated warmth. He didn't seem to mind her small size nor had he become repulsed when he hugged her.

He'd *hugged* her. Twice, if she counted the embrace during the soul-merge.

The first time, she had almost wept at what must have been an impulsive action on his part. He hadn't pulled away or claimed she felt too fragile in his arms. Never would she forget his arms surrounding her.

The second time, she paid attention to the feel of him. He was solid. Gentle even with his muscles flexing around her. She bit her lip. He hadn't even bruised her during the soul-merge, though the hair on his face had scraped and tickled through her cloths. The little nip of teeth on her bottom lip wasn't even worthy of being called a bite. What if he was the same during the mating? That might not be so bad.

She was a coward. When little and still living at the palace, she remembered the clan members coming for healing after mating. Visions of those males and females bruised and bloody ran through her mind. She'd seared shut many a wound caused by a stray spike when she was young. That was before Maman exiled her. Before Maman determined her a danger to herself and others. She snorted. All vladsets were a danger to themselves and others—those spikes of theirs were deadly.

The chief didn't have spikes, though. He hadn't attacked. Hadn't even yelled. And her spikes had never grown in. She just had smooth little nubs where the spikes should've grown. At least they wouldn't impale one another during the mating.

Would he mind that her skin was translucent? Vladsets found the thin network of veins and musculature beneath her skin disgusting. But the veins in both human male's arms were visible—though much fainter than hers. Would he mind her coloring?

Once free from the wraps, she rubbed her chaffed skin. Even after all these years, the cooling cloths still annoyed her, leaving dark marks from the edges of the bands. She took off her veil and released her hair from the black bands, letting the long, stark-white locks fall to her waist, before freeing the rest of her face.

The cool air raised gooseflesh, leaving her feeling vulnerable. While she hated the cooling cloths, she'd grown used to hiding within them.

She donned the chief's shirt and, as he predicted, the hem fell to her knees and the sleeves well below her fingertips. She didn't care. The material smelled like him.

Perhaps she needed to adjust her thinking. She'd battled him before. He'd fought well and fair. He'd treated her well since their marriage. He hadn't attack. Yes, he was different from the vladsets.

Mating with him may well be different, too.

— • —

6

What the hell was he supposed to do with her? His wife. After the fiasco with his fiancée, he hadn't ever expected to have a wife. Much less a wife he didn't know. Didn't choose. Didn't love. Now, in some fucked-up-twist of fate, his body *wanted* her. Oh, he didn't know what she looked like. If she had scales or tentacles hiding under those cloths, if she was covered in tumors or skin-dropping leprosy, but he *wanted* her.

He adjusted himself in his pants and tried to think of something unsexy. Open wounds. Fungal infections. That time Macie drank too much and heaved all over his boots.

"Fuck." He scrubbed his hands over his face and dragged his fingers through his hair as if he could wake himself up. Nope. Still here. Still married. Still had a hard-on to shame all other hard-ons.

She seemed nice enough. Empathetic. Caring. Those traits came through while she cared for him and Macie. She had an adorable laugh. She was intelligent—she'd kept up with the conversation at dinner and . . . and she'd watched them eat before she'd picked up her own utensils. She'd purposely waited to see how they went about feeding themselves.

He shook his head. He'd probably do the same if eating in an alien setting around strangers from another culture. Perhaps that didn't mean anything, but how would she have proceeded if she'd eaten alone? What were vladset customs?

Knowing she'd mimicked their behaviors made him also wonder how much of the real Celeka he'd seen so far.

He snorted. Not enough. Just blue lips and a thick shiny rope of white hair. Those fucking cooling wraps or cloths—whatever the hell they were—they bugged the shit out of him. He stalked down the corridor into the rec room.

"You like her." Macie sang the three words in a falsetto, rivaling nails on glass as he loaded the sonic-washer. He puckered his lips and smooched the air, drawing out the annoying sound.

Donovan crossed his arms over his chest. "Don't start."

"You put her in *your* quarters."

"She needs privacy. I'll sleep in the sparring room." He'd stowed some extra clothes down there when he'd dressed before dinner. He sure as hell wasn't climbing into bed with her.

Macie snorted. "You couldn't tear your eyes from her all night."

"Neither could you."

Macie put his hand to his chest. "*I* was trying to see under her veil."

"So was I, dumbass." Should he ask Macie about the whole soul-merge thing? Hell, she was out of sight now, his cock-stand would diminish and everything would be fine. He took a deep breath. "I thought for sure she'd remove them to eat."

"She's sweet."

"Yeah." He hadn't expected that. Vladsets were an ornery race. Aggressive. Celeka was . . . . "Jesus, I need to come up with a new name for her."

"Why?"

"Her name means wretched in Vladnese."

Macie paused, a dish hanging from his fingers. "The hell you say."

"That's what she said." He shifted his weight, trying to find a more comfortable position. This was getting painful. Sweat broke out on his forehead.

"Give me a minute." Macie finished loading the sonic-washer, wiped his hands on a towel, and retrieved his Saph-link. He flipped the device open and tapped something on the virtual keyboard. "I'll be damned."

"She telling the truth?"

"Yeah." He shook his head. "What I don't understand is why her mother would publicly dishonor her. Offspring are revered by their parents in the vladset culture; children carry on the legacy of the father's clan and they're raised to bring honor to his family name. For the parent to give the child a derogatory name . . . . I've never heard of such a thing."

Prax wanted them to believe she was adored? Right. "It's gotta be whatever's hiding under all those wraps. She's so matter of fact about being ugly." She hadn't been coy. There was no hesitancy or sadness shading her tone. She said she was ugly like she believed it as fact and expected everyone else did, too.

"Yeah, but ugly to a vladset?" Macie plopped onto the couch, his head on the armrest and his feet on the backrest, ankles crossed. "What the hell is that?"

All vladsets were ugly. "That's what worries me. Hell." He let his head fall back against the wall. "She's sweet. What if . . . when she finally lets me see what's under there . . . what if I can't contain my reaction and decimate whatever self-esteem she still has?" Or what if he screwed them both over by acting on whatever she'd done to him when they kissed? He didn't feel right. Was still as hard as forged Glatonian steel.

"Okay, that's heavy." Macie sat up, leaning over the back of the couch. He crooked his arm and rested his chin on his bicep. "Let's focus on what we know: The vladsets take pride in their warriors—size, number, and thickness of their spikes, the darkness of their skin, the red of their eyes. We know she fails in size."

"She's just a bit of a thing."

"She's got a *full* head of hair."

"And then some." He'd never seen hair as thick and long as hers. It must weigh as much as she did.

"I haven't seen any evidence of spikes. Did you notice any when you were feeling her up?"

He leveled a glare at Macie, which earned him a waggle of the eyebrows in return. He hadn't checked. . . . He remembered the sense of delicacy and strength. That didn't make sense and yet, she had a narrow waist, compact torso, thin limbs . . . but good muscle tone—delicate and strong. She wasn't anywhere near as sturdy as her mother. He'd felt her ribs. Her spine. "Nah, no spikes."

"So maybe she's an underdeveloped runt to them. Unworthy of their esteem."

Donovan bobbed his head. Reasonable theory, even Vessa had said something like that, but . . . . . "I think it's something more. You didn't see the queen. The guards. They were terrified of her." Despite the lack of stimulus, his hard-on wasn't going anywhere. This was gonna be awkward as fuck. "I think she did something to me."

"Like what?"

Did he want to have this conversation with Macie? It was embarrassing as hell. Yet he wouldn't get a lot done if he didn't fix his problem. "Find out what soul-merging is."

Macie's lips quirked. "Aw, are you falling in love? That's the sweetest thing—"

Donovan crossed the room, braced his hands on the table, and stared across at Macie. "Look. It. Up."

Macie's misplaced humor died. "All right." He tapped a few things on the Saph-link. "What crawled up your ass and died? From where I stood you seemed like you were enjoying yourself."

"That's the problem." Sweat trickled down his temple. This wasn't normal. Not even when he was a teenager overdosing on hormones had he been like this. All he wanted to do was go to his quarters and sink balls-deep into his wife. "Not happening."

"What?"

"Nothing."

"Found it." Macie read, his eyebrows snapping together. His frowned and glanced up at Donovan. "You . . . uh . . . experiencing some amorous inclinations?"

"If you're asking me if I'm sporting wood . . . yes. How do I get rid of it?"

"Tab A goes into slot—"

"Before you start running your mouth, consider this: It's your fault we ended up on Troon. Your fault I ended up married. All of it is your fault."

"Right, boss. No jokes." He read some more. "Obviously, you're experiencing some aggression."

"There is a seemingly sweet woman in my quarters. One who was shaking so hard, her veil was shimmying around her. So, whatever this is, I know it's not good. She went from talking and laughing with us to terrified of me after one kiss. Why?"

Macie sank down onto the couch, his gaze locked on whatever he was reading.

Donovan paced while he took inventory. He was sweating. Agitated. A little dizzy. Horny as hell. Angry.

"All right."

He gave Macie his full attention.

"Think of this as nature's way of guaranteeing the survival of the vladset race. They produce high amounts of pheromone."

Her scent. "Yeah, I noticed while she patched me up. She smells damn good."

Macie's brows furrowed. "Does she?"

"You didn't notice?"

"Wasn't directed at me. Vladsets target mates they're attracted to. Apparently for your wife, that's you."

"Lucky me." He lifted his arm and wiped the sweat from his forehead on his sleeve. "She's doing this on purpose?"

"Nah. It's a biological function. If she's attracted to someone, her body produces pheromones. Period. She doesn't have any more control than you or I do. Hers are just stronger." He cleared his throat. "You know, like cats. Female goes into heat, her scent changes and all the eligible males come running."

He lifted one brow.

Macie rolled his eyes. "Notice I said, 'eligible males.' I'm not including myself in that category."

Donovan scoffed but something in him eased. At least she wasn't purposely fucking with him. "That explains her scent; what about the soul-merge thing?"

"More pheromones. Her scent diffuses the pheromones—just enough to get you close. A kiss . . . it's like a shot of hundred-proof."

Prax had known. He'd known and he'd demanded they kiss. What was he hoping to gain out of this? More than he was letting on, no doubt. "Fuck me."

"Exactly."

Donovan narrowed his eyes. "Not funny."

"Biologically speaking, this makes total sense. Vladsets have faces only their mothers can love, so they needed something to ensure survival of their species. The pheromones ignite the desire to mate and enough aggression to fight off other affected males."

"My wife's mother doesn't love her face. Doesn't love any of her. She couldn't wait to get rid of her. Now all I want to do is fuck her."

Macie read some more. He swallowed and his gaze lifted. "It's gonna get worse."

Great. "How do I stop it?"

"Her pheromones are the trigger." Macie shrugged. "Her pleasure is the antidote—you know, if you survive the mating."

"Excuse me?"

"Pheromones are unique to a being and they change as you get to know a person and become romantically involved. Give her an O and her scent will change."

"I have no idea what's under those wraps. Or why her people are afraid of her. Or what IgA hopes to get out of this whole thing." He shook his head. "I'm not even sure what all is at stake here for Celeka and me."

"At least she doesn't have spikes—that right there increases your chances of survival."

"Oh, joy." She might not have spikes, but she must have something similar. Something the vladsets feared.

"I've already sent word to Merrick on Asteria to see if he can pick up on any rumors down at the Spaceport. He knows all the bounty hunters and cargo runners. By the time we get there day after tomorrow, he should know something on the IgA front." He tipped his head. "As for Celeka . . . what if I tell her part of marriage for Earthers is a full medical? If I get her in the scanner, I could give you a head's up about what you're getting into. Check out her physiology. Make sure there's no disease or any other surprises."

He grimaced. She was already skittish. Didn't seem to trust them much. "I hate starting things with a lie."

Macie snorted. "There you go talking about 'starting things.' You don't have to stay with her, Reese. Fuck Vessa and fuck the IgA."

He also knew how few people could see past his scars, much less view them as a positive like Celeka did. "I kinda like her so far."

Macie snorted. "You don't want to do to her what Leanne did to you. Don't lie."

"I'm not—" He clenched his jaw and drew in a deep breath. The muscles surrounding his ribs on the left side cramped and his breath whooshed out on a groan. "I do like her *and* I don't want to do to her what Leanne did to me." When Leanne's father had walked in to tell him she couldn't even bear to look at him long enough to break the engagement . . . he was gutted. Destroyed.

"Let me check her out."

"Shit." He pushed himself away from the wall. "I don't know."

Macie held his stare for a full thirty seconds. When Macie didn't budge, Donovan swore. He was right, he needed to know what he was getting into. "Fine. I'll tell her in the morning." He made his way down to the sparring deck. Macie would research the hell out of her. Tomorrow they'd get a scan. One way or another, he'd find out what was under those damned wraps.

7

While dressing, Celeka thought about the night before. Had the soul-merge taken? The chief had left her alone. He hadn't knocked. Hadn't attempted to enter her room. In fact, the ship had remained so quiet, she'd had trouble sleeping.

"Today is a new dawn. My flame is strong and I will endure." She smoothed her hands over her wraps, making sure they covered her skin, and unlocked the door. No more hiding. She'd do good by the chief. If the soul-merge had taken and he needed her, she'd submit. If not, she'd find another way to be useful. She opened the door and headed toward the galley. A rich and bitter scent tickled her nose. Macie stood alone at the counter in a baggy, short-sleeved shirt and loose-fitting black pants with pink lips all over them. His feet were bare except for the murals painted on the tops. Did pictures cover every inch of him between his arms and feet?

"Where's the chief?"

Macie turned, leaned against the counter in the galley and folded his arms over his chest. "You're a glutton for punishment, aren't you, hon?"

She touched the translator in her ear. She couldn't tell if the device was broken, or if they kept using unrecognized words. *You're a feaster for punishment, aren't you, hon.* "You'll tell me what you mean."

One blond brow rose.

Questions, not demands. "Will you tell me what you mean?"

"He wants you to call him by his name, remember?"

Ah, yes. Still, what did that have to do with discipline or gorging? "Where is . . .?" Oh, Dedia, what was his name? "Donovan?"

"Better." He turned his back to her and poured a steamy black liquid from a pot into a mug. "Save calling him chief for when you want to annoy him." He leaned back against the counter and regarded her over the rim of his cup. "I do." He winked. "Want some coffee?"

She eyed the steam rising from his cup. The rich scent was unfamiliar. She shook her head. "I want to find out what my duties are." This morning brought the opportunity to learn new things. Maybe even skills to help her survive on her own. The chief . . . Donovan, didn't seem interested in staying married.

He grunted. "We're gonna make this quick and painless, all right?" He set his cup down and came closer, lowering his voice. "On this ship, my job is to make sure Reese always knows what he's walking into."

"Reese?"

His gaze narrowed. "Donovan Reese, the chief."

How could she have forgotten his second name? "Of course."

"I research languages, customs, societies, laws, you name it. I make sure he has the information he needs to make the big decisions." With each statement, he prowled closer, his expression darkening.

Celeka backed away.

"But you . . . you're a great big question mark and I don't like that. You're not the right size for a vladset. You're not the right shape. You don't dress or talk like them. There is nothing more than your name written into the Royal Vladset Registry."

Celeka's heart pounded. Macie looked like he wanted to hit something. Maybe her.

"I had three armed vladset warriors outside my cell arguing about who had to bring me out. The warrior who escorted me to the ship—and I use the term generously because he mostly dragged me there—sounded terrified he might run into you." Her back hit the wall and he glowered down at her. "Why?"

Because she was the vladsets' secret weapon? Because of the things she could do? Because she was different from them? She had no idea which it was or if it was a combination of factors. She'd never understood. She could hardly catch her breath, her heart thrummed so hard in her chest, and required all her discipline to keep her fear at bay. She *had* to keep a tight control. *Don't hurt him.* She hadn't lost control since she was a youth but didn't trust herself in new surroundings.

"I-I don't know."

"Why did they name you Celeka? Isn't that an insult to the sire as well as the offspring?"

Yes. Maman had hated her father. "M-my sire was part of the spoils of war."

His eyes widened, his lips parted and then snapped shut. His gaze narrowed. "You're still heir to the throne."

Technically, her older sister, Mujara, was, but she wouldn't be for much longer if Maman married her consort. If Maman had led Donovan to think she was heir to the throne, she'd cheated him. Yet another mark against her.

"Vladsets don't let alien species leave, much less with the royal princess. The whole way out of the building I thought they were fucking with us. Thought they'd shoot me in the back or chuck me over the edge of the airpad. Why'd they let us go?"

Because Maman expects Donovan to destroy me. Then Maman would have the right to invade Earth and destroy everything. She couldn't tell him that and she couldn't remain silent. "Maman told Donovan I am a dishonor. I am wretched to the vladsets. Ugly."

"That doesn't explain why they're scared of you. I'll bet everything I own our little interaction with Vessa isn't over. What's coming?"

War. If she told the truth, they'd take her prisoner. She'd be *their* "spoils of war." Theirs to rape and torture. The chief would raise whatever offspring she bore to be an enemy of the vladset. That was the way of war. She shook her head.

"What are you hiding?" He lifted his hand as if to rip away her cooling cloths.

Fight or submit? She didn't want to hurt him. She didn't want to die.

She dropped to her knees, holding her veil to her head. Oh, Dedia, she'd hadn't even been free one day and already they'd discover what she was. "You don't want to see me!"

"What the—?"

His hand circled her arm and she jerked away.

"For Christ's sake, I'm not gonna hurt you." His hands wound around her arms and he pulled her to her feet.

She kept herself pressed to the wall. She liked Macie. Understood his concern and admired his loyalty to his chief. Everything he said was true but she had no desire to get tossed out the airlock midflight. Nothing he did would make her confess. Not out here in the depths of space. "I have no intention of harming anyone."

"Doesn't mean you won't." His blue eyes bored into hers. "I owe Donovan everything. He's saved my ass more than once. You don't want to hurt him. Not even by accident. We clear?"

She nodded.

"Good." His features softened. "You sure you don't want any coffee?"

The change in him was so quick she was left off-balance. "N-no. Just the chie—Donovan."

He crossed the room and picked up his cup of coffee. "He's below in the sparring room."

She turned to hurry away.

"Celeka."

She froze.

"I want to like you." He snorted. "Hell, I do like you. *And* I will keep searching for dirt until I figure this whole puzzle out."

"I understand." Time was running out. How long until they reached Earth? If Macie kept digging, he'd figure everything out.

Then he'd kill her. Or worse, send her home.

Maman would be pleased. If the humans killed her, Maman would not only have the right to wage war against the chief and his clan, the vladset clans would expect her to. The IgA couldn't stop her. No one could. The only thing she didn't understand is what Maman hoped to gain. Was the chief rich? Powerful? He must be for Maman to bother with him.

Would she ever gain control over her own life? Ever make decisions on her own?

She slowed at the bottom of the ramp leading downstairs, the flat smack of flesh on flesh raising the hair at her nape. Who else was on the ship? She peeked around the corner into a large area. Thick black mats padded both the floor and walls. Donovan sparred with a man-shaped pad. He wore baggy gray pants sagging low on his narrow hips.

He hadn't noticed her, so she slid into a shadowy space by the door.

His sweat-slicked skin gleamed in the dim lighting, highlighting the curve and hollows of muscle. Each powerful strike was precise and graceful, except that he favored his left side. How old had the injury to his ribs been? The med-wand had healed the bruised bone, but the surrounding muscle must have been either weakened or also injured. So the injury must've been days old. He probably could've used another med-wand treatment to those strained muscles. Why hadn't he said anything?

Despite his lingering injury, each blow he delivered with his right arm sounded through the space, a heavy, flat whack.

He was good. He threw his weight behind each strike, putting all his power into his fist.

This was Gray Suit. Would he be angry if he discovered she'd stolen his marks? Earth and Troon had been in constant competition for the IgA's attention for the last fifty years, though Earth had been more successful in gaining positive attention.

The vladsets claimed humans were soft. She hadn't felt any softness to him yesterday. Donovan's body was hard, heavy with bone, firm with muscle and sinew, though his skin was thinner than a vladset's and his veins showed through in places like hers. Her gaze traveled over the hard angles of his body and froze. He was erect. Ready to mate.

The soul-merge *had* taken effect. Except, instead of taking his aggression out on Macie and his need out on her . . . he was down here beating the stuffing out of the padded man.

She rubbed her hand over her belly to settle the restlessness. Her breasts ached and her nipples grew taut. What was wrong with her? Instead of standing here admiring him, she should run. He had every reason to hate her and the soul-merge would make him aggressive and demanding.

Worse, the more time she spent around him, the more she *wanted* to give herself to him.

She backed away, stumbled, and landed in a heap on the floor.

The chief's gaze zeroed in on her.

She scrambled to her feet and crossed her arms over her chest. The way he stared made the hair at her nape stand on end. "There's a med-wand left."

"What?" He squinted at the shadows she stood in.

Show no fear. She edged forward into the light and swallowed past the dry lump in her throat. "You're hurting."

"A little tender, that's all." He picked up a towel and blotted his face. Ran it over his arms and chest.

The chief was as stubborn as a vladset. "Why endure pain if it isn't necessary?"

"Why waste a wand that could save a life to heal a little ache?" He winked.

She shook her head. Obstinate male. "You'll tell me my duties now."

For several heartbeats he stared, his jaw working as if he were biting his cheek.

Oh, he wanted her to ask. "Will you tell me my duties?"

He sighed. "Gimme a minute." He unwound the tape protecting his hands as he walked away. "Stay put."

"Gimme" didn't translate to Standard, so she stayed where she was and watched. Waited as he went behind one of the walls.

After several minutes of silence, she padded over to where he'd disappeared and peered behind the wall. He was gone. Must've stepped inside the silver cylinder in the corner. His pants lay pooled on the floor next to it. The door to the device made a noise and started to open. She shot back across the room to the shadowy corner, her heart thumping hard in her chest.

When he came around the corner a moment later, he had on different pants, dark blue with pockets. He had his shirt in his hand which he put on as he walked across the room, leaving the two sides hanging open. "You could've had a seat." No sooner were the words out of his mouth than he sat in the only chair in the room. "Come here."

Perhaps this is why Maman chose him. He had many characteristics of the vladsets. Obstinate. Demanding. Arrogant. But he'd cleaned himself and gotten dressed. Those were not the actions of a male in throes of a mating frenzy. She crossed the room and stood before him.

He frowned. His hand swept out, caught her around the waist, and tumbled her into his lap. "We can share."

My cooling cloths! She straightened her back, perching on his legs and was in the process of checking to make sure nothing had unraveled when he pulled her back against his chest. "Chief!"

Before she could protest further, he held up his taped hand. "Couldn't get this one. Nails are too short. You mind?"

She stared at his hand, uncomprehending. She'd thought he meant to force her to lie beneath him. She blinked. He'd put her into his lap so she could undo his tape? She drew in a deep breath. If he hadn't cut his nails down to the quick, he could've done the task himself. "The tape will stick to my cooling cloths."

"Uncover your fingers. I won't look."

She whipped around to deny him.

His eyes were closed, his head resting on the curved, padded back of the chair. He wasn't acting at all like she'd expected. The evidence of his need to mate was pressed against her hip, but he wasn't acting on the urge. Why? Part of her wanted to escape, but maybe she shouldn't disobey. Not this soon. He was stern today. Less accommodating. Most likely due to the soul-merge. She chewed her lip. If his eyes stayed closed, what was the harm?

"I'm waiting."

Just her fingertips. She slipped the end of the cooling cloth from her wrist, unwound the cloth from her fingers, and tucked the loose end in to keep the rest in place. She repeated with her other hand and took hold of his wrist.

He was not soft. His wrist was thick and while there was enough give to his skin to feel the muscle and bone beneath . . . he wasn't soft. She gripped the sticky tape with her fingers and unwound it from his hand, balling the stuff to keep it from getting tangled with her wraps. She only had one set of cooling cloths, she couldn't afford to ruin them.

Even though humans had no fire, he was warm under her fingers. Once finished, she set the ball of tape on the arm of the chair and petted him. The dusting of red-brown hair on the back of his hands was so sparse she couldn't quite get a feel of it. The sleeves of his shirt covered his arms but he hadn't buttoned the front.

She pressed her lips together. He promised to keep his eyes closed. Maybe she could touch his chest. She turned and came face-to-face with him. She gasped.

"You're a curious little thing."

"Your eyes are open."

"And your skin is blue."

He tricked her! And he meant to make fun of her? She wriggled away. At least the skin on her fingers wasn't as translucent as other areas.

His hands locked around her, pulling her closer. "I'm curious, too."

She flattened her hand on his chest to push away and . . . her gaze dropped. The hair on his chest was coarse. Springy. Tickled her fingers. She dragged her hand though the stuff. "You're not soft."

He chuckled. "Softer than this." He pulled her hand to his cheek and rubbed his face against her bared fingers much the way Limic had done when seeking affection.

"Oh." She jerked away. Changed her mind and put her fingers back. The tiny hairs on his cheeks were rough. No wonder her face had tingled after his kiss yesterday. She shifted her weight so she could put both hands on his jaw.

He grunted but didn't stop her.

Spiky. Bristly. His erection pressed against her hip. His chest was hard against hers. "There's no softness to you." What else had they lied about? "They told me humans were soft."

His lips quirked. He turned his face into her hand and captured her finger between his lips, biting down enough to hold her in place. He stroked his tongue over the pad.

She gasped. *There*. He *was* soft. His lips. His tongue. Warm and wet and soft. Her belly flopped. Tingled. Under her cloths, her nipples tightened.

"Uncover your mouth, wife. I'll give you soft."

This was a dangerous game. "I can't, my Chief." *My* Chief? When had she come to that decision?

"I've seen your lips." His voice was a bare rasp of sound. "I've kissed you already." He lifted her veil and folded the stiff material back over her head. "You'll uncover your mouth."

He sounded like a vladset. He must want to mate. At least he hadn't thrown her to the floor or rammed her against the nearest wall in a frenzy. Her hand trembled while she parted her cloths enough to bare her lips. Her breath shuddered out.

When he tried to pull her closer, she resisted.

"Easy." His gaze searched the cloth covering her face. "Soft, right?"

Her heart pounded under her ribs. Her belly went lopsided. "Soft."

He cradled her face in his big hands and drew her closer. His breath, warm and minty, ghosted over her lips. He pressed his mouth to hers. His lips were firm and smooth and . . . .

"Close your eyes."

She did.

His thumb pressed to the corner of her mouth until she parted her lips. His parted, too. Slanted over hers. He stroked his tongue into her mouth and shivers erupted over her skin. She was cold and hot and tension vibrated deep in her belly. His kiss was better this time. Needy. Coaxing.

When he released her, her gaze dropped to his mouth. "Why do I feel your mouth everywhere?"

He tucked his bottom lip into his mouth as if trying to taste her again.

Liquid heat trickled between her thighs and she stiffened. If she continued to sit on his lap, he'd notice. She tried to get up. "I need to—"

He gripped her wrist in his hand, holding her in place. "How old did you say you are?"

"Twenty-seven."

His brows snapped together. "No one ever kissed you before yesterday?"

"No." She couldn't imagine using something so . . . intimate to hurt someone, not that she had hordes of suitors anyway.

His lips quirked. "Humans do this a lot."

On Troon, vladsets rarely soul-merged since Maman became queen. "How much is 'a lot'?"

"Often." He pulled her closer. "If we stay married, your mouth isn't the only thing I'll want to kiss."

She bit her lip. Humans did this mating thing much different from vladsets. She rubbed her finger over her thumb, remembering the feel of his mouth. "My fingers?"

"Fingers. Toes." His gaze dropped. "Breasts." Dropped again. "Pussy."

That word didn't translate, though he left little doubt what he referenced. More moisture gathered between her thighs. This time she was far too curious to try to escape. "Human husbands do this?"

"Yeah. Wives, too. I'll want to feel your mouth on my skin. To know how hard you bite." He stroked his thumb over her lips. "I'll want to experience these full, pouty lips wrapped around my cock."

Cock? She could ask later, right now she was too focused on the rough pad of his thumb against her lips. When he dipped his thick digit into her mouth, she shivered. Closed her eyes. He was salty . . . she sealed her lips around him and swirled her tongue for a fuller taste. Salty. A bit of tang.

The way he stared at her through heavy-lidded eyes, lips parted, breathing hard, gave the impression of anger except his touch remained gentle. Those blue eyes flicked up to meet hers through the black cloth separating them. "You're gonna give me this."

Give him what? Maman hadn't allowed her to bring any of her posses—

Firm lips sealed to hers and before she could acclimate, his tongue swept into her mouth and licked. No longer gentle, his mouth had turned demanding. Her belly quivered, almost like a gaping hole opened in her gut, wanting . . . something. She wanted something.

"Kiss me back."

Her eyes widened and she stared, hating how her cloths shrouded her vision of him in black. He'd allow her control?

This was not an opportunity to be squandered.

Donovan had no idea what the hell he was doing. He only knew if he didn't touch her, kiss her, fuck her, he'd lose his goddamned mind.

No. He wouldn't let things go too far. Just needed a little relief and then they'd have a heart-to-heart. Figure out what to do.

She continued to stare like a jackrabbit caught in the porch lights.

Damn. He'd pushed too hard, too fast. He was about to let her off the hook when she slipped those cloth-covered hands up his chest, her fingertips silken against his skin in contrast to those coarse wraps.

Come on, you know you're still curious.

Her pheromones had him horny as hell despite all reason. He had no idea what she looked like except she was the same color as a winter sky on a clear day, but he'd be damned if he didn't want her. Unable to focus on her appearance, he latched onto her husky voice, her quiet pride. Her scent and shape. Now he could add smooth, soft skin to his list. Manicured nails tipped with tiny white crescents.

She threaded her fingers into his hair.

He closed his eyes.

Something close to a purr came from her chest. She liked the hair on his head. He did his best to hide his smile of satisfaction and leaned his head back deeper into her palms. Was he so starved for affection he'd gladly accept such from a self-proclaimed mutant?

Celeka cupped his cheeks, her bindings scratchy against his face. Her erratic breath peppered his mouth before she pressed those lush lips to his ruined cheek. Trailed her mouth over scar tissue most people couldn't bear to look at.

His whole body tensed. He'd long since lost all feeling in his cheek and yet her kisses made his throat grow tight. "Sorcha." *Sor-ka.* The name came in a flare of inspiration. He may not be able to see her, but it gave him perverse pleasure to give her a name opposite of what Vessa had tried to make her. Vessa had kept her wrapped in black. Abused and stifled her. Despite all that, Sorcha's passion sure as hell burned bright. He cleared his throat. "That's what I'm calling you."

She pulled away, her head tipped to the side. Her lips parted on an indrawn breath as if she might argue or ask the meaning of the word. She nodded once. Leaned down and kissed him on the mouth.

He needed every ounce of control to resist taking over. Somehow, he remained still for her innocent exploration. She *was* innocent. She didn't even know how to kiss, not that her lack in skill tempered his body's reaction. Every instinct he had urged him to take her to the floor and sink into her heat. She licked his lower lip, nipped him, drew his bottom lip between hers. "Open."

The quiet demand rocked through him. He opened for her, moaning at the first hesitant brush of her tongue. He couldn't be still any longer. His grip tightened as he hauled her up, forcing her to straddle him. He was so hard he was about to burst. Couldn't help the groan that escaped. Those cooling cloths might hide her from prying eyes, but they were thin. So thin the tight buds of her nipples stabbed against his chest and the seam of her sex, wet and hot, pressed up against his cock through his jeans. He might not be able to *see* her, but she may as well have been naked in his lap. Could he part the wraps covering her pussy with the same ease she'd uncovered her mouth?

No. He couldn't do this. Not without knowing what she looked like. Not without knowing if she carried some illness. It was damned near the hardest thing he'd ever done, pushing her back. "We have to stop." He was breathing harder now than after twenty minutes of sparring. *Shit.*

"Why?"

Why? Because in another sixty seconds he'd be balls deep inside of her whether she was aware of what they were doing or not. That bothered him, too. She seemed too damned innocent. He wet his lips, tasted her there, and his balls pulled up tight to his body, ready to explode. "We need to know each other better." Even if waiting killed him. Which it might.

She shrank right before his eyes. Deflated right there in his lap. "You fear me."

"No." He cupped her face, lifted her chin. He couldn't quite tell if she was looking at him or not. "We don't know each other. You may find you don't like me. I may decide we don't suit."

She flinched. "I may be too ugly."

"Sorcha, stop." Even though what she said was dangerously close to his thoughts, hearing them spoken so matter-of-factly made his gut churn.

"What? The truth is the same whether you choose to voice it or not." She pushed away and stood. The straight line of her back showed a fragile pride he didn't want to be responsible for crushing. "I'm strong. I'll tell the truth even if it's not nice." She turned and walked out of the room, winding her cloths back into place, re-covering the tiny pieces of her he'd uncovered. Maybe that shouldn't matter. They'd both been bullied into this marriage. They didn't know each other well.

But he liked her. He liked that she'd trusted him enough to let the tips of her fingers show; it had made him feel . . . worthy. Something that hadn't happened for a long time.

But, damn. He was right back to square one.

— • —

8

By midday, her chief's list of negatives was growing.

He tried to deny her worth by refusing to give her duties. She wasted most of her morning debating the matter. He seemed to think because she didn't know how to cook, or fly the ship, or load the sonic-washer, that learning wasn't necessary.

She scoffed. With the way things were going, she'd be alone once they reached Earth. Her chief didn't want her. Didn't even value her enough to give her duties. She needed to know how to survive on her own. Even more reason to learn everything she could on the flight.

Macie had finally taken her side in the argument and told Donovan he was an ass.

An ass. She wasn't sure what an ass was, but her chief's face had darkened before he grudgingly gave in. She'd remember the saying and use it when needed.

After losing their battle, he'd disappeared. He was a sore loser, which was not a trait to be admired. He left Macie to teach her the duties Donovan gave her. So far, the cooking lesson had been less than pleasant. She pursed her lips together. "Do you only eat dead things?"

His face went blank. "Don't you?"

"I prefer plants. Vladset warriors cook their meat as they eat, preferring the animal warm but alive and struggling. There is no honor in an easy victory."

His lips parted. "I never quite thought of dinner as a battle."

She wrinkled her nose. "Nor I. I can't bear to put something in my mouth that is writhing in agony and screaming." She shuddered. She'd never fit in with the vladsets. She was starting to think she would fair no better on Earth. "Humans are very different from vladsets."

"Yeah." He searched her covered face. "You okay?"

He'd been accommodating all morning despite his earlier warnings. She was starting to think of him as a wary ally. "I want to be a good wife and I'm not. I want to help, but I'm making more work for you. Everything is backward." She let her shoulders slump. Her back ached from holding herself stiff. "I don't understand half of what you say."

"You speak Standard well enough."

"I thought I did, but you and Donovan use words I'm unfamiliar with. Words that don't translate."

"Like what?" He leaned his hip against the counter and lifted his coffee cup to his lips. She might try the liquid soon. He'd been drinking cup after cup all morning. So had Donovan.

"You'll tell me what is cock."

He made a strangled sound and dark liquid dripped out his nose. "Jesus." He grabbed a towel and put it to his face. "Warn a man first, will you?" He coughed. Sputtered. Drew in a deep breath and wiped at his watery eyes. "You're serious?"

Why wouldn't she be? "Donovan would like to feel my lips—"

"Nope!" He held up his hand. "Don't. I don't want the details."

Why did she feel like they were talking at cross-purposes? "Why does this word make you so nervous?"

He laughed. "Okay, forget lunch. I'll cook today and we'll pretend you did."

"I cannot lie to Donovan."

"It's more of a bluff than a lie."

"It would be—"

"Dishonorable. Yeah, well, stuff your honor, we have more important things to deal with." He took her hand and led her across the room. Her heart leapt as they neared the cockpit. Would he teach her to operate the ship, now? That would be a great skill to know.

He guided her right past the door and over to the sitting area. "Okay, so we need some definitions for slang, right?" He nodded, answering his own question. "So the word you asked about—"

"Cock."

"You have to stop saying that." He glanced around. "Reese will have a fucking coronary."

Fucking. There was another one she needed to ask about. "He's asking me for something I don't understand. I'll fail to please—"

"Sit." His features hardened. He pointed to the chair, his tone brooking no argument.

She sat. "I hadn't realized how overwrought humans could get."

"Cele—" He shook his head. "Reese is right, you need a new name."

Again with the name. She wanted answers. "He calls me Sorcha."

"Sorcha." He grunted. "Bright. I like that."

"Can we stay on topic?"

"Listen to me. You don't have to please your husband. Women . . . females have rights."

Was this another trick? Maman had said human culture was like vladset culture, minus the honor. "You'll explain."

He sighed and plopped down on the seat across from her. "Pleasing him is great, don't get me wrong, but only if doing so pleases you, too. You're not his slave. He can't order you to perform . . . . He can't make you . . . . *Fuck*, this is awkward."

Perhaps he needed a little encouragement. For whatever reason, this conversation seemed difficult for him. She patted his knee. "You're doing well. Go on."

He let out a bark of laughter. "If you don't like him or if he doesn't like you, you don't stay married. Even if you do like each other, if you don't suit for whatever reason, you can move on."

Did they want her dead so soon? "Maman will kill me if I dishonor my chief."

He waved his hand in the air. "You don't have to worry about any of that."

"Why?"

"You're married to an Earther now. Earther women don't have to listen to their mothers once they're grown. Nor do they have to obey their husbands."

He couldn't be correct. If she didn't obey, he'd get angry. She'd fight back. Then everyone would want her dead. "We might fight."

"Yeah, and then you get to make up. Sometimes he'll win and sometimes you will."

That sounded good. To have some control. To advocate for what she wanted. Still, it sounded too good to be true. Her gaze narrowed. "How often?"

"What?"

"How often will I win?"

He shook his head. "There's no rule. You win when you're right. If you're wrong"—he shrugged—"you lose. Today, Reese lost."

"Maybe I'll never win again. He conceded because you took my side and called him an ass." She needed clarification on ass, too, but later. Keeping Macie on track was difficult enough with one question at a time. She still had no idea what cock was.

He snorted. "If he never lets you win, divorce him."

"What is this divorce?"

"It's where you go to a judge, tell her you made a mistake in getting married, she un-marries you, and you're both free to stay single or marry someone else."

Like a courting. Did humans view marriage as courting? She was starting to think humans did everything different from the vladsets. "This is common?"

"Common enough." He leaned forward, propping his elbows on his knees. "No one goes into a marriage with the idea of leaving but you and Reese, you were forced to marry. Neither of you had a say."

She flicked her hand up. "He had a choice."

Macie straightened. "He did?"

"Yes. He could marry me or die."

He rolled his eyes. "That's not a choice. It's a threat. What was your choice, marry him or die?"

Close enough. Except her life wasn't on the line. Her sister's was. "If Maman found out we divorced . . . ."

Macie leaned closer. "She doesn't control you anymore. Donovan will protect you from her whether you stay married or not."

He couldn't understand. Maman still had Mujara imprisoned under the palace. If she didn't do as Maman instructed, Mujara would die. "You still haven't told me what cock is."

His face reddened. He picked up a set of goggles. "Give me a minute." He put the goggles on. Waved his hand around in front of him. Poked the air. Took them off and handed them to her. "Put this on."

"What is it?"

"It's a personal holo-screen. Only you can see the holograms. You'll see images that look like they're happening here in this room, except they're not."

Interesting. She didn't want to take off her veil, so she put the goggles under her veil and held them to her face. Inside, a bright green circle hovered in front of her with writing on it.

"You're seeing the start button. Reach your hand out and push it."

She lifted her hand and pushed the button. The scene changed and a naked human male stood before her. He wasn't as muscular as her chief. Had black hair instead of russet brown. The entirety of his naked frame was bare of any hair. "What's . . .?" The man grabbed hold of his growing mating appendage. "Oh. So, that's cock?"

"What in the hell is going on in here?"

Celeka lowered the goggles, keeping them tucked under her veil and stared at her chief. He was angry. Fierce. His gaze bored into the back of Macie's head.

Macie stood and backed toward the front of the ship. "I, uh . . . . She wanted to . . . . Um, I gotta check the maps."

The coward jumped over the couch and locked himself into the cockpit, leaving her with Donovan. It was the aggression part of the soul-merging that was making him glower like that.

Donovan's gaze shifted to her. His eyes weren't red like a vladset's; still, his blue gaze turned as hard and cold as a glacier when he was angry.

She needed to explain and ease his ire. "Macie showed me cock."

From behind her, in the cockpit, Macie moaned. "Tattle-tale."

"Macie, come out here. That's an order."

"Respectfully denied, Reese. You know you'll regret whatever you say, anyway. Better to have our chat later. You be nice to Cele . . . Sorcha. She had no idea what she was asking."

His gaze shifted to her. "What exactly did you ask?"

She wet her lips. "I asked what cock was. You told me you wanted to experience my lips around your cock but the word didn't translate." Her gaze dropped to where his cock pressed against his pants. That's what he wanted to see between her lips. "I didn't know what you wanted." She shifted in her seat, pressing her legs together.

"And now you do?"

"Yes." She lifted the holo-screen.

Macie had showed her a hologram.

He was still gonna beat him until he couldn't walk.

When he'd come in a moment ago and seen the back of Macie's head over the top of the couch, Sorcha in the opposite chair asking if that's what a cock was . . . .

Jesus. He was pretty sure his heart was still lodged in his throat. He sucked in a deep breath. "Next time I say something that doesn't translate, ask *me*." Hell, he didn't know why he was jealous. They didn't even *know* each other.

"Yes, Chief."

Her veil was vibrating again. He'd scared her. This whole soul-merge crap had him tied in knots. He softened his voice. "How's lunch coming?"

"I distracted Macie from the lesson. He's going to finish the job and tell you I did."

"Sorcha!"

Donovan's gaze shot to the cockpit. *Good. He hoped the son of a bitch was pissing himself.* "Music. Oldies. Volume 6." Hard rock thrummed through the ship's speakers loud enough to cut Macie out of the rest of the conversation. He walked around the couch, drew Sorcha up and sat with her tucked to his side on the couch. "You didn't feel like you could ask me?"

"You were being an ass." She stared straight ahead.

He closed his eyes. *Thank you, Macie.* "I'm sorry we argued this morning."

Her head whipped around. "We fought."

"Yes."

"I won."

He cleared his throat. "Maybe from your point of view."

She gasped. Turned to face him. "*You lost.*"

So, she did have some vladset traits. "What did I lose? I have less work. I have an extra set of hands on my ship for free, which allows me time to do other things. The way I see it, you lost. I wanted to give you time to acclimate. To learn the nuances of our culture and language. To get to know me."

"But without duties—"

"Damn it, you have worth whether you have duties or not." He was getting all worked up again. He didn't usually get frustrated so quickly, but trying to negotiate with his wife, living with a perpetual hard-on, having the sense he was in the middle of deep shit but not knowing what side the threat was coming from . . . . Everything was eating at him.

Her head tipped to the side. "Macie says after a fight, we make up."

Thank you, Macie. Maybe he wouldn't be so hard on him after all. "Yeah." He pulled her into his lap.

She fidgeted for a minute, straightening her cloths to make sure her skin was covered like some goddamned puritan.

"I get to keep my duties?"

He nodded.

"And I don't get punished?"

What the hell had the vladsets done to her? There was no emotion to her tone when she asked her obscene question, just a slight tremble in her veil. "Husbands and wives don't punish each other."

"Ever?"

He leaned close. "If I ever say I'm gonna punish you, I promise you'll like it." He lifted her veil.

A tremor rolled through her. She didn't push away.

That's right, get used to me. "It'll involve things like fifty lashes of my tongue."

She put her hand on his shirtfront. Fussed with the wrap on her index finger until the silken skin of her finger caressed his collarbone. The curious part of her wanted to come back out to play.

He gripped the cloth on her chin between his thumb and finger and tugged it down enough to free her lips. Dark blue. Full. They parted to reveal straight white teeth. He caught a glimpse of blue beyond, darker than her skin, lighter than her lips. "Maybe even a bite." He leaned in and nipped her bottom lip. Tugged until she leaned into him. "I might even spank you." He flattened his palm on her ass, letting her feel the heat of his palm. "If you're real nice."

Her lips curved. "I can't tell if you're serious."

He dragged the pad of his thumb over her lip. "Did you enjoy the holograms?"

"I got the answer to my question." She shifted in his lap.

Which didn't come close to answering his. "Did you like what you saw?"

"That male was not a chief." Her one bared fingertip traced a line on his skin at the opening of his collar. "He had no honor marks. No hair."

He grunted. So now chiefs had scars and body hair? Did she make this shit up as she went along?

"He didn't make my insides quiver."

His humor died. Damn, he liked her. She was honest to a fault. A bit literal. Curious. Helpful. Wanted to learn new things. They were all traits he found appealing and refreshing. He didn't even mind how stubborn she got about winning—that could keep things interesting. He wedged a finger under a cloth at her throat. He could see right through the damned thing when he lifted it from the others. They weren't any thicker than cheese cloth.

"Can we take these off now? I want to see your eyes." He needed to see all of her. Was pretty sure he could handle whatever was under there.

"My eyes will disturb you."

She was killing him. His cock throbbed between them. His nut-sack so tight he was sure they'd implode soon. Twice last night he'd stroked himself off. Twice already today. At this rate, he'd be raw long before his erection diminished. He could hardly think of anything aside from her. Sooner or later he'd crack. But not now. Not without her willingness to trust him.

He leaned forward and pecked her lips. "In that case, there's something else we need to talk about." He tugged her wraps back over her lips and lowered her veil. Even without seeing her face, the way she reared back expressed her surprise. Yeah, she knew how uncomfortable he was. Might even feel a little guilty over this whole soul-merge crap.

"I was in the hold doing inventory and—"

"Inventory?"

Now she asked for clarification. "Checking to make sure all the cargo on the ship still matched the list I made when we brought them onboard."

"Oh." She sank back into the chair. "Maman took something."

Interesting how quick she reached that conclusion. "Does she steal often?"

"Of course. She takes whatever she wants from the ships she captures."

Had he expected a different answer? "Well, she's taken something she isn't allowed to have."

"Says who?"

"The Intergalactic Alliance. The IgA sanctioned Troon from off-planet technology. I had an extra antimatter drive onboard. It's gone."

"I see."

"Do you? Because I sure as hell don't." Did the vladsets know how to use the technology? Were their ships capable of withstanding that kind of speed?

Her shoulders turned in. "Will you hold me responsible for Maman's actions?"

"No." He doubted she had anything to do with the theft. Her Maman wouldn't even speak to her directly; they couldn't have conspired together. "If you're honest and tell me what you know, I won't hold anything she's done against you."

She turned her face away. "How long do I have to give my confession?"

Yeah, someday he'd burn in hell for this but he couldn't pass up this opportunity. "Ten seconds."

"I believe she intends *tsangrath.*"

He had no idea what the hell she said. The word didn't translate into anything in Standard. "Music off." He reached back and hit the wall. "Macie, come here."

Macie slid the door aside and poked his head out. "You okay?"

"What's . . .?" He motioned to Sorcha. "Whatever you said?"

She tried to slip out of his lap but he held fast. "*Tsangrath.*"

"War." Macie straightened and came into the room. "Except more. It's the total decimation of an enemy and everything they have, whether they fight or not."

Donovan scoffed. "Vessa may as well commit suicide. If she wars with Earth without cause, the full force of the IgA's allies would take her out." He searched the cloths covering Sorcha's face, trying to see her through all the black. "Why do you think she's angling for war?"

"She killed Limic. She destroyed something of mine. Doing so was a declaration."

No. She must've misunderstood. Not even a vladset would be so brazen as to take on a world allied with the IgA. "Maybe you misunderstood. Maybe she was disowning you . . . or getting in one last dig."

"Yeah." Macie came farther into the room. "Prax said the vladset clans revere you. If Vessa waged war, wouldn't they revolt?"

One of her shoulders lifted. "Perhaps."

She gave in too easy. Did she agree or not want to argue? "If Vessa wanted war with Earth, she could've held me and Macie for ransom. She could've killed us."

"Nah." Macie shook his head. "That would've adversely affected Troon's probation."

"Okay, but the last thing she should've done was marry me to you. If she starts a war now, she'll anger her own people because you're married to an Earther."

Sorcha continued to nod. "What you say makes sense."

He dragged his hand over his face. How could what he said make sense if she still thought Vessa wanted war? "I have to report the loss of the drive to the IgA."

"I understand."

Did she? He wasn't so sure. He was starting to think the vladsets had filled her head with half-truths and biases to make her little more than their slave. Her behavior was odd. She fought hard for things that shouldn't matter—his scars, her chores. Then willingly conceded important stuff—her name, yesterday's kiss, the possibility of war. She was too unemotional about the wrong things. Then again, the way she gripped her hands together showed the conversation bothered her. But she kept her tone modulated. Her reactions muted. Her boundaries were all skewed to hell and it bugged the shit out of him.

Macie cleared his throat. "We land in Asteria tomorrow. I can send another message to Merrick. See if he can dig up any information about a vladset mobilization."

He nodded. The problem was, the vladsets were notoriously secretive about their dealings with the rest of the galaxy. Gaining information would be difficult at best. He didn't think anyone on Asteria would know anything so soon, but it was worth a shot.

Sorcha put her hand on his chest. "We're not going straight to Earth?"

Shit. The medical scan. He eased her out of his lap and stood, putting a little distance between them before he lied. "Actually, I've been meaning to talk to you about that. We have some business on Asteria before we head home and they require current medical scans prior to landing."

Her back straightened. "Why?"

"Well, because . . . ." Donovan ran his hand through his hair. He hated lying. Especially to her. He had a feeling Vessa had lied to her enough. "You see, uh, Asteria—"

Macie cleared his throat. "Has been cut off from the rest of the universe for years. Now that trade has opened, they have concerns about disease and environmental impacts on their planet."

"Yeah." Donovan's jaw clenched. "He's better at explaining."

Silence stretched. She fidgeted her wrap back into place over her finger. "I've never heard of this."

"Well, you haven't traveled." He rubbed the heel of his hand over his chest. "Why would you have?"

She shook her head. "I'll stay on the ship."

Donovan shot Macie a look.

Macie glared, tipping his head toward Sorcha.

"They require everyone to disembark." Now it started. Building the story. Weaving the lie. By the time they finished, he wouldn't remember half of what he said. Lying sucked.

"Mm-hm. For security." Macie lifted his Saph-link and flashed the screen as if their made-up rules were displayed right there. "They scan the ships for stolen cargo and live organisms."

"Why would they do this?"

"Trafficking." Macie folded his arms over his chest and leveled a meaningful look at Donovan.

"Right. See, there are some races . . . who kidnap . . . ."

" . . . and sell . . . ." Macie volleyed back to Donovan.

Right. This was his shit show. "Kidnap and sell other races as slaves."

"To other races." Macie bobbed his head.

She gasped. "That's awful." She picked at the cloths covering her fingers, bowing her head. "What does this medical scanner do?"

Was she afraid of the technology or what they might find? "Takes pictures of your insides. You don't need to worry about any adverse effects. You don't even need to undress."

"How is the scan done?"

"The scanner won't hurt you." Not half as much as lying hurt him. With every response to her questions, her shoulders sagged a little more. He wet his lips. "You step inside and close the door to the chamber. When the machine turns on, a light comes on and scans you from head to toe, providing a full medical diagnostic."

"Will you go first?"

Lord Almighty, she was a suspicious woman. But she was allowing the scan. He chuckled. "If it makes you feel better, I'll go first."

— · —

9

Donovan led her down the hall to the med-bay, but she stopped in the doorway. Her wrapped hand gripped the frame as if she feared they'd drag her inside kicking and screaming.

"It'll take a minute to get everything set up." Macie went around a corner to a glass-enclosed space and powered up the terminal. "I already have Donovan's information entered but I'll need to set up a profile for you." He typed something on the virtual keypad. "Were both your parents vladset?"

Donovan leaned against the wall and folded his arms over his chest.

She turned to him as if silently asking if she had to provide the information. He was starting to feel like a complete ass for putting her through this. "Macie needs to know so he can set the parameters of the scanner."

"Vladsets have thicker skin than humans." Macie tapped something into the keyboard. "They require a longer, more targeted scan. If I set the parameters for vladset and your skin isn't as thick, we could hurt you."

"I am a drek. A half-breed. My father was alien."

Macie straightened. "Do you know where he was from?"

"No." She squared her shoulders. "He was a very important chief. So great he had two titles. Quimet told me once . . . hm . . . oh! Commander *and* Chief." She tilted her chin up. Straightened a little more. "Sounds very impressive, doesn't he? He had a clan one hundred times the size of Maman's."

Did she mean Commander-*in*-chief? Christ, she was human under there. Half-human, at least.

"She's talking about Hobbs." Macie's comment was directed to him, but he stared at Sorcha as if trying to see through her wraps.

"Yeah, I got that." His first mission in the Air Force had been a search and rescue for POTUS. His superiors in the Air Force had always assumed foul play, but they'd never recovered the spacecraft the president had been on, nor the three-hundred-forty-one other people on board, so they never could prove anything.

Sorcha gasped. "You know of him? What planet are the Hobbs from?"

The Hobbs. She thought it was the name of a race. "Hobbs was a person. George Hobbs. He was from Earth. He was *our* Commander-in-chief."

She swayed a bit and he eased her down into a chair by the terminal before she fell. If she was Hobbs' daughter, *she* might be proof of what happened all those years ago. "The vladsets captured him?"

She nodded and when she spoke her voice seemed smaller. Frailer. "Maman soul-merged with him and . . . ."

"You were the product of the soul-merge?"

"Yes."

Macie nudged him with his elbow. "You married POTUS' daughter."

Maybe. There were three-hundred-forty-one people on the flight. He couldn't remember how many were male or female, but any one of the men could be her father. "For all we know, one of the Secret Service agents on the flight impersonated POTUS to protect him."

"You think Vessa wouldn't have ferreted out the real C-in-C?"

True. Vessa would've made sure she had the right one. Tortured them until they broke. He shook his head. "Impossible." That would mean Sorcha was younger than he thought. It meant she might not be deformed under all those wraps . . . she might be *human.* No. He was grasping. Her skin was blue, not any human color. Yet she also wasn't dark vladset gray.

A moment ago, when she told them about her father her shoulders had been back, her spine straight, and her chin up. Now she'd folded. Her posture limp. He'd bet this ship that bitch of a queen had lied about her father her whole life.

"Are you okay, Sorcha?"

"I didn't know. It's good, though, right? I'm a little more like you, less . . . different."

What if they were wrong? What if Vessa had told her Hobbs was her father when it was someone else? The universe was full of biped life once out of the Virgo Cluster—the group of stars and planets surrounding Earth. He didn't want to get her hopes up. "We don't know for sure, yet. This isn't quite adding up for me." He glanced at Macie. "She said she's twenty-seven." He focused his attention on her. "You said twenty-seven, right?"

"Yes."

"You're too old to be Hobbs' daughter. He only traveled into space once and that was twenty-two years ago when he went missing. You would've already been seven years old."

"Maybe not; she did say she was a late bloomer." Macie turned to her. "How long is a year on Troon?"

She shrugged. "The standard ten months."

Macie pulled out his Saph-link.

Two months less than Earth. Donovan cursed. What were they looking at here? Two times twenty-seven was fifty-four months. She was four years and four months *less* than twenty-seven human years. She was a little over twenty-two. A whole fifteen years younger than him. *Damn.*

Great. Now on top of everything else everyone would think he was some dirty old bastard taking advantage of a young woman.

"How many days in a month?"

Macie's question jerked Donovan out of his musings.

"Thirty-four."

"So three hundred and forty days in a year." Macie tapped something into the virtual keyboard.

As opposed to three hundred sixty-five. Holy shit! His gut did a barrel roll. What if she was fresh-faced under those wraps? He'd look pathetic, that's what. An old, scarred battle-hound who'd taken advantage of a naïve girl.

And the Zeros he commanded, what would they think? Most of them had been injured in the line of duty because of his orders. If he returned home married to a young princess . . . even a young, ugly princess . . . . They'd think he'd forgotten them. They'd think he'd forgotten his past mistakes. They'd think he was carrying on with his life after fucking up theirs.

Oh, God. What if she was still a kid? He'd kissed her. Had a hard-on that wouldn't go away no matter what he did.

When Macie met his gaze, Donovan turned away. "Don't say it. Just fucking shoot me." He couldn't even do the math in his head he was so sick.

"When's your birthday, Sorcha?"

"Cintyde." When they both scrunched their brows, she added, "The third day of the seventh month, twenty-two forty-eight."

"Well, I think we've solved the mystery of why you were a late bloomer." Macie winked at her before shooting Donovan a sidelong glance. "She's twenty-one."

His face heated and he went light-headed with relief. At least she was legal. Barely. No wonder she was so innocent.

"Yeah." Macie winked at Sorcha. "In December."

Twenty. Dear God. The good news was her age fit with Hobbs' timeline now. She very well could be his daughter.

"What's wrong?" She had the edge of her veil caught between two wrapped fingers, twisting and untwisting the material. "This is a problem?"

"I'm old enough to be your father."

"You're not." Sorcha and Macie spoke together. "Not really."

He turned to Macie for support, but he just shrugged. "Experience is earned in deeds, not years. How many times have you told me that?"

Hell, he was no help. "Vessa cheated you. She should've married you to someone far younger than me." Hell, Macie was twenty-six. He'd have been a better match.

She shook her head. "We've soul-merged. My flame will keep yours youthful and through you, mine will gain experience."

More soul-merge crap. "That's a fairy tale."

Macie cleared his throat. "It's vladset religion."

"Fine." He flung his hand out to his side. "A fairy tale normalized by mass buy-in."

Her whole frame went rigid.

Donovan wiped the sweat from his brow. "Did you check the thermostat this morning?"

"Yeah. It's fine."

"Then why is it so fucking hot?"

"I'll check it again when we're done here." He motioned to the scanner. "Why don't we get this over with before you say something you'll regret?"

Donovan marched to the scanner with a growl. Flung the door open and climbed inside. Maybe he *was* being an ass. She couldn't help her age. He couldn't help his. They were married and if he divorced her, she'd be up shit creek. Hell, most men his age would be ecstatic, right?

Thing was, he didn't deserve a wife.

Especially not a young wife.

At least she wasn't beautiful.

10

Celeka slipped behind the glass barrier to stand with Macie. Various three-dimensional holograms of Donovan appeared next to them, projected by a small box on the terminal. They showed bone structure, organ health, and musculature. The machine registered everything from temperature to blood count.

They'd see her with this machine. They'd learn what she was. "How does it work? What makes it able to do all this?" She tried to touch Donovan's image and her hand went straight through.

"The scanner uses an isotope from a planet called Lythos. The isotope releases a small amount of radiation and as the arm spins around the outer shell of the machine, it creates images. It gives us views of the body at different depths, depending on how little or how much radiation is released. We can do deep tissue and bone scans, even heat signatures. The machine uses the same isotope in a slightly different way to measure chemical and biological functions." He studied Donovan's images. Frowned.

"What's wrong?"

"His blood pressure is higher than I've ever seen it. Heart rate's up." He shrugged. "I suppose both are normal considering his, uh, current problem." He rubbed the back of his neck.

"Will the effects of the soul-merge harm him?"

"Could." He folded his arms over his chest. "Males with priapism are supposed to seek medical attention." When she shook her head, he added, "An erection that won't go away. This is different, though; his isn't caused by trapped blood, but the effects of your pheromones. I don't have any idea if he'll have lasting effects from the soul-merge."

An unknown. "His body is under duress?"

"His heart is working harder than normal." He blew out a breath. "He's healthy. He can handle a bit of extra stress."

Could he? For how long? She couldn't allow this to continue. She'd have to brave the mating. First, she needed to get out of this scan. If Donovan saw her, he might choose death as a viable option. "Tell me more about the isotope that makes the machine work. Where is it?"

In the other room, Donovan stepped out of the machine.

"Come on, I'll show you." Macie led her into the other room past Donovan, opened a panel on the outside of the machine, and pointed to a glowing pink substance housed in a sealed glass vial in a container of water. He rambled on a little longer, clearly enjoying having someone to impart his knowledge to, but she had the information she needed. She maintained eye contact and made appreciative noises but was no longer interested. "Thank you for explaining. I'm ready for my scan."

Macie and Donovan exchanged a glance. "Step right up here." Donovan held the door open. "Stand in the center, very still until the green light comes on. Then you can come out." He shut the door.

Celeka turned toward the isotope. She couldn't see the pink substance from inside, but she knew its location. She parted the cooling cloths on her hand and placed her palm up against the side of the machine.

Within seconds, a siren blared. She covered her ears. A red light flashed inside the machine. A muffled shout came from outside. Grinning, she adjusted her cooling cloths.

The door flung open. Donovan hauled her out. He lifted her right off her feet and into his arms.

My wraps! She fidgeted, trying to right herself as he strode across the room and sat her on a table.

"Are you okay?" he shouted over the alarm. His hands glided over her covered arms. Her face. He yelled over his shoulder, "Shut it off."

The alarm went silent.

"Does anything hurt?" His gaze searched her. "Burn?"

She shook her head and infused her voice with innocent surprise. "I didn't realize the lights flashed; I couldn't see them from the outside."

"That wasn't supposed to happen." He tugged her against him in a rough embrace. His heart hammered inside his chest and his whole body shook. "Macie, what the hell happened?"

"Don't know." Macie raced past.

"Did you get the scan?" She grinned, doing her best to sound innocent. "Can I see?"

Donovan pushed her away enough to touch the cloths covering her face again.

Her grin faded.

His features were so taut that lines had appeared between his eyes at the top of his nose. More creased around his mouth on the right side. His honor marks had turned white and were pulled taut. His hands shook. Was the machine so important?

"Do you feel sick, Sorcha? Lightheaded?" His questions came so fast she didn't get a chance to answer the first before he asked the second. "Are you sure—?"

"Holy shit."

Donovan whirled toward Macie. She craned her neck to see, too. The hatch on the side of the machine stood open and the glowing substance in the tube had burst and now floated in globs inside the bubbling water.

She should be grinning at her victory over the machine. Instead, her attention shifted to Donovan. He was upset. Worried. A gaping hole opened inside her belly, leaving her insides twisted. A knot burned in her throat. "I'm sorry about your machine, Chief."

"I don't give a fuck about the machine," he growled the statement and jerked her against his chest again. "What do we do for her, Macie? Does she need medical attention?"

Her? He was worried about her?

"She should be fine. The isotope is still in the water. None leaked out. The external tank is sealed tight. Why the hell is the water *boiling*?"

A breath shuddered out of Donovan. "Okay. You're gonna be okay." He pressed his lips to the top of her head. His arms held her flush to his trembling frame.

He wasn't worried about the machine. He worried for *her*.

"When I saw those alarms go off, I thought the worst." He pressed his forehead to hers.

Ah. He worried about the repercussions of her being harmed. "Maman couldn't wage war over an accident."

He reared back, staring. "You could've died and you think I'm worried about Vessa? Fuck her." He dragged a hand through his hair, leaving reddish-brown tufts sticking up in all different directions. "I could give a rat's ass about her."

The vehemence in his tone, the surprise in his expression—he hadn't thought of the repercussions. He worried for her. She wriggled a fingertip free of her wraps and touched the corner of his mouth, trying to ease the stark lines. "I'll endeavor not to make you worry again." She didn't like seeing him upset for her and yet was warmed by his concern. Things had been much less complicated on Erra and Troon. No one cared what happened to her and she never gave a thought about anyone but Mujara.

"This is karma." He shook his head. "I shouldn't have asked you to do the scan."

"Can you fix your machine?" If she had money, she could pay for the repairs. That might be easier to fix than her chief. Despite Macie's reassurances everything was fine, Donovan wasn't calming down. With his already elevated blood pressure and heart rate, this added stress wasn't good.

Macie shook his head. "We'll have to replace the whole part."

"Oh." She'd ruined the machine permanently. She'd upset her chief. Oh, no! She'd also destroyed their plans. She only wanted to keep her secrets. Now they would suffer in many ways. She swallowed past the burning mass in her throat. "What will happen tomorrow?"

Both males stared. "Tomorrow?"

"We can't stop in Asteria."

They shared a glance. Donovan cleared his throat. "I'll, uh, find a way. I'm sure someone owes me a favor." He backed up a step and rubbed his hand over his face. "Shit."

Macie's uneasy gaze shifted between them. He jerked his thumb over his shoulder. "I'll go finish the meal."

"No. Thermostat first." He wiped his brow. "This room was hot as hell ten minutes ago. What if the variation in temperature weakened the glass? That needs to be fixed before anything else happens."

"Yeah, okay." Macie headed for the door. "I'm on it."

Donovan braced his hands on the table on either side of her and bowed his head.

The variations in temperature were her fault, too. She'd allowed herself to get angry twice today. She wasn't used to being around others. Nor sparring to the point her emotions became involved. *Dedia, how do I fix what I've done?* She stroked Donovan's hair while scanning the med-bay. "There's a med-wand left."

He raised his head.

"I know it's not the same as the scan you wished to do but the med-wand will detect any disease."

He blinked.

"Would the port authority accept that?"

The corner of his lips curved. "Maybe." He straightened, turned one way, then the other before he saw it on the counter. He brought the med-wand back to her, calibrated the device for a diagnostic, and ran it over her body. When he finished, a green light blinked from the tip. A heavy sigh escaped him. "Thank you." He lifted it. "This sets my mind at ease, too."

"That I'm not a secret weapon, sent to destroy Earth via incurable virus?"

His lips spread into a smile. "That Macie knows what he's talking about and you're no worse for the scan." His humor faded. "I'm sorry I asked you to do the scan."

"I'd rather you were sorry for insulting my beliefs."

"Yeah, that, too." He set the wand down and paced away. "I guess I don't understand. I mean, if soul-merging was this great thing, if doing so could extend life or add knowledge or whatever, why is there hardly any information about it? Why do vladsets rarely soul-merge? Why did you say kissing wouldn't be a good idea?" He shook his head. "I better go help Macie." He left her sitting on the table, his questions hanging in the air around her.

All valid questions. And all had a very simple answer, one he wouldn't like one bit.

Since Maman had become queen, vladsets only soul-merged their enemies.

11

By the time they finished with the thermostat, she'd finished cooking lunch.

Sort of.

Maybe.

She'd followed the directions, hoping to make up for the extra work she'd given Donovan and Macie, but the food didn't look like the picture. The round balls of meat were blackened, hard, and smelled of charred plastic. The long, thin plant-based tentacles had turned mushy when she slathered on the red sauce. Still, she forced a bright tone when they walked in. "The meal is ready."

Both males stopped dead in their tracks, their noses wrinkling. They shared a glance.

Donovan smiled. "I'm famished."

"Me, too." Macie came over and took two of the trays.

Donovan picked up the three glasses of gray-white liquid.

She grabbed the last tray and they all sat.

"Mm. Smells great." Donovan lifted the lid to the tray. "Spaghetti. My mother used to say anyone could cook spaghetti."

She pulled the top of her tray and stared down into the glop in the bowl. "Are you sure? This resembles the internal organs of some slaughtered creature."

Macie snickered. When Donovan shot him a glare, he bowed his head.

"I'm sure it's fine." Donovan lifted his fork, twirled the prongs into the mess in his bowl and took a huge bite. As he chewed, his eyes began to water.

"Macie said you like those little red flakes, so I added some." She didn't know how much to add, so she coated the entirety.

"Mm." He hadn't swallowed yet. His face was turning red.

Next to him, Macie had his head down. His shoulders shook. He lifted his hand, shielding his face from her.

Donovan elbowed him so hard, Macie was almost jolted from his seat. When he lowered his hand to catch his balance, she caught a glimpse of his face. He was laughing. Silently.

Was he laughing at her food or Donovan's face? His expression was funny. Like the fish living under the ice on Erra. Whenever they got spooked, they'd blow up to twice their size and turn red.

A giggle escaped and she covered her mouth.

Donovan darted out of his seat, into the galley, and spit his food into the compactor. When he came back into the rec room, he was still wiping at his eyes.

She dropped her own gaze to the food. What had she done wrong? "I followed the instructions." She lifted some of the stringy bits with her fork.

"Don't eat that." Donovan snatched her tray away.

How had she ruined the meal? "I followed the instructions."

"I'm sure you did." He put their trays on the counter, opened a cabinet, and grabbed a box before returning to the table. "Do you read English?"

"No. The machine read to me. Macie showed me which button to push to translate to Standard."

"Did any of the directions sound odd?"

She tipped her head to the side. "Most of them."

Macie made an odd, choking sound.

"Macie, shut up. You're banned from teaching my wife how to cook." He opened the box and held it out to her. "Take one."

She pulled out a hard, round, crumbly edible.

"And you"—he pointed to her with the box—"you have one chore on this ship as of now. Learn English. Once you have at least a partial grasp of the language, you can have all the other chores your heart desires. Until then, the galley is off limits unless you're with me."

"Oh, God . . . your face." Macie was all hunkered down into a shaking heap on his seat.

Donovan's lips trembled. He pressed them into a thin line. His eyes started to water again and his shoulders shook. He bowed his head, putting his hand up to hide his face from her. "When we came in and I smelled . . . ."

"I *know* . . . ."

Donovan cleared his throat and raised his head, his face serious. "I'm sorry. I'm not laughing at you."

Yes, he was. "You reminded me of a scared maripod."

His eyes widened and another burst of humor had him lowering his head again.

The two of them . . . . She shook her head. Their laughter was as contagious as a yawn. Just watching them made her giggle.

After a while they all settled down. Celeka bit into the disk her chief had given her. The crumbly food turned sweet in her mouth. She closed her eyes, savoring the flavor. "What is this?"

"Chocolate wafers."

"I like these."

Donovan held the box out to her. "Take a few. We've a way to go before dinner." She took several, warming when he chuckled. "Greedy girl." He winked.

"Where's mine?" Macie snatched the box out of his hand, taking an even bigger handful.

English. She didn't want to learn another language. Standard was difficult enough. "Do they speak Standard on Earth?"

"Nah." He popped a disk into his mouth and chewed. "Earth has allowed interstellar trading for the last fifty some-odd years, but humans are distrustful of anything they don't understand—which includes alien races. For a long time, even human-alien marriages were banned. Now they're just frowned on. Earthers tend to make life as difficult as possible for off-planet races."

Yet another thing to worry over. "Our marriage will cause you problems at home?"

He rubbed his hand over his scarred cheek. "No more than what I already had. Don't worry about it."

"How do you make your living?"

The men exchanged a glance. "We're runners—we run cargo between IgA partner planets, and we're bounty hunters—uh, we take contracts for money to capture marks, men or women wanted for something." He shifted in his seat, wincing. "We pretty much take whatever odd job we can."

"Do you have a trade on Earth?"

He dropped his gaze.

Even Macie grew quiet.

Had she said something wrong? She tried to turn the topic back to something they seemed more willing to talk about. "What kind of goods do you deliver for planets?"

"Anything our clients want." Macie shoved a wafer into his mouth.

Donovan rolled his eyes. "Nothing illegal. Usually exotic food or liquor. Sometimes parts for ships or bulk deliveries of resources." He grimaced and shifted in his seat again, sweat beaded his brow. "We do deliveries to keep up repairs on this ship and keep ourselves fed."

"Most of what we make comes from the money we get for bounty hunting." Macie grabbed another handful of wafers.

Like the ones she stole from them. The only time Maman had ever seemed pleased with her was when she killed those marks, but not even the pride of earning a tiny bit of approval completely diminished her regret for ending lives. "Does it ever bother you, killing for money?"

They both stared.

"We don't kill anymore," Macie said at the same time as Donovan said, "We only take live capture contracts."

Why would they lie? They'd gone after the same targets she had. "There's not much money in no-kill bounties. Sometimes you must . . . ." She trailed off as they both shook their heads.

Her gut churned and she set the remaining wafers aside. Maman said the contracts were posted by the IgA. She said accepting the contracts would increase their chances of having their probation lifted and being accepted fully into the IgA. She said if Troon showed their worth and proved to be an asset, the IgA would lift the sanctions. Had Maman lied or were these men?

Donovan blew out a deep breath. "When I retired from the military, I promised myself I'd never take a life at another's command."

Macie added. "The marks we hunt are high-risk. We get a bonus for bringing them in alive." He sighed. "Well, when someone else doesn't get to them first."

"Oh?"

Donovan leaned his forearms on the table. "We keep running into this one hunter. The bastard kills the marks before we can get them out. The IgA's put a contract on him."

Her body stilled and her face heated. For once she was grateful for her cooling cloths and veil. "They know who the hunter is?"

"Yeah. Blaze."

Donovan scoffed. "Macie calls him Blaze. This hunter wears this black mask shaped like a beast's face. Always covered head-to-toe in battle fatigues. He's got his suit wired somehow so he can set his hands ablaze and he burns his victims alive. He's gotten our last five marks—they were all killed the same way."

She picked at the edge of a wafer. "The contract on Blaze is to bring him in dead or alive?"

"Alive. All the marks he killed were wanted for questioning on the same matter: shipments of an unknown resource that keeps popping up on the black market. The IgA figures Blaze must know something."

Her stomach roiled. Maman had said the men she'd killed had posed a direct threat to the IgA. She wanted to help her people. To keep Mujara safe. And now she had a price on her head? She swallowed past the thick lump forming in her throat. "What kind of resource?"

"We're not sure what it is. Drug. Mineral. Animal. The IgA is tight-lipped as hell about the whole thing, which is why the bounties were so damned high. We got pictures of the marks and enough information to track them, but that's all. We risked our skin to bring these assholes in alive."

"And Blaze killed them." Macie took a drink. "We almost had the son of a bitch last time."

That they had. They'd cornered her in a dead-end alley far from her ship and guards.

"We should've shot him and been done with it."

She stared at Macie. That was the only reason she'd slipped away. Instead of shooting her, they'd tried to capture her. When they'd gotten close, she'd flared her hand and pushed past Donovan. His suit still had her handprint. "Why didn't you?"

"Someone's killing off witnesses. Every time we think we have someone with answers, they end up dead. If we capture Blaze, we can question him and find out who's signing his paychecks. Not knowing what race he is, I was even afraid of using the stun setting—it'll kill some races."

Her gaze locked on his. "The IgA posted those contracts; aren't they paying him?"

"No." Donovan pushed the box away. "*We* held the contracts on those marks and the IgA wanted them alive."

"Who owns Blaze's contract?"

He met her gaze. "Me. I'm gonna get the son of a bitch."

Her husband held her contract. If the IgA discovered her identity . . . if he was harboring her . . . . *Are you compromised?* If Salcedo found out . . . .

Maman had *lied*. Tricked her into doing things that would cause the people of Troon to suffer more in the long run. The clans were eager to become part of the IgA. If they discovered Maman had ordered her to kill the IgA's marks, they would rebel. Why would Maman take such risks? What did she hope to gain? It must be this resource they'd mentioned. Maman had tricked her into killing over a resource.

No longer.

She belonged to her husband now. *Her* chief. To an Earther. And Earthers didn't need to listen to their mothers. She nodded to herself. Her decision was sound and yet her stomach turned queasy. Her chest was full of a stifling darkness that threatened to strangle her flame. Was this why Donovan refused to kill for others? Did he carry this awful feeling for the deeds he'd done on another's behalf?

Perhaps this was another thing they had in common.

"I'm gonna—" Donovan made a waving motion with his hand. "Go." When he stood, he paused, leaning on the table, eyes closed, mouth pressed together in a thin line. Sweat dotted his hairline. He let out a breath, straightened, and limped out of the room.

The soul-merge wasn't treating him kindly. Had he been vladset, he'd have broken long before now. Attacked her. Mated her. Instead, he suffered.

Macie winked. "He's not usually like this. I mean, he tends to be serious most of the time but he's laid back. Easy-going."

"It's the soul-merge."

"Yeah."

"I'll fix the problem." She owed him. For their kindness. For killing their marks. For the machine. She didn't want him to suffer anymore. Not for her.

He started to take another bite, then lowered his hand. "This isn't your fault. You know that, right?"

"The IgA didn't give him a choice. If he hadn't kissed me or if I refused, they would've sent me home." Dead and buried, her and her sister. As Macie said, it wasn't a choice, but a threat.

"Donovan won't force you to do anything. You don't need to *fix* anything. We land in Asteria tomorrow. Donovan can see a doctor. If there's a cure, they'll find it."

There was only one cure for their soul-merge. Her. "What's he like? When he's not in a pheromone-induced cloud."

Macie chuckled. "He's a good guy. He takes care of his people. Works hard. He likes to tease."

Yes, he did like to tease.

"What about bad traits?"

His lips quirked. "Stubborn. He prefers to be in control of everything. Slightly masochistic, which is what's saving you right now. And he's . . . ." Macie blew out his cheeks on a heavy sigh. "I don't know. He's gotten lost somewhere along the way. All he thinks about are all these responsibilities, which shouldn't be his anyway. He used to have things he wanted to do."

"Like what?"

"We'd planned to go into business for ourselves. Only take the jobs we wanted to take. Get rich and find a nice little patch of land on one of the lesser populated planets. Somewhere we could start over."

"But you did."

"Well, yeah. I mean we do work for ourselves, but we don't keep much. He's not done punishing himself." He snapped his mouth closed. "Doesn't matter. Forget I said anything." He got up and collected the remaining dishes.

Why would he punish himself? Was that why he continued to endure the soul-merge without forcing her to mate? "Do you want help?"

"Nah. I got this."

She stood and wandered the rec room. When they arrived at Asteria, she would leave. Not divorce him but leave him. Sooner or later, they'd discover who she was and the things she'd done. After the kindness they'd both shown her, she refused to put them into the situation of choosing between handing her over to the IgA or going on the run with her.

Now that she knew her chief a little, she had no doubt which option he'd choose.

Which left tonight to mate him. Her already queasy tummy erupted into flutters. He'd resist her efforts and she didn't even know how humans went about the mating. From what Donovan had said, their rituals sounded quite different from the vladsets'.

She circled the couch and came upon the personal holo-screen. For a long time, she stared at it. The information she needed was there. She leaned down, grabbed the holo-screen and hid it under her veil. "I'm going to rest for a while."

"All right." Macie didn't even pause in his chore.

Oh, she'd seen vladsets mate. She knew where all the parts fit together, but she was beginning to think human mating wasn't as violent. That's what she needed to know, how humans went about the act so she could seduce Donovan like a human woman.

It seemed she was half human after all.

— • —

12

Donovan couldn't sleep. Couldn't eat. Couldn't do fuck-all without hurting. He managed to shower and change into some sweats; the loose-fitting material helped. He sat on the sparring mat with his back to the wall. Eyes closed. Lips pressed together, arm pressed against his erection.

He kept playing the conversation at lunch over in his mind. When she asked what he did for a living on Earth, he hadn't known how to answer. Anything he said would've pointed out the derogatory slant to a human chief compared to a vladset chief. Macie must've thought the same because he'd kept his trap shut, too.

The vladsets loved their royal hierarchy and chiefs were the dukes of vladset culture. They were rich. Important. Powerful.

That wasn't him.

He and Macie led a group of runners and bounty hunters called the Zeros—a group of old and wounded soldiers—who helped provide money, food, supplies, weapons, infrastructure, and intelligence to Division Command Zero.

He'd retired from the military after the rebellion. He hadn't wanted to fight anymore, but he couldn't abandon the men and women injured during the rebellion under his command. Nor could he leave DCZ to the mess he'd created by leading a coup and not having a replacement ready. As a form of penance, he'd promised to provide the support services DCZ needed to continue to operate until they named a leader and got them into power. After that, they were on their own. After that, he and Macie would take their business and the Zeros and move on.

Three years later and the bastards at DCZ were still looking for someone they trusted enough to put into power. Three long years that the big corporations had taken full advantage of. With no government, wealthy corporations began ruling over their locals, providing infrastructure, law enforcement, and jobs. The Blue Helmets now hired themselves out to the highest bidders—the corporations.

Yeah, DCZ had waited too long and the situation had deteriorated. There were too many enemies now. When DCZ finally found someone to lead, if they found someone, they were looking at a global war against the corporations to get that leader into power.

Once Sorcha figured out who and what he was, she'd see him as nothing more than a male in trade. A poor one. A commoner. A chief with a broken, rundown clan who was beneath her notice.

Hell, he couldn't even walk down the street outside the walls of DCZ without getting noticed by civilians as the traitor who'd led the rebellion against the UN. The majority of Earthers hated him. Hated DCZ. They'd been quite happy with the false peace and prosperity the UN offered and didn't care how they'd secured it.

Sorcha would never understand. Vladsets did not suffer traitors.

A cramp sliced through his groin, bending him forward. He'd hoped he'd be better off down here away from his wife and her scent but distance wasn't helping.

"Vladsets don't soul-merge their mates."

Was he cursed? He cracked his eyes open. Sorcha was lingering in the shadows near the doorway. "Come here and explain."

She strode across the room, stopping before his outstretched legs. "Soul-merging is meant for our enemies."

Considering how he felt right now, he believed her. Should someone attack him, he'd be damned near helpless. Blue balls were one thing, this . . . his groin muscles had started to cramp this afternoon during their make-shift lunch, making him completely useless. "You kiss your enemies?"

"We soul-merge them. After a few days, captives will do anything while under the influence of the soul-merge."

He could well imagine. Right now . . . all he wanted was relief.

"Their captor has complete control, can make them do anything by withholding full mating. When they tire of the game, they can force them to their desire at their ease."

"Why?"

She lowered her voice as if imparting a terrible secret. "The ultimate battle trophy is offspring of an enemy. To hold the child in front of the defeated parent and watch their heart die as they are told the child will be raised to hate their own people. That the child will infiltrate and spy on their people. Maman has spies everywhere."

His wife was one of those children. Raised to be his enemy. Sorcha hadn't even known she was half-human. He remembered the white-haired person in the cell. At the time he'd thought it a woman, but had that been Hobbs? He'd be old enough to have white hair and if they didn't allow him to cut it, it would be very long all these years later. "While the parent sits in prison?"

"No. The vladset soul-devours their enemy—they absorb the defeated soul, killing them."

Not Hobbs, then. Must've been her in that cell.

She pulled a pin from her wrapped hair and lifted her veil off her head.

Why was she telling him this? "Is that what you're doing to me?"

She paused. "You're kind." Folded her veil and set it aside. "I don't wish you ill. I also don't wish to be sent home for execution."

Of course. He'd married her to avoid execution. She'd soul-merged him to avoid the same.

Sorcha stood over him, a foot on either side of his legs.

"What are you doing?"

She lowered herself into his lap, facing him. "I'm preparing to fall on your sword, my Chief."

His lips twitched.

"My joking isn't very good." She ducked her head. "I hoped to hear you laugh."

"Why?"

"I like your laugh. Especially when you're surprised into laughing. Your voice turns hoarse, like you don't do it often, which makes it special." She touched her fingers to his lips. "You don't smile much. You have a beautiful smile."

He lowered his face as his lips spread and his face warmed. Only Sorcha would find his smile beautiful. Due to the scars, his smile was a grim thing at best. He'd gotten in the habit of hiding his humor when around anyone but Macie. Except he didn't need to hide from Sorcha. She was at least as bad off as him.

Why the hell was he fighting this so hard? They couldn't divorce. They might as well make a go of the marriage. They'd only known each other a couple days and had already formed a friendship that never felt forced or fake. He liked her well enough to search for things about her to find attractive.

In fact, he couldn't picture her as a monster anymore. Not now that he was learning her shape. Her colors. Her texture. She may be different but he didn't fear whatever she was hiding anymore.

She unwound the wraps from her hands and tucked the ends into the wraps at her wrists. She was always so careful. Never showing anything more than she had to at any given moment. Being so meticulous must get tiresome. He captured one of her hands in his—another small piece of her revealed. She had tiny hands, her palms a paler blue than the rest of her skin—so translucent he could almost make out her muscles and veins. The cartilage on the backs of her knuckles peeked through her skin.

Yeah, she was different. Not bad. Not ugly. Just different.

He stroked his thumb over the ridges of her knuckles. "Does this hurt?"

She tensed but shook her head.

Had she been full vladset, she'd have small spikes protruding from her knuckles instead of little white nubs. Did she have them down her spine and across her shoulders?

He lifted her hand and kissed her knuckles. Watched as the wrap covering her mouth bowed in with her sharp inhale.

She was young. Inexperienced. He needed to be careful, and right now, he didn't know if he could manage that. "Now isn't a good time to—"

Her hand slid down his chest and abs to the waistband of his pants.

"Don't." He gripped her wrist, holding her still. After being hard for more than twenty-four hours, he wasn't sure he'd continue to do the right thing if she started rubbing up against him.

"What you're experiencing will only get worse." She bowed her head. "I understand you don't want me. I won't take advantage of you, I promise."

Despite his discomfort, he chuckled.

"Nor will I devour your soul. If you want the truth, my own soul is more than I can handle."

He leaned his head back against the wall. "I'm more worried I'll hurt you."

"I'm aware of what will happen. I've seen vladset males take their women. And I stole the holo-screen . . . to learn how humans go about this."

Jesus. "And?"

"In another day, you won't care if you hurt me." She shifted in his lap. "I want to do this now, while you still have control. Please, don't be angry with me."

He pulled her close. "I'm mad at the situation, not you. We're stuck between your maman and the IgA. Nothing but fucking pawns."

"I understand. I've been a pawn my whole life. A tool to someone else's gain. At least this time the choice is mine."

She was gutting him one word at a time.

"I'll make you a deal." She worked her hand free of his grip and stroked his neck. "I'll ease you now and when we get to Asteria, you'll let me go free. You'll let me walk away without the dishonor of a divorce and without sending me back home."

Damn. Here he been starting to think they could make this thing work. Starting to think she wanted him despite his scars. Hell, she was too young for him. It'd probably be for the best if they went their separate ways. Why then, did her request make his stomach twist and his chest ache?

"If you want out of the marriage, fine." He took her chin between his thumb and fingers. "But if we make love, I'll take care of you whether we're together or not. Which means you'll be living on Earth, not Asteria. Otherwise, you're getting nothing out of this deal."

She parted her cooling cloths enough to reveal her lips. "I'll get to feel desirable for once. I'll cherish that always. I need nothing else." Her warm hand dipped inside his pants and wrapped around his cock.

Stars bloomed behind his eyes. "I'm not done—." He blew out a breath and sucked in another. "—talking." The right thing to do would be to remove her hand, but . . . *Christ.* That was way beyond him right now.

"Our deal is made." She stroked up his length, thumbing across the head. "I live. I'm free. So are you. Discussion over." She released him and dragged his sweats down to his thighs. When she wrapped him in her grip again, he closed his eyes. Let his head fall back against the wall.

Without him she wouldn't last two days on Earth, much less Asteria. If she thought—*"Fuck."*

Her mouth enveloped him in wet heat and he jetted into her without warning. His whole body tightened and shuddered, wringing a shout from his chest.

A muffled cry came from Sorcha. She jumped. Drew on him again, swallowing his seed down.

Oh, God. He hadn't even had time to warn her. "Sorry." *Shit.* She probably thought he had no staying power. Must think him a complete brute. He didn't know why her opinion mattered, but it did.

He wasn't softening. He wasn't even close to done. His hands flexed at his sides. All he wanted to do was pull her back into his lap and impale her on his cock.

Still, she worked him with her mouth. Unpracticed. Uncoordinated. She had no damn idea what she was doing and he didn't care.

"Come here." He hauled her up so she straddled his hips. "Let's get these off." He went for the cloths.

She stopped him, her grip stronger than expected. "No."

"It's gonna be difficult to make love while dressed."

"Yet that's what will happen."

His hands tightened on the curve of her hips. "When will you start trusting me?"

"This isn't about trust."

"Then what's it about?"

Her hand curled around his cock again. "Respect. Mutual need. Kindness to those we care for."

Was it? A hollowness settled inside his chest. That's all this was? "Would you do this for Macie? Give him your body?"

She sucked in a breath. "No."

"You don't respect him?"

"Of course, but—"

"You don't find him attractive?" His voice grew harsh.

"He's handsome, but—"

"You don't care for him?"

"He's clan. I'll care for all our clan." Her lips pressed into a thin line. Her muscles tensed as if she might run.

No way in hell was she leaving. He tightened his grip. "Then what's the difference? Why sacrifice your body to me and not him?"

She tried to pull away again. This time he shifted his position, rolling her under him and holy hell those wraps of hers were thin. With no effort on his part, his cock lay right against the heat of her slit. "Why me?"

Her lips drew down at the corners. "*You* are my chief. I'm bound to *you*. You make me want . . . something." Her voice rose with each pronouncement, the edge of panic tinging her words. "My concern for you is *different*. I don't know why."

"That scares you?"

Her chin lifted in silent challenge.

She was raised by vladsets. No way would she admit to fear. The overhead lights glinted off something shining under her cloths. Her eyes? Tears?

"I like you." He stroked his thumb over her bottom lip. "Too much to make love to you with so much stuff between us." The wraps. The distrust. Her damned deal.

"My Chief—"

"Donovan."

"Donovan, this will only get worse for you. For both of us."

He shook his head. "Macie researched soul-merging. I just need to get you off."

"What?"

"Give you an orgasm."

"What?"

He grinned. "Why don't I show you? I won't bare any more of you than I need to. And you're not going to fight me. Deal?"

She gave him a barely perceptible nod. Now for the big question, did half-vladset women have orgasms? She was aroused. Her scent permeated the air around them, driving him to distraction. Her nipples were hard against his chest. He lowered his head and drew one of the peaks into his mouth, cooling cloths and all. The damp material conformed to the shape of her nipple. He sucked and licked and tongued aside the edge of the cloth. He was rewarded with the taste of her skin. She squirmed, her fingers threading into his hair.

He switched sides, sneaking a quick peek . . . her nipple was the same shade of blue as her lips. He sucked the second peak into his mouth. Her breathing changed. Her grip on his hair strengthened. Goddamn, she was responsive. If they ever did make love, he'd enjoy the hell out of her. While she might not trust him to see her without rejecting her, she did trust him with her body. With her pleasure.

He sank lower, nipping her belly through the cloths, making her muscles twitch. "Spread your thighs for me, Sorcha." *Brightness.* His little flame. It was fitting. She scorched the hell out of his senses. Was burning him up from the inside out. Twisting him in knots. He nuzzled her over the cloths at the apex of her thighs.

She jerked upright.

He was ready and pushed her back down. "Easy." He stared up her body. "Soft, remember?"

"Soft." She nodded.

At least he was trying like hell to keep things soft. Easy. He kept his gaze trained on her covered face while he parted the cloths between her thighs. It was strange wanting someone he hadn't ever seen. Kind of erotic, baring one little piece at a time. He lowered his gaze. She was bare. Clean. Wet. She smelled like heaven. Whatever he feared finding under there . . . she was just a woman. "Blue is my new favorite color." He pressed his mouth to her and sucked.

She bowed off the mat. *"Donovan."*

Warmth flooded him to his toes. He teased her delicate hood aside and licked her clit. Slipped a finger inside her and moaned. He needed every ounce of control not to shift positions and bury his cock in her tight, wet, heat.

Her hips lifted with every thrust of his finger. Her hands tangled in his hair, tugging one moment, pushing against him the next. The short tips of her nails scraped his scalp. Oh, yes, he'd enjoy every second of loving on this woman. Her inner muscles tightened around his finger. Little whimpers tore from her throat. She was close.

He threaded a second finger into her. She gasped. Bore down on his hand. Rolled her hips. Her inner muscles fluttered. She tried to clamp her thighs closed and push him away.

"Don't hide." He stroked the flat of his tongue against her. "Let it happen." Her desire bathed his fingers and her inner muscles convulsed. Her whole body tensed, her back arching, and then she eased into pulsing pleasure around him. Heat washed over him, warming him from the inside out. "I've got you."

What he didn't have was himself.

Macie had been wrong. She'd come hard. Her scent surrounded him. He pressed his face to her belly as his balls drew up painfully tight and his cock throbbed. Obviously, more than an orgasm was needed.

"Come here, my Chief."

My Chief. He liked that. She was possessive of him. "Yeah, not a good idea."

Her fingers threaded through his hair, soothing. "I can feel your pain. You'll come here."

He forced himself up. Away. She was too innocent. He was too hard. He didn't want to hurt her. He leaned back against the padded wall, fumbling for his pants.

She crawled right into his lap, straddling his hips. Pressed her mouth to his. Slid against his cock, slicking him in her desire, making the cramping stop, making her impossible to resist.

"I will ease you and then we'll both be free." She took him in hand and a shiver raced over his skin, gathering at the small of his back.

Yeah, he had no idea why he was fighting this so hard. He was halfway in love with her already—wraps and all. She'd sealed her fate when she kissed his ruined cheek. When she claimed ownership over him.

He slipped his fingers under her cloths at her hips and found smooth, soft skin. Nudged her up so she knelt over him. She pressed his tip to her entrance. Christ, she was tight. Her body didn't want to surrender.

She bit her lip. "I don't think you'll fit."

"I'll fit." He would. He had to. He flipped their positions, lying her on her back, coming down over her and repositioning himself. He cupped the back of her head in one hand as he slipped past her entrance. "Goddamn." Her inner muscles contracted around him. There wasn't anywhere else to go. He let his head drop to her shoulder. "I'm not gonna fit."

"You'll fit." She lifted her hips and he slid in another half-inch. She gasped.

Sweat broke out over his brow. "You all right?"

"Mm." She rolled her hips. Spread her legs wider.

He sank in and came up against a barrier. *Shit.* She didn't seem aware of her peril. She continued to move against him, damned near purring. He considered warning her but didn't want her to tense. He tucked one arm under her, gripping her shoulder, tilted her hips up with the other and rammed himself home. She hugged him in a lethal embrace with her inner muscles and stars bloomed behind his eyes. Release broke over him with the force of a tidal wave, sucking the breath from his lungs, making him shudder, lasting far longer than anything he'd ever experienced before. But as the waves of pleasure eased, his cock remained hard. The need to move inside her rising.

Celeka curled around her chief, seeking comfort despite the fact he was the one who'd caused the sharp pain. The overwhelming desire to get closer to him, when he pierced her most delicate flesh, made no sense.

"Sorry." He slipped a finger under the wraps on her face to caress her cheek. His fingers were rough with callouses and yet soothing. Yet another contradiction.

"That's the only bad part." He kissed her lips. "Won't happen again."

She didn't answer. Didn't think she could. The sharp pain where they were joined had stolen her breath and she was still working out why she didn't shove him away. In the past, anytime she was hurt or scared she flared, her inner flame surrounding her in a protective shield. Yet her flame remained deep inside. She didn't push him away. If anything, she held him closer.

He propped himself on one elbow and fidgeted with her wraps at the back of her neck. Unwound the mass of her hair and spread it out. "Beautiful."

Beautiful? When he made the declaration, he stared at her hair, combing his fingers through the ends which made her scalp tingle. Sweat had broken out on his skin and his jaw clenched.

He was distracting himself. Giving her time. Her chief was nothing like vladset males and she loved that about him. Slowly, her inner muscles eased their grip, the pain receded. And yet, he didn't move. After the euphoria she experienced earlier, she'd hoped for more of the same. "Are we done?"

He shook his head against her. Fingered aside her cloths so he could kiss her neck.

She shivered.

He let those fall shut and did the same at her collar bone.

Why had he stopped? The hologram she viewed suggested he should be flexing against her. Did he not know how to do this?

When he continued to do no more than bare tiny sections of skin to kiss, her body relaxed. Her grip on his shoulders eased and she lay back against the padded floor again. He kept his hips still but ducked his head and drew one of her nipples into his mouth, battering the tiny bud with his tongue.

She sucked in a deep breath as shivers erupted over her skin, sparking and flashing like fallen stars down her body to where they were joined. Mm, yes. That's what she wanted.

She writhed against him and he eased out of her. *Oh, Dedia.* He lifted onto one arm. Spread his legs to force hers wider and eased back into her. With his free hand, he pressed the pad of this thumb to her clit, circling and teasing.

Her lips parted on a moan. She took over, rolling her hips against him, easing him in and out of her. Even as she lay beneath him, he allowed her to set the pace.

"That's it." He pressed his thumb harder and lighter against her, teasing. "Take what you need."

She held his hips in a death grip, a silent demand for him to stay still while she sought her pleasure. Her pace quickened with his strokes against her clit, her inner muscles tightening.

Mm, she liked his firm touch, not directly on her clit, but just to the side. She dropped her gaze to watch his engorged cock sliding out of her, her sex stretched tight around his girth. His hips bucked forward of their own accord.

"Yes. Again." Her nails sank into his flanks, urging him on.

He slid out. Slammed home.

"Again." She pressed her heels to the ground, lifting her hips in a demand for more.

Control gone, he thrust into her, his hand trapped between their bodies, thumb to her clit, the scent of sex heavy in the air. He powered into her, making her his. Claiming her like she'd claimed him. Marking her. Deeper. Harder.

She licked his nipple. Nipped him. Sucked . . . His hips jerked forward hard.

Celeka cried out. Her muscles contracted. He pressed his head to the crook of her neck as he jetted into her. Her orgasm seemed to last forever, rolling over her in waves of acute pleasure. She clung to him, shuddering through her release.

After, he rolled over, dragging her with him until she ended up draped over him. His hand stroked over her back once. Twice. And fell away.

He was asleep.

Celeka lifted her head and stared down at her chief in horror. What had she done? How naïve could she be? She'd given herself to him and now she had to leave. She wouldn't remember tonight fondly. She'd remember this with longing and regret. Not regret that she'd fully mated with him. Regret they'd never have the opportunity again. This afternoon, she'd been an ugly female no one wanted . . . but at least she hadn't known what she was missing.

Tonight, she did.

While he slept, she unwound her cloths. He wouldn't wake for hours, not after the first mating, and now was her chance to have everything she wanted. To know his naked body against hers. To put her head on his chest and discover the beat of his heart. To simply lie next to him and allow her body's rhythms to align with his.

She dropped her cloths to the floor, shook out her hair and lay down alongside him. Her ear pressed to his chest, her leg entwined with his, her fingers flattened against his pec. Within a few moments, her heartbeat matched his. The steady rise and fall of their chests harmonized.

What might her life be like if she could stay mated to such a male? She hadn't expected his tenderness. Nor his protectiveness. By all rights, she was the most convenient target for his anger, yet he'd given her pleasure despite his own discomfort. Life with a male like him . . . she closed her eyes against a sudden burn.

Such things were not meant for her. Her chief may not mind her appearance too much. He might get past her coloring. May not even mind the tiny nubs poking through her skin. But he was fully human. He wouldn't understand her flame. Nor the things she'd done to protect Mujara. She couldn't even forgive herself. And now the IgA had put out a contract on her. A contract he owned.

No, she couldn't keep her chief but the memory of him would torture her forever.

                              — • —

                              13

Donovan woke with a smile on his face, feeling better than he had since before his stay with the vladsets. He opened his eyes. He'd fallen asleep on the mat. Sorcha had covered him with a blanket from the bed in his quarters. Next to him, the mat was cold.

Damn. She'd left.

His grin faded. Hell. He remembered pulling her into his arms to hold her but had he said anything? At all? That had been her first time and he hadn't praised her or told her how amazing she was or anything. *Shit.* He hadn't helped her clean up. He should've taken her upstairs to bed.

He rose with a groan, aching in places he'd forgotten *could* ache, and made his way to the CO_2 laser shower. What he wouldn't give for a real shower. This got the job done but didn't ease his tight muscles like hot water did. At least they were close to Asteria. He could offer Sorcha a bath, and they'd be able to replenish their water supply when they landed in port later today.

What the hell had he done? He enjoyed the hell out of his wife, that's what. Now he didn't want to let her go. Not on Asteria. Not on Earth. She could take her deal and shove it where no suns shone.

What would his Zeros think? He'd spent the last three years giving everything he had to them. Due to their injuries, Earthers wouldn't risk hiring them—they were too afraid of backlash from other civilians if they discovered they'd hired employees who'd fought in the rebellion. And they weren't whole, so DCZ had no use for them. He'd hired every last one of them. Found enough ships so they could run cargo and bounty hunt with him for DCZ. Tried to give them purpose and a community where they were welcome. He couldn't ever pay them back in full for what they'd lost, though.

Just this once, he wanted something for himself. Was that wrong?

He needed to find a way to coax her into staying.

Needed to gain her trust so she'd show herself to him.

Hell. He just needed her.

How did he convince her to stay? Honestly, he didn't have a whole hell of a lot going for him. She liked his scars. His title. On Earth, those were marks against him. How would she feel once she realized that?

He could spoil her with attention. She enjoyed sex, if her moans and cries for more were any indication. She could have as much sex as she wanted. A rueful smile broke over his face as he lifted his arms and turned in the chamber. She was a passionate little thing. Which suited him fine. It'd been a hell of a long time since he'd been balls deep in a woman. Even before having his face fucked up, he had a tough time finding women who matched him in the bedroom.

Sorcha would. She liked when he took over. She challenged him, yes, but he liked that—the tug-of-war for dominance. He liked that she allowed herself to completely let go. She trusted him to take care of her.

The chamber went dark and he let himself out, grabbed some clothes from the storage bin, and got dressed. Those wraps had to go. Maybe he'd seduce her out of them. Dominate her out of them. She sure as hell wouldn't remove them on her own. By the time he finished with her, he'd have her begging him to strip her bare. She'd forget that stupid deal.

His muscles tensed at the thought of her leaving. Did she think making her way in Asteria would be any easier than Earth? English was the primary language on both planets, along with a smattering of other Earther languages. And Asteria . . . it wasn't a good place for a woman alone. A woman who didn't know the language. The customs. Hell, she was just learning about her own body. She was naïve. Innocent.

Bastard that he was, he loved that. That he could be the one to help her discover her sexuality. That he could be her first and her last and her everything-in-between.

He caught sight of Macie at the top of the stairs easing the door shut to Sorcha's quarters. Bare-footed, he wore those stupid PJ bottoms with the dancing penguins and a black tee. Donovan froze. Why the fuck was Macie coming out of his wife's room?

Macie straightened and stretched. Twisted around to crack his back and caught sight of Donovan. "You're a lucky son of a bitch, you know that?"

His gaze darted to the door and back to Macie.

"As if." Macie snorted. "You're a lucky bastard because your wife is so pleased with herself that she hasn't even noticed you slept through part of your duties. Apparently, she was so fantastic she made her chief pass out."

He folded his arms over his chest and tried to stifle his grin. "She's not lying."

"I showed her how to fill the bath and use the gravity field in case she's still in there when we start the landing cycle. Thought the warm water might help since she was moving a little stiffly."

He closed his eyes. She was sore. "Thank you." His little flame had turned to wildfire in his arms last night. Something she hadn't ever done before. With anyone. His cock twitched to life.

"That was pathetic." Macie waved his hand in a gesture that encompassed Donovan. "That expression flashing across your face. What was that, euphoric recall?"

"Oh, fuck off." He wouldn't allow Macie to piss him off.

"No, really. After seeing that, I'm thinking about getting myself a wife." His grin widened. "Hell, I finally found a bluff I *can't* say with a straight face."

"You're pathetic." He motioned to the door. "You warned her never to put the gravity field over level two, right?"

Macie sent him a wry glare. "*Yeah.* You warned her she might be pregnant, right?"

His stride faltered. Pregnant? He shook his head. "I've kept up with my shots."

Macie turned down the hall. "Thank God for that."

"Christ, do you have something to say?"

"I'd call you an ass except I know you would've taken care of her yourself if you hadn't been through the ringer." He shrugged. "I've had the last two days to recover from vladset hospitality. You were dealing with . . . ." His gaze dropped. "A different kind of stress."

Donovan followed him into the rec room. "One of these days, Macie, you're gonna get hitched and we're gonna see how fucking perfect a husband you make."

Macie snorted and picked his coffee cup up from the counter. "Single women would cry in the streets."

"Their parents would rejoice."

"I was coming to get you when I got sidetracked with Sorcha. Merrick's waiting to talk to us."

"Go ahead and hail him. I'll be right there." He paused at the counter long enough to pour himself a cup of coffee and grab a nutrient bar out of the cabinet. By the time he finished, Macie had Merrick, the sheriff of Diamond Fjord, Asteria on the com in the cockpit. This close to Asteria the com was far more secure than a vid-call.

"What's your ETA?" Merrick asked.

Macie checked the gauges. "'Bout forty minutes, plus cargo inspection."

Donovan slipped into the captain's chair. "You got any good news for us, Mer?"

"Got news. Wouldn't say it's good."

Not what he wanted to hear. "Go on then, ruin our day."

Merrick's deep voice rumbled through the com. "You have a shit-ton of messages from the Zeros. Rent went up on the first of the month."

Macie's gaze shot to his. He mouthed, *again?*

"From what they say, it's doubled and while they've all hit their monetary goals for the month, they're obviously coming up short."

Shit. Three hundred thousand for that crap piece of land? By his estimation, they had already been paying double what it was worth. CorTech was doing its best to push them out. That wasn't in the budget this month. He and Macie would have to come up with the extra cash on their own. Unless they bumped into a shit-ton of marks on Asteria, that wouldn't happen.

"They received a pay-or-vacate. Y'all have 'til the end of the month." Merrick cleared his throat. "I'm damned sorry to be the bearer of bad news."

"Nah, man." Despite the worry lining Macie's brow, he managed to sound like it was no big deal. "We got this. Don't worry about it."

Thank God Macie could keep the rage out of his voice; he didn't think he could.

"Listen, we caught a glimpse of a guy matching the picture of the mark on one of the contracts you two signed."

"Oh?" Might be promising. Considering their rent just went up, they needed the cash. "Which one?"

"Alexi Popov. A freighter docked here about an hour ago. The captain was livid. He had a stowaway—Popov—who made free with their supplies. Didn't realize it until after they'd lowered the loading ramp and the crew started pulling crates off for deliveries, though."

"You sure it's him?"

"Yeah, the captain showed me the security recordings and our facial recognition software pegged him as your guy. He's here. Somewhere."

"Don't suppose you can put the port on lockdown?" Donovan bit into the nutrient bar. It was a long shot. Asteria was a major port nowadays with a lot of traffic.

"You're funny." Merrick's voice was bone dry. "A fucking riot. We've got hundreds of ships pulling in and out of port daily—a good portion of those are just keeping the town supplied for the tourists," he said the last word like it was the vilest of curse words.

He pouched his food long enough to say, "Was worth a try."

"We've posted guards at the loading ramps of all ships, figuring this guy is searching for a way back to Earth. Maybe once you land, we'll put a sleeping guard at the base of yours and he'll sneak on board."

Donovan chuckled. "I like that. Clever." Yeah, right, as if Popov would fall into their laps that easily. "Where'd the freighter come from?"

"Erra."

He met Macie's gaze and saw the same hope he had. Erra was vladset territory. If they could prove Popov worked for CorTech, they'd be gold. "How 'bout instead of a sleeping guard, you dial Popov's profile into the security system and let us know if you get another hit."

"You got it. I downloaded the feed to my Saph-link, too. Come by Lucky's if you want a peek. I gotta get back to town. Damn Ovvett Races are this weekend and the tourists get rowdy."

Christ. He'd purposely planned this trip so they'd be in and out of Asteria well before the races. Due to their run-in with the vladsets, they'd be landing at the worst possible time.

Macie leaned forward. "What's the fav—?"

"We'll be there," Donovan cut him off. "Thanks, Merrick." He ended the call and punched Macie's shoulder. "No gambling. We're in enough shit."

"I was just making small talk." Macie hauled himself up and out of the cockpit. "What're we gonna do? It's already the tenth of the month. By the time we finish on Asteria and make the trip back to Earth we'll have a day—two at most—to give them another hundred and fifty grand."

"Plus, another three hundred G's on the first." He followed Macie into the main cabin. Fifteen minutes ago, his big idea was to woo his wife? With what? A ramshackle group of misfits no one wanted and a rundown home they were about to lose.

"We'll need a hell of a lot more than Popov's bounty to come up with four hundred-fifty grand."

Yeah. He scrubbed his palm over his face. "It's Asteria, man. The races are going on. Half the criminal population in this sector will be in Diamond Fjord."

Macie shook his head. "It's gonna be so crowded we'll be lucky if we don't lose each other, much less find someone in that mob." His fingers worked at his side—his thumb touching each finger as if counting. Counting money. Counting odds. *Fuck.*

"We're not risking what we have for what we want. Stop thinking about it." The last thing he needed was for Macie to have a goddamn relapse.

Maybe they should bypass Asteria and go straight home. He had no idea how Macie would deal with this much temptation. They needed the money from their deliveries, though. They couldn't pass up a chance at Popov.

Macie sighed. "Look, Division Command Zero can make its own decision, but maybe it's time to sit the Zeros down and tell them it's time to move on."

Donovan stared. "Even if we did, Opal's in no condition—"

"When the fuck are you gonna let go?"

Let go? He wasn't holding on. He just wanted to make up for what he'd fucked up. He'd gotten all of them in shit one way or another and none of them functioned well on their own. Not for long. Not even Macie. "What are you saying?"

Fury glittered in Macie's gaze. "I'm saying I'm wondering how long we're going to work ourselves to death, risking our own skin to provide for people who are taking their own sweet time to hold up their end of the bargain. Three years we've pushed ourselves and the Zeros damned hard. DCZ is taking advantage."

"Come on. It's not like DCZ's living the high life. They're just trying to maintain. To live how they did before—"

Macie's voice rose. "No one else gets to live like they were before."

Right. Before the UN had fragged their base, Macie had disappeared on a mission to spy on the Blue Helmets. For a while, he'd thought Macie had flipped on the rebellion and sold them out, but he hadn't. He didn't know what all had happened but he knew it was bad because when Macie had showed up again, he was a fucking mess. He'd lost everything. After that, Macie had started taking life-ending risks. Gambling. Drinking. Being as impulsive as a cocky youth. He *was* better off now. He lashed out. "*You're* living better than you were before."

Macie threw the coffee cup and it shattered against the wall. "Fuck you."

Shit. Macie meant before they'd met. Before he'd started filling Macie's head with ideas of heroism and honor. Back when he'd been flush and living large . . . until Donovan had talked him into joining the Blue Helmets as a spy. Hell, Macie *had* been better off before he'd gotten hold of him. "I didn't—"

Macie stalked away, noticed Sorcha standing in the entrance, and paused long enough to mutter an apology before storming past her.

"What happened?"

He grimaced. "I fucked up." Hell, and he was doing it again. He pushed his argument with Macie from his mind. Later, he needed to apologize. They'd talk and figure out what they needed to do. First, he needed to make up for his lack of care last night. Needed to give her a reason to stay a little longer. "How are you this morning?" He walked over to her and drew her into an embrace.

"Clean." She melted against his chest. "Macie showed me how to use the bath."

"I should've helped you last night."

"I wore you out." Her voice was quiet, shy, despite the pride in her tone.

"Yeah, you did." He gave her a squeeze. "You were amazing." He pulled away to give her a kiss and had to release her to wrestle with her veil. "Now, if I could find my wife under all this stuff . . . ."

She giggled.

Once he got the veil up, he tugged down the wrap from her mouth. "There she is." He leaned down and captured her mouth.

— ◦ —

14

Her chief was being considerate this morning. He nibbled at her lips, his kiss sweet rather than arousing and despite the aches in her muscles and the soreness between her legs, she leaned into him.

"I missed you this morning, Sorcha."

Things hadn't been this awkward yesterday. She found it difficult to meet his gaze and at the same time wanted to stare at him and soak him in. "Why?"

"Most wives wake up next to their husbands." The rough pads of his fingers slipped under her wraps to stroke her cheek. "Damn, you're soft."

Had anyone else called her soft, she'd have bristled. But the awe lacing his tone and the small smile curving his lips made his words feel like a compliment. "This is desired, softness?"

"Oh, yeah."

She cupped the back of his neck, lifted onto her toes, and pressed her lips to his scarred cheek. "Thank you for last night."

He pulled away to search the cloths covering her face. "I've never been thanked for that before." He stroked his thumb over her bottom lip. The proximity alarm sounded in the cockpit. "You wanna help me land this thing?"

"Yes!"

The cockpit was a tight fit. Two straight-backed flight seats tucked into a control panel that took up most of the space. She wasn't paying attention to that, though, the vision before her held all her attention. Asteria was beautiful. A glowing lavender orb against a sea of pitch black. "It's purple."

"Not once we enter the atmosphere." He pushed a button and the alarm quieted. "They explained it to me once, why Asteria is purple from out here. Something about the way the sun reflects on the blue grass and red water, mixing with the debris in the outer atmosphere. It's pretty, though."

A female voice came over the speaker. "You are entering Asteria's airspace. Identify yourself."

"This is Chief Donovan Reese aboard the *Red Slag* with routine commercial deliveries requesting landing access. Call sign Alpha-Zulu-six-eight-one-Delta-Romeo."

"Call sign Alpha-Zulu-six-eight-one-Delta-Romeo, access granted. Sending signal for beacon at landing pad zero-two-niner-eight on frequency niner-two-point-six-three."

Learning to pilot a craft wouldn't be easy. She'd never watched a pilot before and had no idea what they were talking about.

"Alpha-Zulu-six-eight-one adjust frequency to niner-two-point-six-three." A beeping noise filled the cabin. Donovan pressed a button. "Beacon locked. Altitude sixty-three miles."

"Alpha-Zulu-six-eight-one drop to ten thousand feet within one minute of entry."

The purple blur gave way to orange fire. Her heart leapt in her chest but Donovan didn't seem worried. "Is that normal?" She hadn't ever seen anything like this.

"Yeah. We're all right." He lifted his mug to his lips, winking at her over the rim.

The flames faded and she got her first peek at Asteria. Great swaths of glistening black gave way to bright blue and red. At the same time pressure filled the cabin, pushing her down into her seat. She struggled to lift her hand to grip the armrest.

He flipped a blue switch. "The ship's gravity is off now." The pressure eased, allowing her to lean forward again to stare down at Asteria. He pointed out his window. "There's the Black Desert." He pointed to the right. "The Red Sea. Diamond Fjord is nestled against the mountains by the bay." All the while he pushed forward on a small lever on the panel and the ship continued to dive. Her stomach flopped and her breathing increased until he eased up on the lever and the ship leveled.

"Air control, this is Alpha-Zulu-six-eight-one. Altitude of ten thousand feet acquired. Turning on beacon-guided autopilot." He pushed another button and sat back in his seat.

"Signal locked. You're clear to land, Alpha-Zulu-six-eight-one."

"Now we kick back and enjoy the view." He reached across the space separating them and hauled her into his lap. "Asteria is pretty warm most days unless there's a breeze coming in off the sea. You're going to be uncomfortable."

"I'm used to it."

"Look at me."

She dragged her gaze from the view and gasped as the heat in his gaze registered. Her body tingled to awareness and she squeezed her thighs together as the dull ache from last night's activities morphed into a steady pulse of anticipation. "We'll be getting off the ship soon."

"Yeah."

"We don't have time for the promise in your eyes."

He heaved deep breath in and out. "No."

Ah. "You wanted me to see it, though."

"Yes."

But they had made a promise to each other. Today she would go out on her own. She tried to squirm away.

His hands tightened at her waist.

She froze. What was he doing? "I eased you, didn't I?"

"That's one way to put what happened." His fingers found their way beneath her cloths to stroke her skin.

The rough pads of his fingers coaxed her to give into her need to be held and petted. If he kept this up, he'd ruin her. She'd always wonder what a life with him would've been like if the IgA hadn't had a contract on her. If she were normal. Attractive. Human. "I eased you and now I'll leave you in peace."

He jerked her forward, all her weight balanced on one hip on his legs, her wrapped hands splayed against his chest. So close she could see the striations in his eyes. See how the iris of one bled into the white of his eye.

"Listen well, wife. If you try to leave me, I will hunt you down, put you over my knee, part your cloths, and spank your bare ass until it glows." As if to prove his point, his hand landed a smart slap to her rear.

She squeaked in protest. At least now she knew what an ass was.

"Are we clear?"

The sharp sting eased, leaving a dark new ache between her legs. She could get addicted to him. To the things he made her feel.

Which is why she needed to leave. A flash of heat went through her. "No."

One brow arched on his forehead. "No, we're not clear?"

"No, you can't renege on our deal."

His gaze narrowed. "Technically, I didn't agree. If I did, it was made under duress." He stood and when he sat back in the flight chair, he forced her to straddle him.

"What are you doing?" She glanced over her shoulder. The glittering buildings at the edge of the Red Sea were getting bigger. The Space Port grew larger in the distance.

"Reminding you."

Her gaze snapped to his. "Of what?"

He pulled her core flush with the bulge in his pants. Of their own accord, her eyes closed. She arched her back. A low moan broke from her lips. She was sore, but with his cock tucked tight against her tenderness, a wanting ache overrode the pain, making her restless. "Donovan."

"You remember me filling you?"

Ah, Dedia. In her wildest imaginings, she never thought mating could be so beautiful. "Yes."

"You remember my tongue here?" He ducked his head and drew on her nipple through her cooling cloths.

Pleasure, sharp as a razor's edge sliced through her. "Yes." She wrapped her arms around his head, holding him close. Arched her back until she was sure her spine would snap and she didn't care, not if he kept doing that.

"And here." His thumb dipped between her cloths and stroked the folds of her sex. Spreading the moisture and circling her clit. "You remember?"

"Please." Urgent need coiled through her. Her hips bucked. "Please, Donovan."

He cursed, pressing her tight to his length. "You're like a goddamned brush fire, spark to full burn in three seconds flat."

Heat suffused her cheeks. Was that censure?

"I love that. How quick you respond. How honest you are."

She flipped her veil out of her way with one hand, drew down her cloths with the other and kissed him. She couldn't not kiss him. The taste of him rolled through her, searing itself into her mind.

The heat of his mouth. The rasp of his tongue. "Donovan, please. Once more."

Harsh breaths beat against her lips. "You want me?"

"Yes." She rolled her hips against him, making him moan.

"I can't wait to slide inside you again." He nipped her lip. His thumb circled her clit. "Feel all your hot silk squeezing around me, welcoming me home. You were so tight. Felt so good."

She couldn't wait anymore. She reached between them to the buttons on his pants.

His hand slipped from between her cloths, latching around her wrist. "Tonight."

"Now." She wouldn't be here tonight. She had to leave. Just once more and then she had to leave. Eventually he'd see her. Fear her. Leave her. She couldn't stand that. Or worse, what if he discovered she was Blaze and turned her over to the IgA? Or even worse, what if he discovered who she was and *didn't* turn her in? No matter which option he chose, one of them would get hurt.

"Tonight." The nip he delivered her lip stung, made a shiver race through her. "I want to see you, Sorcha. I want to watch you come apart in my arms. See your face flush with passion. Your eyes dilate when you orgasm."

"You can't. You won't want me."

"I'll want you." His blue eyes were full of heat. Of promise. "Don't you worry about that." His chest rose and fell as if he'd just finished sparring, his cock rigid against her softness. All his muscles bunched around her prepared to fight. "Don't you doubt me."

He stood, holding onto her until she had her feet under her, then helped her navigate the tight confines of the cockpit. By the time she sat, the traffic tower had a clear line of sight into the cockpit. Her gaze shot to Donovan's.

"They didn't see anything." He winked. "I'll always protect you. No one needs to know what we do but us."

She drew in a shuddering breath and lifted her cloths to cover her mouth. Lowered her veil. He watched and there was no mistaking the displeasure in his expression. The stubborn press of his lips said he'd be relentless about seeing her now.

Why would he want to keep her? They'd made a deal last night. They were supposed to part as friends. Now he'd watch her and wait for her to slip up.

They couldn't disembark until after an inspection.

Celeka had paced in the rec room, worrying the inspectors would discover they had no scan for her. They'd have to go on to Earth. She'd have to spend more time with Donovan and by the time they reached Earth, leaving him would destroy her.

Donovan appeared in the doorway, wearing his battle suit, minus his helmet. The suit hugged his frame, emphasizing his wide shoulders and narrow hips. A utility belt hung low on his hips, his blaster holstered against his thigh at arm's reach. A frown marred his good looks, tugging the scars on the left side of his face taut.

She'd ruined everything. "They're making us leave?"

His face went blank. "What?"

"We didn't get a scan of me."

"Told you not to worry." He couldn't seem to meet her gaze. "Everything's fine. You ready to go?"

Was she? She'd been to other planets before. Usually, in the dead of night. Usually, to some remote, rural area her handlers had lured her target to. Always in her body armor, covered from head to toe. This would be her first time in a city. The first time she wore her wraps in public during the light of day. Or explored a new place with her husband.

And it would be the last. It had to be.

She nodded, checking her cooling cloths to ensure everything was covered.

"Come on." He waited until she reached his side. His hand warmed her lower back as they left the ship. He hesitated on the ramp. "Shit."

"What?" She followed his gaze to a tall, trim male standing on the airpad. He had a wide-brimmed hat pulled low on his forehead and thick round pieces of glass held together by wire covering his eyes. "Will he cause us trouble?"

The corner of his lips tugged up. "Grady? Nah. He's gonna be damned disappointed, though." He strode toward the other man, holding his hand out as he neared. "Grady."

Grady seemed to take forever to extend his arm and take hold of Donovan's. They shook hands. "How the hell are ya, Reese?" Grady spoke slowly, his words slurred.

"Well enough. You?"

One shoulder edged up close to his ear. "Be doing better once I got my goods."

Donovan dragged his hand down his face. "Tell you the truth, we ran into some trouble."

"Oh?" Grady took out a metal container from his clothing, uncapped it and drank some of the contents, swaying on his feet.

Celeka was fascinated by the slow, purposeful way Grady moved and at the same time she had the urge to take over and do things for him to get them done quicker.

"We were captured by vladsets."

His eyes widened and, already magnified by the thick glass covering them, they looked like they'd pop right out of his head. "Ya don't say."

"They took the drive, man. We didn't notice until later."

Celeka's face heated. By vladset law, Maman had a right to take what she wanted from a captured ship. She'd never considered before what the collateral damage from such an action might be.

Slowly, Grady nodded, the corners of his mouth pulled down.

"Hell, I know how important the delivery was. I can get another and be back here next month."

Grady's nod picked up speed. "Yep. Good enough. Has to be." He drew each word out to its breaking point.

Celeka watched the two. Something more was being communicated than their spoken words allowed. A tension between them that set her hair on edge. She wasn't worried about Grady attacking. He didn't seem to have enough energy in him for such an endeavor. At the same time, she now understood why Donovan was upset about disappointing Grady. It was kind of like kicking an old, worn-out warrior.

Donovan cleared his throat. "No extra charge."

"Well, that I can't allow." Grady lifted his arm, paused, and then flicked his hand as if swatting an insect . . . one that had flown past thirty seconds ago. "Paid insurance on that package, so I'm thinking they'll be reimbursing me for my trouble. No sense making ya pay, too."

"Yeah?"

"Yep."

The tension eased out of Donovan.

"What about the rest?" Grady folded his arms loose over his chest. "They take that, too?"

"No, sir. Got three cases of hundred-proof absinthe and a case of sugar cubes. What the hell do you do with all the liquor, Grady? I know you can't be drinking that much. Lucky's doesn't sell the stuff. Where's it going?"

"Now, ya don't know nothing of the sort." He hiccupped, and his glasses slid down to the tip of his nose. Celeka almost reached forward to adjust them before Grady finally got around to it. "Got me a hollow leg, I do."

Her gaze dropped to his legs. They were both covered in the rough blue material Donovan liked to wear. How . . . Why would his leg be empty?

Grady leaned over and touched her shoulder. "I'm joshing him, honey."

She lifted her gaze. "Joshing?"

"He's teasing me." Donovan grinned. "Grady, this is Sorcha. Sorcha, Grady here helped Chief Payne and his woman take out the Parnells."

She stared at Donovan with wide eyes. This man, the one who seemed to take ages just to talk, helped in a battle? And lived?

Grady waved away the last. "Don't listen to him, darlin'. He makes me sound dangerous and I'm nothing of the sort." He held his hand out. "Glad Reese finally hired him some help."

Celeka slipped her wrapped hand into his as Macie had shown her. "I'm his wife."

Grady froze, still holding her hand. "Well . . . now . . . ." He swallowed, his Adam's apple bouncing. "You're a purdy little thing, ain't ya?"

She leaned toward Donovan, lowering her voice. "Do those pieces of glass affect his vision adversely?"

A bark of laugher burst from him. "Those are glasses. They help him see."

"I don't think they work."

Grady gave her a squeeze before releasing her. "And funny to boot. How do ya rate, Reese?"

"High on the luck scale, I guess." He drew her closer. "We're heading over to Lucky's to meet Merrick."

Grady hiccupped. "Might as well join ya. Could use me a drink."

Donovan turned back to the ramp. "You coming, Macie?"

"Yeah." A moment later Macie bounded down the ramp in his green and black battle suit. "Where to?"

Why were they both armed and prepared for a fight? Did they expect trouble on Asteria?

"Lucky's."

As they walked, Donovan and Macie matched their pace to Grady's slow meander, the three men chatting about Diamond Fjord. She was pretty certain that was the town they were in, though they spoke in a mix of English and Standard so half of what they said had no translation. She was beginning to see why Donovan was adamant she learn English.

Their slow pace allowed her a chance to soak in the sights. Small shops lined the spaceport's walkways. She couldn't read the signs but the items in the windows were fascinating. Jars and bottles, various kinds of clothing, and quite a few items she hadn't seen before. All around them humans co-mingled with various races of aliens. Occasionally, she caught bits of Standard, but mostly other languages.

She'd thought she was so worldly, having traveled more than most of the residents of Troon. But Maman had been smarter than her, keeping her cultural experiences to a minimum. Maman made sure her handlers never let her see too much or learn enough.

How would she get by on her own?

They came out of the Spaceport onto a narrow road filled with people. Humans came in all sorts of colors and the aliens present completed the spectrum. Maybe blue skin wasn't that unusual. Nor white hair. She scanned the crowd, focusing on eyes, looking for someone like her.

A group of five children stopped them. She couldn't understand what they said, but they all vied for Grady's attention, chattering and bouncing around him.

She nudged Donovan. "Who are they?"

"War orphans. Grady sponsors several of the kids, making sure they have everything they need. I think a few of them live with him."

"But they're not his?"

He shook his head. "Their parents died. Other adults can adopt them and become their parents."

Fascinating. On Troon, a child was part of a clan. If the parents died, the clan cared for the child.

Just as they started walking, Donovan pulled her to a stop. "Hey!"

She jerked to attention, but his gaze was locked onto Macie, not her. He stood a few feet back, staring at words and numbers handwritten on the glass of a building. A black-and-white-checkered flag hung from the store front.

Donovan released her and went back to get Macie. "Come on, man. That's not gonna help. Let's get some food."

"Look, you big control freak, back off." Macie pushed past Donovan and walked ahead of their group, straight into what she assumed was Lucky's.

Lucky's was a rectangular wooden structure surrounded by a covered porch and was full to bursting with people. A huge male with a ponytail and tightly clipped black facial hair motioned to them. Donovan led her through the crowd to the back of the room.

"Hey, Merrick." Donovan shook hands with the big male. "Sorcha, this is the sheriff here in Diamond Fjord."

"Ma'am." He tipped his hat. "How did you come to be tagging around with these two miscreants?"

Miscreants? Not knowing what else to say, she told the truth, "The chief married me."

Merrick's eyes widened and flashed back to Donovan. "Someone finally tied you down, eh, Reese?"

"Yeah, you could say that."

Celeka's attention shifted to Macie. He hadn't teased Donovan, his attention fixed on something over Merrick's shoulder. She tugged on his arm.

Macie smiled and came closer. "How you doing, man?" He shook hands with Merrick and made small talk about the crowds and the weather.

Whatever had happened between Macie and Donovan still sat between them. They were acting happy but an underlying tension hung in the air and she didn't like it.

As they sat around a table, a woman with a toddler came to the table. She leaned down and kissed Macie on the cheek. Then did the same to Donovan before sitting down. "Griffin's at the Spaceport. He said he'll catch up with you later."

Donovan made small talk with the woman for a few minutes which gave Celeka time to study her. She appeared almost human except for her lavender eyes. Celeka leaned forward. "Where are you from?"

Donovan and the woman both stopped talking and turned to her. "I'm sorry I interrupted."

"Nah." Donovan scooted back a little. "My wife just reminded me of my manners. Angel, this is Sorcha."

Angel's smile deepened and she reached her hand forward. "I'm from Lythos."

She shook her hand. "Is your husband also from there?"

"Griffin? No, he's from Earth. I grew up there, too."

"Really?" Maybe Griffin didn't mind how different Angel's eyes were, but at least she looked human, otherwise.

Donovan put his hand on Sorcha's knee. "Angel is Chief Griffin Payne's wife and Merrick's sister-in-law."

She looked at the woman with renewed interest. She was petite and beautiful, her maternal side in full force while coddling her toddler. This was the woman who killed one of the leaders of the UN?

Donovan leaned over and ruffled the baby's blond hair, grinning.

The little girl stared, her bottom lip quivering. Then she let out a wail of distress. "Oh, silly girl." Angel patted the baby's back. "You know Donovan."

Donovan's cheeks turned pink. "Oh, it's no problem. Been, what, a couple of months since I was here last." When the little girl continued to cry, he started to get up just as another male joined them. Angel introduced him as Lucan, Griffin's brother. He shook hands around the table, picked up the little girl, walked to where Merrick sat, and kissed him before sitting down.

The quick melding of lips hinted at the kind of intimacy she'd always longed for. "How long have you been together?"

Lucan bounced the little girl on his knee. "Almost four years."

Somehow she thought it would take much longer to find such comfort with another.

Donovan leaned toward her. "Are same-sex couples common on Troon?"

She tipped her head to the side. "Males mate with females for offspring, of course, but marriage is different. Some marry one person and mate another."

His brows drew together. "In your culture you could take another mate even though we're married?"

"We're soul-mated, so no. But if we weren't, a male could challenge you for the right to mate me. If you lost . . . ." She shrugged. "Marriage is about connections, money, love. Mating is about producing the best offspring. They're not always the same thing."

Queen Vessa sat back in her chaise lounge and waved her hand to the guard to allow the communications through. Nothing was working right. She should've never gotten involved with the humans. Williams had finally broken and given her a frequency and then she'd devoured his soul. His blackened, scorched body lay where she'd left him in his cell but the scent of his burning flesh had followed her all the way to the throne room.

Unfortunately, the frequency had proved incorrect and the sempisim was worthless without it.

The screen changed, showing Quimet on board *CorTech 12*. He bowed.

"We are in Asteria, my Queen."

"Good. Celeka's chief may already be dead. My spies tell me she was instructed to soul-merge her mate."

"I'm sorry, but if that is true, Celeka failed to follow through and soul-devour him. I saw her and her chief walking through town."

Vessa cursed. That girl couldn't do anything right. Soul-merging was a weakness—sharing energy and life with another. Power came with devouring the weaker partner's soul and taking what was theirs for her own.

"I have assigned a warrior to follow Celeka and her chief. We'll lure them away from the city and kill the chief as requested. I also took the liberty of bringing the remaining CorTech bodies to dispose of."

They'd worked their way through several of CorTech scientists, trying to get the frequencies for the sempisim in recent weeks. They all refused, preferring to die.

If Celeka was soul-mated, that complicated matters. She frowned. "Celeka must soul-devour the chief. If you kill him instead, she'll become weak." And too soon, she'd die. Vessa wasn't sure how long she'd need Celeka, but she didn't want her dying before she'd secured her position.

"Williams didn't give you the frequencies." His lips pressed together. "That would've been the easier way."

"The frequency Williams gave was not accurate." He'd lied like all the others. Humans had no honor.

"She's become attached to the chief, my Queen. The longer they're together, the less likely she'll follow your directives. The guards have seen them. There will soon be talk that your daughter's loyalty has shifted."

She snorted. "She'll do as I ask. If you must, threaten her with Mujara's life. She'll protect her sister."

"My Queen, she hasn't laid eyes on her sister in years. Eventually, she'll question whether Mujara is even alive. If she has to choose between someone tangible and someone she hasn't seen in years . . ."

So now even Quimet questioned her.

"Then we'll remind her." Vessa paced away with a flick of her arm and then returned. "We'll force her to get rid of the humans she's grown attached to. All of them." She nodded once. "I'll prepare the arena for Mujara and you can show Celeka her sister—alive and in peril. You'll demand Celeka kill her chief, his second, and destroy the ship. That'll convince the guards where her loyalty lies." She liked this plan. "You'll take her to Earth and demand she get the frequencies."

Quimet shifted his weight. Nodded.

"You'll not fail me, Quimet. I'd be most disappointed."

"I'll not fail, my Queen."

Donovan took a big bite of his sandwich.

Goddamn, he'd missed good food. For the week they'd spent on Troon they'd only gotten water, some slimy gray stuff, and flat bread. And ship food was . . . well, it wasn't half as bad as the shit they used to serve in the chow hall on base.

This, though, was home cooked. Fresh. Damned fine. He didn't even know for sure what he was eating. Meat from some local animal stacked with veggies and slapped between two grilled slabs of bread. It was good. That's what mattered. Even Sorcha had perked up as the waitress slid a plate in front of her. After three days of picking at the food on the ship, she finally showed signs of an appetite, finishing everything on her plate.

"I wonder what Vessa wants the antimatter drive for." Merrick leaned back in his seat, sipping his beer.

He shrugged. "I sent Prax a message while I was waiting for the cargo inspection. He's gonna have the IgA come down on her like a ton of bricks." Prax had also wanted to talk to him alone, but he never did find out why because Salcedo had walked in and Prax acted like they'd been saying goodbye. Something was up with Prax.

Merrick picked at the label on his beer bottle. "Hasn't he been Troon's inspector for the last ten years? Despite the sanctions, he's given the vladsets a hell of a lot more freedom than he should."

Yet another reason to mistrust Prax. He touched Sorcha's hand to get her attention. "Did you ever meet any of the IgA inspectors?"

"Prax comes to the spaceport on Erra twice a year."

He leaned his forearms on the table. "Erra? What needs inspection on Erra?"

Her shoulders tensed.

Merrick tipped his head to the side. "You were on Erra?"

The slight tremble had returned, making her veil shimmy. He shouldn't have asked here. Now Merrick was interrogating her. "She didn't get along well with Vessa. Sorcha preferred Erra."

She'd turned her face to his when he'd started talking and he gave her a slow nod. *Lie. Lie for me.* No one needed to know what Vessa thought of her. No one needed to know Vessa had exiled her.

"Isn't that right?"

She nodded. "I like watching the ice flows on the ocean. Erra is beautiful. Peaceful."

"It is remote." Merrick's gaze flashed to Donovan and one brow rose. "You saved my entire family, Reese."

After the rebellion, he'd hauled ass to Asteria with DCZ to help free the exiled. He'd arrived in the nick of time. The Blue Helmets had Chief Payne, Grady, Angel, Merrick, Lucan, and a few others at gunpoint and were planning to kill them via firing squad. Had they arrived ten minutes later, they'd have all died.

"As far as I'm concerned you, Macie"—he jerked his chin toward Sorcha—"and your wife—you're family."

"Yep." Grady pouched the food in his mouth in his cheek. "We're loyal to family 'round here."

The tension in him eased. Merrick and the others would help them. If they needed it. If he asked. He'd rather not drag them into his and Sorcha's problems, though. "I appreciate that."

Macie leaned forward. "Seems odd. How everything keeps coming back to Troon. They're not supposed to leave their system and yet somehow have their fingers in everything."

"How'd you end up in vladset airspace anyway?" Grady hiccupped, lifting his flask to his lips for another swig.

He'd said he wanted to come to Lucky's for a drink, but he hadn't ordered one. Just kept nipping at that damned flask. Hell, maybe he did drink all that absinthe himself. He couldn't ever remember seeing the man sober.

"We were following *CorTech 12*, Jerrod Williams' ship—he's Larkin Astor's assistant at CorTech." Macie handed his empty plate to a passing waitress. "I was hoping if we caught him alone, he'd talk more freely about some contracts we own. Donovan and I remember the marks on those contracts as CorTech employees, but CorTech has erased any connection to them."

Where the hell was Williams now? Had Vessa captured him, too? Had he escaped and returned to Earth? Was he dead? They hadn't seen him while imprisoned.

Sorcha paused with her sandwich halfway to her mouth. "He's been to Erra, too."

Prax *and* Williams had both been to Erra? And Popov—the-stowaway—had arrived in Asteria via a freighter coming from Erra. "When freighters land on Erra, do they pick up or drop off?"

"I wasn't allowed down to the airpads."

Dead end. What he was thinking was insane anyway. The vladsets hated humans. They wouldn't willingly work with a human-run corporation, would they?

Macie frowned. "Vladsets can trade, just not in tech or weapons." His eyebrows crept up. "You're wondering if this is linked to the resource the IgA wants information on, if it's a weapon."

"Yeah." He took Sorcha's hand. "Does the name Alexi Popov mean anything to you?"

"No." Her brows drew together. "Erra's made of ice. There's hardly any landmass to mine resources. Just ice."

"There's a whole universe of undiscovered planets out there."

Everyone turned to stare at Grady.

"What?" He sniffed and took another swig. "Troon lies on the outer rim, don't it? Everybody avoids that sector like the plague 'cause they don't want to run into the vladsets. Which means everything on the other side of their sector is unexplored territory. Not like space stops on the other side of Troon like it does on IgA star maps."

Donovan sat back in his chair. "Jesus." What if the vladsets had found a new planet in the unmapped sectors beyond Troon and hidden the discovery?

"I don't know how you do it, Grady." Merrick tipped his hat back on his head and chuckled. "Most times nothing but rubbish comes out of your mouth but every now and then I swear you're smarter than all the rest of us put together."

Grady hiccupped. "Stop, now, 'fore ya embarrass me."

The IgA had sanctioned the vladsets from having antimatter drives specifically to keep them from terrorizing other planets, but he doubted his was the first ship they'd taken, searched, and stolen from. "Have you ever heard of your people expanding their territory?"

The tremble was back. Either she was afraid of getting into trouble herself or afraid of selling out her people. "Troon can travel to and trade with any planet they can reach with their own technology. There's no rule preventing Maman from doing so. That sanction is specific to wormhole travel and antimatter drives."

Which didn't quite answer his question. He tried a different angle. "They're sanctioned against warring with other races."

"There was no war. The people on Senna aren't very advanced. Maman said she traded them something and they swore allegiance to her."

"Ah, hell."

Macie swore.

He sat back in his chair. Vessa *had* discovered a new planet. Senna. A new race. All this time the vladsets could've been raping and pillaging to their hearts' content. Or was Sorcha correct about Vessa trading something—technology, maybe? That was almost as bad and totally against IgA law. Outsiders were discouraged via threat of sanctions from interfering with undeveloped cultures. The vladsets were proof of what could go wrong when a society gained technology before modernizing their culture and beliefs.

Did Prax know? He could've manipulated the hell out of the system from inside the IgA if he'd profit from doing so. Is that why he'd been so intent on Donovan kissing Sorcha? He must've known about soul-merging. How did ensuring their marriage continue to benefit Prax? Or was he looking at this from the wrong angle? If vladsets only soul-merged enemies . . . . Had that been a message to Sorcha to kill him? If so, what would happen when they discovered she hadn't?

Damn. He'd told Prax about the missing drive. If the son of a bitch was playing both sides, they were in trouble because now he knew they were both alive. He'd even asked how he was getting on with Sorcha. He'd probably been wondering why he was still alive.

Merrick leaned forward. "If I were you, I'd keep my trap shut."

Right. Going up against the IgA was a quick way to get dead. On the other hand, his conscience wouldn't allow him to turn a blind eye. "Until I have evidence."

Macie swore again. "The UN wasn't enough? You want to take on the whole goddamned IgA?"

Hell, if the vladsets were doing what he suspected and Prax was making everything a-okay then somewhere, a world the IgA didn't know about was suffering under Vessa's brutality. He couldn't *not* do anything. "You don't have to get involved."

For a split-second, the badass crumbled and hurt flashed over Macie's features. Then he was back, his eyes blazing. "Fuck you."

"Maman has spies everywhere."

They both turned to Sorcha. Her soft-spoken words were eerie and out of place with the conversation. He couldn't quite tell, but he didn't think she was looking at any of them. She leaned to the side to see around Merrick.

Donovan stood, scanning the crowd for vladset warriors. "Here?"

"Everywhere."

There were too many people. He pushed his chair back. Macie was already on his feet. Merrick stood.

"Grady?"

"I got your lady, don't ya worry none."

"Thanks." He dropped his gaze long enough to point at his wife. "Stay with Grady."

Sorcha shook her head. "You stay here. No good will come of this."

His chest tightened a bit as he left. Last time a woman asked him to stay instead of fight . . . by the time he returned, broken and burned, she hadn't wanted him anymore.

— · —

15

Outside, Donovan stopped on Lucky's porch. There were people everywhere. Seller stalls. Hover cars. All blocking his view. Still, a vladset should stand out. He should be a head and shoulders taller than the crowd.

Maman has spies everywhere.

"I don't see him." Macie turned to look back inside Lucky's. "Why can't we see him?"

"Tech?" Merrick asked.

Donovan shook his head. "They don't do science. All the tech they have is from somewhere else. They steal, borrow, or barter for it." Individual cloaking devices were banned on most planets, so it would've been difficult for the vladsets to come across it. So why couldn't he see him? The porch gave them a higher vantage. The vladset should be taller than the crowd.

The sun glinted off a curved black spike. "Got him." He vaulted over the railing and dove through the crowd. He'd seen a spike, but nothing else that should've gone with it.

When he reached the spot where the spy had been, he paused and scoured the crowd again. Someone shouted. Several people were jostled as someone pushed through. "There." He hoped. This was like chasing a goddamned ghost.

The lady who'd fallen to the ground had a long gash across her back. Blood soaked her blouse. *From the spike.* The son of a bitch had pushed through the crowd, his spikes cutting people as he passed.

He upped his pace. Behind him, Merrick called for medics on his Saph-link, giving the location of the injured woman.

"You're on to something." Macie kept pace next to him. "I still can't see the fucker."

Maman has spies everywhere.

How? How could vladset spies mix in with the rest of the population and not be seen? They were so big, so easy to spot. They'd make horrible spies.

Unless they're like Sorcha.

Fuck. "I think we're searching for a human with some vladset characteristics."

Macie swore. "They're like her."

"Yeah. Except this one has spikes." He shouldered through a group.

"Griffin, pick up." Merrick was right behind them. "Griffin."

"Yeah." Griffin's voice was hard to hear, the connection full of static.

"Where you at?"

"Spaceport."

"A guy . . . maybe a gal, is gonna be coming through the main gates. Human-looking with some vladset traits."

"Spikes." Donovan pushed passed another tightly packed group.

"He's got spikes," Merrick repeated.

"You want me to stop him?"

"Nope. Watch him. Tell us where he's going."

"Got it. I'm at the gate."

Donovan hadn't caught a glimpse of the bastard in a while. *Shit.* "I can't see him." There was no commotion ahead. "I don't know if we're still following him or if he ducked out of the crowd." He spun around. Had the bastard circled back? Maybe to come up behind them? Maybe to get to Sorcha?

"Stop." Merrick's hand gripped his shoulder. He stepped in front of Donovan, motioned Macie over. "Take him up."

Both men positioned themselves so he could use one of each of their legs to stand on. He put his hands on their shoulders, a boot on Merrick's thigh, and hefted himself up, putting his other boot on Macie's thigh. Above the crowd, he scanned the area. Where was the spy? The spikes.

"Back off, asshole," a big human shouted into the crowd.

He caught the flash of spikes. "Bald male. Black leather jacket with silver eyelets to allow the spikes through." To someone who didn't know, the spikes looked like part of the jacket. Clever bastard. He jumped down and ran. Behind him Merrick relayed the information to Griffin. "He's headed straight for Griffin."

"I got him." Griffin's voice came through the Saph-link. "He's passing right by me. I got a picture of his face. Uploading to security cameras."

"Hey." Merrick's hand landed on his shoulder again, slowing him. "We got him. I don't need him getting desperate and freaking out in this crowd."

"I don't want to lose him. I wanna know why he's watching us. If he's reporting to Vessa, and why the fuck he's here."

"We'll get your answers." Merrick patted his shoulder. "No need getting anyone killed in the process."

"Breathe." Macie clapped him on the back. "He's not near Sorcha. She's safe."

He nodded. Was that what had his adrenaline pumping through his veins? When he realized someone was watching them, he reacted. Hadn't stopped to think why, just went after the perceived threat.

"Uh, guys?" Griffin's voice came through the Saph-link.

Donovan turned, glanced at Merrick and then down at the Saph-link in his hand.

"He's headed straight for a ship. There's a logo on the loading ramp—a star fractal."

A star fractal. That was one way to describe it. To him it'd always had the shape of nine-armed sea star with its legs curled to the left—except the fractal made it look dangerous. Sharp. Like a weapon. It was the CorTech logo. "Williams' ship?"

Macie grunted. "Maybe."

Merrick spoke into the Saph-link, "What pad?"

"Eight-seven-six."

"I'm grounding it." Merrick cut the call and made another. "This is Merrick Andersen. Make an announcement: We're grounding all outbound air-traffic on a Code Four-eight. All off-planet communications goes through a recorded line."

Donovan cocked his brow. "Code Four-eight?"

"Missing child, possible abduction." He grinned. "Common practice at events like this. We shut down everything until we find the kid. Shouldn't raise any flags for your guy."

He sure as hell hoped not.

16

This was the perfect time to leave.

Vladsets were here. Were they here to take her back? To kill her?

She could be well away from here before her chief returned with more questions she had no answers for. Part of her was curious what Maman wanted, another part of her didn't want to know. Though she didn't know Maman well, she still felt responsible for the things Maman had done. For the things she'd done *for* Maman.

Celeka shifted in her seat. This was her chance to go. To be free. To live her own life.

For the first time, the idea terrified her.

She leaned toward Grady. "Is there a"—what had Macie called it?—"bathing chamber here?"

His brows crept up high on his forehead. He blinked. "Bathroom?"

"Yes."

"Sure. 'Round the corner." He pointed along the back wall to a door with a cloth draped over it.

"I'll be right back?" She winced. She hadn't meant to make that sound like a question.

"Yeah, ya will." His lips spread in a slow grin. "Five minutes or I come in after ya." What would five minutes translate to for a man who took forever to do anything? Would he require another five to cross the room? To open the door?

She slid out of her seat and stood, straightening her cloths while walking to the covered door. She paused before going through. Grady had taken off his glasses and was polishing them on his shirt. Still, his gaze seemed to lock onto hers . . . could he see at all without his glasses? Donovan made it sound like he was half-blind without them.

Two men passed between them and she ducked down, pacing them as they crossed to the front door. Once there, she slipped outside into the dense crowd.

She had no idea where to go. *Away from the spaceport.* Yes. She didn't want to risk running into Donovan. Or the spy. She made her way through the crowd quickly, her gaze darting from one face to the next, hoping she wouldn't see Donovan, Macie, or any of their friends. Her chest got tighter with each step, squeezing the air from her lungs until she was panting.

What would happen to Mujara? To Donovan? She didn't know. Her hope was if she disappeared, Maman wouldn't do anything but search for her.

Was that naïve? Was she being too optimistic?

She broke through the crowd onto a pier. This one was different from the one on Erra. She used to like to walk out on the pier over the frozen sea. Sometimes the ice was so thin she'd see creatures swimming beneath. This pier didn't go straight out, but off to the side with store fronts along one side and water on the other before jutting into a lagoon where the water was a paler red. The pier was deserted and out of sight of the large vid-screens showing the Ovvitt races placed throughout the main street.

She bit her lip. Turned to the crowd behind her. The idea of threading herself back through all those people didn't appeal. Her gaze followed the wooden planks to where they ended. A small craft floated in the water and to her left, there was a spot where she could jump down to the ground.

Boat or land? Both were risky. Either way, she wouldn't have much cover.

She scanned the calm waters of the sea. What if she took the boat straight out to the left where land jutted into the sea before the water opened into a vast ocean?

Then what? How would she survive? Could she make a shelter? Find food? Initially, she'd hoped to get lost in a large city. But Merrick was the sheriff here. It'd only be a matter of time before their paths crossed.

She wandered down the pier to where the boat waited and stared down. Nothing but a thick rope held the small craft to the pier.

"You running from something, or to something?"

Her gaze shot up. *Grady.* How had he gotten out here so fast?

"I warned ya, darlin'." He opened his arms out to his sides. "Five minutes. So I'm thinking, since yur still here, *here* is more appealing than what's out there." He lifted his flask and took a swig.

If she wanted, she could take him down. Unfortunately, she liked him. His easy acceptance had endeared him to her. She turned back to the view. To the great big unknown. "What's out there?"

"Wild, untamed land, mostly. Ain't no one out there to bother ya." He shrugged. "'Cept for the scarecrows. If ya want isolation and adventure, that'd be my pick."

"Adventure?"

"Mm." His head bobbed. "Think about it. No one to help ya. No one to cook for ya. No one to tell ya how to live. Hell, ya'd have to come up with yur own code of ethics, yur own laws, and police yurself, 'cause there ain't anyone else to do it."

What might that be like? "No one to tell me what to do. No one to manipulate me or hate me."

"No one to love ya, neither." He leaned his forearms on the wooden rail. "S'pose it'd be lonely. No one to talk to or laugh with. No one to hold ya though the night."

A week ago she wouldn't have cared. She wouldn't have known even what he was talking about. Now she did.

"For yur husband, neither."

Donovan would be lonely. *If you try to leave me . . . .*

"Have you ever been out there?"

"I live out there."

She turned to stare. He told her doing so would be lonely.

"That there"—his gaze shifted to the craft—"is my boat yur thinking of stealing."

Why would he choose to live out there? He hadn't made it sound appealing. "You really do drink all that liquor, don't you?"

"Yep."

His first question came back to her: "Which one are you? Running to, or away?"

"Me? Oh, I ain't no one important. We're talking about you." He'd volleyed the question right back to her.

"Both. I don't want to go back to how things were, so I'm running away. And things can't stay as they are, so I'm running to the next thing before I get too caught up in how things are right now."

"Why can't things stay as they are?"

"I'm different. I'm not human like Donovan." Nor vladset like her people. "Our marriage will cause problems." What would Donovan do when he realized who she was? What she'd done?

He sipped from his flask, started to put it away, then changed his mind and held it out. "Liquid courage?"

She stared at the offering. She didn't want to offend Grady, but she had no idea what was in there.

"Ain't poison." He hiccupped. "Just absinthe."

Ah. The liquor Donovan brought to him. She accepted the flask and drank.

Pure fire burned down her throat. She swallowed. Coughed. Sucked in a breath and then wished she hadn't—that only fanned the flames. Her eyes watered at the bitter, herbal flavor. "Donovan brings this to you?" She pressed her wraps to her eyes to blot her tears as warmth flooded her system, loosening her joints. Ah. She saw the appeal.

Grady chuckled. "Try a smaller sip next time." He set the flask on the railing, pulled off his glasses and used the end of his shirt to polish them. The whole while he studied her as if trying to see through her cooling cloths. His eyes were a clear, bright blue. Without the glasses deforming his face, he was handsome. Younger than she first thought, too. She plucked his hat off his head.

"Hey, now." He scowled. "What're ya about?"

Thick, yellow hair. Not gray as she'd assumed. "You're young."

"Not very." He put his glasses back on. "Not as young as I'm thinking you are."

"Am I immature?"

"Nope. But a woman Donovan's age wouldn'ta been so impertinent." He snatched the hat out of her hand and slammed it back on his head. "Sassy little thing, ain't ya?"

Armor. He was hiding. "Those are your cooling cloths."

"That what ya call what yur wearing?" At her nod, he winked. "Like always recognizes like, don't it?"

She put her hand on his. "You're clan, Grady. Tell me what you're running from. I'll help."

"Know what, darlin'? I believe ya would. Thing is, ya have enough trouble." He chuckled. "When Donovan gets aholda ya." His laugh grew and he shook his head. "I saw the look he leveled at ya when he told ya to stay put."

One minute he was laughing at her expense, the next he was sprawled on the ground. Blood blooming bright on his chest.

A shooter.

She dropped to her knees and gave a quick glance around but didn't see anyone. "Grady?" When she reached for him, he scooted back.

"Damn it, woman, don't touch me."

Did he fear her? His words were no longer slurred. He struggled a moment. Pulled his glasses off. He glanced around. Searched the roof top. Turned to peer between the planks in the rail. "Ya see 'em?"

"No." She moved closer.

"Don't." He waved her back. He coughed and blood spattered his lips.

Oh, Dedia. He was dying.

"Run." He pulled his gun from its holster, sliding it across the deck to her. "Go on."

All those kids relied on him. He'd been nice to her. He was Donovan's friend. "I can help. I can seal the wound and stop the bleeding. Let me." She edged closer.

"They'll be comin' now. Ya gotta run." His gaze lowered. He held up his hand. "Stop."

Bright red blood smeared the wood from when he'd scooted away. Except the wood was . . . degrading. Disappearing. She scooted back, her gaze jerking to his. He was trying to talk. His bloody lips forming the same word over and over, though no sound came out. *Run.*

Trembling, she snatched up the gun and pushed back onto her feet into a squat, glancing around for the shooter. "I'm not leaving you, Grady. You're clan." She had to get him to safety at the very least. If she could touch him, she could sear the wound closed, but . . . what was wrong with his blood?

White flared behind her eyes and her teeth clamped together. Pain slashed through her as all her muscles locked tight and froze. Her fingers convulsed, and her weapon fired once. She felt herself swaying, tilting, and she couldn't stop her fall. The rough wood scraped against her shoulder. Her cheek. Her body twitched but she couldn't make herself move. Couldn't blink. She stared at Grady, unable to blink or look away. His eyes wide. Blood spattering his lips and chin.

Had she hit him? Someone else?

He reached out, straining to get to her. His hand went limp. His eyes closed and his body deflated as the last of the air left his lungs.

No.

She shouldn't have left Lucky's. Shouldn't have backed away from the blood. She could've saved him if she hadn't hesitated. Now he was gone and it was her fault.

The planks trembled beneath her as someone approached. Thick black boots and dark-gray legs. Vladset. She tried to force her gaze higher but couldn't. Rough hands grabbed her legs and dragged her back down the planks. Her throat closed as Grady's body disappeared from her sight.

Grady had been right, she should've run. They'd have followed her and left him alone.

Her heart thudded heavy in her chest. She couldn't regulate her breathing nor the roiling in her gut. Tears blurred her vision, leaving itchy trails down her face. The vladsets wouldn't harm her. If that had been their plan, they'd have killed her already. They wanted something, which was far worse.

He dragged her down the alley and dropped her legs. For several moments, he didn't touch her. She lay there, staring at a gutter. Listening to the clank of metal and rustle of cloth. What was he doing?

A shadow fell across her as he squatted next to her. Quimet. He picked her up and dumped her into the back of a hover car. A blanket followed, covering her from head to toe. He got in, making the whole vehicle sway. "The effects will wear off soon."

Quimet had always been a neutral in her life. The one who spoke between her and Maman. The one who provided the necessities she needed to live. He always lowered his tone when he spoke Maman's words as if trying to soften the blow. He hadn't been part of her missions. Nor her punishments. She'd counted on him to be the steadiness in her life.

The rumble of the crowds grew louder as the hover car slowed, easing through the laden streets. She blinked and for a moment her eyes wouldn't open again, tears flooded under her lids, lubricating them after the stasis.

The hover car kept moving farther from the pier. From Lucky's. From Donovan. They'd be long out of Diamond Fjord before the stun wore off enough for her to fight. She had no doubt about that. Quimet was precise about everything he did. He would've bound her if she had a chance of evading him while still in town.

By the time she struggled into a sitting position, they were in the middle of nowhere. Blue fields stretched in all directions. She couldn't see Diamond Fjord or the spaceport. Mountains rose high behind them. There were no craft in the sky. How far had they gone? She should at least see ships taking off and landing. Hear the roar of the engines. "Where are we?"

"If you try to run, you'll get lost. Asteria is a dangerous place. You don't want to be alone here, Princess." He'd removed the driver's seat to accommodate his size and spikes and sat on the floor of the craft.

"This dishonors my chief, Quimet." Her voice was thick, her tongue heavy in her mouth. "You're not my clan. We shouldn't be alone."

"You didn't seem to mind being alone with that other male."

Grady. Tears pricked the back of her eyes and she sniffed. "He was clan and in charge of my protection."

"He failed."

Her voice rose. "You shot him in the back like a coward."

Quimet slammed on the breaks, throwing her forward. She caught herself on the back of the passenger seat. He swung around, capturing her face in his hand. "Be careful, Celeka." The sound of her vladset name made her flinch. "You failed your mission."

"Maman said not to dishonor my chief. I haven't."

His lips thinned. "Then you were told to soul-merge him."

Prax had told her to soul-merge Donovan, not Maman. Had Prax betrayed her, too? Was he one of Maman's spies? She didn't want to believe it. Prax had always been kind to her.

"You'll tell me what we do with those we soul-merge."

"Devour their soul." She swallowed. Only since Maman had become queen. Long ago, soul-merging had been part of a love marriage, to prevent challenges for the right to mate the female.

"Yet you didn't." His lip curled. "I know you didn't because he is walking around. You mated him fully as only a weak female would."

"I didn't know."

"You knew." His gaze narrowed and he hissed between his teeth, "You failed. Now I'll watch as you do what you should've done already."

"Killing my chief will start a war." She tried to shake loose of his grip and his hold tightened, digging into her skin. She stifled her cry of alarm and tried to keep her voice steady. "My chief is a hero on Earth. A hero here. Our people will suffer because of Maman's hurt pride."

"Our queen said you needed a reminder of what's at stake. I'll remind you today."

He shoved her away so hard her head bounced off the metal behind her seat. Pain blossomed through her skull, dimming the light from the sun.

17

Donovan peered over the crate. "Yeah, definitely a CorTech ship."

"I haven't been away from Earth so long I was likely to forget." Chief Griffin Payne hunkered down between him and Merrick, his expression full of affront at the possibility they'd doubted him.

"Not just any CorTech ship, that's *CorTech 12*. See that?" Macie pointed to a blackened streak on the side of the ship. "That was me."

Donovan scowled. "You took a potshot at William's ship, too? Anything else you forgot to tell me?"

"Yeah, I scratched my ass last Tuesday."

Griffin snickered.

Donovan nodded to the ramp. "Someone's coming."

Jerrod Williams? Alexi Popov? The half-breed? Thick, dark-gray legs encased in boots appeared first. A vladset warrior. The male swung a cape over his shoulders and lifted a hood over his head. The spikes gave him a misshapen silhouette.

Behind him two more caped vladsets appeared, pushing a long box on a levitator toward a waiting hover car.

Merrick lifted his saph-link and recorded them. "Want me to grab them?"

"Nah." He wanted to see who they were meeting. Figure out why they were here. "Would love a hover car, though."

Griffin tossed him a small card key. "Come on. There's only one way out for hover car traffic and it'll take them a few minutes. You can be waiting outside."

They left the way they'd come in, staying low until they were out of sight of the vladsets.

"You want us to tag along?" Merrick glanced behind them.

"Macie and I can handle it. If you're headed back to town, though—"

Merrick nodded. "I'll check on your missus."

"Thanks."

They followed Griffin to his parked hover car. "I have a tracker on this, so if you need help, call me. We'll find you."

"Thanks, man." Macie plucked the keycard from Donovan's hand. "I'll drive." He pulled a small thin one-shot tacking pistol out of his backpack. "Here, you're a better shot."

This was one of the few things he didn't need his left eye to do. It'd taken him a while to learn to shoot with only one eye open—it fucked with his depth perception—but he learned to be a good shot despite his injury. He took the pistol, climbed into the convertible hover car and stood on the seat, leaning his leg against the backrest for balance. He checked to make sure the tracking pistol was loaded.

Griffin stood across the street watching the tunnel leading to the spaceport.

"He'll signal you." Macie started the engine.

Donovan kept his gaze on Griffin. Lifted the gun. Griffin raised his hand in a slight wave before dragging his fingers through his blond hair.

Taking a deep breath, Donovan held it. He closed his bad eye and, as the hover car slid past, he fired. The tracker hit the back of the craft with a dull *thwap*.

The vladsets looked around, then settled back into their seats.

"Keep back." Donovan lowered himself into his seat. "There's not much cover once we're out of town."

Macie eased into traffic.

Forty-minutes later, the vladsets stopped. Macie guided their hover car to an outcropping of trees and parked. Together, they crept over to a ridge that dipped down into the valley below. The vladsets pulled the box from their hover car, dumped it, got back in, and drove away.

"What do you think?" Macie jerked his chin up at the scene below.

"Evidence?"

"Yeah, but of what?"

"There's only so many things you'd take to another planet and dump in open country in a box that big."

Macie smirked. "Bet you at least one of our marks is in there."

"I'm not betting fuck all and neither should you. Come on." The vladsets disappeared over the ridge on the other side of the valley. "Let's check out the box."

He threw his legs over the edge, pausing when his Saph-link pinged. "Hang on." He picked up. "Reese."

Merrick said, "Give your link to Macie."

He pulled the device away from his face and stared for a heartbeat before holding it out to Macie. *What the fuck? Why can't he talk to me?*

Macie's eyebrows rose. "What?"

No. Something was wrong. He put the phone back to his ear. "Where's Sorcha?"

"Put Macie on."

Heart pounding in his chest he put it on speaker. "You're talking to both of us now. What happened?"

"I'm sorry as hell, man." Grady's voice. "I don't think they'll hurt her. They stunned us both. I couldn't move. Couldn't stop them."

His mind felt like it was flying ten miles over his body. His hands went cold. Sweat pricked his skin. Then he was crashing back inside himself and white-hot rage filled him to bursting. "Who?"

"Vladset. Older one, I think. Smallest one I've ever seen."

Quimet? Another half-breed? "Which way did he go, Grady?"

"Don't know."

"The crew we're following stopped not far from here." Macie lifted his Saph-link and wiggled it.

Okay. There was a fair chance all the vladsets would end up together at some point. "You two watch the ship to see if they take her there. We're gonna see if the guys we're following lead us to her." Donovan ran back the way they'd come, ignoring the voices on the other end of the com. He shouldn't have left her alone. How the hell had they gotten her out of Lucky's?

Macie reached the hover car first and had the engine revved before he even climbed in. He snatched the Saph-link from Donovan. "Merrick, we're maybe five minutes out from their final stop."

Merrick cursed. "Grady, Griffin, and I are headed to you."

Macie hit the gas and the hover car went over the ravine, scraping the ground and bouncing as they landed on the valley floor.

Donovan huffed. "You won't make it in time." They were forty minutes out from Diamond Fjord. He wasn't waiting. Once they found the vladsets, he was getting Sorcha back.

"We're almost there," Merrick said. "Right behind you."

Donovan stared at the Saph-Link. How were they . . .? "You *bastard*. You waited to call. What if they took her back to the ship?"

"Reese, I've got people searching Diamond Fjord. I got people watching their ship. All I have so far is a video feed of a weird-shaped guy driving a hover car out of the alley behind Lucky's. He had something in the back, but I couldn't get a good look. He headed out the same direction we're going."

"Okay." He rubbed his chest. "All right. That's him, right?"

"Timing would've been right." Macie eased off the accelerator.

"What are you doing?"

"We're close. We should walk the rest of the way."

Walk? He wanted to drive right into the middle of whatever was going on.

"Look." Macie pointed to where the sun glinted off metal between the trees. "A building."

Once Macie pulled the craft to a stop, Donovan climbed out. Grabbed a fully auto assault blaster from the back and checked his sidearm. "Tell him we're headed . . . ." He looked around to get his bearings. "Due south."

Macie relayed the message, adding, "I'll keep you posted, Mer, but you stay quiet."

They crept up through the stand of diamond-bark trees. Three hover cars sat in the front of a two-story cabin built with a combination of wood and old ship-siding. A river crossed in front of the property, with a little wooden bridge between the hover cars and the house. Donovan pointed to the closest hover car.

Together, they edged up to the craft, taking cover.

"There're six," Macie whispered into his Saph-link.

Donovan corrected him. "Seven. Plus whoever's inside."

"Seven. Maybe more. Shit."

"What?" Donovan turned to look at him.

Macie jerked his chin toward the house. "On the ground, next to the door."

Black cloth had snagged on a bush like a massive spider web. Sorcha's veil. She was here. Donovan withdrew his ocular from his utility belt and focused on the house, zooming in on an uncovered window. There was no movement inside. Where was she? "How long?"

"Coming up behind you."

About time. "I don't see her." He expanded the view. All but two of the guards were full-blooded vladsets. Then there was the spy and his buddy. Both had vladset spikes, but otherwise they appeared human. Maybe a little boxier around the torso, but not enough to announce their heritage. "I don't like this."

The vladsets carried their traditional war staffs. The two half-breeds wore blasters at their hips.

"We need to take out the two half-breeds first. They'll go down easier than the others."

Macie nodded. "They got extra chargers on the backs of their belts in case we need them."

Right. They'd learned the hard way it took several shots to take down a vladset. Christ, he promised himself he'd never drag another man into war and yet here he was. "Macie, you don't have to—"

"Don't." Macie pointed at him, his expression stern. "Not another word." He glanced over his shoulder. "Here they come."

Merrick, Griffin, and Grady kept low to the ground, hot-footing to where they'd hunkered down. "What we got?" Griffin asked.

Donovan summed up the situation. "Seven vladsets, two are half-breeds. Haven't seen who's on the inside."

"She here?" Grady took off his glasses to polish the lenses, his gaze scouring the layout.

"Yeah." Donovan looked him over, searching for signs of a violent fight and didn't find any. Except . . . "Did you change clothes?"

Grady's gaze locked onto his as he put his glasses back on. "That's what ya want to talk about?"

Kinda. Why had he changed? Because he had blood on his clothes? Because they got ripped in a scuffle? He was scared shitless of what condition Sorcha would be in by the time they found her. Hell, they didn't have time for twenty questions. "I'm thinking we'll each get one, maybe two shots off before they're on us. The bigger the vladset, the more shots you'll need to take him down."

Merrick blew out a breath. Checked his weapon. "I'm ready."

"Let's go." Griffin got up close to the hood of the hover car and stared over it for a second. "I'll take the one by the door."

Donovan grinned. "Half-breed on the roof." They all sounded off, naming their marks. "Count of one, boys. Three. Two. One."

The heavy, blunt report of blaster-fire filled the meadow. Donovan's mark fell from the roof, landing in a heap next to Griffin's downed mark. The two by the other hover car and one closest took multiple shots.

Five warriors left, three of which were wounded.

The vladsets went on alert, searching for the threat. One of them looked their way, his red eyes locked onto Donovan.

Shit. He fired another shot. The vladset dodged. Ran at them full throttle with a battle-cry.

The rest of the vladsets locked onto their position.

"Spread out." Donovan stood, firing several rounds. The others scattered as they fired.

One warrior staggered and fell. As did another. But they couldn't get them all.

His heart throbbed in his chest until the organ echoed in his ears. He backed away, firing. Three warriors bearing down on them. One was wounded, but that wasn't slowing him down.

Something slammed into him with the force of a wrecking ball. They tumbled and he lost his grip on his blaster. He pulled the blade at his hip. The warrior stood, dragging Donovan with him until his feet dangled off the ground. Shook him like a rag doll.

Donovan pulled his legs up and kicked out at the bastard's groin. The move gained his release. He fell flat on his back. Shit. He scrambled up, knife in one hand, and he withdrew his sidearm from its holster.

The warrior ran at him.

He fired three shots. Hit him three times. The warrior was still coming. Donovan lifted his knife.

The warrior slammed into him.

He sank the blade into the warrior's chest. The full weight of the larger male bore down on him, pushing him to the ground.

"Fuck's sake." The son of a bitch was heavy as hell and dead weight to boot. The hilt of his own knife pushed against his chest, trapped between them.

Griffin's face appeared over his. "That didn't look fun." He grabbed hold of a couple of the spikes and hefted the vladset's weight enough for Donovan to crawl out from underneath.

"Thanks, man." He straightened and his eyes widened. A vladset was running straight for Griffin. "Down."

Griffin ducked and spun, firing at the same time Donovan did.

The fucker didn't slow.

Macie barreled in from the side, dropping and sliding as if making a run for home plate. The vladset tripped over him and tumbled. Macie stood and all three fired, the vladset's prone body jerking as it absorbed the shots.

Donovan pointed at Macie. "You're reckless."

All he got in response was a shrug and Macie jerking his chin up.

Donovan turned. Four more vladsets poured out of the building. "Shit."

Celeka stood in the center of the small room. One chair faced a table. Gold curtains covered the two windows and a dark brown carpet covered the floor. The stun had worn off but she was surrounded now. Vladset warriors patrolled the property.

Pain sluiced through her, not physical but just as potent. Grady was dead because of her.

"Your queen bids you to kill the chief, his second-in-command, and destroy the ship."

A choice: Kill Donovan or watch Mujara die. This wasn't a choice, it was an ultimatum wrapped up in a threat. Quimet paced in front of her.

"I don't understand why."

"They can hurt us, Celeka. You'll tell me if it's acceptable to you, your people suffering."

The only reason Donovan could hurt them was because Maman had made poor choices. "Maman did that. Maman and her spitefulness. Sneakiness is not the vladset way. To lie. To be one way to our enemy's face and another way behind their back. You'll tell me if pride fills you when you see how she behaves."

Something flashed in the depths of his red eyes. Shame? Fear? Disregard? "You've changed. Sit."

"Why would Maman marry me to him if she wanted him dead? The IgA will question me. Killing him will draw attention."

"Our queen discovered your chief can do much damage to her. While marrying you off should've been a boon for her, your chief is more than she bargained for."

She'd been right. Maman wanted to get rid of her so she could re-marry and have pure offspring. Who told Maman Donovan could hurt her? Had she learned he'd hunted the same marks she'd sent Celeka after?

"Who told her this? Jerrod Williams?"

"Williams is dead." Quimet pulled out the chair. "I told you to sit."

She sat. Flinched when he leaned over her with a Saph-link. "Where did you—? You're not supposed to have that, Quimet. The IgA will put more sanctions—"

"Watch." His red eyes bored into her. Had she truly seen warmth in those eyes at one time? Had any of her perceptions of her encounters with him been real?

On the screen, vladset guards escorted Mujara down a hallway toward an arena. She hadn't seen her sister in years. They were twins, with the same hair and eyes but Mujara was taller, curvier, and more muscular, her skin a rich, creamy sienna.

One guard opened the door, the other shoved her sister out into the arena. They slammed the door and leaned against it while engaging the lock.

The guards feared Mujara even more than they feared her.

"If you kill her, I'll never do anything for you."

"Mujara is heir to the throne. She won't die." Quimet smiled. "But we can hurt her. We can make her life agony until she wishes to die."

The picture shifted to a shot from another camera. To the view of the empty benches in the stadium. Down to Mujara standing alone in the arena. Cages surrounded her, filled with all sorts of terrifying creatures. Big creatures. Fast creatures. All with claws and sharp teeth. All predators.

Quimet walked around behind her, leaning over her shoulder. "They're hungry, Celeka. You'll tell me which one we should let out first."

Mujara, though bigger and stronger, was not a fighter. She never had been, hating to see anything suffer. Standing amid the cages she looked like a lost swahali, only wings were missing. Glossy white hair fell to her waist. All she wore was the traditional ribbons all vladset women wore. They rose from the v of her legs, over her breasts to her shoulders.

Mujara was never shamed, not like Celeka. Mujara was strong. Instead, Maman kept her locked away where the vladset people couldn't rally behind her. The guards would shock her with electricity until she had no strength and lock her in a box she couldn't escape from.

"Mujara can best all those creatures."

"Which is why she won't die." Quimet's gaze narrowed. "You'll tell me if you think she can escape injury."

Despite Mujara's strength, she'd get hurt. She'd feel pain. Maybe even be maimed. Mujara's skin was nearly as thin as hers.

Beneath the table, Celeka began to unwind the cooling cloths from her hands. "Quimet." She drew in a breath. "I want you to know until today I always thought of you as my friend."

His lip curled back. "My loyalty belongs to the queen alone. Someday, Mujara will earn my loyalty."

"You think Mujara will forgive you?" She tipped her head toward the screen. "For this? For everything you and Maman have done to us over the years?"

He made a slash in the air with his hand. "You even sound like the humans now. Questioning. Pleading for what you want." He spat on the floor. "You never had my loyalty. You're weak. Fragile. You have one strength, one asset to give to the queen, and you balk at using it."

She and Mujara would never be free. "Maman is destroying any hope of the vladset people improving their lives. She'll have them sanctioned for life. She'll bring war to a people who barely have food. Who barely have resources to trade. All because she bends to her spite. *That's* weak."

He leaned forward, speaking into the Saph-link. "Release them all."

Celeka's gaze darted to the screen where the doors to all the cages began rising. "No." Heat swamped her body and her hands caught fire. She lifted her arms, standing so quickly her chair toppled. "I'll not balk at using my strength on you." She threw herself at him.

Quimet's eyes widened as he raised his arms. His robe burst into flame and they both tumbled to the floor. "This is for Mujara."

With a snarl, he rolled with her, trying to smother the flames between the floor and her cooling cloths. He struck her back and pain lanced down her spine. He pounded her shoulders. He rolled the other way, catching the curtains on fire as they passed. All the while she hung on, her arms squeezed between the spikes on his back.

Quimet squealed. Thrashed. His fists beat on her back and head. The smell of burnt flesh filled each breath. When he weakened, she pulled away. "That was for Mujara." She put her burning hand over his face. "This is for me."

Marked. He'd go into the afterlife with her mark for all their ancestors to see. He'd exist in shame in the Beyond. "Because you lied. Because you were not true to yourself or to me. Shame to you." She kneeled over him as his eyes widened and he tried to wriggle away.

She allowed her flame to draw his soul into hers. "My flame is stronger than yours."

Her heart rate increased. She closed her eyes and allowed the energy of his soul to course through her veins, making her lightheaded. When it was done, when Quimet's body had gone still and stiff, his skin brittle and crumbling, she stood on unsteady legs, staring down at what she'd done. He was dead. His skin had charred and curled away from his smoldering spikes, his lips pulled back in a blackened snarl. He'd been her only friend, but it was all a lie. A trick. She took his knife from his belt, parted her cloths on her upper arm and cut his first initial into her arm—a straight line with a diamond at the end.

She turned, searching the burning room for the Saph-link and picked it up. The metal was melting in places. Part of the screen had gone dark, but part of it still played. Mujara had transformed to protect herself. She was bleeding. Moving stiffly. But the bodies of most of the creatures lay unmoving on the ground. She was winning, though there were several creatures stalking her still. In the background, vladsets poured into the arena, fists raised. What happened? Why were—?

The device burst. Sparks and bits of plastic and glass hurtled in all directions, pelting her body. Her hands! She folded in on herself, tucking her hands to her torso. Oh, Dedia, that hurt. She lifted her hands. Blood coated her palms from ragged cuts.

"Mujara." The whole room blazed now. Scorching hot and yet chills coursed through her. Mujara would survive, wouldn't she? Could she fight the vladsets attacking her?

Blaster fire shot through the door, drawing her attention. She backed away. More shots made a hole and all the flames around her rushed to that one spot before settling back to consume the room.

The door slammed inward and Donovan shouted for her. "Sorcha!"

She ran to him, tears filling her eyes. Stupid male! His flesh would boil. She threw her arms around his neck and he hissed. His arms locked her to him. "Christ, you're hot." They were moving. She lifted her legs and wrapped herself around him so she didn't hinder his movements.

Sunlight broke over them and something heavy and wet wrapped around her from behind. She closed her eyes, not wanting to see the dead vladset warriors who must be littering the grounds. Had they been alive, Donovan would never have gotten inside.

"Gotta let go, little flame."

She shook her head against him. "You'll tell me if you ever lied to me."

"No." His grip tightened. "Yes. I did. I lied to you once and I'll never do it again. Not ever."

"Reese, we need to get the towels around you both." Macie smoothed the wet blanket over her back.

"No." Her grip tightened.

"Okay, okay." Donovan pressed his lips to her head. "The river." They were moving again. He stumbled. Righted himself and kept going. "I've got you."

Cool water enveloped her, making her shiver.

"I want these off." He tugged at her wraps.

"No." Her chief had come for her. He was holding her. That's all she wanted.

"Goddamn it."

Even if he was cursing.

Donovan rocked with her, his hands searching, feeling over her head, her shoulders. "I've got you." He'd aged twenty years in the last twenty minutes he was sure. How he made it into the room in time, he'd never understand. He was old. Slow. They'd been outnumbered.

He needed to pull her away from him. Needed to take care of her burns. The room . . . it'd been an inferno. Everything had been on fire. She'd been smoldering when he first pulled her out. She must be a mess. Her skin . . . .

Christ, he was a coward.

He knew all too well what happened to a body on fire. After his base had been fragged . . . Ah, God. Mangled burnt bodies flashed through his mind. Jesus, some of them had still been alive . . . burnt down to the bone and hanging on to life until someone was there with them. How many had died right after he'd arrived? And here he was holding her, probably making her injuries worse.

"Tell her to let me see her hands. She keeps pulling away."

Macie, as always had his back.

"Honey, you gotta let Macie have your hands."

"No."

"I'm not gonna let go. I'll keep holding you. Let him see." She didn't obey, so he barked his next order. "You'll do what your chief says."

She obeyed. She didn't move her arms from around his neck, but he felt her turn her hands out for Macie to inspect.

"Where the fuck is the medic?" Macie shouted the question, making his breath stall his lungs. How bad were her burns?

"Here." A female voice. He couldn't see the medic. Didn't want to turn and impede their progress.

"Her palms." Macie's voice. "You see?"

"Got it," the medic said.

He held Sorcha still. "No moving. No pulling away. I'll be very angry with you if you don't obey."

"I-I'm sorry." She let out a sob against his neck.

She was breaking his goddamned heart. "Why are you sorry? This wasn't your fault."

"Grady's dead." A shudder wracked through her.

What? She must be in shock. "He's fine. It was a stun shot."

She shook her head against him and he winced. Was she pulling her skin off? Rubbing the brittle, blisters away? "Stay still!"

"Grady was bleeding from his chest. He coughed and there was blood on his lips."

Macie came around behind her, wading deeper into the stream. "Grady!"

Another man approached and he knew right away from the slow, easy gait who it was. "There he is. Don't move, just open your eyes."

Instead of relief, disbelief laced her tone. "You're dead!"

He expected Grady's quick denial, but he didn't get it. "Now, darlin', sometimes we just gotta let things go. I'm here and I sure am sorry I didn't protect ya better."

"You owe me now, Grady." She sniffed. "Are you running from, or to?"

Grady chuckled. "Well, now, I suppose it's a bit of both, just like you."

Donovan's gaze flashed to Macie's. He'd caught the oddness of the exchange, too. They were talking in riddles. Hiding something.

Macie's gaze slid back down to Sorcha's back. He lifted her wraps; his fingers grazed Donovan's arm as he checked the skin beneath.

"He was a coward." Sorcha sniffed. "He shot you in the back." Another shudder wracked though her.

Donovan turned his face, kissed the cooling cloths covering her cheek. "Who was?"

"Quimet." Her voice broke. "I trusted him. I thought he was a friend."

Ah. That's why she was worried about him lying to her.

Macie's troubled gaze met his. He shook his head.

What was that supposed to mean? Was she dying right here in his arms? "Tell me."

"The wraps are intact. Everything looks fine but her hands."

His knees damn near gave out and he started shaking like a day-dry drunk. Jesus. She was fine. Not dying of shock. Not burned to the bone. "You're okay." Tears pricked the back of his eyes and he cleared the thickness from his throat. "You're fine."

Macie leaned closer, lowering his voice to the barest whisper. "She was smoking like a wet fire when you brought her out. *You have* light burns on your neck and cheek from holding her." Macie held his gaze.

What he said was important. Must be. He couldn't wrap his head around it, though. She *shouldn't* be fine. There hadn't been anywhere for her to hide. There wasn't anything but a table and a chair in the room. Everything had been ablaze. The walls. The carpet. Everything but his wife.

Blaze.

Macie mouthed the name even as it flashed through his mind. "No." He adjusted his grip on his wife. She was silent. Maybe listening. Maybe asleep. Her arms had gone lax. Her legs loosened around his hips.

"You're reaching." Except the thought had passed through his mind, too. They'd assumed Blaze was a man because of the sheer brazenness of the hits and the grizzly condition of the bodies, but he'd have to be a petite male. Or a woman. Sorcha was the right size. All he needed to do was put her hand on the burnt spot on his suit to verify.

He didn't want to know. That would fuck everything up.

Her leg slipped from his hip and she jerked in his arms. "I've got you. Sleep." He altered his grip, pulling her legs to one side so he could drape them over his arm. "I'm taking her back to the ship. Get her some clothes."

Macie's brow lifted.

"They're coming off." He tipped his head at the woman in his arms. The cloths were history, she just didn't know it yet. He wouldn't sleep until he made sure she had no other injuries. He refused to force her into another scanner. Not after what happened last time.

"I'll drive you back and then go into town."

Donovan waded out of the water. He was shaking hard and she'd grown heavy in his arms. He was dealing with the aftermath of the fight. Of the shock of finding her in that room. He didn't want to put her down, though. Didn't want to give her to anyone else. Macie seemed to understand. His hand braced under Donovan's elbow, helping stabilize him as they climbed the bank.

Grady waited, hat in hand. "I'll sit guard outside your ship. Won't fail again, Reese."

He had a feeling Grady hadn't failed the first time. They weren't telling him everything. "I appreciate that."

They all climbed into the hover car and while Macie drove, Donovan settled Sorcha in his lap and closed his eyes. That had damned near been a disaster he wouldn't have recovered from. Jesus, he didn't even know what she looked like. Wouldn't recognize his wife on the street without her wraps, but he'd fallen in love with her. He knew the important stuff. Her kindness and honesty. Her sensuality and helpfulness. The sound of her voice. Her shape and scent.

"It was a kidnapping, plain and simple, Reese."

He cracked his eyes open and glanced back at Grady.

"Thought you should know, seeing on where she came from. She weren't disloyal. Maybe she wasn't where she was supposed to be, but I think she was planning to come back before I let her know I was there."

Ice rolled through his veins. "What?"

"She's scairt she's too much trouble. Think she was comin' around to the idea maybe that's not true all on her own, though."

"She snuck out of the bar?"

"Tried to. I stayed right on her heels."

Macie swore. "Grady, shut up, man. Can't you see you're pissing him off?"

No wonder she was so upset. None of this would've happened if she'd listened. Was that why she held onto him so tight? Was she trying to dodge telling him what happened?

"Don't see why. Like I said, she was coming around to staying all on her own. She's loyal to a fault, that one. If she hadn't been checking on me, she'd have gotten away."

Donovan shifted in his seat to better see Grady, his gaze narrowing. "What are you trying to say?"

"I'm saying your wife earned my loyalty. She stayed." He dropped his gaze. Shrugged. "Anybody else woulda run." He took a swig from his flask, his eyes glittering in the twilight. "Don't be upsetting her none."

Well, shit.

Macie laughed outright. "You got some competition, Reese."

Yeah. Looked like he wasn't the only one falling for his wife.

— • —

18

Celeka drifted awake as Donovan got out of the hover car.

"I can walk." Though she offered, she tucked her face to the warmth of Donovan's neck, inhaled his familiar scent, and held on tighter. Still, the events of the night wouldn't be banished.

Quimet was dead.

Her stomach churned. Before, there had always been the quiet praise from Maman to chase away the awful feelings from killing, the idea she was a hero who'd protected her people.

Quimet *was* her people. She'd never killed a vladset before.

"I've got you," Donovan whispered the promise, giving her a gentle squeeze.

This time she couldn't even tell herself she'd protected someone. Last she'd seen, Mujara had been injured and still fighting. Vladsets had been swarming around her. Was she alive?

Donovan was. Macie, too. And Grady. Did that make up for the life she took? Quimet's screams still echoed in her mind. The smell. The bubbling of his skin. Her whole body shuddered.

"Hang on, Sorcha. You're not alone."

No. She wasn't alone. She had Donovan. Her chief. She wrapped her arms tighter around his neck. How had she survived so long without hugs? She didn't ever want to let go. Just wanted to lose herself in him so she could forget.

"Macie, you remember what you're doing?" With her face pressed to his, Donovan's voice sounded deeper than usual.

"Yeah. I'll be back soon."

"What's Macie doing?"

Donovan headed up the ramp to their ship. She opened her eyes long enough to see Grady wobble to a stop at the base and give her a little salute.

"Running errands." He carried her down the hall to her quarters . . . *his* quarters and shut the door. He sat on the bed, rocking them both. Though he didn't say anything, the way he pressed his cheek to hers, keeping her engulfed in his strength made tears spike behind her lashes. His sigh sounded as if the burst of air had come from fathoms deep.

Had she intended to leave him? Perhaps she should've run while she could because now . . . leaving would be like cutting out her own heart. *He'd come for her.* In the last couple of hours, he'd given her so much she'd never known before. He hadn't asked her what she'd done, he'd asked her how she was. He hadn't taken her to task for defying him, he'd demanded she allow medical treatment. He didn't question her loyalty after being found with a militia of vladsets, he held her as if he couldn't let go.

He toed off his boots. Took one of her hands in his and ran his thumb over her palm. "Does this hurt?"

"No." The jagged cuts from when the Saph-link exploded were nothing more than thin scars now. Someone had used a med-wand to heal her.

He grabbed the trailing end of her wrap where it hung loose at her wrist. "I want you out of these."

She wound her arm around his neck again, out of reach and shook her head.

"Come on." He tried to coax her arms from around his neck. "I need to see for myself you're okay."

"No." He was insane if he thought she'd allow him to ruin everything. She liked how things were. He liked her, *desired* her, even, because he didn't know what she looked like.

Everything would change.

"Now." His voice turned stern.

Everything she'd been taught urged her to obey. She'd already denied him twice in quick succession. She forced herself to shake her head.

"You'll obey your chief."

She flinched. Macie told her she didn't have to obey. She pushed away and stood.

Her knees buckled.

"Jesus." He stood, catching her around the waist. Pulled her back against his chest. "What hurts?"

My heart. "Nothing." He was going to ruin this. Steal away everything he'd given her tonight by ordering her around like Maman. Even as a flash of anger simmered through her, she pressed her cheek back against his chest. "Why can't you just hold me?"

He kissed her forehead through the cooling cloths. "Because I'll die a little bit if I find out later you're hurt and I did nothing to help you."

She squeezed her eyes shut. "I might die a little bit if you see me."

"That's all right. I know CPR. I'll bring you right back."

CPR? Was he teasing? His tone said he was, but she didn't understand the word and she wasn't ready for teasing. She pushed his arm away and stood.

"Sorcha."

Warning rang in his tone. Her legs were steadier, though, and she didn't want to give in. Not on this. "You have no right to tease." Her tone was far more challenging than she'd intended. She dropped her gaze.

"I'm not belittling your concern, I'm trying to instill a little levity. You might be hurt and that's far more important than your modesty."

"Modesty?" She gasped. "I'm not being humble you . . . you . . . ." Ugh. What was that word? "*Ass.*"

Donovan stood.

She blanched. Maybe name-calling hadn't been a good idea. She held her arm out to keep him back and retreated. "Macie said I don't have to listen to you. Not you or Maman or anybody."

"True." He stalked forward. "It's also true that you'll obey me when your safety is an issue." He wasn't stopping. "They're coming off. You can do the honors, or I can, but I'll look over every goddamned inch of your naked skin."

She backed away. "I'm not letting you boss me around like Maman did."

"*I am nothing like your Maman.*" If his expression had darkened when she'd called him an ass, it turned downright menacing after comparing him to Maman. "You never minded my orders before."

"You were helping me then."

"I'm still helping. They're coming off and I'm burning them." He reached for her.

"They won't burn." She slapped his hand away.

His gaze narrowed.

"I'm not hurt."

"You'd say whatever you need to keep yourself hidden under those things." He reached out again and when she went to smack his hand, he snagged the loose end of her cloths and tugged. The wrap on her left arm unwound.

"My Chief!" She stopped moving. If she backed away, she'd only aid his cause.

"Donovan." He kept coming at her, forcing her back.

"Stop." She came up hard against the wall and before she could dart to the side, he had both her arms pinned above her head.

His nostrils flared. "I have no problem tying you up if needed. I'll be damned if I let you hurt yourself running away from me."

She gasped. "You wouldn't."

"Try me." He leaned in and tugged the cloth covering her lips down with his teeth. "Kiss me."

A shiver tore through her. "I'm angry with you. You shouldn't tell me what to do."

"Mm. Refresh my memory. When have I given you an order?"

"You told me not to cry when Maman killed my pet. You told me to present my hands to Macie."

"Both safety issues."

"You said I had to learn English."

His brow lifted.

She supposed he considered that a safety issue. So maybe he wasn't like Maman. That didn't mean she had to obey him.

"When else?"

"That's all." She refused to admit she was being unfair, she still wasn't sure she had been.

His lips curved at the corner. "You sure? I remember two more."

What other . . .? Her breath caught. He'd told her to stay with Grady at Lucky's. He'd told her if she tried to leave him he'd spank her ass. She lunged forward and kissed him, hoping to distract him.

The rumble of his laughter morphed into a moan. *This.* This is what she wanted. Needed. "We're revisiting that later, Sorcha." His fingers ran up and down her arms. "Damn, you're soft."

Sorcha froze. He'd released her arms so she could put them around his neck, but sometime during the kiss, he unwound the rest of her armbands. "You tricked me."

"Mm." Her arms were bare. Blue. Silky. Translucent enough that he could make out the lines and shadows of what was beneath the skin but not so translucent to be see through. Her skin was . . . . brighter near her shoulders. She had a small scar on her right shoulder, and another on her right thumb, but he wouldn't have noticed either if he hadn't been searching for flaws. On her left bicep she had six . . . sigils, of some sort. Five old scars and one still raw and seeping. The bands from her arms wrapped around the bands at her shoulder. Not one long piece of material, but five . . . maybe six. He let the bands hang from those at her shoulders. They'd been too tight and left marks on her skin, but he wasn't seeing anything to account for Vessa demanding she stay covered. His finger stroked over one tiny nub just above her elbow on the back of her arm, right where a spike should be. "Come here." She was shaking so hard he worried she might pass out. He eased her down into a chair near the bed.

"Please, there's no reason for this." She pushed his hands away. "I'm fine and I don't wish to sh—"

He got right down into her face. "If you tell me one more time that you'll shame me by showing me your skin I'll not be responsible for what I do to you." He gave her his meanest expression, turning the scarred side of his face toward her like he did when trying to intimidate someone. "You understand?"

She bit her lip. Her gaze slid to the side.

"I'm your *husband*. For Christ's sakes, I'm the only other person aside from you who *should* see all your skin. Now, I'm seeing what the damage is, and if you interfere in any way, I *will* tie you up."

He couldn't miss the sharp breath she sucked in, but she didn't argue. The tremors coursing through her seemed to jump right into him. Now that he was finally about to see his wife, he was the tiniest bit afraid *he* might shame *her*. After wondering for days what was so awful her own mother felt she should go around wearing these shrouds . . . what if he didn't conceal his reaction well enough?

He slipped off her shoe, found the end of the binding cloth and began to unwrap her. Her toes were well groomed with tiny crescent nails made especially for her dainty feet. Both her heel and the ball of her foot had blisters.

"Why didn't you say anything?"

Her chin tipped up. "My shoes are new."

He pressed his lips together. Her ankles were so slim he could wrap his hand around her and have room to go. She was just a bit of a thing even for a human, so at odds with the rest of her people. He smoothed his palm over her pale azure calf. "You wear them too tight."

"If they aren't tight, they'd slip." Irritation made her answer snap.

He placed her foot flat on his thigh and massaged her calf, trying to knead away the red stripes marking her. "You scared the shit out of me tonight."

"That wasn't my intention."

"What did Quimet want?"

She tipped her chin up a notch. "He wanted me to kill you."

He sat back, letting his hand settle over the top of her foot. "Did he."

A single nod.

Not a muscle so much as twitched. Her hands remained folded into a tight ball in her lap. Why would Quimet think she'd be willing or capable of murder?

Blaze.

Right. The petite female who shook like a palsied old maid every time he so much as raised his voice had burned his marks alive in cold blood. He'd believe that when hell froze over.

He unwound the cloth from her thigh. His body taking notice of all the silken skin he uncovered. He traced the outline of a vein he wouldn't have been able to see on anyone else. Her leg was muscular but slim and he couldn't help but remember how they'd felt wrapped around his hips, squeezing him while she came. He shifted. "Obviously, you denied his request."

"I'm reconsidering."

His gaze flicked up. "Why?"

"I like you."

"So you're gonna kill me?" His lips quirked.

One shrouded shoulder lifted. "Killing you would be easier than watching you change."

The wrap ended at her hip where the end had been tucked under the bindings wound around her torso. He slid his finger along the seam of her leg, smiling when she jumped.

"When am I gonna change?" He repeated the entire process with her second leg. There wasn't a flaw anywhere. No burns. No bruises. Her legs were shapely and smooth as satin. Granted, if he hadn't already been in love with her, he might find the translucence of her skin unsettling. He dragged his hand over her thigh, trying to rub away the dark lines.

She shifted in her seat. "When you see me."

"Mm. What if I don't?" He wrapped his fingers around the base of the chair between her thighs and tugged her closer. Her legs ended up on the outside of his. He spread his, forcing hers wider. "What if I don't have a problem with how you look?" So far, he hadn't seen anything he'd be averse to. She was different with her translucent, sky-blue coloring and the little nubs. He didn't mind different. His gaze flicked over the remaining wraps. He plucked at a few bands, searching for the end.

She huffed. Slid her finger under two bands at her hip and emerged with an end clutched between two fingers.

"Thank you." He reached around her to pass the band to his other hand. "What did Quimet say when you told him no?"

"His screams were incoherent."

Okay, right. She wanted him to believe she killed him. Burned him alive. Except she wasn't wearing the armor rigged to set fire to the wearer's gloves, so the fire couldn't have been from her. *Are you Blaze?* The question hung in his mind, dancing at the tip of his tongue. Part of him wanted to know . . . but what then? Cart her into the IgA and collect the reward? He snorted.

She jumped.

"Easy." He reached around her, passing the band to his other hand, unveiling the small divot of her navel on a flat belly, bracketed by the gentle curves of her waist. Again, her skin was brighter here. Almost as if lit from within. He could just about make out her abs beneath her skin. "Still thinking of killing me?"

"Yes." She sniffled.

"You know I won't hurt you, right?" *Even if she's Blaze? Even if it's your duty?*

She nodded.

Underneath the bands, she wore the same skimpy V ribbons her mother had worn. They went from her shoulders to the v between her legs and up her backside. The higher up her torso he ventured, the brighter her skin grew. The next couple of trips around her torso revealed beautiful, full tear-drop breasts, her nipples hidden behind the ribbons. The center of her chest glowed from within, the light flickering beneath her skin like an open flame. As the remaining bands fell away, his breath hitched. She had a beautiful body. God help him, he could smell her arousal. He leaned forward and kissed the swell of her breast. Her skin was far warmer here than it should be.

Her hands flew to his hair.

"You shouldn't."

"I'm gonna lick every inch of your skin." To prove his point, he stroked his tongue over the same spot just to the left of her ribbons. "I hated this on Vessa, but it suits you." Keeping her most private secrets while highlighting the curves of a fit, feminine body. Why in God's name did she think herself ugly?

As he sat back, his gaze flicked over her covered face. *Oh, God.*

"I'm scared."

Holy Christ, he was, too. "I won't ever hurt you."

"Not intentionally."

No. Not intentionally. Whatever was under there must be bad. Awful. Inwardly steeling himself, he began unwinding her head wrap. On the first go around, he found the heavy sack at the back of her head holding her hair. He untwisted the bands until silken white hair dropped to her waist. He revealed the sharp edge of her jaw and a thin, pointed chin.

Faint discoloration marred her skin with what looked to be a small pool of blood beneath. Bruising? Or was this part of what made her "ugly?" "What happened here?" He brushed his lips over the spot.

"Quimet grabbed my face."

Rage flashed through him. "The bastard's lucky he's dead."

Her lips parted. Perfect, bowed deep-blue lips. Straight, white teeth. Another pass around her head and he uncovered a pert nose and damp cheeks.

His gut rolled into a tight knot.

The next pass revealed thick white crescents of eyelashes, and as her lids lifted, the most amazing eyes. Rainbow eyes. The striations around her pupils were streaked with red that faded to orange, yellow, green, blue, and purple before returning to red. She had mesmerizing eyes; he could see a whole universe suspended in their depths. Unusual, not disturbing.

The last of the bindings fell away and he stared at her in horror.

She was gorgeous.

Perfect.

And children cried when he smiled at them.

"Is this a fucking joke?" Her eyes filled with fresh tears but he wasn't buying her shit anymore. "A trick? A trap?" He stood, pushed her chair away. "I don't get it." His voice dropped to a bare whispered. "Where are your flaws?" The fact that her skin was so thin, he could see bits of vein and muscle? That light in her chest that seemed to flare brighter even now? Big fucking deal.

Celeka collapsed in on herself until she knelt before him, her inner light highlighting the shadows of her ribs and spine. "I told you not to. I told you I would shame you."

Oh, that was rich. This whole time he'd felt sorry for her. This entire flight he'd protected her, made excuses for her, damned near killed himself and his friends trying to rescue her and why? For what? Because her beauty should shame an ugly, maimed bastard like him. Because, what, her mother was jealous?

"Fuck you." He turned on his heel and left the room.

— • —

19

What the fuck was wrong with him? He headed for the ramp, then realized he'd taken off his boots. Shit. Fuck. "Goddamnittohell!" With nowhere else to go he stormed into the rec room, almost plowing into Macie.

"That was quick."

"Fuck off." He grabbed a beer out of the cold cabinet, removed the lid, and downed half the bottle on his way to the couch. Paused long enough to sit and then chugged the rest.

Macie must've had a hearing problem because he came over and plopped onto the armchair. He tossed a heavy cloth-wrapped package to Donovan—probably the clothes he'd asked for. "She wouldn't let you see her, huh?"

"Oh, I saw her all right. Every perfect inch of her." He lifted his beer, remembered it was empty, and set it aside.

"Perfect?"

"Gorgeous. She puts Leanne to shame. She's—"

"Stop." Macie sat forward, resting his elbows on his knees. "What's the problem?"

"She's fucking with me, right? I mean all this shit about her being ugly and shaming me. It was all bullshit. Even her fucking mother had me convinced she was a train wreck under those wraps."

"Help me out here, what does she look like?"

"Human."

Macie's brows lifted.

"Except the blue skin. You can kinda see through her skin actually—the shadows of muscle and the lines of veins. She kinda shines on the inside. She has little nubs where vladsets have spikes. Perfect body. Insanely gorgeous eyes—I've never seen anything like them."

"White hair."

Donovan let his head fall back onto the back of the couch and stared up at the ceiling. "She's different, not ugly. She's not scarred. Not maimed." *Not like him.* She could do so much better than him. Was that why she tried to run when he left her with Grady? Had she realized she could do better? Did she have someone, somewhere that was better? Hell, did she want Grady?

"I know you're not an idiot, so something more is going on."

Was it something more? He should be happy, shouldn't he? Married to a knock-out. She was sweet. She even liked things about him everyone else hated.

"Fuck-off, Macie." There was no heat behind his words, though, so he may as well have invited him to carry on. Shit, maybe he had overreacted. He'd just expected her to be like him. Assumed they were at least on a level playing field. Talk about a train wreck. Her life would be hell being married to him.

"She's not Leanne."

He closed his eyes, trying to ignore Macie. No, she wasn't Leanne. And she wasn't from Earth. Leanne had done what she had to do to protect herself. The UN, had they continued to retain control, would've shipped his sorry, scarred ass to Asteria. Things weren't much better now. The UN had been in control long enough for the civilians on Earth to get used to their perfect utopia. They rejected anyone who was scarred or disabled. Sorcha had no idea what she was getting into. How difficult her life would be married to him.

Macie drew in a deep breath. "Vladsets hate weakness—they revere the biggest, the most muscular. The longest, thickest spikes."

He pressed his lips together. Granted, Earthers didn't like aliens. She'd earn their venom for that, but far less than for being associated with him and the Zeros.

"They hate humans—sounds like she resembles her father's people, right?"

Damn it, why wouldn't he shut up? This would be different if Sorcha had been from Earth. If she'd decided she wanted him despite understanding all the shit Earthers would give her for being with him. Did he want to continue to get close to her? She was beautiful. He wouldn't blame her any more than he'd blamed Leanne for leaving him. But damn it, he didn't want to go through that again.

"They hate pale colors—it's a sign of sickness."

And her skin was the color and translucence of a winter morning. "I get it, she truly believes she's ugly." His stomach knotted. "I fucked up."

Macie shook his head. "You look guilty as hell. Tell me walking out was the worst thing you did."

What had he said before he left? Had he verbalized how beautiful she was? *Is this a fucking joke?*

"The woman I've been talking to the last few days has zero self-esteem." Macie slouched back in the chair, throwing an arm over the back. "I mean I'm not saying I don't have concerns about her, because after everything that went down today, *I have concerns*, but she's been blossoming since she's been with us, don't you think?"

Killing you would be easier than watching you change.

Is this a fucking joke?

How much abuse had she taken at the hands of the vladsets? Then he got her, starts building her up only to totally decimate her. The blood drained from Donovan's face. "Oh, my God."

Decimated her and left her alone. He raced back to her room. The door was locked. "Sorcha!" He pounded on the door. Listened. Was that water running? He slammed his fist on the door again. "Get the master key."

Macie dashed toward the front of the ship.

Should she cleanse herself of the scent of smoke and death or cleanse the world of a cold-blooded killer no one could stand to see?

Donovan's horrified expression flashed through her mind and she flinched. She'd never forget. Not even Maman's disgust hurt so much. Donovan was the only one to be nice to her and now, after seeing his reaction, all the sweet tenderness that came before only made his rejection more severe. He'd confirmed everything Maman had ever said.

She huddled in the center of the tub, knees drawn to her chest and stroked her thumb over the remote control for the para-gravity device.

Macie said never to increase the power past level two, but there were several other buttons. She could wait until the water filled the tub and then push the last one. The strongest one. What would happen? Would the gravity increase, slamming her down to the bottom of the tub and hold her there? The water would engulf her, ensuring she didn't catch the ship on fire when she began to panic. No one else would get hurt.

She wouldn't hurt anymore.

For a few minutes, she'd been so overcome she'd thought somehow, miraculously, he had found her attractive.

But no.

She couldn't blame him. He'd tried. He'd tried so much harder than anyone else. For that, it saddened her to shame him by taking her own life. Maman, not so much. Maman could suffer with the shame. She hoped she choked on it.

Yet she wanted to see more of Asteria. She wanted to see Earth. Doing so would be easy if she was like everyone else . . . *anyone* else. Like Angel. She was alien and yet similar enough to the humans that they accepted her. She had a husband who loved her and a sweet little girl who trusted and adored her.

What she wouldn't give for the same.

She stroked her thumb over the smooth buttons on the remote. She had no idea how a child of hers might turn out—vladset or human or something in between. She'd have to think long and hard before bringing a child into the world.

She might be better off to care for one of the small beings with no parents, like Grady did. Children with no clan. Like her. If she raised the child, he'd grow accustomed to her, he might love her anyway.

What was she doing? She could leave Donovan. Divorce him. Either would shame those associated with her, but *she* didn't have to suffer further. As Donovan would say—fuck them.

Her physical appearance wasn't *her* fault.

Donovan burst into the room, making her jump. His gaze darted around the room, zeroing in on the remote. "What are doing?"

Macie burst in right behind him. His eyes widened.

"Out!" She covered her face.

"That's not the part you need to cover." Donovan shielded her with a towel as he plucked the remote from her hand. "Get it out of here and don't give it back to her." He shut off the water.

"Damn, Reese, you weren't exaggerating, were you?."

"Get out, Macie." Donovan hauled her up, covered her with a towel, and shook her. "What are you thinking?"

My physical appearance isn't my fault. I'm not hiding anymore.

She lowered her hands and forced herself to smile while reciting her plan. "I'm staying on Asteria. I won't bother you or Maman or anyone." She poked him in the chest. "I don't need you. I don't have to keep putting myself around people who don't want me."

"Good for you." Macie raised his fist in the air. "You go, girl."

"Get out." Donovan growled the words, chasing Macie out and slamming the bedroom door behind him.

She was in the process of closing the bathroom door when he reappeared. "Nah." He pushed through. "You, you're not hiding from me anymore and you sure as hell aren't going anywhere."

"Why?" She backed to the far corner of the bathroom which only put a handful of feet between them. "You don't want me. Macie said women on Earth can get a divorce. And after, Maman won't expect me back. It'd be a death sentence to go back."

"We. Are. Not. Getting. A. Divorce." With each word, he stalked forward until he stood entirely too close. She reached out to stop him, saw her hand would land on the spot where she burned his suit, and lowered her arm, instead.

"Why not?" Had she said the wrong word? "Would it be an annulment? You'll tell me the correct word."

"That's for freedom from religious unifications. We didn't marry in a church."

"Divorce, then."

His nostrils flared. "Stop saying that."

She straightened her back. "I don't have to listen to you."

His eyelid twitched. "I'm gonna kill Macie."

"I'm divorcing you and living on the other side of the Red Sea next to Grady. I'm going adopt the war orphans and they'll like me because I'm giving them a home."

"You can't adopt children willy-nilly." He dragged his hand down his face.

Willy-nilly? She huffed. He was trying to confuse her with slang. "Grady did."

"Quit talking about Grady." His voice crept up in volume. "You're not living out there with him."

"Why? He's clan."

His brows snapped together. "What?"

"At lunch. Merrick and Grady vowed their loyalty. They're clan." She pointed. "You may be chief, but the female takes care of clan."

He closed his eyes. "How can they be your clan if they're loyal to me and you're divorcing me?"

Now he was being obtuse. "I'm keeping them." She propped her hand on her hip. "Macie, too."

"Macie—" He lifted his hands to his head, fisted them, as if mimicking the act of pulling his hair out. "You're not divorcing me." He shook his head. "Not over this."

"You've wanted a divorce since we got married." Her voice raised. "Why are you being fickle?"

She didn't think he intended to answer. His gaze clashed with hers, his lips pressed into a thin line stretching the scars on his face. His tone dropped to a bare grumble. "I got to know you. I like you."

"I saw your face." Maybe he liked her, but . . . "You don't want me."

"That's the hell of it, I do. I want you." He dragged his hand down his face. "You're making me fucking insane. I don't deserve you, but I want you."

She bit her lip, unsure how to resolve this now. Fickle male, changing his mind once she settled on a plan.

"What were you doing with the remote?" He crowded her body until he was pressed against her length.

"Nothing." She craned her neck to meet his gaze.

"Don't lie." He tipped his face down to hers so his words breezed over her lips. Flutters erupted in her belly. He cupped her face, stroking his thumbs over her skin. She couldn't think straight when he did that. All she wanted to do was lean into his touch. Absorb his strength. Kiss him until neither of them could stand. "One of the things I like best about you, is that you don't lie."

How could he touch her? His gaze was direct and intense. He snuggled close, searching her features. If the hard cock pressed to her belly was any indication, he wanted her still.

She wanted him. Even knowing how much he could wound her without even lifting a hand, she still wanted him. "You hurt me." She closed her eyes against the prick of tears.

"Sorcha." He tried to pull her into his arms.

She smacked his shoulder. "Don't do that. You don't get to be mean and then switch back to being nice."

"Look at me."

"No." She turned her face away, if she looked at him, her determination would crumble. "If I raise a small human like Grady, they'd grow up seeing me every day. I might not be odd to them. An adopted child might love me anyway. Macie said I can live on my own once we're divorced so I don't need you."

"Why am I hearing all about Macie and Grady? What about me?"

She lifted her gaze. "What do you mean?"

"Who's going to love me?"

Oh, yes. She would lose this battle. His features drew taut. She thought her solution would solve everything, but now she was hurting him as much as he'd hurt her.

He cleared his throat. "Gimme time, Sorcha. I know I don't deserve it. Give me a month."

A month? She wasn't even sure how long that was. What if he asked for a divorce at the end? He'd break her heart. She shook her head. "That's—"

"Two weeks." He nodded. "I'll make you want to stay."

She bit her lip. "Are weeks shorter than months?"

He nodded. "Months, weeks, days."

"I don't know."

"Fourteen days, then. That's all.

Days were less than weeks. She almost asked him to explain the number fourteen, then decided it didn't matter. Fourteen days filled with his warmth and his scent. Fourteen days of kindness he might rip away when the time was up. But it was better than weeks. She didn't know if she could survive two weeks of his attention if he decided he didn't want her at the end.

She didn't get a chance to answer. His mouth crashed down on hers and she was hauled higher against the wall and pinned there with his hard body. His lips were firm against hers and when he nipped her, she gasped. What was he doing? She saw his absolute horror. How could he kiss her like this after seeing her? He trailed his lips across her cheek. Nuzzled the sensitive curve of her neck. "I don't understand you."

"Sometimes, I don't understand myself, so you're pretty much up to speed." He pulled back enough to meet her gaze. "I'm sorry. You surprised me. I was geared up, bracing for the worst . . . I thought you'd lied to me." He stroked his thumb over her cheek. "You're beautiful."

How could he say that? Did he think her stupid, too? "Now *you're* lying."

He shook his head. "Gorgeous."

Tears pricked the back of her eyes. Was he teasing? Didn't he understand how much it hurt? "Stop it."

"Do you think . . .?" He looked away. Swallowed hard before his gaze came back to hers. "Do you think I'm ugly?"

Her chief was a beautiful male. Half his face ruggedly handsome, half bearing the marks of his honor. The sculpted muscles on his body proclaimed his strength for all to see. "Of course not, you—"

"—made a small child cry because I smiled."

Was that why the child had reared away from him? She curled her hand around the side of his throat and stroked his jaw with her thumb. "My Chief, I—"

"All this time, I thought you were like me, but you're not."

No, she wasn't like anyone.

"You're so much better."

She started to shake her head but his hands cupped her face, staying her.

"Where I come from, I'm ugly. Where I come from, children cry when they see me and adults avert their gazes, but you find me attractive?"

She nodded.

"So maybe, even though your people think you're ugly, even though they hid you away and call you wretched . . . can't you understand to me, you're beautiful?"

Could that be possible? She bit her lip. Searched his face and found only intensity and promise. He wasn't flinching. He leaned into her instead of shying away.

Fourteen days? Even if she agreed, this solved nothing. They couldn't be together forever—she'd cause him far too many problems. With Maman. With the IgA. The rational part of her screamed, *No!* She'd suffer more from the loss after those fourteen days.

But with his gaze steady on hers, with his body pressed close, his heat surrounding her, denying him was impossible. "I fear I'll cause you trouble."

"Endlessly." The corner of his lips curved, taking out the sting. "Even then, you won't cause me half the trouble I'll cause you."

How could he cause her trouble? There must be some truth behind his teasing, though: He averted his gaze. "What do you mean?"

"Later." His mouth sealed to hers. Something dark and needy began to grow deep in her belly. He had the flavor of decadence—maleness, heat, and something even better yet unknown to her. She held his head, twining her fingers in his hair to hold him close while she explored his mouth. "Take this off." She tugged the collar of his body armor.

"Not yet." He leaned away from her, drawing in an unsteady breath. "We have one more thing to discuss."

She rose on tiptoes to kiss his neck. "Now?"

He swallowed hard and held her away from him. "You put yourself in danger today because you refused to listen."

Stay with Grady.

If you try to leave me, I'll spank your ass.

That had been an idle threat, right? Except his features were drawn into hard, determined lines; the scars near his left eye twitched.

She pushed him back. He didn't budge.

He trapped her hand against his chest. His gaze dipped down to where her fingers were outlined by the scorch marks on his suit.

Oh, Dedia. She'd shoved his opposite shoulder, putting her hand right over the scorched handprint.

His whole countenance hardened, something unreadable flashing through his eyes. He stepped back, pulling her with him.

"It's not what you thin—"

— • —

20

"Don't." He shook his head. "Not another word."

Maybe he hadn't noticed. He and Macie both thought Blaze was a male. Maybe he was still focused on her disobedience.

He led her to the center of the bathroom and turned her, stepping behind her and dragging her towel off her body.

A chill broke over her skin, tightening her nipples. She averted her gaze from the mirror. Shivered as his heat pressed against her back. He gathered her hair, making her scalp tingle, pulling the heavy mass from her shoulders, and ducked his head to whisper in her ear. "At the end of fourteen days, you're repeating your marriage vows. Earther vows."

Her breath caught. "Why?"

"The important ones were left out of our wedding." He drew her earlobe into his mouth, sucking. Gooseflesh lifted on her skin.

What was he talking about? "Which vows?"

"To love, cherish, and *obey*." His palm flattened low on her belly, holding her to him.

The first two wouldn't be hard . . . but *obey?* That couldn't be part of Earther marriage vows. "Macie said—"

His hold tightened and their gazes clashed in the mirror. "The only name I want to hear on your lips tonight is mine."

Was he jealous? If his people saw him as ugly and he truly thought her beautiful, was he worried about *her* leaving *him?* Maybe, feeling undesirable? She bit her lip. As arrogant as he was, insecurity seemed farfetched. Keeping her gaze on his, she arched back, pressing her rear to his groin.

A moan rumbled through his chest.

"You're overdressed."

Heat filled his gaze and with the change, she realized he *had* been worried. Her chief questioned his value. She refused to allow that. She held his hips to her. "I've never seen all of you, either."

He stepped back, bringing her with him. "Put your hands on the counter, little flame."

He kept his palm flattened against her belly, refusing to let her get closer.

"Go on."

She widened her stance, reaching out to grip the counter. The position left her butt flush with his groin, her torso stretched, and her arms extended in front of her. Her breasts tingled and ached.

"Don't move." He stepped away, unzipping his body armor.

Her gaze followed him.

"Eyes on the mirror."

She faced forward, searching out his reflection. He stood out of range but the rustle of clothing indicated he was undressing.

When he returned, the heat from his legs warmed the back of hers. He stroked his hand over her back, his palm tickling over the nubs along her spine.

She stared at his reflection. He was beautiful. So different from her. His body was a mixture of planes and angles compared to her curves. His skin tan to her blue. His hard to her soft. His hairy to her bare. His cock brushed against her hip, hot and smooth and fiercely hard.

"You never told me, how much of the holo-vid did you watch?"

He wanted to talk about that? She tried to press back into him, but his hand on her ass prevented that. Her breath caught. Would he carry through with his threat? No. He was hard so he must be thinking of mating, not punishment.

"Enough to understand what was expected by a human."

He stroked down the back of her leg. Up again. Settled his palm over her pussy, making her inner muscles clench. "Are you sore?"

A little. She shook her head.

"Good." His fingers slid between her folds, and he pressed one into her.

An unsteady breath shook out of her lungs as his finger entered her. Despite the slight sting, ripples of pleasure rolled through her.

"Look at me."

She met his gaze in the mirror.

"You have no problem following my orders here."

"I thought . . . ." *He'd forgotten.* She tried to straighten, his palm on her back stopped her. Her heart rate picked up and with it, her flame grew brighter.

"Tell me why?" His finger slid out of her, two plunged back in.

The combination of pain and pleasure had shivers coursing through her. He wouldn't hit her. Not when he was busy making her feel so good. "You know more about mating than I do."

"Yeah." He spread his fingers inside of her.

She closed her eyes, lowering her head. *Yes.* A soft moan broke from her lips.

"Eyes on me."

She forced herself to meet his gaze in the mirror.

"I know how to keep you safe, too."

She shook her head, pressing against him, taking his fingers deeper. He didn't have all the facts. Didn't know who she was or how her identity could ruin everything.

He pulled his fingers from her and his palm landed with a resounding smack, echoing around them.

Her eyes widened. "Donovan," whooshed out on a sharp breath. He rubbed the sting away. In its wake, heat flooded her pussy. Her lips parted. Maybe she should have watched more of the hologram. "Donovan?"

He leaned over, kissing his way down her back while his fingers found her entrance and thrust in. He pressed his forehead to her back and moaned. "Christ, you're wet." His other hand cupped her breast. "You can tell me to stop."

Did she want him to? The *idea* of his "spanking" her had terrified her, but now . . . She bit her lip. "No."

His teeth grazed over her back. He nipped her hip. "When I give you an order you'll obey without question."

He might be punishing her, but he was also giving her control by asking her if she wanted him to stop. By asking a question that would force the punishment to continue. She rolled her hips against him, fighting back a grin. "No."

"Damn it." This time, he continued to play with her nipple when he pulled his fingers from her. His palm grazed over her bum once, twice. She gasped as his hand landed just to the side of her pussy.

What if he'd smacked her pussy? What would that have felt like? Suddenly she wanted to know. Needed to know.

She was killing him. His dick was so hard he could hammer nails with it and she was teasing him. His innocent wife had upped the ante. He sank his fingers back into her wet heat, wishing his throbbing cock was balls deep, instead. Her inner walls squeezed and gripped him, her desire coating his fingers.

Hell, when he burst in here, he'd had every intention of being honorable and giving her the choice of staying or leaving. He'd planned on telling her everything.

But she'd been naked and wet and so damn sad. When she'd pasted on that fake smile and told him she was divorcing him—

He'd lost his shit. Totally and completely.

Obviously.

"Tell me what I want to hear."

"I'm close."

Oh, God. She was getting off on this. Christ Almighty, he was in trouble. She was knocking down every assumption he'd made about a young vladset princess, turning out to be nothing he expected and everything he wanted. He knew how their relationship would end, how it had to end, but he couldn't give her up. Not yet.

He circled her clit, teasing.

"Donovan." Her hips bucked. Her knuckles whitened from her grip on the counter. Now that she was so focused on pleasure, the light in her chest had dimmed and her skin had cooled to a normal temperature.

"Tell me you'll obey." Again, he withdrew his fingers, flattening his palm on her rounded ass in warning.

She shook her head, shifting her hips so his hand ended up against her pussy. "Please."

His breath caught. He cupped her, pressing against her heat. "Here?"

She pushed into his palm.

Hell, she was supposed to agree to obey to avoid the light smacks, not for more of them. "Tell me you'll obey, first."

"No."

He slid his fingers into her heat. "When it's a safety issue." Pinched her nipple, drawing the swollen bud away from her body. Put the flat of his palm back against her heat. "Say it."

She gasped. "Yes."

He let his hand fly.

She came, all pulsing wet heat against his hand, her strangled shout echoing around them. She was gorgeous. He pulled her up and she sagged against his chest. He angled her face to the mirror. "Open your eyes." Her heavy-lidded gaze met his. "Do you see how beautiful you are?"

Those gorgeous eyes of hers widened, but her gaze never left his. "I see."

Stubborn woman. "You're supposed to look at yourself, little flame."

She turned and wrapped her arms around him. "I don't need to. I can see desire on your face." She rose on her tiptoes and the heat of her mouth skated over his throat, his scarred cheek. She tipped his face down to hers. "Do you see my desire?"

Those multi-colored eyes were dilated. Quick shallow breaths escaped swollen, well-loved lips. Yeah, he could see her desire. His throat tightened, so he kissed her instead of answering. He lifted her and she wrapped her legs around his waist. He carried her into the bedroom, knelt on the bed, and laid them both down. "Touch me."

She reached up with her right hand to push against his right shoulder. Fighters did that to make it harder for the other person to hit—a block and an attack all wrapped into one.

Damn, his wife was Blaze.

His wife had an IgA contract on her head.

A contract *he* owned.

If he wanted to keep her safe, she needed to listen to his orders. He might not always have time to explain and there were plenty of other hunters out there who had no qualms about impinging on another's contract.

He allowed her to move him, rolling onto his back.

She straddled his legs. He was already wet, had been leaking pre-come since he'd bent her over in the bathroom and her pert ass had snuggled up to his groin.

He flexed his hips so his length slid against her wet heat, catching at her entrance.

Her nails sank into his chest and her lips parted. She leaned forward until the head of his cock angled into her. Slowly, she sank back.

That was the most erotic sight—his dick disappearing into his tiny wife. "Good girl. Take me."

It was damn near torture. She pushed down until there was resistance and then eased up before sinking deeper, slowing fucking herself on his cock.

"God, Sorcha, that's good." She eased off him, her inner muscles clenching. He moaned. "Come on, take all of me." She slid back down his length. "So fucking tight. I love being inside you." With a wiggle of her hips, she pressed down the last little bit until he was fully sheathed inside her.

Her head tilted back, lips parted, the long locks of her hair tickling his thighs.

He'd fallen in love with her before he'd seen her beauty. He didn't stand a chance in hell of protecting his heart now. Somehow, he needed to find a way to keep her safe. Keep her off the IgA's radar. Off the vladsets' radar. Somehow, he needed to shield her from the hell of his existence back on Earth. Everything was against them. Letting her leave now would be so much easier.

Maybe he was a bastard but he wasn't letting her go.

Donovan sat up, twisting her hair around his fist and brringing her mouth to his. "You feel me inside you?"

"Yes. So deep." She rocked against him.

He thrust up. "I'm part of you."

"Yes." Her head lolled to the side and she let out a little mewl.

"One with you."

"Yes."

"You're mine."

Her eyes opened, all those brilliant colors focused on him. She stroked her palm down his left cheek. Traced the line on his bottom lip. "For now, my Chief. As agreed."

Not good enough. What if she never loved him like he loved her? What if he poured everything into the next two weeks only to lose her anyway? He had two weeks to convince her to stay. Two weeks to make her love him.

He angled his mouth over hers, sinking his tongue deep, trying to possess her in every way. She threaded her fingers though his hair, kissing him back with abandon. Rocking against him. Her nipples stabbing into his chest with each thrust. He kissed his way down her throat. Bowed his back so he could take one nipple into his mouth and sucked until her movements became jerky and uncoordinated. Until her nails bit into his scalp and her sighs turned to urgent cries. Until that flame of hers brightened once again.

His balls drew up tight to his body, ready to explode. Shivers ghosted over his skin at the warm flex and release of her pussy. He wouldn't last much longer. He pressed his thumb to her clit, rubbing slow circles in counterpoint to her thrusts.

"*Stloke ke lithie.*" Her grip tightened on his hair.

He grinned. His little flame was losing control, so far gone she was using words that didn't translate to Standard. Yeah, he wouldn't ever grow tired of this. Two weeks would never be enough. A lifetime wouldn't be enough. "Take it, Sorcha."

Her gaze locked with his and she pressed against his thumb, angling his cock to sink deeper.

"*Inteka svelte, Donavan.*" She trembled in his arms, her inner muscles pulsing around his cock. "*Dedia.*"

He flipped their positions, hooking one of her legs over his arm, desperate for release. "God, I love you."

He thrust into her, his balls slapping against her and she clung to him. Stroked his face, his shoulders. With her hands on his chest, her gaze on his, and her body hugging him tight, stars bloomed behind his eyes. He buried his face in her neck as his orgasm crashed over him.

God, I love you.

Celeka rubbed her cheek against her mate's as they fought to catch their breath. Did he even realize what he'd said? She'd put far more stock into the declaration had they not been uttered as pleasure consumed him. She couldn't form coherent thoughts much less speak them when orgasm crashed over her. Maybe it was best to pretend the words hadn't been spoken.

Donovan lifted onto his elbows and brushed her hair from her face. He gave her a lingering kiss. When he lifted, he winked, rolled over, and dragged her with him. She ended up sprawled over his chest, her legs tangled with his.

He gathered up her hair and moved the length of it out of his way so he could stroke his hand up and down her back.

"Hey."

She lifted her face.

"I won't ever stop wanting to be inside you."

Her belly did a little flop. She couldn't imagine ever not wanting him, either. A slow smile spread on her face.

"Who's Dedia?"

"You know of Dedia?"

He grinned. "You cried out the name when you came."

Her face heated and he laughed.

When she tucked her face against his neck he gave her a squeeze. "Tell me about Dedia."

"In the beginning, Troon was a cold desolate place. The only colors were the white of the snow and the blue of the ice. Dedia came to Troon because she was lonely. She searched everywhere for life, trudging through the snow until she came upon the giant penitents in the South."

"What are penitents?"

"They're hard cones of snow, like a stalagmite. When she first saw them jutting out of the glacier through the heavy snow and raging winds, she thought they were a great army marching across the valley. She ran toward them, sure she'd find a mate among their number but when she arrived, she discovered her mistake. She breathed her fire into them—her passion for life and the fire of her spirit—and they came to life."

"That's the vladset creation story?"

She nodded. "Dedia tried to soul-merge many of the males but none could hold her flame, each of them burned from the inside out as her flame devoured theirs." She held onto him tighter.

"She devoured their souls?"

"Yes. The vladsets, fearing she meant to destroy them all, chased her away into the sky where she was trapped and has burned ever since."

"A harsh story for a harsh world."

"Her light brings little warmth from where it burns in the sky, but all vladsets carry her flame." She put her hand to her chest. "It heats them from the inside out, their thick skin keeping the flame deep inside them."

"I still don't understand. You told me soul-merging wouldn't be a good idea, but we're both fine."

"Before Maman's rule, we celebrated soul-merging as complete commitment between two souls. After a time, the couple's biology changes to complement each other. They'd sense each other's pain or joy." She trailed her finger down his chest. "When one dies, the other follows. Soul-merging was considered a beautiful offering to each other. But there was a dark side, too. If a wife betrayed her husband, the husband could soul-devour her—take her soul as his own, which killed her while saving his own life. If a husband betrayed his wife . . . she could do the same to him."

"This was done before or after the guilty party was forced to watch everything they held dear destroyed?"

"After, of course." She fidgeted with the hair on his chest. "After Maman soul-devoured her mate and became queen, she proclaimed soul-merging was never meant for mates, but for enemies. She prohibited the people from the tradition and turned it into something awful."

He lifted his head to look at her. "So they just die?"

"No. The life is scorched out of them with a kiss. Soul-devouring is terrible."

Distressed with the conversation, her inner flame flared and she started to pull away. Instead of letting go, he tucked her closer to him.

"All vladsets pray to this goddess?"

Hadn't he listened? "Dedia isn't a goddess, she had no control. She's . . . feared."

He frowned while he played with strands of her hair. "She's, what, like a demon?" He searched her face. "But you pray to her. I've heard you say her name before."

She supposed she did pray to her. She had a lot in common with Dedia. Much more than the cold, controlled gods and goddess the vladsets worshiped.

His Saph-link saved her from having to explain. She shifted to Donovan's side so he could get up. He stood there at ease with his nakedness, lifting the device to his ear. "Reese."

While he listened, his gaze stroked over her from toes to face, lingering at the places on her body where he tended to devote most of his attention. Her whole body warmed.

"Now?" He sighed. "Do I have time for a shower? How urgent is this?" He pulled the device from his ear to look at the screen. "Thirty minutes? Fine. We'll meet you down in the landing pad." He hung up and let the device fold in on itself until it was a rectangle small enough to fit into a pocket. "Griffin needs to meet with me. Why don't we take a quick shower"—he winked—"together, get dressed, see what Griffin wants, and then go to dinner?"

As if on cue, her belly grumbled. After all she'd eaten at Lucky's that afternoon, she hadn't thought she'd be hungry again for the rest of the day. "Can we go back to Lucky's?"

He grinned. "Told you the food was good."

Celeka rolled out of bed and followed him to the bathroom. If the next fourteen days were like this, she'd never want to leave.

21

What the hell had Macie been thinking?

Donovan did his best to hide his absolute horror at his wife's attire. She was going to start a goddamned riot. He'd made passionate love to his wife in the shower until he could barely stand and, in the act of *dressing* her, he was stone hard again.

The clothes Macie purchased were . . . indecent. The black cargo pants hugged her ass so tight he wouldn't be surprised if the seams burst when she bent over and they rode so low on her hips that if she had pubic hair, it would've shown. The top wasn't any better—the sleeveless black vest ended below her ribs, leaving the curve of her hips and flat belly exposed. The deep V of the vest left the tops of her full un-bound breasts visible. And while her flame was barely visible now, should she flare, everyone would know.

But the fucker had bought her a hat and thick leather boots. Her hair and feet would be protected well enough.

His hands shook a little as he gathered her hair and threaded the thick silken stuff through the hole in the back of the hat and settled it on her head. The hat was black, too, and it made the brilliant colors in her eyes pop. Her white hair hung down her back to her waist in a thick braid which did nothing more than enhance the curves of her hips on either side.

Biting her lip, she looked down at herself, lifting her arms to the side. "I wish I had my veil, at least."

"No. You look amazing. That's the problem. I'm gonna spend all night making sure everyone knows you're taken."

Her lips trembled, curved in a shy smile. "I'll allow, perhaps, you like my appearance, but you're outrageous to suggest others will."

He grunted. After so many years of being told she was wretched, it would take a hell of a lot more than one night to convince her otherwise, but he *would* find a way to get her to accept how beautiful she was.

Her whole attitude turned cagey, the light in her chest increasing as her attention shifted toward the door. "I'm ready."

Hell, she was scared.

"Nah, not yet." He pulled her into his embrace. Was he being a bully for making her wear different clothes? His friends would never say anything negative about her appearance. He didn't think anyone could, but now he was starting to worry his plan might backfire and cause her more pain.

"We try this my way for fourteen days, right?"

She nodded, the top of her head bumping his chin. "If you want to come back to the ship, tell me. We'll come back. No big deal."

"I'll not shame—"

He pulled back and tipped her chin up to see her beneath the brim of her hat. "You can't shame me. Get the idea out of your head. It's an impossible feat."

With a jerky nod, she lifted and gave him a quick kiss. She always gravitated to his left side, his scarred side, and every time the pressure of her soft lips on his ruined flesh damned near unmanned him.

"Can we go? The wait is making me nervous."

That was his little flame—she burned right through her fear. He threaded his fingers with hers and opened the bedroom door. They walked down the corridor in silence and when they reached the ramp she tried to slip her hand from his.

He tightened his grip.

"It's rude." She hissed her criticism under her breath.

That was rich. He'd knelt in front of her in the shower while the last of their water supply rained over them both, teasing and kissing her sweet spot until she'd come on his face with wild abandon and now she feared someone seeing them hold hands? "It's expected." He lifted her hand and kissed her knuckles. "And it's happening."

She made a distressed sound as he pulled her along.

Grady turned as they approached. His lips parted and he tipped his face down, looking at them over the rims of his glasses. "Well, now . . . ."

Oh, hell no. "Don't start. She's married."

"I'm thinking ya better take good care of her else someone might steal her away." He folded his arms over his chest, his posture full of challenge.

"Don't tease my chief, Grady. He's in a strange mood."

Donovan gave her hand a squeeze. "Griffin show up yet?"

"Yep." Grady jerked his chin off to the side. "Got a right mess, ya do."

Looked like it. Griffin sat on a crate and Macie stood in front of him, looking pissed as fuck. His lip was split and he had a shiner on his cheek. He couldn't quite tell from this angle, but he was pretty sure Griffin had Macie cuffed. Half a dozen rough-looking men stood off to the side, talking and throwing stink-eye at Macie. They were all sporting bruises. One had a bloody rag to his nose.

As Donovan headed toward them, one of the men met his gaze and started forward. He pointed. "That's our—"

"I said, I'll take care of it." Griffin stood, pulling his weapon and pointing it at the guy. "You lot shut up and stay over there. Anyone interferes and you'll be sitting in Merrik's jail tonight." Griffin held the short chain between Macie's cuffs and used his shoulder to nudge him forward.

Yeah, this didn't look good.

As soon as they could talk without being overheard he asked, "What's going on?"

Griffin's expression was grim. "I was passing by the Checkered Flag when a ruckus broke out inside, and—"

Macie's lips curled. "I had a winning hand—"

"Ah, Christ. Not again." Not *now*.

"—I counted the fucking cards. I watched them. Learned their goddamned tells. It was a sure thing."

"Jesus, Macie." Donovan let go of Sorcha and lifted his hands to his head. Son of a bitch! He knew better than to leave Macie alone for so long. He hadn't gambled in a while, but it was a constant struggle to keep him away from the tables. "What'd you lose?" Whatever it was, he'd cover it. Then they were getting out of here before anything else could go wrong. He just needed to resupply the ship with fuel and water. Hell, he should probably double check their food supply.

Macie turned his face away, mumbling under his breath.

"What?"

"The *Slag*."

Donovan blinked. He couldn't possibly have heard right. "What?"

"The *Red Slag*. The ship. I lost the fucking ship!" He turned, dragging Griffin along with him, raising his voice. "But those fuckers *cheated*."

"Settle down, Mason." Griffin strong-armed him back where he wanted him, facing away from the men who apparently now owned their ship.

Macie lowered his voice. "I'm telling you, they cheated, man. You know me, I don't lose."

"Except when you do." Like when he was running from his demons. When he drank, he tended to lose big.

"No. Not this time. It was a winning hand. Everything lined up perfect. I wasn't drinking. No drugs. No nothing. I had the suicide king, the queen of hearts, and the one-eyed jack, *my* cards."

Donovan grunted. Despite how smart Macie was, like any gambler, he held certain beliefs about luck and omens. Why the fuck had he let him go off alone?

"They *did* something."

Griffin shrugged. "I shook 'em down. They didn't have anything on them. No extra cards, no devices. Cards weren't marked."

His gaze shifted back to Macie.

"We would've been good with this win. We'd have had rent for the next six months, no problem."

Always searching for the easy fix. Always wanting to make up everything he'd lost.

And whose fault is it he lost everything?

He never should've talked Macie into joining the Blue Helmets as a spy. Whatever happened to him during that time had fucked him up.

The sharp prick of an on-coming headache lanced behind his eyes. He pinched the bridge of his nose. "What exactly was the wording of the bet?"

"Just the ship. That's it."

That's it? *Just* the *Red Slag*. *Just* their livelihood. Their *fucking home*. Donovan hauled back and punched him. Pain reverberated across his knuckles and down his wrist as Macie staggered back. If

Griffin hadn't held him up, the dumb fuck would've landed on his ass.

"You done?" Both Macie and Griffin asked at the same time.

"No more." Sorcha snuck in-between him and Macie, flattening her hands to his chest. "Enough."

He didn't know if he was more pissed off at Macie or himself. *He lost everything because of you, you can damned well suck it up.* He drew in an unsteady breath and the red haze started to ease back from his vision. He was pissed, yeah, but this was nothing compared to what Macie had endured because of him. "Yeah, I'm done." He lifted his arm and wiped the sweat from his brow on his sleeve. Why was it so hot in here?

He put his hand on Sorcha's hip. What must she think of all this? Knowing her reaction would give him an idea of how she might react to all the shit going on back home, but he couldn't quite bring himself to look at her yet. He focused on Griffin, instead. "You giving us time to get our shit?"

"Yep." Griffin jerked his head back. "I'll sit right over there and make sure everyone behaves." He used the back of his hand to wipe the sweat from his eyes.

The hand resting on Sorcha's hip had grown warm. Unnaturally warm.

He forced himself to look at Sorcha, bracing for her disappointment. She'd twisted slightly to glare at the males waiting to take their ship. Her chest was glowing bright, her cheeks had turned bright blue, and her beautiful eyes were full of animosity. She wasn't sweating, but he and the others were.

"Sorcha?"

Her voice was whisper-soft and lethal. "If all of you go back to the ship, I'll take care of them."

He squeezed her hip and she jerked a bit. Blinked. Turned her face up to his. The brightness in her chest dimmed.

The air cooled.

Shit. The hair on his nape lifted. It was *her*. She was changing the temperature. Did she know she was? Any lingering doubts he had went up in smoke. She was Blaze. He glanced up to find Macie watching her more closely than he would've liked.

Griffin chuckled. "While I would love to see nothing more, I can't condone violence in the spaceport."

"Come inside with us." Macie tore his gaze from Sorcha to glare at Griffin over his shoulder. "Let her at them. They fucking cheated."

Griffin's gaze settled on Sorcha and his humor faded. He searched her face. Probably trying to figure out what they knew that he didn't.

Wonderful. This had dipped into a fast downward spiral. Donovan pulled Sorcha around and pressed her face to his chest. "You gonna let Macie get his stuff or do I have to suffer through packing for him, too?"

Almost reluctantly, Griffin's gaze shifted to Macie. The tableau faded. "You gonna behave yourself?"

Macie rolled his eyes. "Yeah."

Griffin unlocked the cuffs. "You guys have cargo on there? I can call for a storage container to be brought down."

"Yeah. I'd appreciate that." The enormity of the last few minutes settled over him like a cold, wet blanket. What the hell were they going to do? They had no way to get back to Earth. Or find the marks on the contracts they held. Which meant they had no way to make rent.

They were homeless. Shipless. Damn close to broke and a hell of a long way from home. And somehow he had to protect his wife from the IgA discovering she was Blaze while keeping his own head out of vladset sites.

Oh, and somehow convince her to stay.

Right.

Karma, it seemed, pulled no punches when she came calling.

He gave Macie a little shove toward the *Red Slag* but then stopped to eye the men who'd be taking their ship.

They stared back defiantly. Smug bastards. They'd better do a diagnostic before they took off because he'd be damned if he was going to warn them the ship was dry of water. They probably *had* cheated. Macie had a problem, yeah, but Donovan had never known him to lose when he was sober. Anywhere else, he'd have fought the sons of bitches. But here on Asteria, he had friends. Friends he'd put into a shitty position if he acted on his need to retaliate.

Sorcha flattened her hands on his chest. "My Chief, if you want them dead . . . ." She trailed off, leaving the thought unspoken.

What? If he wanted them dead, she'd take care of it? Burn them? Nah. He didn't want her to end up like him.

He shook his head. "They're not worth the emotional capital."

"What do you mean?" Her brows furrowed.

"We all have a certain amount of . . . self-worth stored up inside us. When we kill, we spend some of that. We become less optimistic. Less resilient. Less capable of connecting with others." *Less worthy of someone good.* "Emotional capital isn't self-replenishing, so eventually, we run out." He jerked his chin up toward the men. "They're not worth a cent."

Her lashes lowered. "That's why you only take live-capture contracts?"

His emotional capital was all but gone. If he spent any more on ambiguous kills, there wouldn't be anything left of him. "Yeah. It's easier on my conscience."

She slipped her hand into his. "Then let's go inside and pack."

"I'm sorry about this."

"This isn't your fault." She looked over her shoulder. "Their fires burn low."

"What do you mean?"

"There's no light in their eyes."

Donovan paused. She was right. They had dead eyes. Jaded eyes. "Come on."

—·—

22

Damn, he was tired. Hungry. Heart sore.

Midnight was approaching as Donovan wound through the crowd, Sorcha's hand in his, Macie and Grady trudging along behind them, headed toward Lucky's. They'd packed up their belongings, stowed their freight, and left before Griffin gave the other crew permission to board the *Red Slag*.

He paused and looked up. Every time a ship took off, he turned his face toward the night sky to see if it was theirs. An old six-engine Crawler, not the *Red Slag*.

"There's an old Xuit ship for sale." Grady was searching through postings to see if there was anything that might fit their needs. "Slow as shit, though. Take you near six weeks to get home."

"Which is four weeks too long." He was leading Sorcha up the steps to the bar, when another engine roared in the night. That was her. The *Red Slag* powered through the sky, orange light flaring from the four engines. Funny, after all these years, he'd never watched her take off before.

From somewhere east of town, a yellow beam of light shot up from the ground, touched the *Red Slag*, and tracked her through the night sky.

"What in hell?"

The ship exploded into a bright fireball. People screamed. Sorcha grabbed hold of his arm.

Streams of flaming debris fell from the sky, trailing into the Red Sea.

"That was our ship." He couldn't quite tear his gaze away. "That was our fucking ship." Their ship blew up.

Great peals of laughter drew his attention. Macie. Had he lost his mind? He wrapped his arm around his middle and bent forward with his mirth, drawing everyone's attention. Dear baby Jesus, had he done something to the ship?

"Hey." He stormed over to Macie and lowered his voice. "What the fuck did you do?"

That only made Macie laugh harder.

"Mason." He thumped him on the shoulder.

Macie waved Donovan away. "Don't be stupid. Just realized I—" He was laughing too hard to be intelligible.

"What?"

Grady chuckled. "Said, he just realized he won after all."

"Won?"

Macie tucked his face to the crook of his arms, wiping away the tears. "I told you I had a winning hand. The queen of hearts, the suicide king, and the one-eyed Jack—they never steer me wrong."

"Hell, are you still on about that?" He shook his head. He didn't believe in omens; he made his own luck.

"That would've been us." Macie pointed to the ship. "Instead, those cheating bastards are frying in the sky. *That* was luck."

Someone had tried to kill them. He dragged his hand down his face. If he'd followed his plan and had taken off tonight, they'd all be dead. In trying to protect his wife, he'd have ensured her death. His gaze dropped to Sorcha. Narrowed.

Why did she look so guilty? "Sorcha?"

She stepped back, bumped into a guy ogling the fiery sky, and muttered an apology in Standard. Quimet had wanted her to kill him. Had he given someone else orders in case she refused?

"Tell me exactly what Quimet wanted."

"He wanted me to kill you both. To destroy the ship." She shook her head. "But I wouldn't. I didn't do this, I swear." Her flame flared brighter except for two twin stains of dark blue on her cheeks. Tears welled in her eyes.

When the hell would she start trusting him? He pulled her into his arms. "I didn't suspect you had." He dropped a kiss on her head. "I kept you busy all evening, remember?"

With his reassurance, she sighed and returned his hug.

"You ever seen that yellow light before?"

She gripped her hands together. "On Erra. I don't know what it is. Maman came with visitors. They didn't come to where I was, they went out onto the ice fields, but I saw the yellow light. The explosions. Please don't tell the IgA."

Was Vessa using Erra as a testing ground for a new weapon? His insides went cold. "Sorcha, I can't promise that."

"But, if you don't know anything . . . ."

She left the sentence hanging out in the ether. If he didn't know anything, he couldn't tell the IgA anything. Except he *knew* she was Blaze. He knew and he didn't think he could turn her in. She didn't fit the profile of a cold-blooded killer. She wouldn't cover up illegal activity. Not as disappointed as she seemed every time they discovered the queen had broken another law. "Okay." He breathed deep and exhaled. "We'll leave this alone."

She grinned.

"For now."

Her smile faded which made his gut churn. Oh, he was in trouble. Eventually, he'd have to disappoint his wife and that had him in knots. "Let's go eat."

He'd never seen Lucky's so empty. Everyone must've run outside to watch the excitement. They took one of the larger tables and ordered their food. He winked at Sorcha.

Somehow, he had to get her to talk to him. He couldn't protect her if he didn't understand what was going on.

Grady and Macie sat on the other side of the table, searching the ads for ships for sale. They weren't paying them any mind, so he leaned toward Sorcha. "Did Quimet say why he wanted you to kill me?"

"Quimet said something changed after we left. He said you could hurt Maman. Hurt our clans."

Yeah, something had changed all right. He just wished he knew what. What happened in the last three days to change her mind?

Now what? He had a wife with a bounty on her head and a mother-in-law who wanted him dead. "Why did she want you gone?"

"At first, I thought she was fulfilling her duties, ensuring I settled into an honorable house, so she could move on with her life."

"You told me she wants to marry, didn't you?"

"Oh, yes. She'd do anything to prevent Mujara or me from taking the throne."

He sat back. Blinked. "Mujara?"

Her gaze shifted away.

"Sorcha, tell me who Mujara is." If either of them could take the throne, it had to be a sibling, right? "Brother or sister?"

"Sister."

Sister. The white-haired person huddled in the corner of the glass-encased cell on Troon. "She's in a cell under the palace?"

A slight nod.

"Hey." He used his finger to guide her chin toward him and up. "I need you to tell me everything, Blaze."

Her eyes widened. She pushed away and made a lunge for freedom.

He tightened his grip.

Her gaze slid to Macie and Grady who were both staring back with open curiosity.

Yeah, much more and the two of them might decide to play hero. "We'll be right back." He stood, pulled Sorcha up, and led her out the back door and into the alleyway. "I can't keep the three of us safe if I don't know where the danger is coming from. If Macie hadn't lost the ship, we'd be dead. I need you to trust me when I say nothing you tell me will change what's between us."

"You won't understand."

He crowded her against the wall, trapping her. "I need to know what your Maman has on you." Vessa must have something to hold over her. "You're not a killer. You don't even like confrontation. Talk to me." He needed a reason to not hand her over . . . something other than his own selfish reasons.

"I wouldn't know where to start." She looked away.

"How did Mujara end up in a cell and you end up on Erra."

Her lips pressed together.

He stroked his thumb across her cheek. "Trust me."

"When I was seven—"

Seven years old . . . but their years were only ten months, so seven times ten months equaled seventy months. She'd been five years and eight months. Had she been exiled most of her life?

"—Mujara got in trouble for saving dinner and—"

Wait. What? "You mean she didn't want to eat and put her dinner away for later?"

"No, I mean she released an entire crate of Trytini."

When he continued to stare at her uncomprehending, she sighed. "They're small." She held her finger and thumb about two inches apart. "Hairless. Four legs. Their skin is see-through and they're more cartilage than bone. Vladsets warm them over a fire until they blister and eat them alive."

Well, that was disgusting. "That's what you're used to eating?"

She shook her head. "Maman was always vexed because we refused to eat anything but plants. Mujara is more soft-hearted than I—"

He couldn't quite wrap his head around that—Sorcha was extremely soft-hearted.

"—and she freed a week's worth of Trytini. Maman was furious. Punishments were always swift and painful, but she was enraged. I was scared for Mujara. I ran up behind Maman with the intention of pushing her." She held her hands up, fingers spread wide and made a pushing motion. "But I was upset. I flared and I burned her." She shrugged. "It was the first time."

Oh, hell. His gaze dropped to her hands. "Your suit doesn't make the flames, does it?"

"No." She held up her hand and a flame no bigger than the flare from a match sprouted from the tip of her finger. "It's easier when I'm upset, but I have better control than I did when I was younger."

He covered her finger with his hand, stifling the flame. That's why she wore *cooling cloths*. Why she prayed to Dedia. "*Just* your hands?"

She bit her lip and her gaze dropped to the side.

Okay. His wife could spontaneously ignite herself. All right. He should probably be as terrified as everyone on Troon. Probably would be if he found out before he knew her, but . . . .

An image flashed in his mind of a six-year-old girl running up behind Vessa with arms held up, fingers spread . . . His lips twitched. "Vessa has your handprints scarred into her ass, doesn't she?"

"Yes." Bright blue bloomed on her cheeks. That's why Vessa wore the bustle thing covering her ass when the rest of her had been on full display. He chuckled. "Oh, God. I'd have loved to have seen that."

She swatted him. "This isn't funny."

"It is." He tried to stymie his mirth, but another chuckle escaped. "I'm sorry, it really is . . . ." Two tiny handprints scorched into the arrogant bitch's ass cheeks.

"Not funny." She gave him a stern frown. "Maman turned and backhanded me."

His humor died. Vessa's backhand had landed him on the other side of the room and he was a big guy. The bitch could've killed Sorcha at the tender age of six. "You're right, I'm not amused. I'm gonna kill her."

She rolled her eyes. "Do you want the rest of the story?"

God, he loved being able to see her face. Her expressions. Her eyes. He stroked the back of his fingers over her cheek. "Yeah."

"Mujara was protective of me too. So she fought Maman."

"How?"

She tucked a strand of hair behind her ear. "The *how* isn't important, the fact she protected me is."

Interesting. She was hedging. Why? Did her sister also "flare," or did she have some other defense mechanism?

"Mujara almost won."

"She would've become queen."

"Yes, but I was hurt and we always protected each other, because we were so similar. Copies of one another. The same in a world where everything else was different."

"You're twins."

She nodded. "Vladsets don't bear multiple children. Not ever. They think we're two parts of one whole."

I'll kill you. All of you.

He'd been confused when Vessa issued that threat. Now he understood. She'd been telling Sorcha she'd kill her sister if she shamed her.

"So what happened?"

"Instead of finishing the fight with Maman, Mujara came to help me. Maman called the guards and I was sent to Erra. Mujara was taken to a cell below the palace. I haven't talked to Mujara since then."

"I'm glad she didn't kill you both."

Sorcha shrugged. "She would've lost the support of the clans. Maman had just taken over as the queen when she intercepted my father's ship. She soul-merged him, got pregnant, and devoured his soul. It was a great victory, to her mind. Bearing her enemy's child to raise us as spies was yet another sign of her power. She broadcast the birth to show her people how strong she was to bear two offspring."

"So her arrogance saved you? She couldn't kill you after everyone had seen the two of you."

"Exactly. Instead, she hid us away and claimed we were serving her will, destroying her enemies. The palace guards are sworn to secrecy. They fear us as much as Maman and she threatens to seal them in a room with us should they betray her. The rest of the clans don't know what happens in the palace."

"She broadcast the wedding to show her people you were infiltrating Earth?"

She shook her head. "When we wed, you became her extended clan. She cannot fight you. Not unless you hurt me. She broadcast the wedding to prove she was free to marry."

"So something changed? Something that made her risk the wrath of both her clans and the IgA?"

"Jerrod Williams must have told Maman something, I'm not sure what, that made her decide it would be better if I killed you and Macie and destroyed the *Red Slag*."

She bit her lip. "I think she wanted me to do another mission. That's the only reason she'd insist I kill you."

"What do you mean?"

"We're soul-merged. You die, I die. Unless I soul-devour you. If she wanted both of us dead, she only has to kill one of us."

Well, shit. He shook his head. He couldn't think about that right now.

"Could she be involved with CorTech? Maybe fear that I'd figure it out and tell the IgA?" He shook his head. That still put her in shit with both the IgA and her clans.

She shrugged. "I don't know. She hates Earth. Hates that she's been stuck with me and Mujara for so many years. Her ultimate victory turned into a nightmare."

"Well, apparently, a vladset's nightmare is a human's dream." He leaned down and kissed her. A quick melding of his lips and hers. A taste. A promise for later. "Are you Blaze or is Mujara?"

A shiver shook through her. "I am."

Mujara was just as protective of me as I was of her. "She's holding Mujara against you." It wasn't a question. Sorcha wasn't a killer, but he imagined she'd do anything to protect those she loved.

"Yes." A tear slid down her cheek and he thumbed it away.

"What did they threaten?"

She lifted her hands between them, staring at them. "Quimet had a Saph-link. We're not supposed to have them, but he did, and he showed me Mujara."

His whole frame tensed. "He wanted you to kill me in exchange for her safety?"

She nodded. "The guards took her into the arena and left her there with several creatures."

The arena had become a too-familiar place during his time on Troon. "Creatures?"

"I'm not even sure what some of them were. They left her there to fight or die. The arena was empty at first, but toward the end . . . warriors were running down the stands toward Mujara when the Saph-link broke."

Ah, hell. He pulled her into his arms. "Okay. All right." How did he fix this? Mujara was probably dead by now. "Is there someone on Troon we could contact?"

"No." She pulled away. Instead of tears, rage lit her eyes. "We must fight Maman."

As if they were in any position to do that. "Sorcha, I know you're worried about your sister, but—"

Someone cleared his throat. Macie was leaning out of the door. "Food arrived."

"Let me think about this, okay?"

She nodded.

"Come on." They followed Macie inside.

Once at the table, Macie leaned forward, waggling his brows. "So, you have a sister?"

Donovan's gaze jerked up. How much had Macie overheard?

"Mujara." She nodded. "My twin."

"Twin?" Grady's eyes lit up. "She single?"

He sighed. The two of them could duke it out over Mujara to their heart's content if they left his wife alone.

"As the oldest, she was betrothed since before she was born."

Damn. "And Sorcha's already married." Donovan turned his gaze away. He scanned the dwindling crowd, maybe fifty people were scattered throughout the bar, some sitting, some standing, all three-sheets to the wind and talking far too loud. His paused, his attention captured by a middle-aged man with a receding hairline who was staring back with wide eyes.

Alexi Popov.

"Macie." Donovan tapped his palm on the table to get Macie's attention but didn't look away from his prey. Donovan rose.

Popov's gaze darted left, then right.

As Donovan started across the room, the man jumped up and bolted toward the front doors. He pushed past several revelers. A man shouted.

He took off after him, unclasping his holster and palming the handle of his blaster, pushing his way toward the entrance. Without taking his gaze from his prey, he thumbed the setting slider all the way to the top position—stun.

Popov vaulted over the porch railing, losing his balance and staggering when he landed.

Donovan hoisted himself up to stand on the railing and aimed. The crowd wasn't as thick out here now. He took his time, lining up his shot, making sure he didn't take out an innocent bystander. He fired.

Popov dropped mid-sprint, sprawling flat on his belly. The stun attacked the nervous system, temporarily paralyzing the victim.

"Good shot." Macie jogged down the steps, heading for the downed mark. "Who is it?"

"Popov." Donovan jumped down and followed Macie. "Maybe we can finally get some information."

"Jesus, Reese, you're getting kind of high-brow, expecting actual facts to work with."

He chuckled, waving some bystanders back. "You should've seen his face when he saw me."

Macie stopped at the guy's feet. "I bet." He glanced around the crowd. "Interesting he was hanging out at Lucky's instead of trying to hitch a ride home."

"Maybe. Might be trying to lay low." He motioned for Macie to grab one of the guy's arms. "Merrick grounded air traffic for a few hours this afternoon. Might've thought they were looking for him."

Macie snorted. "That would've been a perfect time to become a stowaway." He bent down to grab the other arm and pulled. "He could've hidden until the ship took off."

They'd barely lifted him before the side of Popov's neck burst open with a spray of blood and bone. Donovan dropped him, taking a step back. "Sniper!"

They both turned and hauled ass for the cover of Lucky's porch as the shooter opened fire. Blaster shots peppered the street, forcing them to zig-zag. Sorcha had wandered out to see what was going on. Their eyes locked.

Hers widened.

There wasn't any sense in trying to verbalize instructions. He bent at the waist and hauled her over his shoulder as he passed.

Her soft "Oof" reached his ears past the shouts in the crowd and the din of people fleeing.

Once under the porch awning, he set her on her feet. The blaster fire stopped. He stroked his hand down the side of her face. "Okay?"

"Only surprised." She ran her hands over his chest, her gaze searching him for injury.

He should go after the shooter, but she'd given him a scare and he needed to touch her. He pulled her close and pressed his lips to her forehead. "You didn't stay put. You know what happens now."

"You didn't tell me—"

"It was implied." He scowled.

"I think you're making up reasons now." Her lips curved in a secret smile and just like that he was hard as stone.

"What the hell happened?" Griffin stormed up the porch steps. "You three have been nothing but trouble since you got here."

Donovan forced his mind from all the things he wanted to do to his wife. "We found Popov, one of our marks. I stunned him."

Griffin stacked his arms over his chest. "Then why's he bleeding all over the damn street?"

"Sniper. The shot came from above and behind us." He tipped his head up toward the roof.

"Goddamn it." Griffin sighed. "Merrick's still investigating the explosion. He's out at the wreckage site." His eyes narrowed. "Why don't you come help me out." He headed around the side of the building.

"Stay put." Donovan gave her a stern nod and nudged her toward Macie and Grady before following. Griffin was halfway up an access ladder built into the side of the building. Donovan climbed on top of a crate sitting near the porch, jumped to grab the edge of the wood awning, and pulled himself up. The awning sat several feet lower than the roof of the building. He stayed low and peered around the corner at Griffin.

Griffin nodded. Held up one finger. Two. Three.

Donovan launched himself over the low wall to the roof.

Nothing moved. Shadows stretched across the dark surface. The streetlights didn't quite reach up here. There were no moons tonight. He could barely see Griffin's outline. The sniper was probably long gone. Still, they spread out, walking the perimeter of the roof until they came face-to-face again. Griffin kicked something as he walked, sending it skidding across the roof. He picked it up and studied it.

"What is it?"

"In a minute." Griffin tucked whatever he'd picked up into his pocket. "First, tell me what's going on."

"Damned if I know."

"Merrick filled me in on Williams, Troon, and your marriage."

When Griffin continued to wait, Donovan cursed again. "Apparently, Queen Vessa has changed her mind about having me for a son-in-law. She sent those guys to convince my wife to kill me and when that failed . . . ."

I think Maman wanted me to go on another mission. That's why she wanted me to kill you. Otherwise, we'd both die.

Donovan shook his head. "I don't know. Someone blew up my ship."

"The vladsets were dead, so it wasn't them."

"Maybe one's still alive."

"And decided since Sorcha wouldn't kill you, she should die, too?"

"Maybe." He frowned. "No. It must've been someone else."

Griffin grunted. "I found three people listed on your CorTech contracts this afternoon."

Donovan quit pacing. "Where? I want to talk to them. I need answers."

"They were in the box the vladsets dumped. We checked it out on the way back to town."

Un-fucking-believable. "So, what? They were on the ship with Williams? The vladsets nabbed Williams and his crew when they got me and Macie. Killed the crew. Kept Williams. Stole the ship." He didn't like it. "Why would they bring the bodies here?"

"CorTech chips their employees. Hell, most of their security staff are Blue Helmets—they were already chipped. Thing is, the chips make the bodies easy to trace."

"So they brought the bodies and his ship here to make it appear they'd all left Troon alive."

"Except here's the catch, Reese. The bodies were, well, they were burned from the inside out."

The life is scorched out of them.

Donovan kept his face expressionless. "Oh? How's that work?"

"The skin and hair still contained some fluid, but the organs . . . especially the adrenal glands, were dry, shriveled, black bits of nothing."

He nodded. "What do you think happened?"

"Well, now, the body in the house . . . you know, where your wife was trapped. His body was in the exact same condition."

Wait. She'd kissed that ugly bastard? Kissed him and . . . devoured his soul? Unless he'd misunderstood when she'd told him how soul-merging happened? No. She was clear. He'd been listening intently. Damn. He'd assumed she'd burned Quimet. His heart pounded in his chest, a wary anxiety forcing adrenaline to pump through his veins while he waited for Griffin to continue.

"Recently, we've found other bodies outside the city in the same condition; fifty, all told. The scarecrows got to most of them, so there wasn't enough surface tissue left to identify the bodies. One of them had a chip intact—a CorTech employee, but there wasn't a contract on him." He cleared his throat. "It's my understanding your wife lived on Erra."

Griffin thought Sorcha had killed them all? *I think Maman wanted me to go on another mission.*

He'd known of five marks that had been burned alive. *But fifty?* Donovan's grip tightened on his blaster. *Shit.* He didn't want to hurt Griffin but he didn't like where this was going. No way Sorcha killed fifty people.

Griffin held up one hand, palm out. "Don't be stupid."

There was hardly any light up here, just enough to glint off the other man's eyes. Enough to make out his outline.

"Sorcha didn't do all that. It's gotta be Vessa. You know that, right?"

"You know we've got *your* back, right?" They'd help him, not necessarily Sorcha. "Do you trust your wife? Are you sure I won't find *your* body out there one of these days?"

"She wouldn't hurt me."

"Yeah, but you may be serving a purpose right now."

True. The marriage allowed her to escape Vessa. But she could've gone with the vladsets. She could've burned a hole in the wall of the room and escaped before he arrived. She could've left before Grady stopped her. She had ample opportunity to leave him . . . or soul-devour him. He swallowed. "We're soul-merged."

"Well, that has a permanent ring to it." Griffin turned away and blew out a breath that puffed his cheeks. "Look, all I've got on your wife is the guy in the house. Far as we're concerned, that was self-defense. So how 'bout you put your weapon away?"

Relief made his head spin. Donovan holstered his weapon and shook his hands out to his sides.

"Now, help me out. What happened to these bodies? And why the hell did you look like I shot your best friend when I told you about the guy in the house?"

He explained about soul-merging and soul-devouring.

"And you kissed her willingly?"

Donovan smiled. "Didn't know all this then, not that I had much choice. Prax demanded we kiss. He made sure we couldn't walk away from the marriage."

"Well, that explains a few things." He pulled the item he'd found earlier out of his pocket and handed it to him.

Donovan turned the small metal device over in his hand. A weapons charger with a logo of six planets orbiting a sun. "IgA issue."

"Yep." He pulled his Saph-link out. "And there's this." He opened the device. "Play last hologram."

Their corner of the roof lit up as a three-inch hologram of Prax hovered over the Saph-link. "Queen Vessa, in a magnanimous gesture of cooperation, provided the IgA with the identity of one of the IgA's most sought-after criminals." He gestured behind him, where petite red body armor hung on the wall with a masked helmet. "We have the identity of the assassin killing CorTech marks. The queen's daughter, Celeka. We do not have a description; however, she's traveling with her husband, Chief Donovan Reese of Earth. We'd be most indebted to you if you would detain them on Asteria."

Could tonight get any worse? "Who all's got this?"

"Just us." Griffin closed the Saph-link, tucking it away in a shirt pocket. "They knew you were here and know Asteria wants a seat on the Council."

Asteria was still going through the long, tedious process of becoming part of the IgA. Handing Sorcha over would speed things up. "What are you gonna do?"

"Well, up until your fucking ship made a mess in our harbor, we didn't think we had many choices."

Did that mean they weren't giving them up to the IgA?

"Thing is, best we can tell, we killed all the vladsets this afternoon. No one's returned to *CorTech 12*. Which made me wonder, who else have you pissed off enough to blow up your ship? Then we get this message from Prax . . . ." He braced his hands on his hips and stared up at the starlit sky. "Merrick started asking around and lo and behold, there's an IgA ship docked at our spaceport. Don't know who all's on board."

"Prax."

"Doubt it."

Donovan opened his mouth to argue.

Griffin waved his argument away. "Even if he was behind the order, he wouldn't personally come to see it through. He'd retain deniability." Griffin shrugged. "I can't very well hand your wife over to the IgA when they're our top suspects in the explosion." He shook his head. "I also can't detain that ship or whoever's on board without more proof."

"If they're here, they'll be looking for us."

"Yep. Shame you couldn't just steal *CorTech 12*." Griffin stared at him, rocking back on his heels. "No one's watching it."

Donovan grinned. "Might need a little help with Macie."

Vessa's heart hammered in her chest. "We're away?"

"Yes, my Queen."

She lowered herself to her throne aboard the *Warrior Maiden* before her knees gave out. That was close. Too close. For the first time in her life, she was on the run. Her. Running.

No. She could salvage this. Regain control. She just needed Celeka. "You'll hail Quimet again." Her chamberlain was missing in action as were the warriors he'd taken with him to Asteria.

Oolock, her consort, shook his head. "Quimet isn't answering our hails, my Queen. None of them are."

Then she'd have to find Celeka herself. "We'll have to assume they're dead. Continue to Asteria." She needed Celeka. Needed her to get the frequencies. And now she needed her if she wanted to regain control of Mujara.

Everything was falling apart.

Mujara was free. How she'd coordinated a coup while imprisoned, she couldn't fathom. When the warriors first breached the arena, Vessa thought they'd attack Mujara. Instead, they'd rallied behind her. Even some of the palace guards had joined the coup. Vessa had no recourse but to flee before Mujara could reach the throne room.

If she could get her hands on Celeka, she could use her to regain control of Mujara. The two of them always protected each other. Neither would do anything to hurt the other.

The vid-screen signaled an incoming call, a wicked-looking star fractal appearing on the screen. "That's Quimet. He was in a CorTech ship. Answer."

Oolock allowed the call.

Quimet wasn't on the screen. Larkin Astor was. The older male's hair had turned white at his temples. More white threaded through his goatee. His lips quirked. "I heard you got us all in a bit of a pickle. I'm calling to let you know it's been taken care of."

These humans. Half of what they said was unintelligible. "You'll explain."

"You had Donovan Reese on Troon and instead of killing him, you married him to your daughter." He shook his head. "I'm assuming this is the same daughter you've been sending out to kill my contracted employees."

Perhaps she'd underestimated Astor. He seemed to have almost godlike powers to know everything she'd been up to. "You knew and you didn't try to stop me?"

"Why would I? They were told to stay under the IgA's radar and they failed. Why do you think I fired them all on paper? If they screwed up, I didn't want it coming back to me. But you . . . you find the one person who could tie it all together with the right information and then hand-deliver that information to him in the form of your daughter. You're an idiot." He shook his head. "They're dead. All of them."

The breath stalled in her lungs. Celeka was dead?

"Interested parties shot the *Red Slag* out of the sky with your weapon. I just got the news and couldn't think of a better way to celebrate than to call you."

Interested parties? What interested parties? "You plan to implicate me."

"One of the first things a good businessman learns is when to walk away from a losing situation. You lost. Walk away."

No. He took her product. Killed her daughter. Implicated her to the IgA. She stood, her hands fisting at her sides. "You stole from me."

"Have a nice life, Vessa." He smiled. "At least what's left of it."

The screen went dark.

He'd dismissed her. Insulted her, threatened her, and dismissed her.

"We're changing course." She turned to Oolock. "Take us to Earth. To CorTech. Now."

— · —

23

Celeka narrowed her gaze on Grady. "You aren't a vladset."

"Not last time I checked, no."

"You're not human, either. So, what are you?"

Grady's gaze shifted to Macie. "'Scuse us." He pulled her away and leaned down. "I've helped ya, right?"

She nodded.

"So drop it already. I gotta ask ya not to repeat anything ya saw. Not even to Reese. You two don't need any more trouble."

Was he afraid for her? "I'll promise that for now. Once we've confronted Maman, I'm asking Donovan to bring me back here and we'll fix your problem, too."

He cursed. "Get it out of yur head." He scowled and jerked his chin up. "Yur man needs ya. Focus on that."

Celeka turned and her insides twisted. Lines of strain crossed Donovan's forehead, making him appear older than he did yesterday. He and Griffin checked something on their Saph-links. They put away the devices and shook hands.

She bit her lip, glancing at Macie.

He shrugged. "I'm sure everything's fine."

Griffin left and Donovan turned their way.

Macie asked, "Did you find anything?"

"Nothing I was looking for." His gaze locked onto her, scanning her face as if searching for something.

"What happened?"

"Later."

She had no choice but to nod. Whatever was bothering him, he didn't want to discuss it now.

"We've got a ride home." He laced his fingers with hers and tugged her into motion. "We need to move fast."

She turned back to say goodbye, but Grady had disappeared.

Macie snorted, falling in step beside them. "Do I want to know what's going on?"

"Probably not. Not out here."

"Fucking psychopath."

Celeka tightened her grip on Donovan. They were walking fast; she took two steps for each of theirs. Both their faces were drawn into the hard, cold masks they wore when fighting. Her belly did a little flop and she sucked in a deep breath.

They made their way swiftly down Main Street, walking past groups of people who were still celebrating. Most of the shops were closed. Droids made their way down the sidewalks` sucking up debris as they went. By the time they reached the Spaceport, sweat dotted her upper lip and her legs burned. They strode through the gates and down to the landing pad, not stopping until they came to Air-pad 876.

Macie stared at the docked ship for several heartbeats before turning toward Donovan. "You're fucking kidding me."

Donovan shook his head.

"It's illegal." Macie threw up his hands, turned, and took two steps closer to the ship. "What the—" A blast came out of the shadows. Macie dropped like a brick.

She opened her mouth to scream.

Donovan's hand snaked around her face, covering her mouth. "It's okay. Everything's all right. We didn't hurt him."

Griffin strolled out of the shadows, holstering his weapon. "You need help getting him inside?"

"Nah, we're good."

Her gaze bounced between the two men. What had they done? Was this because of the *Red Slag*?

"Your gear is on board. Don't switch on the power until you're ready to leave—oh-five-hundred sharp. Merrick and I will cover the tower. You'll have a very small window of opportunity."

"Thanks." He held out his free hand and shook Griffin's hand. "Tell Merrick I really appreciate this."

"Will do." He winked at Sorcha and strolled away.

Donovan leaned down. "Can I move my hand without you causing a scene?"

She nodded and he let her go. "What did you do?" She pushed away. "He made a mistake, he doesn't deserve this."

"It's for his own good. I'll explain inside. I would've warned you, but I didn't have the chance without putting Macie on guard." He cursed. "Help me get him up. We need to get out of sight."

Warily, she followed Donovan over to Macie's prone body. He turned Macie over and Sorcha dropped to her knees. Macie's eyes were open and staring straight ahead. With a trembling hand, she felt for his pulse. A shuddering breath shook free—he was alive. Stunned.

"Grab his arm and pull him into a sitting position."

Together, they hauled him upright. Once sitting, Donovan took both arms, jerked Macie to his feet and hauled him over his shoulder. "Come on." He led the way onto the ship. The loading ramp had a star-shaped logo, with sharp points and edges. Red emergency lights lit the inside. Donovan started to lead her down the hallway to the right, cursed, then squeezed past her to go down the hallway to the left. They went down a flight of stairs, past a med-bay, several closed doors, through a kitchen, and into another hallway that turned into a ramp leading down another level. They ended up in a circular room with seven metal-and-glass pods.

"What is this?"

"When traveling at warp-speeds, it's safest to do so in a life-pod. There's less stress on the body." He slapped his hand on a red button at the head of one of the pods and the glass lid hissed open, lifting to stand on one end above the pod. "They provide oxygen, nutrients, and flex the muscles of the occupant so they don't lose muscle mass during the flight."

"You're putting Macie in there?"

He sat Macie down and then eased him back so his head rested on the small pillow. Donovan straightened, arched his back, then stretched from side to side. "He's got a phobia about small spaces. I can never get him into a pod without drugging or stunning him. He wasn't trained as a warp-pilot. Doesn't do well outside the pod on long hauls like we're gonna do. This is better."

"He'll be angry."

"Yeah. We had a special pod made on the *Red Slag*. Had it set up to put him under before the lid closed, but now . . . ."

Now they didn't have that option. Now he had to do what was best for Macie with or without his permission. "I understand. How do I help?"

"Strip him to his drawers so we can hook him up."

She leaned over and stared into Macie's eyes. He hadn't moved an inch, but she had no doubt he was furious. "You'll not be angry with our chief. He's doing his best to take care of you and I think you've caused trouble over this in the past." She paused. This felt strange. "I can't undress him while he's watching."

He chuckled. "By all means, close his eyes."

"May your flame never flicker." She eased his eyelids down. "I'm ready."

Undressing an unconscious Macie was like trying to skin a live maripod. He was all unwieldy limp limbs and awkward weight. At one point, she crawled into the pod with him as they pulled up his shirt so his weight could lean against her shoulder. "He wears his clothes too tight. This would be easier if . . . ooph!" His arm fell across her.

"I've got him, get outta there." She crawled over the edge, turned, and gaped. "Why does he decorate his skin?" The same bright-colored ink covering his arms extended over his shoulders and down his torso.

"They're tattoos. It's a common practice on Earth." As Donovan lay him down, she leaned closer. Images of women, planets, animals, buildings, and a variety of symbols covered his skin. Her brows furrowed and she leaned closer. Touched his shoulder and found the skin wasn't smooth, but streaked with long, thin, deep scars.

When she stepped back, Donovan had removed Macie's shoes and was dragging his pants down his legs. There were fewer tattoos on his legs, but they were all strategically placed. "He covers his honor marks."

Donovan tossed the pants onto the heap of clothing at his feet. "Not all scars feel honorable. If mine weren't on my face, I would've covered them." He took the bundle of wires anchored at the side of the pod, attached pads to the ends of each and handed half to her. "These send a small shock to his muscles which make them flex while he sleeps." He began placing them, one on the back of his calf, one on the front of his thigh, the back of his thigh.

"I do the same?"

He nodded and she distributed her section of pads in the same places on her side of Macie's body. By the time she finished, Donovan had inserted a needle into his arm and a mask over his nose and mouth. He leaned down. "I know you're pissed at me and I'm sorry, all right? For everything, our argument the other day, the past, *everything*." He closed the lid, sealing Macie inside.

"He'll be all right?"

"Yeah. We've done this too many times to count. He'll be fine."

"Will I?"

Donovan came around the side of the pod and took her by the shoulders. "These pods calibrate by species, understand?"

"How do you know whether to set it for vladset or human?"

"I don't." He curled a strand of her hair around his finger. "I need to ask you a question and I want you to be honest."

She nodded.

"When you were in the scanner, did it malfunction by itself?"

She shook her head. "I didn't want you to know how different I was."

"I'm more concerned with keeping you alive. If we can get a good scan, I can use the data to calibrate your pod and keep you safe."

"I don't have anything to hide anymore. I won't break the machine, I promise."

He took her by the hand and led her back to the med-bay, letting out a low whistle as they entered. "Fancy."

The bay was larger than the one on the *Red Slag* and had much more equipment. She wandered the space, studying the various gadgets while Donovan went to the terminal.

"Don't you need Macie to do the scan?"

"No." He typed something into the terminal and a hologram rose behind him showing various settings for the scanner. "I've been trained, my eye just gives me a hard time. It's easier for Macie to do anything requiring computers or reading."

She stared. It hadn't occurred to her his damaged eye didn't function well. "You seem to see fine."

"I learned to make adjustments." He punched a couple more buttons.

And Macie had always done anything that required reading or computers without being asked. Had Donovan ever noticed?

"All set. I'm ready when you are."

She closed herself into the chamber. This time, a soft blue glow emanated from the walls. A soft knocking worked around her, dropping lower and lower along with the light before raising up over her head again. The lights went dark and she stepped out.

She walked to Donovan, her belly twisting. The hologram had changed to show a three-dimensional image of her. He clicked through various images, some showing musculature, some bone, some internal organs, and paused on one that turned red and flickering. When she drew close to his side, he winked before returning his attention to the hologram. "Have you ever traveled at warp-speed before?"

"No."

He smiled. "Well, you're a perfectly healthy female."

Perhaps, but something in the scan was giving him pause. "What's bothering you?"

"It wants to set the temperature in your pod considerably lower than for a human."

Ah. "My flame will keep me warm while I sleep."

"It wants me to set it at thirty-three degrees Fahrenheit." When she frowned, he added. "Rain turns to snow at that temperature."

"A warm day on Erra. An average day on Troon." She smoothed her fingers over the lines forming on his forehead. "What has you worried?"

Aside from the fact he was about to deep-freeze his wife? Yeah, he was still trying to wrap his head around the fact that she had planted a kiss of death on Quimet.

His temper ignited like a flashfire. Vladsets might view a kiss different from humans, obviously it wasn't anywhere in the same universe as an affair, but that didn't make it any easier to stomach. "Did you soul-merge Quimet?"

She stepped back. "Not exactly."

"How did he die?"

She touched the scars on her arm and he followed her action with his gaze. Six individual rune-like scars that looked similar, and one of which was still scabbed over that was a different design.

Maybe they were words in the vladset language. Or names. She'd killed five of his marks, plus Quimet. It made sense. Except she'd told him she'd never been kissed before.

"Let's try this again." He dragged his hand down his face. "Did you soul-merge Quimet?"

"That's the same question."

He stalked forward, backing her up until her bottom came up against an exam table. "Kissing might be an aggressive action on Troon, but where I come from, married couples don't kiss anyone but each other. Did you kiss him?"

She chewed the corner of her lip. "That would upset you?"

"Oh, yeah." His eye twitched.

"I didn't."

Little liar. "You said soul-merging required a kiss." He folded his arms over his chest and scowled, waiting.

She twisted the fingers of one hand with the fingers of the other. She was nervous. Good. "I'm not like the others, I don't have to kiss someone when I take their soul."

His head tipped to the side and his gaze narrowed. "If that's true, why didn't you clarify the difference before?"

"I didn't want you to fear me." Her gaze remained locked on his chin.

He placed one of his hands on the table on either side of her, leaning in until he was eye level with her. "I'm not afraid of you." Jealous, yeah. Hurt, sure. But not scared. "I'm pissed as hell, so you better start explaining."

"Full vladsets have thick skin, almost more of a hide. It contains their flame, keeping them warm. When they take their enemies soul, they require intimate contact, for example, through a kiss."

He gave her a brisk nod. So far, her story aligned with what she'd said before.

"My flesh doesn't always hold my flame. I don't have to be intimate with my enemies to devour their soul. I just have to consume them with my flame."

The scan had showed several anomalies. Her body was different. Her organs . . . unusual. Not entirely vladset, not entirely human. The scan showing her internal body temperature was off the charts. Her surface temperature was considerably lower than her internal temperature—by almost thirty degrees Fahrenheit. "How did you do it?"

She shifted under his gaze.

"I didn't kiss him." Moisture shimmered in her colorful eyes. "I've never kissed anyone but you."

The violent rage simmering inside him eased. "Is that why they fear you, because you don't need to soul-merge to soul-devour?"

She didn't seem to hear him, she slid past him, pacing. "I embrace them. Their clothing catches fire and when they are too weak to fight, I put my hand on their face so they're forced to inhale my flame. It terrifies Maman, that I can devour anyone without warning."

She hadn't kissed Quimet. The knots in his gut eased. "You killed him, but you didn't kiss him."

"I had no choice!"

"Stop." He pulled her close, holding her tight as if he could still her trembling by force. "Everything's okay."

"Quimet wouldn't stop until you and Macie were dead. He had no qualms about sacrificing Mujara to force me to Maman's will."

"Okay." He kissed her hair. "You defended yourself. It's okay. You were protecting the people you care about. No one can prosecute you." If they had to face a day in Diamond Fjord's court, Merrick wouldn't view Quimet's death as a crime. Now for the big question. "What about the others?"

She didn't ask for clarification. "I believed they were hurting people. I thought the IgA wanted them dead. I thought I was helping my people to become assets to the IgA."

He stilled at her soft-spoken confession. That fit with what he knew of her. She didn't like to see others hurting. She championed her people whenever the subject came up despite how they'd treated her. "How many?"

"Five." She sniffed. "Not including Quimet."

Five. She had the same number of scars on her arm. She must've cut the names of her kills into her skin, like badges of honor. "They were all human?"

She nodded. "They were your marks. I got to them first."

"They've found over fifty bodies."

"Fifty?" She pulled away. "They were soul-merged?"

"They were in the same condition as Quimet—burned from the inside out."

"Maman must be stopped. If anyone finds out, the IgA could declare war. Earth could declare war." She squirmed out of his embrace and paced. "We should return to Troon. Fight her. Free the vladsets from her dishonor."

Griffin was right, there was something she still wanted from him. A use for him beyond being her husband. He shook his head. If he denied her, would she no longer have a use for him? "I'll find a way to get Mujara out of there, but I'm not fighting for people when I don't know if they want our help."

Her gaze turned fierce. "If they knew what she was doing, they'd want help. Honor is everything to the vladset people."

No. He wasn't having this argument. He wasn't starting another war to overthrow an oppressive government only to discover the very people he tried to help hated him for it.

"You're still angry. You don't believe me."

"Does the future of our relationship depend on whether I'm willing to overthrow your queen?"

She gasped. "Of course not. It's just . . . ."

The tightness in his chest eased. "Just what?"

"Never mind. You wouldn't understand."

"Tell me."

She poked his chest. "Why should I express my opinions to you, if you make them sound unworthy?"

"Because I want to know you." He pulled her into his arms. "I want to know what you think." She tried to squirm away and he tightened his hold. "I want to know your dreams and desires. Even if I can't make them come true, I want to know them."

"My dream is to keep Maman from hurting anyone else." She tilted her chin up. "My desire is for you to help me. My opinion is we need to act quickly before she starts a war." Her gaze clashed with his. Steady. Strong. Challenging.

He closed his eyes. "And then?"

"What do you mean?"

Who would replace Vessa? Who would keep Troon from falling into anarchy? How would she feel afterward if someone worse than her Maman took over her rule? How would she feel if her people detested her for destroying the illusion of their well-ordered lives?

"I—" He shook his head. This wasn't a discussion for now. They had to get moving. "Right now, we need to get you in a life-pod and get out of here before we get caught. This ship is impounded pending the investigation into your kidnapping and the vladset deaths."

He led her back downstairs and checked on Macie while she got undressed. He made a couple adjustments to his life-pod and when he turned toward Sorcha, his breath caught. She stood next to a pod in nothing but her ribbons, looking for all the world as if she lost her best friend.

"Sorcha, I promise we'll work through this." He walked toward her.

"You're angry with me."

"I'm not . . . ." Was he? Frustrated, yes. Aroused, absolutely. Worried, definitely. "Look at me." When she refused, he tipped her chin up. "One thing at a time, okay? We need to get off Asteria before anyone finds us. I have to get the Zeros sorted—we can't abandon them."

"I understand."

And it would be good for her to see what happened to a world with no leader. She might change her mind about trying to overthrow Vessa. He gave her a quick kiss. "Hop in."

While she got comfortable, he studied the options on the pod. Maybe he could get her mind off rebellion for a little while. "Let's see. Most of these things come standard with educational recordings . . . yep." He glanced up. "How would you like to learn English in-flight?"

Her eyes widened. "While I sleep?"

"Mm." He adjusted some setting. "It'll give you a dose of a Nootropic drug to increase cognitive function and play an audio recording nonstop while you sleep. You'll have to work on pronunciation later, but . . . ."

"Yes." The one word exploded out of her so hard, she seemed surprised with her vehemence.

Donovan chuckled. "Okay. Hang on."

She blushed. "It'll teach me all of the words you say that don't translate in Standard?"

"I can set it to include slang terms, sure." His lips quirked.

"Yes. I'm tired of feeling inferior." Her lips spread into a wide grin. "I'm going to learn English." Her shoulders straightened and he suddenly felt like king of her world.

Once he finished, he leaned over her. "You're not inferior." He snuck another kiss before grabbing the bundle of electrodes.

She helped him attach the pads and then lay back while he inserted the peripheral parenteral nutrition line into her vein.

"Relax." He stroked his thumb over her cheek. "You're taking a long nap. That's all."

She sucked in a deep breath. "While we travel faster than I've ever gone."

"This is old hat to me, little flame. I'll keep us safe."

"I know." She pulled him down for a quick kiss.

He bussed her lips one last time, winked, and lowered the lid. "I'll see you soon."

Time was running out. He still needed to suit up and prepare for takeoff. Instead, he remained where he was, palm pressed to the glass of Sorcha's life-pod. Something kept him there. Maybe the intensity in her expression—as if forcing herself to be still while inside raging with the urge to claw her way out. He didn't blame her. Life-pods were scary, especially the first time. Knowing she was locking herself into sleep, making herself helpless while he hurled them through space. . . . She must be going out of her mind.

Her eyes grew heavy as the glass began to fog from the temperature difference inside the pod and the rest of the ship. Ice crystals formed at the edges of the glass. He didn't like this. Dropping the temperature in her pod made sense in some twisted fashion, considering the temperature of the ship would jack up a considerable degree once they were underway . . . and with her internal temperature . . . *shit*. He had no idea. Had to trust the fucking computer with her life, with all their lives.

He gave her a reassuring smile and her eyes closed.

The alarm on his Saph-link went off, and he jerked upright. They were out of time. His gaze darted around the room, found a glass cabinet containing flight suits. He hustled over, grabbed one of the suits, stripped down, and dressed. Tossing the gloves inside the helmet, he tucked the helmet under his arm, and did a quick inspection of the rest of the room.

This was a nice ship. There were plenty of rations, first aid, and facilities for more personal matters—while underway, this would be the only room with gravity, oxygen, and full temperature control. A terminal sat in the corner to allow him to monitor their progress. It'd be a hell of a lot more comfortable than the set-up they'd had on the *Red Slag*.

He made his way to the cockpit and pulled his gloves on while he familiarized himself with the control panels. "Hope you're in as good of shape as you look, darlin'."

The second alarm went off on his Saph-link. The shifts were changing. Merrick and Griffin should be causing distractions at the tower so he could take off safely.

He powered up the ship, which allowed him to close the loading bay doors. Sweat trickled down his back. Once the internal computer registered all green lights, he engaged the engines. Seconds ticked past while the six engines fired up one-by-one, tiny green lights glowing as they came online. The sixth gave him a green light, then flickered out.

Oh, hell no.

He tapped the light and it glowed green again, this time staying that way. "Thank God." He deactivated the magnetic lock, took the ship off autopilot, and took off.

He'd barely left port before a voice came over the speaker. "Ship Zulu-eight-alpha-two, this is tower. You do not have clearance for takeoff."

He climbed higher, pushing the ship to its limits, faster than was safe, his gaze swiveling from side-to-side, watching for other aircraft. Asteria's Spaceport was busy as hell this time of year. He needed to avoid the patrol ships, break through the atmosphere, and then through the security ships orbiting the planet.

"Ship Zulu-eight-alpha-two: Pilot, identify yourself."

Man, they hadn't bought him much time. "This is CorTech Commander Tashi with orders to return Zulu-eight-alpha-two to Earth for a new assignment." He started warming the antimatter drive. When he glanced up, it was to see the oncoming hull of a landing freighter.

"Fuck." He jerked his ship to the side and down, narrowly avoiding a collision, then increased his speed and continued to climb. Above, the crafts patrolling Asteria's outer atmosphere converged, creating a barrier between him and freedom.

If they opened fire . . . .

"Ship Zulu-eight-alpha-two is under impound pending a criminal investigation."

He sighed. "Tower, this is Zulu-eight-alpha-two. My orders are to return this ship to its owners. Take it up with CorTech." That might buy him another five minutes. Maybe. Hopefully.

Above, the patrol craft parted enough for him to push through, though they maneuvered to follow and flank him.

A shockwave rolled through the ship as he breached the sound-barrier.

"Ship Zulu-eight-alpha-two—CorTech has denied knowledge of your orders and identity. Security craft are en route for intercept."

They hadn't bought his bluff, the ships flanking him flew closer, trying to box him in. Griffin wasn't kidding when he said he'd only have a "narrow window of opportunity."

"Computer, begin calculations for Earth orbit." He tapped Earth's coordinates into the system.

"Antimatter drive is not online."

His lips quirked at the sultry voice of the computer. "Computer, begin calculations for Earth's orbit."

"Coordinates received. Antimatter drive is not online."

Jesus. He knew that. "Computer, begin calculations for Earth's orbit." This was all he needed, a computer with an attitude.

"Calculations complete. Start destination for wormhole travel not yet attained. Antimatter drive online in fifteen seconds. Fourteen."

He wet his lips and pulled on his helmet, sealing it to his suit around the neckline. He'd have to cut life support in this part of the ship prior to engaging the antimatter drive.

"Twelve."

A large security cruiser was coming at him head on. "Ship Zulu-eight-alpha-two, this is Asteria Spaceport authority. Turn off your engines and prepare for boarding."

"Eleven."

Did demands like that work? He fired up the ship's cannons and aimed a warning shot over the cruiser's nose. Instead of the expected weapons blast, a yellow beam of light shot out and held, just like the beam that shot down the *Red Slag*. The cruiser flew straight into the beam before Donovan could take evasive action. Nothing happened. The light hit the ship, bouncing off. Harmless.

"Jesus." The light that blew the *Slag* hadn't come from the Spaceport. How many ships were equipped with the weapon? And why'd the light blow up the *Red Slag* but not that cruiser?

The computer's voice filled his helmet. "Weapons online. Antimatter drive offline."

Goddamnit! He forgot Macie had jimmy-rigged the *Red Slag* to allow both to operate simultaneously. He deactivated the weapons, restarted the antimatter drive warm-up, and gunned the engines, diving below the cruiser.

"Antimatter drive online in ten. Nine." Thank God it hadn't started the count at the beginning.

"Ship Zulu-eight-alpha-two, weapons activation noted. Your aggressive maneuvers are unacceptable."

"Eight."

"Well, shit." He slammed his hand against the control panel. "Come on, you fucking computer, get your ass in gear."

"Seven."

A warning shot sailed over the nose of his ship.

"Six."

"About fucking time. Computer, drop life support and activate drive with new calculations."

"Drive activated in five. Four."

He buckled himself in as the gravity field turned off.

"Three."

"Ship Zulu-eight-alpha-two, power off your engines."

"Two."

Closed his eyes. *Come on, let's go.*

"This is your last warning, Zulu-eight-alpha-two."

"One."

The antimatter drive activated with a whir, giving him a green light.

— • —

24

The one thing Donovan had always hated about being awake during jumps was there was no way to hide from his thoughts. He couldn't read for long without getting a blinding headache and there was nothing worse than the droning monotone of an audio book. There was no view to watch. No communications.

There was time. A shitload of it. While traveling to Earth only took two weeks, his reality—awake during a jump—was considerably longer. Time slowed. Seconds stretched. Not in his mind, but in his reality.

Back in his father's day—the time stretch amounted to years per day, but technology had advanced. He was only looking at weeks per day. Roughly two weeks per "day" of travel. Fourteen days equaled twenty-eight weeks of nothing. He was already half out of his mind with boredom, and they were only halfway to their destination.

In truth, this trip was far worse than others. They had a plethora of trouble on their hands and all he could do was think about the problems; he couldn't do anything to mitigate them.

So, he sat and mulled over their situation day-after-day until his head throbbed. He was missing something important. He pulled up his notes on the terminal and reviewed them.

What did he know?

He knew Vessa had originally wanted Sorcha gone, and if he'd divorced or killed her, she'd have been happy with that, too, because her clans would've backed her in war. He knew the vladsets had captured, and probably killed, Jerrod Williams because the vladset warriors they'd encountered on Asteria traveled in *CorTech 12*—William's ship, his ship now. The vladsets had also dumped three bodies of ex-CorTech employees, people he had contracts on.

So he knew Vessa and CorTech were connected. Not allies, considering the bodies. Were they both after the unknown resource? Willing to kill each other for it?

How did it work? Why did the yellow light blow up one ship and not another? Was the weapon the light itself? Something that used the light as a homing beacon? He shook his head. He'd have to wait for those answers.

He also knew the IgA, or at least Prax, was connected to Vessa. He was Troon's inspector. He'd ensured that he and Sorcha soul-mated. He had to be the one feeding Vessa the names of the marks on his contracts.

And he knew CorTech wanted Division Command Zero off its property. Why now? Was it because he was hunting marks that had once worked for them? Maybe. They'd gone to a lot of trouble scrubbing those employees from their databases.

Now that he considered that, was it possible that after he and Macie had raided CorTech, Williams had given Vessa the names of their marks? Nah, that was the action of an ally, not an enemy.

Either way, motivation for all three was solid, considering they were all after a weapon. Vessa could wreak havoc with anyone who opposed her. The IgA depended on the fact that their weapons were better than everyone else's—a good arsenal came in handy when a rogue civilization started making threats. And CorTech . . . well, they knew DCZ was searching for a leader. They knew other Corporations were looking for ways to become that leader. One way or another, Earth was in for another war and CorTech would fight tooth and nail to keep what they considered theirs. A weapon like the one that blew up the *Red Slag* would be beneficial.

Damn it. He knew it was all connected, he knew it all had to do with the unknown resource, but he couldn't figure out how. He needed evidence. A confession. He just needed a goddamned break.

Had the IgA determined if they were still alive yet? Would they be there, waiting, when they arrived in Earth's orbit? If they'd investigated, they would've watched the security footage from Asteria's spaceport. They'd know he stole this ship and their destination wasn't hard to guess. Nor was alerting CorTech of the theft.

What about Vessa? Did she know they'd lived? That Sorcha had killed Quimet? If so, would Vessa leave them alone, or would she see this as a challenge to pursue even more fanatically?

And he still had to talk to his Zeros and Command Zero. He'd gone over the figures time and again and there was no fucking way they could come up with the rent. He wasn't looking forward to coming home empty-handed. Both his Zeros and DCZ would have to decide if they wanted to go off on their own or find a new place. Then again, maybe Macie was right. DCZ hadn't held up their end of the bargain. They hadn't found a new leader. Maybe he should take his company, his Zeros, and cut his losses.

He sighed. How the hell were they going to get through all this without any of them ending up dead or in prison? Stealing this goddamned ship certainly hadn't improved their odds. Even if they avoided punishment, would Sorcha still want to remain married to him once they reached Earth and she discovered he wasn't quite so honorable?

Honor was a big damn deal to the vladsets. To her. While Asterians considered him a hero . . . war wasn't cut and dried. One man's hero was another's villain. Honor to some was fanatical resistance to others. A soldier without military backing was nothing more than a terrorist.

Which is how the civvies back home thought of him. DCZ and the Zeroes held enough sway to avoid being killed by a mob. *Sway* . . . he chuckled . . . the truth was, the civilians back home feared them. The civvies taunted, jeered, and attacked if they caught one or two of them alone, but they didn't dare take on the group. They never tried to breach the walls around DCZ.

Why in God's name had he decided he and Sorcha could work? Why had he thought bringing her home was a good idea?

Because she was his. He couldn't leave her behind. Yet she didn't do well in heat, according to her scan, so she'd hate his home—the remnants of a fragged air base in the middle of a desert. She was used to life in a fucking palace on an ice planet, for God's sake. And their "clan"—how would she react to a bunch of burned-out, disabled rebels who couldn't even walk down the street without being spit on?

Donovan pulled a chair over to Sorcha's lifepod as he did every evening before he went to sleep. Damn, she was beautiful. He paused the conversational English lecture playing in the pod and set the device to an open mic. She needed to learn English, true, but she couldn't survive on English alone. He put on the headset, adjusting the mic to hang in front of his lips. After leaning back and kicking his feet up on the corner edge of the pod, he began.

"I'm beautiful and feel comfortable in my own skin." He swallowed, feeling ten kinds of an idiot. "I'm in control of my flame and choose when I use it." He wasn't even sure these affirmations would have any impact being delivered in *his* voice. "I'm an intelligent woman and my opinions matter even if others disagree."

What if she woke up thinking he was a conceited pig instead of feeling empowered herself? "I'm a capable woman. I can do anything I set my mind to." His lips quirked, remembering her cooking disaster. She'd get better. "I'm the only person in charge of my life. I must do what is best for me and my future." That was an important one. She might decide she needed to leave him. "No matter what happens, I know my chief will always love me."

Christ, he couldn't let her leave him.

— · —

25

When Macie woke, he came up swinging.

Donovan dodged the blow and pushed him back down. "Sit still or you're gonna rip out the IV."

Macie slumped back and rubbed his eyes. "Where are we?"

"Sonoran Desert National Monument." The nature reserve sat on two thousand acres in what was once Glendale, Arizona. He'd landed there with the hope no one would notice them this far out into the desert. He pulled the needle out of Macie's arm, stuck a cotton swab over the tiny hole and folded Macie's arm at the elbow to hold it in place. "I cloaked us on the way in, but this was the only place I could think of. We've got a twenty-five-mile hike to base."

"You look thrilled."

His mouth quirked from Macie's wry tone. "Oh, yeah."

"How's Sorcha?"

"Asleep."

Macie swung his legs over the edge of the pod and bowed his head, stretching his neck muscles from side to side. "You seem to be avoiding the obvious question, but why the hell are we parked in bum fuck Egypt instead of the spaceport?"

Yeah, Macie wasn't all the way awake yet. He snorted. "Aside from the fact we're in a stolen craft?"

"I need coffee. I can't think when I'm this fucking groggy. Stolen? How did you . . .?" A string of vicious curses punctuated the air. "Now I remember. Did we actually steal CorTech's ship? And who the fuck shot me?" He stood. "What the hell were you thinking? The fucking thing must have a tracking—"

"I disabled it." They'd already been mid-jump before he considered the possibility of a tracking device. Most corporations used them to protect their assets. Disabling the device hadn't been easy. With gravity and life support off in most of the ship, and traveling near the speed of light . . . Hell, he passed out a few different times during his foray into the guts of the ship. He had no idea how much time he'd spent in there. He'd easily shaved off a year or two of his life.

"Before we left?"

He shook his head. "There wasn't time."

Macie snapped his mouth closed. Blinked. "How'd you . . .?" He must've read the answer in his expression. "Jesus, Reese. That's the most hair-brained, risky bullshit I've ever heard."

"It's done."

"You okay?"

"Yeah." He folded his arms over his chest. "So that's the good news."

Macie moaned. "You're killing me."

"The bad news is because of our rapid departure, there was no way for me to choose what time we landed and because we're now wanted by multiple parties—"

Macie's gaze narrowed. "Multiple? What the fuck else did I miss?"

"There's the vladsets." He held up his thumb. "Possibly Asteria Spaceport Authority—" Held up his forefinger. "—I'm not sure if they know we're the ones who stole the ship. And possibly CorTech." Held up his middle finger. "For the same reason—though we already owe them a shit ton of money we can't pay, so it's kind of a moot point." Help up his ring finger. "And the IgA."

"Jesus." Macie raised both hands, dragging them through his hair as if he wanted to pull it all out by the roots. "What the fuck did you do to the IgA?"

"Vessa informed the IgA that Sorcha is Blaze. They have her body armor."

His eyes closed and his head dropped back. "If I could get ten minutes alone with that bitch . . . ."

"Get in line." He drew in a deep sigh. "Anyways, I couldn't schedule our timing or risk a lengthy orbit and we're sitting ducks if we stay here. CorTech must know we stole the ship by now. They'll be scanning the area for heat signatures . . . ."

"What time is it?"

"Eleven-hundred, Saturday, July eighteenth."

Macie threw up his hands. "We'll hit town just in time to march right through the goddamned market."

"Yeah."

Macie nodded. "All right. Okay. Have you explained how things are to Sorcha?"

"No." He ignored Macie's curses. "She'll walk ahead of us in case they have anyone watching for us. They'll leave her be if they don't know she's mine."

"Have you seen your wife?" He shook his head. "I'll be amazed if she makes it through the gauntlet without being accosted."

No. He'd thought this through. "She's alien. They might talk smack, but they won't touch an exotic."

"Hope you're right."

He folded his arms over his chest. "What's the alternative?" He'd considered having Macie walk with her, but the locals had seen Macie and him together too many times. Someone was bound to recognize him. "The people in town know our faces."

Macie opened his mouth and then clamped it shut.

"You know what'll happen if they see her with us. She *will* get accosted."

"You know you can't control everything, right?"

Donovan clenched his jaw. "I'm gonna wake her up." He *had* to control everything. If he didn't, he'd lose his wife.

You are beautiful and comfortable in your own skin.

Celeka rolled onto her side and curled into a tight ball. Her body was stiff, achy, and her mind felt like it was covered in the silky strands of an Obookay's net. She tried to ignore the insistent hands trying to draw her from sleep. The fingers poking and prodding all over her body. All she wanted to do was sleep.

You must make decisions based on what's best for you.

" . . . Let's go, Sorcha. Open those beautiful eyes."

Everything blurred, even so, she couldn't mistake the face hovering above her for anyone's but her chief's. "I'm tired."

"You slept for two weeks, little flame. It's my turn to have you." His hand stroked over her cheek.

"You missed me."

"You have no idea." He leaned down and nibbled kisses at the corner of her mouth. "If you hurry, I can give you a whole ten minutes in the bathroom for a quick clean up."

"Are we home?" She stretched her stiff muscles.

His gaze slid away. "Mm-hm."

Dedia, they were home and she was groggy and achy and hadn't bathed in two weeks. "Yes, I want ten minutes." She was going to meet their clan! She struggled up, put her feet on the floor, and pitched forward. Donovan caught her with a chuckle and lifted her into his arms. "How 'bout I carry you?"

"Good idea."

He lifted her into his arms, nuzzling her neck. "The English lessons took."

"What?" She turned her gaze to his.

"You're speaking English."

"I am?" A trembling smile tugged at the corner of her mouth. "*I am.*"

He chuckled. "You are."

She threw her arms around his neck. This would raise her chances of being accepted by their clan. She could speak to the Earthers without using translators!

"Here." He set her down, handed her a stack of clothing—she hadn't even seen him grab them—before pulling the door shut.

She made quick work of her ablutions and dressing. They were home. This is where she'd live out the rest of her days with her chief and her clan. She couldn't quit smiling, nor the insistent fluttering in her belly. So far, Donovan's friends had accepted her, would the clan here on Earth be the same? When she finished, she practically bounded down the corridor but came to an abrupt halt. Donovan and Macie were both frowning. Were they still arguing?

"Hello, Macie."

He smiled, but it didn't quite reach his eyes. "You ready to stretch your legs?"

She frowned. She understood the words, but the context didn't make sense.

"He's asking if you're ready for a long walk—it's a saying."

"Yes. A walk sounds nice."

Donovan lowered the ramp. "We've got a twenty-five-mile hike, during the hottest part of the day. It won't be easy."

She barely heard him. Twenty-five miles—she had no understanding of the measurement, but her attention was captured by the glaring light flowing into the ship. The sun was so bright, she had to squint her eyes. "How many hours?"

"Eight." He held up his fingers to show her the number. "Here." Donovan handed her a pair of dark glasses that allowed her to open her eyes all the way.

Her jaw dropped.

There was no ice or snow like at home. No grass or trees like on Asteria. There was dirt. Lots and lots of reddish-brown dirt. The vegetation was sickly yellows and browns except for some oblong, spiky green plants. "What's wrong with your world?"

Macie chuckled. "This part of Earth is a desert. There's very little water."

A tiny brownish-gray slithery creature scuttled past on four legs, its long tale swishing from side to side. "This is natural?"

They both nodded. Donovan added, "The brush lizards won't hurt you."

She stepped outside and gooseflesh broke out on her skin as the heat seared away the chill from the ship.

Donovan led her a few yards away to the edge of a cliff and pointed out over the perfectly flat valley below. As deserted as this area was, the valley was full to bursting with buildings. Never had she seen anything like it. The roads ran in straight lines, like a grid, with buildings clustered together inside perfect squares stretching into the horizon. Everything had angles.

"You see this trail, the one right below us?"

A narrow dirt path carved out by decades of use. "Yeah."

"I want you to walk carefully down this ridge." He motioned off to the side, where the narrow dirt trail curved down the side of the mountain. "*Carefully.* Don't touch the bushes or cacti—the plants with needles poking out of them."

She nodded.

"Don't try to interact with any of the wildlife and, for God's sakes, if you hear something rattle, back up the way you came."

Her eyes widened. "What kind of animal rattles?"

"Snakes." He held his thumb and finger up in a circle. "They're kind of like long tubes. No legs, they slither . . . Jesus." He brought both hands up to his head. "This isn't safe."

"I won't touch anything."

"Not even the bugs—most are poisonous." He blew out a pent-up breath and nodded. "When you get to the paved road, stick to the middle—stay away from the alleys and storefronts."

Something wasn't right. "I won't walk with you?"

"Don't worry." He dragged his hand down his face. "Walk straight. Don't talk to anyone. Don't look anyone in the eye. Walk straight through town until you come to a wall and you can't walk anymore." He pulled a band out of his pocket and attached it around her wrist. "This shows you where you're going." He pointed to a star. "You head toward this."

"Then what?"

"The Zeros will see you coming. They'll let you in from behind the gate." He rubbed his hand down her arm. "Tell them you're my wife. They look scary as hell but let them take your weapons. Let them scan you. No one there will hurt you and I'll be right behind."

Macie interrupted to hand her a backpack with a long tube sticking out from one of the straps before walking away again.

Donovan put the pack on her, adjusted the straps and then curled the tube toward her. "Suck."

She lifted her brow, which made him smile. She put the tube between her lips and drew on it. "Water?"

"Yeah." Donovan nodded. "It'll get hotter and there's no shade. Sip as you go. This—" He lifted her wrist to show her the device again. "—will beep when it's time for you to take a sip. Drink even if you aren't thirsty. You have more than enough, you won't run out."

Macie came back, this time with a loaded holster on a belt.

Donovan took the holster, put it around her hips so the weapon hung down her thigh at arm's length. "Don't draw unless you have no choice. You probably won't need it but I want you to be safe. It's a long trek home."

This wasn't like him. Up until this moment, he always wanted her to stay with him, or with a friend of his—wandering alone wasn't an option. She bit her lip. Now he wanted her to walk alone, armed, and through what sounded to be hostile territory. "Did I do something wrong?"

"No." He tugged her into his embrace. "God, no. I'm trying to keep you safe, that's all."

"And safe is away from you?" She tried to see his face, but his hug refused to allow it.

His whole body tensed. "I'll explain later. Right now, we have to move."

She cupped the back of his head and pulled him down to press her lips to his. "See you soon?"

"Count on it." He flashed her a smile, but it wasn't real. Didn't reach his eyes. "Go on, now." He smacked her bottom.

After shooting him a scowl, she followed the narrow dirt trail, winding her way down the ridge. Her gaze kept trying to tug back to the scene below—to the pretty glass buildings, to the straight lines of the roads. The Earth's sun glared down, shining off the glass and metal, dazzling her eyes to the point that dark spots began to haze her vision. She forced her gaze to stay away from the glittering oasis below and focused on the red dirt and the rocks sliding under her boots on the steep slope. Bleached-out, spindly shrubs lined the hard-packed path. She didn't see any tube-shaped animals or hear any rattling, but she did see lots of plants with needle-like stickers. She even saw one with thick white fur. She stopped to admire the plant, which looked as though it would be soft to the touch. She reached out her hand—

"Don't touch that!"

She snatched her hand back and peered up to where Donovan watched over her. She smiled and waved as if she hadn't gotten caught doing exactly what he'd said not to do. With a baleful glance at the tempting plant, she continued down the incline until she reached the bottom. Down here, the distance to the tall square buildings was daunting. Dwellings with sharp angles and slanted roofs lined the way. The broken windows and crumbling exteriors pronouncing them vacant. Why? Where had all the people gone? Rows and rows of dwellings sat off to each side, but there was no noise aside from the distant caws of black birds circling overhead. No movement aside from more of those little brush lizards—they were everywhere.

She stared at the faded black road. Cracked and uneven, it must've seen better days. Heat rose off the road in waves, cooking the soles of her shoes and searing her legs. She stepped back onto the dirt. They had to walk on *that*? It was like an oven with the sun beating down overhead and the heat rising from the road. She glanced back and up.

Donovan nodded. Macie gave her two thumbs up.

Fine. Into the oven she'd go.

"I warn you, Earth. My flame is stronger than yours."

26

Today was hot as fuck, which appeared to be a good thing. For most of the trip, they'd walked past the suburb wastelands between the Sonoran Desert Monument and the Air Force base. The population had gone from over four hundred thousand before the UN, to just shy of one hundred thousand after. Between the exiles to Asteria and the loss of life from the wars, the population had taken a major hit. When he was a kid, this place had been bursting with people. There hadn't been enough housing. Not enough resources. Now, miles and miles of empty tract homes, shopping centers, and office buildings sat dried and crumbled in the blistering sun.

However, as they'd crossed through the wrought iron arches onto CorTech land, people became a more regular occurrence. Dogs barked. Hover cars slid through the streets. Pedestrian traffic increased. The tall apartment buildings and converted businesses were maintained. Farther in, the occasional maintenance droid bustled down the sidewalk, tidying everything in its path.

The people they'd encountered so far, were too uncomfortable from the heat to do anything more than sneer or spit as they passed. Macie might've walked through anonymously, but him, with the goddamned scars on his face, he was infamous. The UN had exiled the majority of the disabled and deformed—it wasn't hard to guess someone with scars or missing a limb had been part of the rebellion.

Macie kicked a rock, sending the stone skittering over the broken asphalt. "Don't you ever think of leaving here?"

He grunted, not in the mood.

"I mean we work non-stop for what? To be spit on?" Macie shook his head. "Don't you ever get tired of this shit?"

"Shut up."

Macie's gaze shot to him, mouth open no doubt to spew a bunch of his nonsense. Donovan tipped his head forward.

The market. Sorcha had slipped into the crowd, disappearing. So far, no one had given her a second glance, but if anyone was going to give her problems, it'd be here. The buildings shaded the street, which meant the place was packed with people trying to escape the heat. The curved tops of blue helmets bobbed among the crowd.

The Blue Helmets—the UN's private army—had sold out after the UN fell. Once they realized there were no more Parnell's left to sign their paychecks, they took their training and equipment and hired out to the highest bidder in their area. CoreTech had a big pocketbook. They had no problem hiring Blue Helmets to patrol the market and protect their corporation.

The Blue Helmets didn't usually give the Division Command nor the Zeros a hard time. Then again, they didn't exactly go out of their way to keep anyone else from doing so either. Their purpose was to protect CorTech assets and they took their job seriously. Everyone else was on their own.

Every time he saw those pale-blue domed helmets his gut knotted. The civilians, however, loved them.

"It's getting worse." Macie lowered his voice, tipping his face down. "There weren't this many vendors out here when we left. It's starting to resemble Diamond Fjord's market."

His gaze slid from the crowd to the rows of carts on either side of the road. "Seems we're not the only ones CorTech is putting a pinch on."

With rents flying sky-high, more and more retailers were offering their goods out of carts and trailers. If they wanted their families protected, they needed the stability of a corporation like CorTech who had enough clout and money to ensure the lights stayed on and the riffraff stayed out—but living within the boundaries and laws of a corporation was expensive. CorTech would raise rents on homeowners and retailers, the homeowners and retailers would move onto the streets or into smaller dwellings, then CorTech would say they had to raise rent to make up for the missing renters. The cycle wasn't sustainable. Eventually, what was left of Glendale, Arizona would implode.

"We could—"

"No." He wasn't fighting CorTech for these fucking people. No-fucking-way.

"—leave."

He turned his face to the side, his gaze tangling with Macie's. Leave? Not even Macie understood. This. All of this. It was his fault. He'd taken up Chief Payne's call to arms. He'd recruited a rebel army and they'd overthrown the UN. Except he hadn't thought beyond that. No one had. They didn't have a replacement leader to put into power. Everything had crumbled. Was still crumbling.

If he'd kept to his own business and left the UN alone, these people wouldn't be in this predicament. They'd still have a real government and all the protections that had been afforded them. Most of these people hated him for it—either because they liked the way things had been, or because they hated the way the corporations took advantage of them now that there was no government—he couldn't walk away, leaving them to the mess he created.

"What the fuck are you doing in town?"

Donovan kept his head down, not looking at the man who'd spoken, and eased into the crowd. Sorcha was almost through the worst of this. She only had a couple blocks to go. When she reached the wall, the Zeros would take her in. They took in anyone who came to them.

Someone shoved Macie and he stumbled into Donovan. He lost his balance and shouldered another guy in the back. "Sorry. My fault." Normally, he'd take the fight. Hell, he wanted the fight. Anything to escape his thoughts.

They hadn't gotten two steps before a big hand settled on his shoulder. "What'd you say?"

Hell, the guy was built like a pro-wrestler with a mug to match. "I apologized."

Macie added, "Fuck-face," under his breath.

Donovan closed his eyes. "Not yet." Give Sorcha time to get to safety.

Big Ape's eyes narrowed. "Not yet, what?"

The crowd around them started pushing back, making room. Guess he was getting his fight. Still, he needed to stall a little longer. "In a few minutes, I'm going to use you as a human shield until you asphyxiate and pass out at my feet." He grinned. "But not yet."

Ape-boy continued to stare, his eyebrows scrunching down.

"I think the big word confused him, poor guy." Macie cracked his knuckles. "Chief here is gonna choke you out." Macie turned to Donovan, giving Ape-boy his back, his gaze scanning the area behind Donovan. "I think it's a bad plan, personally. I mean did you see his neck—it's too thick, you're gonna end up hurting your arm and you'll still have these two assholes to deal with."

Donovan nodded toward the two guys who'd strutted up to flank Ape-boy behind Macie. "Those two?"

"Nah." He shook his head and pointed behind Donovan. "Those two."

So five. Five guys who wanted to be heroes.

"Three." Macie nodded. "Now it's three."

So six. Great. "Not yet."

"We wait much longer and—"

Ape-boy let out a war cry and his ruddy face turned an incinerating red.

Donovan grabbed Macie's arm, put a booted foot on his braced thigh and launched himself at the giant. He latched onto his throat, swinging around to his back, and pinched his larynx between his bicep and forearm. Macie was right, the son of a bitch's neck was as thick as a saguaro cactus. He used his other arm to lock the choke hold tight. Let his full weight dangle off his back.

Ape-boy flailed with his fist, trying to get a punch, trying to reach back and grab Donovan's head. His fingers locked onto Donovan's collar at the back of his neck, latching on. He bent forward, trying to haul Donovan over his shoulder. With Donovan's weight hanging down his back, he couldn't get the momentum he needed.

Someone punched him in the back. Pain seared straight up his spine. Fuck.

Donovan kicked back with one leg, while trying to dodge Ape-boy's fists. The son of a bitch behind them caught his booted foot and started to pull. Ape-boy stumbled. Donovan tightened his grip, using the leverage to kick back with his other foot just as Ape-boy landed a fist on Donovan's jaw.

Black checkered his vision for a pain-filled second. Ape-boy may as well have had sledgehammers for fists. He'd thrown the punch over his shoulder, had Donovan taken the hit head on, he'd be down for the count.

His kick missed, but the dumb ass behind him grabbed that foot, too. From the feel of it, both his legs were around the guy's neck. Donovan bent his knees, bringing his calves up behind the guy's head and drawing him closer. Once his neck was between his knees, he locked his ankles and squeezed.

He glanced up in time to see Macie wrestling with one of the other guys. Two were already on the ground, not moving. Another was sneaking up . . . . "Check your six!"

Macie hauled his opponent up and swung him around, toppling the guy sneaking up on him.

Behind Donovan, the guy locked between his knees was punching his thighs. Donovan twisted his lower body, leaning more of his weight onto his legs and squeezing hard. His whole body jerked as the guy fell to his knees, making Ape-boy stumble again. He held him for a few seconds more, then dropped the guy behind him, letting his body dangle from Ape-boy again.

Ape-boy showed no sign of going down, but he wasn't punching anymore. He was trying to pry Donovan's arms from his neck. Donovan jerked his knee up, ramming it into the guy's kidney. Again. And again. Finally, Ape-boy gasped. Sputtered. He went down to one knee. Then struggled right back up, clawing at his arms and face.

"Fuck sake."

"I'm about done." Macie shook his opponent off, turned, and threw a punch at Ape-boy. His nose crunched and wet heat slid over Donovan's arm. Blood. He tightened his arm, jerking him back until he got his feet on the ground. Ape-boy's hands continued to claw at his arm, getting weaker

"Hey, now."

Donovan turned at Macie's voice. The last asshole had pulled a gun.

Everyone froze.

Everyone except one gorgeous white-haired woman who ran right into the middle of the tension. Sorcha lifted her hand toward the guy with the gun. "Stay back."

All the blood left Donovan's head and he went cold. What the fuck was she doing? "Walk away, lady."

Her reply was instantaneous, "No, my Chief."

Donovan winced.

Murmurs went through the crowd. "She's with them," and "They brought a fucking exotic home," and "Just what we need, another Zero," and "Grab her!"

Macie's gaze slid to his and he nodded, reaching down to pull his blaster with his right hand while keeping his choke hold on Ape-boy. When the fuck was he going down? They both leveled their weapons at the dick with the weapon. "Sorcha, come here." He put every ounce of mean he had into the command. He couldn't let go of Ape-boy. Didn't want her between him and them. "Now!"

She backed a step closer, staring at her palm as if she'd never seen it before.

"Let Jonesy go," the guy with the gun said.

"Jonesy?" Macie snorted.

"When he's down," Donovan said. "Not before." Ape-boy was finally starting to list to the side. Donovan leaned his weight on his shoulders, pushing him to one knee. "Now, we're just walking through. We'll drop Jonesy at the end of the street."

Another gun whirred to life. The muzzle sitting just inside Donovan's peripheral vision on the right.

Sorcha spun and glared. "You shoot him, I'll shoot you."

Donovan's gaze dropped. She had her gun pointed at the guy's dick. Good girl.

Next to her, Macie turned a slow circle, checking the rest of the people around them, both his weapons out and pointed low. "Anyone else? I've got two weapons minus targets; we can take two more heroes."

Jesus, he never shut his fucking mouth.

A Blue Helmet strolled up. "Problem?"

Donovan shook his head. "No, we were just squaring off, having a little fun. We're done now. No one's hurt bad. No one needs to die." He eyed up the two men with guns. "Back up."

Both men backed off. Neither lowered their weapons.

The Blue Helmet sighed. "You can't take him." He lifted the muzzle of the semi-auto he carried to indicate Ape-boy.

"Don't want him. I'll leave him at the edge of the crowd."

The Blue Helmet leveled a glare at one of the men. "You heard the boss this morning, no fighting with DCZ."

The guy powered down his blaster.

Everyone turned to the guy who'd first pulled his weapon. "You, too, Morton."

Morton winked. "Yeah, you boys'll be gone soon." His lips curved. "Real soon."

That didn't sound good. Was he referring to the raise in rents or something more nefarious? What the hell had the boss said this morning? Was he referring to CorTech's CEO or the Blue Helmet commander? *Shit.* He didn't recognize any of these guys and had no idea who their boss was.

Donovan dragged the now sleeping Ape-boy through the crowd, walking backward, covering Sorcha and Macie until they reached the edge of the crowd. Their feet pounded asphalt as they ran toward home. He waited a heartbeat or two, staring down the fifty or so sets of eyes watching his every move. Then he dumped Ape-boy, turned, and beat feet.

Ahead of him, Macie had Sorcha by the arm, forcing her to keep pace as he hauled ass for the gate. She kept trying to look over her shoulder. Damn, Macie would give him an earful later. If Sorcha hadn't returned, they'd still be kicking ass and taking names, and ridding themselves of all this damn tension. Then again, it was probably for the best. They didn't need more trouble right now.

"Oy!" Macie shouted the one syllable.

The metal gate set into the wall began to rise, the dusty gears shrieking in protest. As the gate rose, booted, pacing feet came into view.

Celeka's heart raced double-time in her chest.

They brought an exotic. Thanks to her English lessons, she understood what those people had called her. Exotic: unusual, different, and strange. Other.

She wasn't going to fit in on Earth, either.

What had happened? No one had paid much attention to her at first. She'd strolled through the market, pausing to look in a cage housing a small, furry bug-eyed creature when a rattle had drawn her attention. After Donovan's earlier warning, she had to take a closer look. When she approached the glass cage the long tube-like creature—the snake—curled its body into a spiral with its head lifted and swaying and its tail shaking in warning. There was no softness to the creature. It was solid muscle like her chief. Awful and beautiful all at once, leaving her feeling unsettled and awed. When she dared a step closer, the snake struck the glass, its hinged mouth wide open.

She'd frozen for several moments when the crowd had erupted into jeers and shouts behind her, Donovan's commands echoing in her mind. *Don't talk to anyone. Don't stop. Don't look anyone in the eye.*

But when Macie had shouted she ran back because . . . *I'm the only person in charge of my life.*

She thought she'd go back, let her hands flare, and run with Donovan and Macie while the humans fled in fear. Except she couldn't flare.

Why?

She'd spent so much time hating that her flame showed when she was angry or scared. Spent so much effort wishing it would stay hidden . . . . Had she finally willed her flame to remain within?

If so, the timing was terrible. She needed that ability more than ever now.

Or was this the result of two weeks sleeping in freezing temperatures in the life-pod. Or traveling at light speed? Or some effect unique to Earth?

If her chief thought her defenseless, he'd be doubly protective if he discovered she couldn't flare. Maybe it was the heat. She'd never been anywhere so hot, and while she'd been worried it would make it more difficult to control her flame, perhaps it had smothered it, instead.

She turned her gaze to the massive wall of Donovan's palace to avoid his scowls while they waited for the gate to rise. Steel-gray and several stories high, it was an imposing structure. Great slashes of red- and black-painted symbols scattered the surface near the gate.

"What's that say?"

Macie shrugged. "It's graffiti." The gate ground to a halt, high enough to allow them through, but she held her ground.

An angry hand had drawn the graffiti. "What does it say?" Did it have to do with the awful humans back there?

"Come on." Donovan nudged her in motion. "It's safer inside."

"You'll tell me." She shoved away from him. "What does it say?"

A female answered, "Traitors."

Donovan cursed.

She swung around to stare at the woman on the other side of the gate. Taller than Celeka, with her dark hair pulled back from her face and trailing down her back, she was imposing in her gray-and-green-splotched uniform. With a gun on a strap slung over her shoulder, she looked from Macie, to her, to Donovan and back to her. "Below, it says 'Heroes to Zeros.'"

Zero: naught, nothing, zilch. That's why they called themselves the Zeros? They accepted this?

Heat bloomed under her skin, so hot it made her hair lift as if a swift breeze had caught the strands, though no flame erupted over her skin. Her chief was dishonored? Or was he dishonorable? He wouldn't give her the answer willingly. Even now, he refused to meet her gaze, staring off into the distance, his chin tipped up, his body braced for attack.

Celeka forced the heat away. Strode past her chief and stuck her hand out in greeting.

The woman took her hand, pumping it once. "Marigold."

That must be her name. "Sorcha."

Marigold's gaze shifted to Donovan. "We keeping exotics now?" Her lips curved and she winked at Celeka. She didn't seem to think "exotics" a bad thing . . . still, she hated being pointed out as different. She wanted to belong.

Donovan pulled Sorcha back against him. "My wife."

The woman's cheeks turned a bright red and her gaze jerked back to Celeka's. "A pleasure to meet you." And back to Donovan. "Congratulations, sir."

Odd, he received the same deferential treatment here he received in Asteria, but out there . . . . She glanced back, but the road behind them was empty.

"Any problems, Marigold?"

"Aside from hearing news that you were dead?" She smiled. "Nah. Nothing we couldn't handle, sir."

"Good." He nudged Celeka forward.

As they walked past the small security shelter, her eyes widened. This was not a palace. The gate led to more outside. A long, wide stretch of rubble. Most of it decimated building material, but there were vehicles, too, some for the land, others with long wings made for the air. Broken. Burnt black in places. Tossed about as if playthings discarded by an angry god-child.

"This way." Donovan's hand settled on the small of her back.

She jerked away. He'd lied to her. Brought her to this place. Subjected her to those people. *Goddamn traitors. Get them the fuck outta here. They brought an exotic. Grab her!*

His gaze dropped and he swept his hand out, indicating a narrow trail through the rubble. She walked forward. What kind of man was he, truly? A man who couldn't land his ship in the local spaceport? A man who strangers jeered as he walked by? This was about far more than the scars on his face.

They walked in silence. Not even Macie had anything to say. Maybe because they knew she was angry. Maybe because they were ashamed of this place. Maybe because it felt like a tomb. The scale of the damage . . . this was a dead place. No trees or bushes grew here. Not even weeds tried to sprout up through the rubble. *What is this place?* Part of her wanted to ask, most of her wasn't ready for the answer. Had he done this?

In the distance, well off the cleared pathway, her gaze snagged on a bright swath of pink blowing in the breeze. A piece of cloth hanging off a shrouded figure.

"I got her."

She paused. Donovan jogged ahead and squatted next to the figure, reaching up to touch the face. Spoke in tones too low for her to hear. "He knows her?"

"Opal was in his unit." Macie nudged her into motion. "He'll catch up."

Donovan stood and hauled the woman into his arms. He made his way back to them through the rubble with cautious steps, unable to see over his burden, but eventually he rejoined them. "She must've had a good day today."

Macie nodded. "She made it pretty far out."

What was protocol here? Her chief should've introduced them. Should she introduce herself or was there some other social obligation that needed to be met first? She glanced back. The woman was frighteningly thin, bundled in clothes in dire need of a wash, her unblinking gaze staring into the distance.

Celeka faced forward, feeling like an interloper.

"Hey, where'd you find her?"

Her gaze shot to the side where a male with a missing limb limped toward them with the aid of wooden braces under his arms. He was young, fair. Thin and wiry.

"Hey, Josh. She was out by the BX."

She sidled closer to Macie. "What's the BX?"

"Base exchange. Used to be a store where military could buy clothes and household items."

Josh nodded. "Trying to go see Delmar at work again."

It wasn't a question. She searched the area, but there was nothing there, no store, no humans, nothing but the outer wall.

"How'd she get out of the infirmary?" Donovan asked.

Josh wiped the sweat from his brow. "Blue Helmets brought prosecutors through to serve the eviction notice. She must've slipped out while we were busy with them."

This time Macie clarified before she asked. "Prosecutors are a cross between police—kind of like your vladset guards—and lawyers. Clients hire them to settle legal disputes. They're kind of like cop, lawyer, and judge all in one and they're independent of local corporations and Blue Helmets."

She took in each of their somber expressions. "This isn't what I expected Earth to be like. And this place . . . ." She motioned around them. "Why are we here?" Her gaze shifted between Donovan and Macie and settled back on Donovan.

"This is Luke Air Force Base—or used to be. Now it's home to Command Division Zero. Our home." He sidled past her and walked ahead with Opal cradled in his arms.

Air Force base. A military base. The UN had bombed the bases, they'd said. *Dedia.* When they spoke of the disaster, she'd pictured a building being destroyed, but this . . . Thousands must've died on this base alone.

Josh held his hand out to her. "Welcome, Miss . . .?"

She slipped her hand into his and he pumped once. "Sorcha."

Macie winked. "Donovan's wife."

Josh's blue eyes widened. He released her hand. "Oh." His gaze ran down the length of her before shifting back to Macie. "This should be interesting."

— • —

28

Donovan had known today would suck. He'd replayed the possibilities over in his mind until his gut had roiled and his head ached. Now, seeing everything through Sorcha's eyes, he felt worse. Her every thought seemed to manifest in her expressions.

Christ, they'd tried to grab her.

Even him, with his fatalistic imaginings hadn't conjured such a possibility. Jesus, had he thought he could hide all this from her? That she wouldn't figure out who and what he was?

He had to let her go.

Find someplace safe to send her so no one would associate her with him. How could he have been so fucking selfish? He shifted Opal in his arms and held her tighter, trying to take strength from her, even as he tried to instill some strength into her. "They're gone, sweetheart. I'm so sorry, but I can't bring them back."

He strode through their encampment, toward their compound. Only two buildings stood on the grounds. The infirmary was positioned in the Zeros' camp, and the Command Room was dead center in DCZ's camp. Some of his Zeros were milling about, taking their owed time off between cargo runs and bounty hunting.

He caught sight of one of his runners walking alone. "Jaybird."

The woman jogged over, the cloud of tight black curls bouncing around her face. "Good to see you alive and well." She used to be the Air Force's best damned fighter pilot, now she had skewed depth perception due to a missing eye. DCZ didn't want to risk their assets with her, but Donovan hired her as one of his pilots. Just like him, she had learned to compensate. They all teased that the black eye-patch gave her a devil-may-care air that was sexy as hell. Honestly, she didn't need any help. At six-foot-two her lean curves were packed with muscle and she had a pretty face to complete the package. "Can you take Opal up to the infirmary? I've got to get my wife settled."

"Wife?" She took Opal from him, her brows creeping up her forehead.

He nodded. "I'll introduce you later."

She grinned. "Looking forward to it, Chief."

Chief. Chief of what? His gaze searched the cleared-off quad in front of the infirmary where his runners had built shelters and dragged in trailers . . . reminding him of pictures of the Old West where pioneers circled their fucking wagons to create a false sense of safety against the threats of the world. His band of wounded, maimed, and morally injured men and women—*his* Zeros—lounged in small groups, some standing, some sitting as they shared a pot of grub. Division Command Zero—twenty-five thousand strong—resided over the rise.

This was all he had . . . and he was about to lose this, too. Hell, maybe Macie was right and he couldn't let go. He sure as shit didn't like change.

"Reese?" He turned toward Macie's voice. Sorcha stood in front of Macie, her eyes wide as she scanned the area. Lips parted. Her breaths coming faster than normal. He pressed a hand to his chest and rubbed as if he could ease the ache deep in his chest. He'd already lost her. At this point, he just needed to give her the explanations and figure out where to send her that would be safe. "Hungry?"

She shook her head.

"I'll take you to our quarters." He held his hand out to her.

She stared as if she'd never seen the like.

Macie cleared his throat. "What about tonight?"

His gaze searched Macie's face.

"After what happened?"

Right. After that near riot. After they'd tried to grab Sorcha. "Extra guards. I'll take a couple double shifts later this week after—" *After she's gone.* "Tell them I'll make it up to them."

Macie nodded. He started to walk away and then turned back, his gaze shifting to Sorcha and back. He lowered his voice. "You know, Reese, maybe you don't want to make any decisions right now. Wait a day or two. Don't do anything stupid."

Stupid? Like risking Sorcha's safety to bring her here? That kind of stupid? He nodded. Instead of trying to touch his wife again, he pointed to the trailer across the quad. "That's us. We can talk there."

As he passed the communal dinner table, he snagged two bottles of beer out of the cooler. The ice sliding off the bottles and rattling back into the cooler seemed unusually loud. All the conversation in the camp had ceased. He turned. Sorcha stood by the fire pit, waiting for him. His Zeros stared at her, no doubt wondering what kind of hellfire her presence would bring down on them from DCZ and the people outside their walls. He went and stood next to her.

"Everyone, this is my wife, Sorcha. Sorcha this is . . . . ." He waved his arm out to indicate all the people around them. "Everyone." He motioned for her to follow. "Come on."

The low buzz of conversations returned as they walked to the trailer. He tried to open the door and the latch stuck. Damn! He thumped his fist against it, jerked up hard on the handle, and the door opened with a rusty squeal. With a wry twist of his lips, he motioned her inside. "Our castle."

She poked her head in as if expecting something to leap out of the shadows before cautiously climbing the two steps and going inside.

"Power up." The lights kicked on and the air conditioner grumbled to life. He tried to see his home though her eyes. A fine layer of dust coated every surface. He hadn't come home for over a month and out here in the desert, dust crept into every crack and crevice. The tiny living room/dining room combo consisted of a small table—a blaster lay there, the damn thing wasn't working right and he'd been repairing it—two chairs, a beat-up loveseat and a La-Z-Boy with a ripped arm. The floor was nothing but plywood with a rug thrown between the recliner and couch. A couple of Lucan's paintings—Griffin's brother was a damned savant when it came to painting and could remember and replicate landscapes he'd seen down to the tiniest detail—decorated the walls. The gutted kitchen only contained a counter and sink which, last time he'd used it, he'd cooked up IEDs, improvised explosive devices, instead of food.

She walked through the kitchen into the tiny bathroom, backed out and went into the last room—the bedroom. A king-sized mattress thrown onto the floor, a closet, and one window looking out onto the quad covered in nothing but a sheet.

Some castle.

After twisting off the lids to both beers he lifted one to his lips and took a swig, wishing he had something stronger.

"You lied to me." She stormed back toward him, stopping in the little kitchenette, her eyes flashing, the light in her chest flaring.

The hell he had. "I never claimed Earther chiefs were anything like vladset chiefs."

She pointed. "You knew the difference and said nothing."

"I didn't lie. Never told you I was rich. Never said anything about where I lived or who I lived with other than they were called Zeros." That was the truth. He'd been real careful not to lie.

"I don't care about that. You let me believe you were honorable."

He stepped back, reeling as if she'd hit him. That was his wife; she didn't pull punches.

"You said you led the resistance against the UN."

"Macie said that."

"You didn't contradict him."

"It's not a lie." He lifted the bottle to his lips and downed the remainder. He *had* led the rebellion. He'd led them to victory. Except he'd had no fucking plan beyond winning.

"Then why does everyone here call you traitor?"

That's what she wanted to fight about? Semantics? "You gonna drink this?" He held out the second bottle and when she declined, he lifted it to his own lips.

She must've flown across the room because before he got more than a swallow, she smacked it right out of his hand. "Answer me!"

Beer dripped down his face to soak the front of his shirt. The bottle smacked against the far wall before falling to the floor. The remaining liquid glugged out of the bottle in a pulse-like foam onto the plywood. He lifted his hand and wiped his face. "There's a shitload of things you should be mad at me about. This isn't one of them. We're poor."

"I've always been poor." She braced her hands on her hips.

"If you leave this base, those people out there will hurt you."

She stepped back. "Because of how I look?"

"Because they know you're with me. You shouldn't have come back. You shouldn't have called me your chief. Not out there."

Her features hardened. "Because you're a traitor."

"In their opinion."

"A traitor either is or isn't, there's no opinion."

"Well, here there is." He pulled off his shirt and mopped up the remaining liquid from his chest and face. He smelled like a goddamned brewery. He dismissed the mess on the floor with a brief glance. This place would never be home. Who the hell cared about a stain? He strode down the narrow hall to his bedroom, tossed the shirt into the basket in the corner and grabbed a fresh one from his closet, yanking it on. She sounded just like them. *Traitor.* He couldn't do this. Not with her. Couldn't watch her expression change and shudder as her opinion of him disintegrated.

He turned to find her blocking his exit. God, what the hell had he been thinking, bringing her here? What if she'd flared in the market? They would've killed her. What if one of those guys had shot her when she ran up instead of waiting to see who she was? What if that mob had been a fraction braver?

He could've lost her. She could've died or ended up as grievously injured as any of his Zeros.

"In your opinion, you're not a traitor? What are you then?"

"I . . . ." He threw up his hands. Great question. What was he? A human who'd lost his humanity? A husband who'd withheld information from his wife? A washed up, burnt-out soldier? Nothing good, that's what he was. "You saw Opal. What did you think of her?"

"I think you have no manners." Her gaze narrowed. "You didn't introduce me."

He scoffed. "She was out of it by the time we found her; she wouldn't have heard me. If she was having a good day, maybe, but . . . ."

"What's wrong with her?"

Lay it out. Give the truth and let her go. "Picture this. Seven years ago, this base was functional. Four thousand, two hundred acres of prime US military power. I was a Chief Master, second highest-ranking non-commissioned officer on base." He pointed out the window. "Most of those men and women were soldiers. Their families lived on the base. We were the US and we were fighting with everybody."

"The US?"

"America. Our big clan. We had troops overseas doing God-knows-what in more countries than you and I can count on our fingers and toes. Christ, we were spread thin. The world's biggest military rationed out into forty-plus countries, trying to contain the violence and keep the worst from our shores. There was so much fighting the IgA suspended our membership—we got cut off from our interplanetary allies. We were in a tough spot. Everyone was. Then Alfred Parnell, with his grand promises of a utopia, took over the UN and started collecting the governments of all our world's countries like he was picking up jacks off the sidewalk. Easy pickings. All the governments were fucking desperate. Even ours."

He leaned back against the wall. Tired. Sick over everything that had happened. "So here the Air Force was, thinking, 'Yeah, this Parnell guy is bad news, but he's picking up the shit.' We figured we'd have to keep an eye on him, but he seemed less of a threat than all the fighting, right? As governments collapsed, our troops overseas started helping the UN to smooth the transition.

"Meanwhile, here on base, we're watching it all happen, thinking maybe this is okay. Maybe the UN really is helping. Our president, not your father, he'd long since disappeared, but President Amira Zaman, started talking about strengthening our relationship with the UN. Partnering for this, partnering for that . . . and, you know, before Parnell, that would've been A-okay. Before Parnell, the UN was a mostly benign organization. Back then, shit made sense. As bad as things were, you could at least follow the goddamned story line and knew who the good guys were and who the bad guys were."

His story sounded similar to what was happening on Troon. Maman had forsaken her people for her own gain. "But you had a plan, right?" He must've. He'd stopped the Parnells.

He stared at her for so long she didn't think he'd continue. Now that she finally had him talking, she wasn't sure she *wanted* him to continue. He seemed so lost she almost went and hugged him. And she wondered, for the first time, how much of his emotional capital he'd spent on becoming a hero. . . or a traitor.

"Macie was a friend of a friend. He was a bounty hunter—hunted down soldiers who went AWOL and brought them back for courts-martial—he was a shadow. People didn't know him. So I talked him into joining the Blue Helmets as a spy. I ruined everything for him."

I'm sorry, man. For everything.

She wrapped her arms around her middle. He'd hurt Macie, that was plain in the tense lines of his face and she didn't want to know. Except he was *her* chief. Part of being a chief's wife was sharing their burden. She might not want to hear this, but he needed to say it. So she braced herself. "What do you mean?"

"Macie found a way to make war work for him. Made a fucking fortune bounty hunting. Was living the high life. Then I came along and convinced him to join the Blue Helmets in hopes he could get the lowdown on what was going on with our government."

The argument they'd had on the ship came back to her.

No one else gets to live like they were before.

You're living better than you were before.

Fuck you.

She wet her lips. "What happened to him?"

"To Macie?" He shook his head. "Don't know. He joined the Blue Helmets about the same time the UN came into power. Countries—the big clans—had ceded power."

"And your clan?"

He gave a wry laugh. "Americans are a lot like rattlesnakes. They'll lie in the sun, leaving everybody at peace until you tread too close."

"Americans?"

"My old country. My big clan. Americans used to live in the United States, back when there was one. And we were like rattlesnakes. Cold-blooded critters that laze around, soaking up the heat of the sun. Prideful creatures. Arrogant."

"Until the UN came."

He gave her a single nod. "It was all speculation and conspiracy theories at first. Parnell was meeting with President Zaman—our last Commander-in-Chief—on a regular basis. People got antsy. Didn't like the idea of change. There were protests. Riots.

Small militias popped up all over the US. People started dying. Disappearing."

He sighed. "No one knew what the fuck was going on. The whole country started tearing itself apart—the haves against the have-nots. It was like the slow burning of a fuse—we all knew the explosion was coming, we just didn't know when or how everything was going to blow. For a while, Macie reported in on a regular basis, then one day . . . nothing. We all thought . . . ." He shrugged. "*I* thought he'd turned on us. He was one of the 'haves,' after all."

No, Macie was loyal. He'd never betray Donovan. *I'm sorry, man. For everything.*

Oh, Dedia. "What did you do?"

"I left him." He closed his eyes, letting his head rest on the wall. "I did what my Commander-in-Chief told me to do—fought the guerilla militias. Killed my own countrymen trying to stop a civil war that happened anyway. State and local governments militarized their police forces, trying to protect what was theirs. Soldiers went AWOL to run home and protect their families. Our president wasn't calling our forces home from overseas . . . . What we didn't understand was they weren't *her* forces anymore. Our Commander-in-Chief was nothing more than a talking head at that point, trying to calm Americans and rally the troops behind the UN. The bitch had already sold us out. I wasn't fighting for the US, I was a hired gun for the UN; I just didn't know it."

She leaned against the doorway, folding her arms over her chest. *What happened to Macie?* No, she wasn't ready, yet. Was terrified she might not get past whatever he'd done. "What happened to Opal?"

"Opal's family lived here. We got pigeonholed onto the base. She and I were up on the roof of the BX. The building was full of military families." He scrubbed his hand over his head. "We sat there sniping enemies over our troop's heads. Suddenly, this little guy comes racing out of the fight. Ben. Eight years old. Flying straight for us, his little legs going a mile a minute, tears streaming down his face, screaming for his mama." His lips twisted and he pressed them into a straight line. "The fuckers had strapped a bomb to his chest." He shook his head. "I don't know how they nabbed him. Maybe he snuck out looking for Opal, or Delmar, his dad."

Celeka blanched. "The boy blew up in front of his mother?"

"Nah." He turned to the window. "I shot him."

Before the child could carry death to those in the building he protected. "You had no choice."

"See those two—the two guys smoking out there?"

She looked out the window. Josh sat with another man who was missing both legs. "Yes."

"Week after I shot Ben, they went out on my orders and came back like that." He pointed again, refusing to meet her gaze. "The boy there. The skinny one with scars on his face."

She closed her eyes. "Stop."

"No. You wanted to know. I'm telling you. You want to know if I'm a traitor. I felt like a traitor back then. I killed my own. I killed the people I vowed to protect, and, in the process, I hurt the men and women I commanded."

"Your Commander-in-Chief gave you orders."

"That contradicted my vows. When I took my oath to the military, I vowed to protect the Constitution of the United States of America against threats foreign *or domestic*—which essentially means protecting the people protected by that Constitution—and I failed that duty. No matter which side I stood on, I wasn't ever gonna win. Every time I gave a goddamned order, I stole life or limb or moral conscience from each of them." He pointed out the window. "They're not part of Division Command Zero now. They're not fit for that kind of duty. The Zeros are my employees. *My* responsibility. I owe them. *All of them.*"

"And Macie?"

"I left him—" His voice cracked and he turned away. "When the UN came I refused to relinquish our base. We were the first bombed. Ground Zero."

The Zeros. Now she understood where the name came from.

"C-fucking-M.D. Controlled Munitions Destruction. That's what the press called the bombing of our bases. I was wearing my body armor but had taken off my helmet."

His scars. She closed her eyes. He'd never told her how he'd gotten them.

"There were bodies . . . everywhere. Seemed like everyone I tried to help died as soon as I arrived. Then I . . . I woke up in a make-shift infirmary. Two days later, they brought Macie in. He was . . . not good. The Blue Helmets had tortured him for months. There wasn't much left of him. I didn't think he'd survive. All I could think was *I left him.* I assumed the worst and I didn't check. I just left him."

He sniffed and dragged his sleeve over his face. When he turned to face her, his eyes were red.

"So, when I heard that Chief Payne tried taking on the Parnells on his own, while I was lying on a cot healing from this"—he jerked his finger toward his face—"I thought: *I can help.* I can make things better. Return everything to the way it was when I was a kid."

He's not done punishing himself. Obviously, Macie didn't hold any of this against him. Nor did the Zeros. The only one who wouldn't forgive him, was him.

Dedia, this wasn't good for him. He didn't deserve any of this. Best she could tell he'd done everything he could and still blamed himself for not doing enough.

"You did. The Parnells are no longer in charge."

He'd freed all the humans exiled on Asteria. He'd gotten his people out from under the Parnells' thumbs.

"See, that's what I wanted. I thought, if we stage a coup, if we got rid of the sons-a-bitches who turned our world upside-down, everything would go to rights again." He shook his head. "But it didn't. The Parnells are gone. And now we're dealing with this anarcho-capitalist pseudo-government bullshit. The Parnells are gone, but their beliefs about the undesirables lingers. They're gone, and it's no better. The people on the other side of that wall, they call me a traitor because they blame me for the UN's fall.

"They *wanted* what the Parnells provided. The false stability of their fucked-up utopia. They didn't care if exiling half the population wasn't right. That segregating what they determined as undesirables to Asteria was unethical. They didn't care if the system was corrupt. They wanted their comfortable fucking lives. They wanted to lie in the goddamned sun."

There was her answer. That's why he wouldn't help her overthrow Maman. He feared her people were the same. What if they were? What if she did everything in her power to help them only to find out they didn't want help?

"So, yeah. Here, on this planet, I'm a traitor. Here, Chief Payne is considered a terrorist. Here, if you get caught with us, you could be beaten, raped, or killed just for being with us."

This was what she still didn't understand: He risked what he had with her for another chance at punishing himself. "And knowing that, you brought me here?"

His mouth opened. Closed. He held his arms out to the side. "I knew you being here would be bad, but I didn't realize how bad. I thought we could handle it, but . . . ."

He didn't get it. He should've explained all this sooner. "You let me walk through town unprepared!"

"Away from us. If you hadn't come back, if you had followed my directions, you'd have been inside the walls, safe, before any of them figured it out."

She stared at him for several heartbeats. It was his fault she'd been ignorant. She shook her head. This place was poison. He was different here and not in a good way. "We should return to Asteria."

He pointed at the floor. "This is home. I won't fight for them anymore, but I promised Division Command I'd provide support services until they got a new leader in power. Someone who could rein-in the corporations and secure peace again—at least here in the States. The Zeros and me, we make sure they have what they need. Pay the rent. Macie and I can keep our crew running cargo and bounty hunting for years yet."

"Years? How long do you expect them to take?"

His lips pressed together.

A long time, then. Must be. It had been three years since the rebellion. "Do they have a candidate?"

"They have to make sure whoever they choose is committed to bringing back a democracy."

"It's been three years."

"It takes time."

Did he even hear himself? Macie was right, he was punishing himself. That was more important to him than anything else. "Even the vladsets know better than to fight a war they can't win. Asteria would be a better hom—"

"Asteria isn't safe. It's too close to Troon. We'd always be looking over our shoulders."

"Then we fight Maman!"

He snorted. "I'm not staging another coup."

"But—"

"You've seen what it's like here. You want this for Troon? You want your people to suffer? To live with the knowledge you fucked up what the majority wanted because *you* didn't like it?" He paced away and then came back. "There is nothing, *nothing* that would make me *ever* step foot on that fucking planet again. I'll not be coerced into another fight. If the vladsets want to be free, they'd better step up their game and take Vessa out themselves."

She stepped closer and glared. "I'm not staying here." She needed him to see reason. Find a way to take away his hurt but that wouldn't happen here. "I refuse to live where you're dishonored. I refuse to live here where you can hide from life and punish yourself, and—"

"Is that what you think?" He motioned outside. "I have responsibilities here."

"You're running away. Hiding."

"Excuse me?"

"You pitied me when you thought I was ugly. Worried over hurting my feelings." She tilted her face up, staring him down. "Until you realized I wasn't ugly. Then you ran away."

"I explained. I thought you were fucking with me. Trying to trick me."

"No, you ran away because you were scared." She poked her finger into his chest. "You were scared I wouldn't want you anymore when I realized I'm not ugly. Our marriage was okay when *you* were the prize."

His jaw flexed. He swallowed. "And now I'm not. Is that it?" He pushed past her, stormed into the living room, but she wasn't letting up.

"This is the problem." She paced him. Shouted her truths. "You don't dare live anywhere where you might enjoy life. You place all your value on how much others need you and, in the process, do a disservice to both yourself and everyone else. You make your flame small. You allow others to determine your worth on your appearance or how much you can do for them."

He snorted. "Pretty speech from a woman raised by vladsets. What do you do with *your* Zeros? Burn them alive?" He threw open the door and escaped to the outside.

She gasped and dashed outside. "Vladsets honor those who fought to the point of permanent injury and they honor their old for the valuable contributions they've made to our society. When their flames grow small they walk out onto the ice fields and die with pride."

Several curious gazes watched her. Her voice faded.

Donovan lowered his voice. "So what? All us poor injured humans have small flames?"

You have to do what's best for you. She had to make him see reason.

"The only person here with a small flame is you." She poked him. "I think your Zeros are like Macie. They stay because they don't want to leave you alone, because they feel they owe you." *Your opinion matters and should be voiced.* "And in turn, you give them value only based on what they can do for your cause.

"That's what you said, right? They're not fit for duty so you hired them. As if you're doing them a favor. They have value on their own, not because you gave it back to them. This is all for you. For your sense of guilt. You're the only one who's given up. A strong chief does what's best for his clan even if it scares him. A strong chief would take his clan somewhere they're wanted. Where they can belong and thrive. But not you." She poked him again. "Because you gave up. *You* should go walk out into the ice fields." She glanced around at the hot red dirt. "Or desert. Whatever this barren place is. You're as bad as the Parnells, trying to force the world into the way you want it to be."

His mouth opened. Closed. Something awful passed over his face and he turned away.

She'd gone too far. "My chief . . . ."

Macie pulled her back. "Let him be."

Donovan climbed down the wooden steps, pushed into the side of a crater, his shoulders stiff and unyielding. She hadn't noticed the crater before, not from the other side of the trailer. The sunken area was massive and filled with rows of small, orderly, makeshift dwellings surrounding a one-story building. That must be Command Division Zero.

"I didn't . . . ." She shook her head. "I don't want him to go out there to die."

The low rumble of Macie's laughter made her bristle. She pushed him.

"Relax. He's going for a walk to think things over. He'll be calmer when he comes back."

"You're sure?"

He nodded. "You'll win this fight, Sorcha. Maybe not today, but eventually, you'll win."

Macie sounded confident. "How do you know?"

"Because you're right. I've told him the same things for years."

She glanced at the trailer. "You heard?"

"Thin walls. You were both yelling."

Mortified, she looked around the camp, finding several humans staring back. Some turned away, others nodded or winked. "They must think I'm awful."

"Nah." He leaned against the trailer. "Remember I told you Donovan and I had plans?"

"You said he wasn't done punishing himself."

"Yeah." He sighed. "We're liaisons between Command Division Zero and the IgA; we can operate from anywhere. We can assign the Zeros jobs from anywhere. Everyone seems to realize that but Reese. He's stubborn as hell."

"He feels guilty."

"Which makes everyone else feel like shit, too." He stomped the heel of his boot into the dirt a few times, making a divot. "I'm proud of you. You gave him hell in there."

"I don't know what's wrong with me. It's the strangest thing. I keep hearing Donovan's voice in my head telling me I'm beautiful and strong and intelligent. Telling me my opinions matter and should be voiced. I don't know why I keep hearing him, but it made me braver than I otherwise might be." Maybe that wasn't such a good thing.

Macie's gaze narrowed. "You heard all that in Reese's voice?"

"His voice." She frowned. "In English."

He laughed, but it was a rueful sound. "Son of a bitch."

"What?"

He shook his head. "Just remembered something I need to talk to Reese about, is all." He looked up. "You really leaving him?"

What? "We're married."

"He was almost married once before. Beautiful gal named Leanne. After he was injured, she had her father break the engagement. She couldn't look at Reese because of his injuries."

She closed her eyes. "That's why . . . ." *Our marriage was okay when you were the prize."*

His jaw flexed. "And now I'm not. Is that it?" Dedia, she could still see his expression. That's when he gave up on their argument and walked away. "I accused him of only wanting me when he thought I was worse off than him."

Macie's lips twitched. "Oh, from what I heard you were much harsher."

She groaned. "I never should've—"

"Yeah." He pulled her hand from her face. "You should've. He might listen to you." His gaze shot over her shoulder. He tipped his chin up. "He's back."

She whirled and would've run to Donovan to apologize, but someone stopped him. "Chief Reese, Commander Sak would like to speak to you immediately."

Donovan's gaze caught hers and tangled for a heartbeat before he nodded to the soldier and walked back the other direction.

"Hey, Jones." Macie waved the soldier over. "What's that about?"

Jones shrugged. "Dunno. Rumor is the IgA wants something Reese has. The whole command has gathered."

Macie cursed.

"What do they want?" Celeka asked.

"You." Macie dragged his hand over his face. "Come on." They followed Donovan at a quick clip. "Your maman sent your body armor to the IgA and named you as Blaze."

Dedia, help them.

"Reese told me when we landed."

"He'll have to hand me over. He's retired, he has no power here."

Macie snorted. "Don't listen to Reese. What he said was true; he's not in charge here. He's not even a part of DCZ. Still, some would argue he has more power than anyone else."

She stopped. "He said he's a contractor, a tradesman."

Macie grinned, tugging her into motion. "Yeah, but this place is like East Berlin."

"What's that?"

"It means DCZ is totally cut off from the rest of the planet. The civilians outside our walls won't trade or work with them. The IgA won't even take them seriously. Donovan came up with the work-around by creating the Zeros and allying with the IgA. Now we control the food, the money, and the ships. DCZ is fucked if they piss him off."

It seemed Donovan had lied to her again.

29

Word of their return must've spread like wild fire within DCZ.

Donovan strode into the command center. Inside, makeshift workstations were positioned around a square, glass-walled, soundproof structure they called the fishbowl, where the top brass was gathered.

At least twenty uniformed men and women were waiting for him. This didn't look good. Even though he wasn't technically part of DCZ, they usually invited him to their pow-wows, considering his team made sure they had the weapons and ships needed for their campaigns.

DCZ was led by Commander Sak, who oversaw two Division Chief Masters, three Division Chiefs, nine Brigade Master Sergeants, twenty-seven Brigade Sergeants, and fifty-four Regiment Captains—they were all a mix-match of what was left of the various military branches.

Commander Sak sat at a table at the front of the room, and the rest sat in chairs facing her. He turned the outside corner of the fishbowl, pulled open the door and entered. Someone coming in behind him caught the door, probably the grunt who'd come to fetch him.

Everyone stood, saluted.

Donovan cursed under his breath. Saluted back. He hated this shit. "As you were."

Commander Sak motioned to an isolated chair sitting in the middle of the floor between her and the rest of the brass. "Take a seat, Chief Reese."

Hell, no. "I'll stand." He folded his arms over his chest. Catching movement in his peripheral vision, he turned. Macie was leading

Sorcha toward the back of the room. All he needed was for her to watch him get a dressing down. "Hey."

They froze. Turned.

Donovan scowled. "Out."

Macie let go of her hand and walked back to Donovan, leaning close and lowering his voice. "Jones says you have something they want. I think the IgA contacted DCZ. If so, she's safer with us, in here. Someone might try to grab her out there."

Shit. He thought they'd have more time. He gave Macie a single nod. Gave Sorcha what he hoped was a reassuring wink.

Macie led her to the back of the room where they stood behind the seated group. Her shoulders were slumped.

When he turned back to Commander Sak, rage churned his stomach. "Why am I here? And before you answer, I'll remind you I'm not enlisted and therefore you have no right to bring me to a Courts-martial or Non-Judicial Punishment . . . or whatever this is."

Commander Sak cleared her throat, her dark eyes penetrating. "The IgA has informed us you brought a mark into our Corps, instead of delivering her to the IgA. An exotic, no less."

His gaze narrowed. "Again, IgA marks as well as any bounty contracts fall under my purview, not yours. You have no right to intervene."

Sak's lips pressed together. "Watch your tone, Chief. What does fall under my purview, is the safety of our Corps and one man, no matter how respected, will not endanger them while I'm in charge. The IgA has contacted us with concerns you're compromised."

"I'm not."

Sak stood. "Chief Reese, despite the honor and respect we have for—"

Oh, he'd had about enough of their bullshit. If they wanted to play those cards, he'd throw them right back in their face. "You wouldn't have a division to command if not for me. You'd be hiding." His gaze swept the room. "All of you. Hunted down one-by-one as the UN tracked your chips." He may have fucked up as far as the rest of the world was concerned, but he'd done good by these soldiers.

A murmur went through the group.

"That doesn't mean we'll stand by while you destroy our alliance with the IgA. Without their support, we're dead in the water."

"Without me you have no alliance." His friendship with Salcedo was his ace in the hole.

A bitter smile briefly lifted her lips. "Yes, since you've never allowed anyone but yourself to contact them directly."

His contacts were the only bargaining chip he had. Many a time he'd worried if he or Macie had stepped a toe out of line, DCZ would hand them over to the civilians outside their walls and allow them to be tried for treason. Macie said he was paranoid, but his psychosis was saving their ass right now. "You're welcome to start at the beginning, bowing and scraping and going through the years of vetting it'll take for the IgA Council to allow another Earther close."

"We're getting off track, Chief. We shouldn't strain our alliance. If I understand correctly, the IgA only wants the woman for questioning, nothing more. I see no reason why you'd refuse to comply unless you're hiding something."

Donovan went cold. "Sounds to me as though you've tried and convicted me already. I'm disappointed in how fickle DCZ's loyalty is. You should hope I don't become as fickle, considering you've yet to put forth a candidate to put into power. You touch my wife and I will no longer run cargo or bounty hunt for you, but at the end of the day, I'll retain my status at the IgA. You can count on that."

A hush fell over the room.

That's right, asshole. I know how to play this game.

Sak leaned forward, her silver-streaked black curly hair clipped close to her scalp, and gave him a warm smile. "Chief Reese, I'm simply briefing you on the IgA's accusations. I'm giving you the benefit of the doubt. I've allowed you to come here of your free will and want to hear your side of the story. I'm sure we can work together to find a solution agreeable to us all."

That's right, back the hell off.

"I want you to speak freely. Only those with the highest security clearance are in this room. Why didn't you turn her over to the IgA?"

"I believe the IgA is compromised."

Conversation erupted throughout the room.

Sak pounded her hand on the table. "I will have order." Once the room quieted, she scowled at Donovan. "That's quite the accusation. Explain."

Donovan relayed the facts of what had happened since they'd followed Williams to Troon.

Sak snorted. "You believe, because Prax ordered you to kiss your wife, he's on the vladsets' side?"

"He ordered my wife to soul-merge me, which, with the way the queen runs things, is equivalent to a demand to execute me. Remember President Hobbs? The queen captured the ship and soul-merged our president."

"Now you're going too far. You can't make that kind of accusation, even against an un-allied planet, without proof."

He nodded to Sorcha. "My wife is proof. She's the daughter of the vladset queen and President Hobbs. DNA testing will prove my claim." He hoped.

"Prax has been on the IgA Council for the last ten years. He wasn't part of the IgA during Hobbs' time."

"I'm not saying he was party to that. But now Prax is the liaison to the vladsets. He visits Troon and Erra twice a year to ensure the vladsets are abiding by IgA sanctions, which they obviously are not. I couldn't figure out why he wanted the union until the vladsets tried to blackmail my wife into killing me and Macie.

"I believe Vessa ordered the soul-merge with the intent Sorcha would treat me as an enemy and kill me. When that failed, someone from the IgA had our ship blown up. As of now, the sheriff on Asteria believes the IgA is behind it. We found one of their coms on site.

"I don't know how or why the IgA got involved, but someone has been feeding Vessa the names on those contracts so she could have them killed before I got to them. Prax is the only connection between Troon and the IgA. I believe Prax and the queen are trying to encourage a war."

Sak sat back. "And CorTech is involved?"

Donovan nodded. "We followed Williams to Troon—he was in a CorTech ship. When we went to Asteria, the vladsets were in that ship. They dropped three CorTech bodies outside town. I think they had a deal that went sour—something to do with the resource the IgA wants information on—and I intend to find out what it was. All the contracts I've signed related to the resource are for ex-CorTech employees. It's all connected."

Sak raised a single brow. "And your wife's bounty?"

"My wife is innocent and I plan to prove it. Her mother had her convinced she was fulfilling IgA contracts by killing those marks. Prax, if he's the one feeding the queen the names of our contracts, knows she's innocent. If we turn her in, Prax will probably have her killed to ensure her silence to protect Vessa."

All eyes turned toward Sorcha. "Mrs. Reese, do you have information that could aid the IgA?"

She shook her head. "I've told my Chief everything I know."

"Mrs. Ree—"

Donovan moved to block Sak's view of his wife. "DCZ has no right to question civilians." The reminder was growled more than spoken and she stared back at him through incredulous eyes. "She's not a criminal to be interrogated."

Sak folded her hands on the table. "How will you prove your theories?"

"I'll go to CorTech tonight and get the information we need."

Her lips thinned. "Before you left, you questioned them and didn't find anything."

As soon as he and Macie got the contracts they'd gone to CorTech to look for evidence and hadn't found any. However, they'd asked. This time, they would go in and take. "I was polite last time."

"You ransacked the place. They're still complaining of the inconvenience."

Donovan shrugged. "As I said, I was polite. This time, I won't be."

Sak stared at him without speaking for several heartbeats. He needed every ounce of control not to squirm.

"Your actions put me in a difficult situation. On the one hand, you brought a mark here without permission. You broke Interstellar laws, stole a ship which resulted in a warrant issued for you on Asteria, and have showed disrespect to your superior." As she ticked off each grievance, he counted minimum sentences for breaking each ordinance. Yeah, if he was still military he could spend the rest of his life in the brig. "I'm not part of your Corps." The worst she could do was fire his ass.

Sak tipped her face to the side, raising a brow as if to say, "You see, you just did it again."

He cleared his throat. "No disrespect intended."

She nodded. "On the other hand, your record speaks for itself. You are an asset to the Corp."

His gaze shifted away and he forced it back. "If you lock me up and send my wife to the IgA, you'll be in a worse position than you're in now." She'd lose the income from the Zeros and keeping this place running wasn't cheap. She'd lose his contacts, too, which provided the base with everything they needed.

"Yes, and if it turns out you are not being entirely truthful, or your wife has withheld pertinent information, we stand to lose all of that *plus* any chance at future positive interaction with the IgA."

Fuck.

Sak gave him a tight-lipped smile. "This is what I propose. I'll give you twelve hours to prove your theory. Twelve. No more."

He gave a single nod as his heart hammered in his chest. How the hell was he gonna pull that off?

"I'll also lend you manpower for your . . . questioning at CorTech. You'll want to talk to Larkin Astor."

The CEO? He lifted a brow in question. "He's here?"

"He works nights, mostly. When you visit CorTech, question him, get your answers, and do what you need to do to ensure they back off trying to kick us off our land." She was using him. If he failed to prove his theories, she could deny any participation and hang him out to dry.

"Volunteers only." He swept his gaze over the twenty brass in the room. "No one gets ordered to follow me." He refused to fight at someone else's command, he'd be damned if he allowed anyone to fight with him at someone else's command.

"How many?" Sak asked.

He shrugged. He couldn't imagine many who would want to go on this little suicide trip. CorTech would fight to the death to protect their assets. If this mission failed, they might find themselves convicted of treason right along with him. "I don't expect our visit to be as easy as last time. They'll be ready for us. I'll take whoever wants to go."

Sak nodded. "I'll have a crew waiting at the back gate at oh-four-hundred. CorTech should still be on a skeleton crew."

"Thank you." He motioned to Macie and headed for the door, holding it open until he and Sorcha came through. "What the hell just happened?"

"You won." Sorcha nodded. "My Chief is fierce."

Macie chuckled. "You did good."

"You realize we'll probably be raiding CorTech with half a dozen adrenaline junkies, right?"

"You have no faith, Reese. Quit worrying."

"If we get at least twenty volunteers, I'll be amazed."

"Count me among your numbers."

She planned to stay? "Absolutely not."

She shrugged. "I'll either walk into battle by your side or I'll follow behind with you unaware, but I will fight with you."

He shook his head. "You can't flare around humans; you'll freak them out. Hell, the troops on our side might decide to shoot you."

"I won't flare." She propped her hands on her hips. "I'm combat trained. I can shoot a target from two-hundred paces."

Macie chuckled. "Quit being a control freak. At least you'll know where she's at and what she's up to."

Christ. "Full body armor for everyone—"

"Enough. I'll sort everything." Macie slapped him on the back. "Go get some rest. I'll meet you at your place at quarter to four." Macie veered away, heading for a group of Zeros and stopped. "Reese."

Macie was staring at an electronic board attached to the side of the infirmary building that listed their current contracts. He walked over, studying the faces. Each picture had a list of stats next to them along with the amount of the bounty. "What're we looking at?"

"Look familiar?" Macie tipped his chin up.

Again, Donovan scanned the faces, coming to rest at the one on the top. Bradley Weston. A heavy-set blond male with blue eyes and a thick beard. "He owned WestCorp, didn't he? I thought he died in the war."

"Look again. The eyes."

They were blue. Crinkled at the corners.

Sorcha came up next to him, and gasped. "Grady."

He looked at her and then back at the picture. Shit. "Maybe." He didn't sport a beard anymore and he must've lost weight. His glasses usually distorted his eyes, but . . . he'd taken them off several times.

"He's getting sloppy. I've never seen him take his glasses off before this trip."

"I'm thinking our Sorcha captured his fancy. He kept trying to get a better look at her."

Macie nodded. "How much you want to bet the reason he moves so slow and is such a klutz is because he doesn't need those damn glasses." He let out a low whistle. "Three-point-five million for live capture."

Sorcha came around to stand in front of them, hands braced on her hips. "No. I don't care how much that contract is worth. I promised Grady we'd go back and help him once we sorted out our own lives and I meant it."

He shared a look with Macie. "He's clan, right? We take care of clan. Better let the Zeros know he's off-limits." He jerked his head to the side. "Come on, Sorcha, we'd better get our lives sorted."

— • —

30

Donovan was subdued as he walked her toward their home. He held the door open for her and let it fall shut behind them. He searched her gaze. "I, uh, I'm sorry for earlier."

"You. Yelled. At. Me." She poked his chest with her finger with each word. "In front of your clan." At his raised brow, she motioned to the walls. "They heard *everything*."

He wandered over to his worn couch and sat. "I did yell. I was angrier at myself than you, thinking I could hide all this from you." He motioned to the walls around them. "This isn't exactly a palace."

"I don't care if we're poor or how small our abode is. I care that these people treat you badly. I want to be where we have friends—a true clan. The Zeros deserve the same, don't they?"

He nodded.

"What are we doing here? This place is dead. There's nothing here for us."

"You don't understand. This is my home. I was born here. Grew up here. I thought I could make everything how it was before."

"Should I pine for Troon?" She stood in front of him and propped her hand on her hip. "I was born there. I should go back and make my planet the way I want it to be?"

He pulled her into his lap with a growl. "No more talk of leaving me. Your home is where I am."

"And yours is where I am." She pressed her forehead to his.

"I can't abandon DCZ."

She smiled. "You are a contractor. Macie says that means you can work from anywhere."

He sighed. Nodded. "Not yet, though."

"No." She slid her thumb over his bottom lip. "First we'll punish CorTech and clear our names. We'll level them."

"Bloodthirsty much?" Donovan chuckled. "How 'bout we take their power, get our proof, and walk away?"

"Devious. We will force them to live in shame." She nodded. "Very well. You're wrong about Maman, though." She shrugged.

"How so?"

"Maman hates humans almost as much as the IgA. I find it difficult to see her associated with any human, but the IgA? She'd kill herself before entangling with them beyond what's required by the people of Troon. She never even accompanied Prax when he inspected Erra. I think maybe you're wrong about him, too. I led his tours of the prisons. He always acted honorably. Kind."

"With the right motivators, anyone can be compromised."

He brushed his thumb over her lips and all she wanted to do was kiss him. But this was important. She needed him to understand. She needed his help. "What would it take to compromise *you*?"

His brow lifted.

"Maman is part of our clan whether we like it or not. She's our responsibility. *We* should deal with her treachery. Giving the duty to someone else is . . . wrong."

"Does your maman find traitors herself? Does she go into the prison and punish those in the cells?"

"Never."

He stared. Waiting.

Arrogant male. "I'm not Maman."

A small smile curved his lips and he touched the corner of her mouth. "I didn't mean you should be like her. Those in authority delegate. As princess of Troon, it's not your place to bring your maman to justice. It's your place to delegate the duty."

She stared. Waiting.

"Fine. You delegate to me and I'll delegate to those who are better equipped to deal with her."

He had no problem with marching into CorTech with the Zeros and raiding the place, but not Troon? She didn't understand him.

"I already have one world that would love nothing more than to try to kill me as a traitor. I'm not going to Troon. Once we figure out who we can trust at the IgA, I'll see if they can intercede on behalf of the people with Vessa and get your sister back."

"Vladsets are not as fickle as humans. Killing Maman wouldn't leave them without a government."

"If I understand correctly, whoever kills Vessa becomes ruler of Troon. So if a vladset kills your maman, the people would follow her."

It was unlikely Maman would allow herself to be in a position where she could be challenged, but . . . . "Yes."

"If the IgA kills your maman, they might follow the IgA, because they want the sanctions lifted."

Her brows furrowed. She didn't like the idea of the IgA ruling Troon. "Maybe."

"If I kill her . . . a human chief . . . what happens?"

She closed her eyes. He was right. They would never follow a human male. The royal line would appear weak. All the chiefs would thrust their females forward to fight for the honor of ruling the clans. "But if we could get to Mujara—"

"God, you're stubborn. We can't get anywhere near Mujara without killing Vessa. That's why she keeps her locked under the palace. Eventually, someone will champion your sister. I'm shocked it hasn't happened already." He scrubbed his hand over his face. "The only hope Mujara has is the IgA. The best I can do is to prove Prax a traitor, uncover whatever deal your maman has with CorTech and let the IgA loose with the information."

She nodded. He wasn't heartless. Hadn't abandoned her concerns. He was doing what he could and unlike a blooded vladset warrior, he'd thought out his plan instead of rushing head-long into battle. His plan might work. She threw her arms around his neck. "Thank you."

He held her close, brushing his lips over her temple. "Do you still hate me?"

Is that what he thought? "I don't . . . I could never *hate* you."

His shoulder lifted and he couldn't quite seem to meet her gaze. "You did a damn good imitation."

"I was angry because you lied to me. You didn't trust me to understand or to fight for you." She shook her head. "Allowed me to carry wrong impressions. I'm still not sure I understand."

"What?"

"You said you have no power here, but when you stood before Commander Sak, you wielded all the power."

"I'm not a chief anymore. I'm not a soldier. I'm not rich. Macie and I put most all our earnings back into our business. It'll be another year or two before we start seeing true profits."

"And yet, without your business, without you and Macie, they can't function."

"Sak would've figured out a way."

"You threatened her with sanctions, and they bowed to your will."

He chuckled. "I wasn't so sure that would happen. Sak could've told me to fuck off and used you as leverage for future access to the IgA." He shook his head. "To be honest, I'm not so certain she wasn't talking through her ass with every intention of fucking us over tonight."

So their position wasn't secure. "You don't trust Sak?"

"Her job is to do whatever is in the best interest of the DCZ."

"Perhaps you are in their best interest. Should any of them be wounded to the point they can't battle, where will they go?"

"They'd come work for me. Become part of *my* Zeros."

"Exactly." She nodded. "They need you. They'll follow you wherever you lead from. No matter if it's here, Troon, Asteria, or somewhere else."

She pressed her hands to his chest and spread her fingers wide. His heart thumped steady under her palm. "I knew you were a strong chief. You'd only forgotten."

The corner of his lips curved. "What the hell did I do before you came along to boss me around?"

"You floundered, as did I. Now, we burn brighter together." She peeked up at him through her lashes. "But not here, right?"

"No." His lips spread into a grin. He hauled her against his chest and rubbed her back. "How does Asteria sound?"

"Perfect, my Chi—" She grinned ruefully. Now she understood why he didn't like her calling him chief. "Donovan."

"I don't mind anymore."

"No?" Good, because he embodied the title.

He shook his head. "The way you say *my* Chief, it sounds like you're claiming me. I like that."

"To the vladsets, a chief is a strong leader, a powerful male." Her smile widened. "But despite a chief's superior strength, the woman, the wife, is the one who claims a chief for her own." She stroked her hands over his shoulders, down his chest. Now that he'd seen the wisdom of her argument, perhaps he was done hiding his feelings from her.

"Ah, so the woman gets all the control."

Mm. She liked the sound of that. Of having her chief bend to her will. She got to her feet. "Take off your clothes."

His head tipped to the side, but otherwise he didn't move. "I should prep for the raid."

"You'll trust Macie to do that and stay with me." She let her fingers trail down the buttons of her blouse. Plucked the top one free. The second one. Stopped and fingered the third. "*Now*, my Chief."

He stood, his gaze never leaving hers and stripped with quick, efficient motions. Even in disrobing, there was something predatory about him. Something a little untamed that only obeyed because he wanted to. Once naked, he sat on the sofa, taking up all the space, waiting, goading.

She took her time undressing, letting her gaze stroke over each slab and bulge of muscle until it lingered on his arousal.

They'd fought and now they'd make up. He'd finally opened himself to her. Allowed her into his past, his home. When they mated this time, he'd let himself go. Let her take care of him. She grinned.

He spread his hands wide. "I'm at your mercy, little flame. What's your command?"

Her breath caught and her heart pounded a rapid tempo. She had all that sexy masculinity at her mercy, willing to obey her command, and she had no idea what to demand. What if she asked for something silly? What if she misspoke? What if he didn't like what she thought he might like? Her tummy flopped. She bit her lip.

"Know what I think?"

She shook her head.

"I think you like when I'm in charge. You like not having to think while I feed you pleasure."

Moisture gathered between her legs.

"Give me the command and I'll take care of everything."

What command? She reviewed the conversation in her mind.

"Tell me to take over. Tell me to pleasure you. I'll make sure we're both satisfied."

"Yes." The one word came out on a husky sigh. "Take control, my Chief."

The slow smile curving his lips was almost cruel. He hitched his finger at her.

Her gaze snagged on the thick erection straining up from his lap, the heavy weight of his balls between his spread thighs.

"Kneel over me."

Her gaze jerked up. With his legs spread . . . A flash of heat flared through her, tightening her nipples. She knelt over his lap, the position keeping her spread wide above him, the kiss of cool air on her damp folds making her shiver. She tried to edge forward, to snuggle over his hips.

"Uh-uh."

Celeka froze. Waiting. Her chief's gaze stroked over her from the crown of her head to her knees. "You're so sexy." He skimmed his hand down her arm. Over her breast. Up the inside of her thigh. His fingers ghosted over her pussy. "Should I spank you? I know you like that."

"Yes."

"Nah." A wicked grin twisted his lips. "I think I'll make my proud warrior princess beg."

A shock wracked her. Beg? "I commanded you to give us pleasure."

"Mm-hm." His fingers slipped inside her.

Her breath caught and she swayed. Wanted nothing more than to lean into his strength. He pumped in and out of her slick channel, twisting his fingers to hit every sensitive spot she had. Her hips twitched, trying to force a quicker pace, a deeper penetration, but with her knees spread so wide, she had no leverage.

Donovan chuckled. "You'll disappoint me if you move." He pulled his fingers from her, right up to his mouth. His eyes closed and he hummed low in his chest.

A shiver coursed through her. Her inner muscles clenched. Liquid heat flooded her pussy. Dedia, she loved him. He always knew exactly how to give her pleasure. How to comfort her. How to make her feel cared for.

She only wished he'd allow her to do the same for him. Her gaze dropped to his cock. A bead of clear liquid broke from the seam, trailing down his length. She reached for him.

He lightly slapped her hand away. "Did you want something?"
I'll make you beg.

"No." He couldn't truly make her beg. This was another game—like how he let her fear spankings only to discover the light smacks were delicious. She'd make him work for his prize. Maybe even make him lose a little of his control. Make him open himself to her.

He slipped his fingers back into her, rotating his hand, watching his fingers disappear into her through heavy-lidded eyes. Chills coursed over her skin, lifting gooseflesh. Tightening her nipples to sensitive points. Of their own accord, her hips began rocking in a narrow rhythm, her thighs straining. She wanted him to meet her gaze. To be here with her. "Donovan."

"Yes?"

Part of her still feared issuing that particular demand. What if he didn't want to look at her? She clamped her mouth shut.

I'm beautiful and comfortable in my own skin.

He found her attractive. Her thighs trembled. Release was close. Her inner muscles tightened. She closed her eyes, letting her head fall back. *Oh, Dedia . ..*

He withdrew his fingers.

The tension receded, leaving an empty ache in the pit of her stomach. Her eyes flew open.

"Want something?" He licked over her nipple. Blew his warm breath over the tight peak.

Dedia, he was doing everything right. Making her burn, but still holding back himself.

The tension wound low in her belly. She tangled her fingers in his hair, drawing him closer. He suckled her. Sharp arrows of need flew through her body, straight to her pussy. Just when she didn't think she could stand anymore, he shifted to the other side. Took the bud between his teeth and battered it with his tongue. She leaned forward, pressing her hips to his chest.

"Uh-uh." He nipped her.

She hissed in a sharp breath.

"Are you close?"

"No." She stared right into his eyes and lied. He was holding back from her. She was sure of it. He wasn't anywhere near losing control.

He grinned. "Let's see." His blunt fingers prodded her entrance. Slipped deep inside. Just a little friction would send her over the edge. His thumb stroked over her clit. Circling round and round.

Her rapid breaths peppered his hair, her nails scraping his scalp. Her inner muscles tightened, gripping him until his fingers filled her completely. Her lips parted as the first pulses of orgasm quivered toward realization. She jerked her hips and . . . .

"Not yet."

The noise escaping her sounded almost animalistic.

He chuckled. His palm flattened against her pussy. "You're so damn wet." He pressed, rubbing her. "I bet if I were to slap you . . . ." He pulled his hand away as if to follow through with his threat.

"Yes. Yes. Yes." She couldn't stop the chant. She wanted the sharp sting that would send her over. She waited. Panting. Needing. Instead of a slap, his damp fingers tickled her inner thigh where her muscles shook.

"You're tiring."

"I gave you a command."

"Mm." He lapped the underside of her breast.

She was shivering. Panting. Desperate for release. And he was . . . not. She wanted him there with her. "The wife's responsibility . . ." He sucked her nipple into his mouth. *Ah, Dedia, yes.* She wet her lips. Drew in a shaky breath. " . . . is to care for her Chief." He ran his teeth over her nipple and she gasped. "Sometimes that means reminding him who he is and who he is not. For instance, you have big hands." She drew his hands to her breasts, pressing into his palms. "You can build with your hands or destroy with them." He slid his thumbs over her nipples, making her breath hitch. "But you only have two."

His fingers stopped their movement. His open mouth froze against her throat.

Sorcha sent up a quick prayer to Dedia for strength. One way or another, her chief would open himself to her.

He hadn't been listening, not well enough apparently, because he couldn't have heard correctly. His little wife had his attention now.

"And you have the shoulders of a warrior; broad and strong. You could carry the wounded or allow me to lean against you."

"But I only have two?" Where the hell was she going with this?

She grinned. "But you can't do both at the same time."

What the hell was going on? He thought they'd finished their argument. "Enough."

"And you have a strong, steady heart. So strong you could run forever." She ran her thumb over his lips. "Or you could love me." She rested her forehead against his. "But I fear, you cannot continue to do both."

"I'm not running anywhere." He tried to get up, done with . . . whatever the fuck this had turned into, but her hand on his chest stopped him. The light in her chest shone bright and her palm was hot. Unnaturally so. A tendril of alarm shot through him. "What are you doing?"

"Exercising my rights as your wife. You'll listen. You'll allow me to care for you." She fisted his cock, stroking him. "I think you listen better when I have your full attention."

"You have it." He tried to lay her back onto the couch.

"No." She pushed him back, settling into his lap. "You always take control."

"You like that about me."

She grinned. "I do."

What was this? She didn't sound angry. And yet, he had no idea what had gotten into her. "Then let me—"

"No." She let her hand warm against his skin.

Maybe she wasn't angry, but she was clearly threatening him. "What are you up to?"

She kissed his cheek. "I think you like control too much. Like an addict." She ran her tongue along his jaw, pumping his cock in her hand.

And Christ, he was hard and aching despite the fact that she was starting to piss him off.

"Your drug of choice keeps you from letting go and truly mating with me."

What did she want? He'd told her he loved her. "You're not making any—"

She pressed him to her entrance and sank down, enveloping him in her body and making his thoughts scatter. "God, you feel good."

She rode him, trailing her lips over his cheek. He bracketed her hips with his hands, and every time he tried to force her to a faster pace, she nipped him. "Tell me what this feels like for you."

"Liquid fire."

Squeezing her inner muscles, she slid down his length.

He moaned through clenched teeth. "Jesus, you're hot and tight as a second skin." His hands tightened on her hips "I want . . . ." A shudder ran through him and he thrust hard into her, holding her tight to his body. "I want to get so deep inside you . . . ." His grip eased and she slid up his length. "But it feels too damn good to stop moving." She rotated her hips, sliding back down. He couldn't help but hold her there, all her heat squeezing around him. Then slowly, she eased up. "So it ends up being this sweet, desperate torture I never want to stop."

He rolled his hips, thrusting up, pulling her down tight until their bodies nearly fused together. "I could turn myself inside out trying to get deeper."

"It's like that for me, too." Her hands gripped his shoulders, her nipples dragging against his chest. "When you're deep inside me, it's like being complete. So full I almost can't stand it, and yet love it." She lifted and this time cradled his head to her, drawing him to her breast. He was so out of his mind he took her offering with what sounded far more like a growl than a groan. She couldn't sink all the way down while he suckled, so she took him in shallow dips, teasing them both to the point of madness.

Then he had to release her. He had to let go so he could sink all the way in.

"Look at me."

He did. Almost got lost in those kaleidoscope-colored eyes. Almost came as she eased down his length, her thighs quivering against his, her insides hugging him in a scorching embrace. He tried to hide, dropping his gaze to where they joined, but her palms on his cheeks brought him back. Demanded he stay. The loss of that last little barrier left him raw. Naked down to his soul. Wide open.

That was hard. Hardest damn thing he'd ever done—meeting his wife's gaze while she accepted him into her body.

What was worse, what was making his throat tight and his eyes burn, was the absolute trust staring back.

She'd forgiven him.

He told her what he'd done. Laid bare his sins and thrown them at her feet like a goddamned dare and she'd forgiven him like it was nothing, welcoming him home with no conditions. She didn't understand. She couldn't.

She lifted her body, sending shivers over his skin. Met his gaze with no hesitation. Made love to him as if he deserved this. Her. "I can't." He couldn't accept her forgiveness. Couldn't forgive himself.

Her palms squeezed. "You can." Her breath came in sharp little gasps. "You will. For me, you will."

He wasn't sure they were even talking about the same thing. When it was just him, the past, present, future all blended together. None of it mattered. A shiver ghosted over his skin. Christ, she felt good.

"We can't have a future if you're living in the past." She lifted, dragging her breasts against his chest. "Be with me here."

"You deserve better than me."

"I'm the only person in charge of my life and must do what's best for me." She threaded her fingers through his hair and jerked his head back against the headrest, forcing him to stare up into his fierce little wife's beautiful face. "I'm in charge of my life and I chose you, my Chief. If I deserve better, give me better."

He found himself nodding. She was right. They were married. Soul-mated. He was the only one who could give her better. He *wanted* to give her better because she was so much more than he deserved. "Okay."

"Now that you're here with me, will you make love with me?"

Right. *Yes.* He flipped their positions, laying her across the couch. It wasn't right, her back landed on the arm of the love seat which forced her head back over the edge and her breasts up. He still held her tight, an arm behind her, the other tunneling between her and the cushions to grip her ass.

It wasn't right. She couldn't be comfortable and yet he couldn't stop. Not with her thighs spread so wide to accommodate him. Not when she was arching against him. Not with her drawing him closer, her nails digging into his shoulders. Not with those desperate whimpers and pleas teasing his ears.

So he made fucking love to his wife. His mouth rough against her breast. His hand kneading her ass. His hips slamming against her. He completely lost his mind. Taking everything she had to give. Giving everything he had back. And when her body squeezed his, when she shouted her release, her hands caught in his hair in an unyielding grip. He let go. The world went dark except for the flashes of light behind his eyes, his whole body locked up, and then he was cussing. Cursing the vulnerability even while reveling in it. Cussing and telling her he loved her and pouring himself into her until he was pretty certain he *had* turned inside out.

He held her hips tight and dragged them both down until the armrest pillowed her head. She was smiling and sloe-eyed. Her lips were bruised and her breasts had turned soft. Every now and then a lingering pulse of orgasm tightened her pussy around him. He stretched out over her, all those sweet compact curves against his bulk, and nuzzled her neck, feeling wide open and wounded and somehow . . . at peace.

She wrapped her arms around him, her hands gentle, her fingers lifting gooseflesh as they trailed down his spine. "You fucking love me?"

His cheeks heated. Not the most romantic of gestures. "I fucking do."

"Mm." She giggled.

He propped himself up on his elbow. He'd never heard her giggle before. "You're beautiful."

"I feel beautiful when you look at me." She cupped his scarred cheek in her hand. "I love you, too, my Chief. And if I ever leave you . . . ."

His entire body went rigid.

" . . . it'll be with the expectation that you'll follow."

31

They'd gotten lucky for once. When they arrived at the rendezvous, they discovered they had just shy of fifty on their team. Fifty. Granted, most of them were his own Zeros outfitted in full armor for the first time since their injuries. Macie had already split up the troops into teams and outlined a plan.

They were south of the DCZ's wall, where CorTech's five skyscrapers and six landing pads were located. The building they wanted—the one with Larkin Astor's office—sat right smack in the middle and had four landing pads attached to the roof. That building was the tallest—sixteen stories. The entire backend of the property was surrounded by chain link and razor wire.

Josh finished cutting an opening in the fence and Donovan held it open for the others to slip through before going through himself. Josh was doing good. With his prosthesis on, his limp was hardly noticeable.

He checked his watch. Team One and Team Two should be at the security huts at the front and back of the property. They'd take down the guards, silence any alarms, and watch the vid-screens, feeding them information over their coms.

Two other teams, Three and Four, would secure the ground floor and roof of Astor's building, providing sniper cover when it was time to exit.

Donovan led Team Five: Sorcha, Macie, Josh, Jaybird, and two DCZ soldiers, Wrecker and Acosta. They were going for the big prize: the CEO, Larkin Astor. They all hunkered down behind some tarp-covered shipping crates.

"You know, if CorTech hadn't raised the rent, we wouldn't have so much help." Macie grinned. "It's almost like . . . fate."

Jesus, that's all he'd talked about tonight. Fate. "I control my own destiny, thank you." Donovan turned on the mike in his helmet. "Everyone in position?"

Each team sounded off.

"Team One and Two, move out." This was the part he hated. Waiting, unable to help, while someone else risked their lives. Their com remained silent. His heart beat faster until he started breathing hard despite doing nothing more physical than squatting.

Sorcha put her hand on his. Their gazes met. She didn't say anything. Didn't have to. She knew exactly what was going through his mind.

"Hut Two, secure."

A quick, reassuring smile flashed over her face.

Team One hadn't checked in. Shit. They might've underestimated the number of guards. The Blue Helmets could've seen his teams in the security cameras. What if—

"Hut One, secure."

A breath burst out of him, making him lightheaded. He was too old for this shit. He gave Sorcha's hand a squeeze. "Stay close."

"Always, my Chief."

"Let's go."

They hot footed around the shipping crates, between two buildings, and across the landscaped lawns to the center building. "Head for the delivery entrance."

Macie got there first. Checked the door. Shook his head. "Wrecker."

The burly male shouldered past Macie, wired a device to the door, and motioned them back. A second later, there was a pop and a tiny flash of light. The door swung open.

No alarms went off. The teams stationed at the security huts had done their job.

Wrecker motioned them in with a haughty bow.

The loading docks were empty. They had at least three more hours before the employees showed up for work but Larkin Astor liked to get ahead of the day, finishing his work while the grunts were rolling out of bed. "Where to?"

Josh already had his Saph-link out and a holo-schematic of the building displayed. "All the way to the top. Astor's office is in the center of the sixteenth floor."

"Of course, it is."

"We can take the service elevator up to the fourteenth. That's R-and-D." Josh shrugged. "Should be empty this time of morning. It'd be best to take the stairs the rest of the way so we don't get caught in the elevator with no exit." Josh turned left, then right. "There." He pointed. "You'll see the elevator in about a hundred feet."

Donovan only got about forty feet before he ran into a Blue Helmet coming around the corner. The guy's eyes widened. He lifted his weapon.

Donovan fired.

The Blue Helmet slammed back against the wall, bounced off, and crumpled to the ground.

Donovan's heart pounded in his ears. There was no blood. No . . . .

"Still on stun." He closed his eyes. The damn thing was still on stun. The shots came slower when on stun. If there'd been more than one guy . . . .

While the others secured the body, Sorcha came around his side. "Are you sure you want to do this?"

No. "Yeah." He flipped the switch off stun.

"You made a vow. There's no shame in wanting to be true to it."

There'd be shame in losing his wife because he couldn't protect her. "I'm good." He almost sounded convinced. His voice was steady. He even forced a devil-may-care grin. Except she missed it because she was staring at his hands.

He was shaking.

Shit. "I'm good." *You better be, dickhead, you only have twelve hours to find proof.*

She opened her mouth to argue, but the others returned. Jaybird winked. "You lovebirds ready?"

"Yeah."

He led the way, almost bypassing the door to the elevator. Christ, he had to get his shit together. "Macie, take point."

Macie quirked his brow.

He shook his head. Held the door open and let the others pass before entering the elevator. He didn't know why he was reacting like this. He hadn't had this problem when fighting the vladsets. Didn't have this problem when hunting marks.

Then again, he never killed his marks when hunting. And those vladsets had taken his wife. This was his first live-ammo fight with humans since the rebellion and he was going in for info, not to save a life.

Her life will be in danger if you fuck this up.

He'd push through. He was fine.

Sorcha sidled up to Josh. "Tell me how you walk."

The kid looked startled. Laughed softly. "It's a prosthesis. I don't like wearing it during the summer unless I have to because it's uncomfortable in the heat." He paused and lifted his pant leg to show the steel bar underneath. "It's a fake leg."

She gave Josh a wide smile. "The warriors on Troon would make good use of fake limbs."

"Enough chatter." How could they be so calm? The place was damn near empty and he was close to a panic attack. "This is us."

The doors opened and Josh led the way across the hall to the stairs. They quietly climbed the last two flights, with Donovan bringing up the rear. Macie led them through the door to the sixteenth floor and came to a full stop. He held up his arm.

There were voices ahead. There shouldn't be at four in the morning. What the hell was going on?

"Hey!"

Donovan whirled around. Three Blue Helmets stood in the hall behind them.

They opened fire.

He returned fire, diving for the stairwell door. His shoulder hit the door before it clicked shut and he slid onto the landing. Scrambling up, he eased into the doorway. Peeked around the corner.

Blaster rounds scorched the doorjamb. "I'm pinned." He leaned against the wall and looked out the other way.

Sorcha huddled in an adjacent hallway. She winked. Held up one finger. *Hold on.*

He released a slow breath, trying to slow his heart and quiet his breathing.

Another round of blaster fire lit the hallway. A male shouted.

"We're clear." Macie's voice.

He came out of the stairwell. Wrecker, Josh, and Acosta were with Sorcha. Macie and Jaybird had circled around and ambushed the Blue Helmets. "Good job."

Macie shrugged. "You took the first one out."

Josh motioned down the hall. "We want to turn right at the third hall."

They'd only gone a few steps when a voice over the com said, "Stop."

They froze.

"This is Team One Leader, You're gonna come to some double doors when you turn the corner. That part of the building is full. It's set up like a maze, with your target in the center surrounded by lobbies, workstations, and labs."

"Ten-four." Donovan shared a look with Macie. Not good.

Team One Leader continued, "Something's going down. Maybe a board meeting. Several employees are in the main work area. They got a shit-ton of security in there."

Macie lifted his visor. "All that security and no one's noticed us?"

"I'm missing something," Leader One said into the com. "They're all focused on the interior doors by the south entrances near the boardroom, but I'm not seeing whoever they're waiting for. Someone not chipped, maybe."

Sorcha must've looked confused because Josh explained. "CorTech chips their employees to make them easier to monitor. They program their chips with security clearances and record their whereabouts during the workday. Instead of live holo-projectors, they trace the chips through the building."

"Team Three Leader here." The voice was accompanied by a bit of static. "Might know what they're waiting for. We got some unusual activity on the landing pads. An unknown ship at pad four and an IgA ship at pad two."

Did they have a visiting dignitary?

"The Blue Helmets are running around out here like pissed-off ants, trying to protect their hill."

"Team Two Leader in position. Permission to continue distraction?"

"This might be good." Josh lifted his Saph-link. "They're focused on the other direction. Their forces are split."

Yeah. He'd love nothing more than to catch Prax and Astor together. Donovan nodded. "Team Three and Four. Can either of you spare soldiers to send to the south entrance, sixteenth floor?"

"Team Four, I can spare three."

"Team Three, sending seven."

"Have them hustle. Team Three, permission to continue mission is granted." He looked up at his own team. "If you're low on power, replace the charger now."

They all obeyed without comment, except Macie who cocked his brow. "Thanks for the reminder, Mom." Yeah, overkill, maybe, but he wasn't taking any chances. As it was, he needed every ounce of discipline he had not to order Sorcha to go back. She'd see that as a lack of trust, though. "Let's go."

They turned the corner and the double doors came into view. Secure blast doors. No wonder no one came running—those doors were thick and soundproof. "Wrecker."

"On it."

Wrecker wired the door and waved them back. Way back. "We're giving them some shock and awe. Take cover."

Donovan pulled Sorcha into an alcove with restrooms, curling his body around hers and spoke into the com. "Blowing the doors." The floor trembled with the force of the explosion. Smoke filled the hallway. "Go! Go!"

They ran into the room under the cover of the smoke and spread out. An alarm drowned out the screams and shouts before being silenced. The lights shut off and red emergency beacons lit the room. He squinted. Switched the power in his visor to night vision and everything came into crisp focus. Civilians ran for the exits. The Blue Helmets came at them from two different hallways across the room.

Sorcha ran and dropped to her knees. Slid across the wood floors, shooting, taking out four Blue Helmets. She was fucking brilliant.

Donovan opened fire, taking out two others. She was damned good with her weapon which made some of the tension ease out of his shoulders. "Teams Three? Four?"

A voice came over the com. "ETA three minutes on Team Three."

Donovan grabbed the edge of a worktable and flipped it, motioning Sorcha closer and drawing her down beside him.

"Team Four here . . . we can't get the landing pad blast doors open. Stand by."

"This is Team One . . . landing pad doors are unresponsive. Be advised Team Five, they'll need to be manually opened from the inside."

Great. "We need to get those doors open for our reinforcements." The smoke started to clear. Blue Helmets were pouring into the room. "Stay down." He glanced behind them. A crew of Blue Helmets approached their rear, coming fast.

He stood, fired at a Blue Helmet who had Sorcha in his sights. Used the butt of his weapon to slam another in the face. He aimed at a third, but his fucking power clip had ejected. He hauled up the guy he'd dropped, using him for cover and did a kamikaze run at the next Blue Helmet. He hefted the body up and shoved it away from him into his opponent. Took his knife out and slammed it hilt-deep into the last guy's neck as they all tumbled to the ground.

When he stood, he grabbed one of the Blue Helmet's weapons. He turned—

Where the fuck was Sorcha?

His gaze searched the room. Blue Helmets outnumbered them four to one. "Sorcha!"

Her voice came over the com. "I'm with Josh. We're getting the doors open."

His pent-up breath exploded from his chest. "Right." Okay. At least she wasn't in here. He lifted the weapon he'd commandeered and went back to work.

Celeka wasn't sure what she'd expected, but it wasn't this.

"Watch it!"

She ducked back behind a wall as a blast glanced off her helmet. The acrid scent of scorched plastic and singed hair tickled her nose. Was it burning? Hurting her? She yanked the helmet off and let it fall to the floor.

Josh jerked his head to the opposite hallway. "I'll give cover, you run."

When he let off a bevy of shots, she darted across the hall. She leaned around her corner and fired, providing Josh cover.

"Keep going, I'll watch our backs. Take a right two halls down. Get those doors open!"

Gunfire erupted as she turned, her team caught by Blue Helmets. She had to get the doors open. She ran around the corner and stumbled to a halt, her eyes widening. "Maman."

Dedia, why was she here? CoreTech employees, Blue Helmets, and Zero's bodies littered the hall.

Donovan was right about everything. Maman was in league with CorTech. Rage welled inside her and she lifted her hands.

Maman shrank back.

The guards shrank back.

Her hands warmed, but no flame appeared.

She brought her hands to her face, focusing all her energy into bringing her flame to the surface. Nothing. Not even a sputter.

You're a disgrace. Pathetic. Wretched. Donovan finally trusted her, let her fight for him, and she was letting him down. Letting everyone down.

Maman straightened. Smiled. "Take her."

You can do anything you set your mind to.

No, she wasn't giving up. She lifted her weapon and fired.

When the first shot hit Maman, she stopped smiling. Celeka ran, a war-cry on her lips, firing at Maman.

One of the guards stepped in front of Maman, protecting her from the barrage of fire. She tried to dodge past. He grabbed her weapon, wrenching it from her hand, throwing her off balance.

Celeka withdrew the knife on her belt and leapt to her feet. She wouldn't go down without a fight. She'd take at least one of them with her. She ran at the wounded vladset. Swung her arm and sliced down his chest.

He backhanded her. She slid across the floor and into the opposite wall. Her face throbbed as everything spun. Up. She had to get up. Had to fight. She rolled onto her side and pushed up into a squat. Her knees gave out, sending her back to the floor.

The guard grabbed her by the hair, dragging her along the slippery floor behind him. She reached up with the blade. Tried to slice his arm. His leg. Whatever she could reach.

Josh careened around the corner and froze. Eyes wide. Indecision crossing his expression as he took in her position.

Oh, Dedia. "Run!"

Josh opened fire. Vladset skin was thick and required multiple shots before one would fall. He didn't seem to understand. He kept aiming for a new target after hitting one. The warriors raced forward; war staffs raised.

The guard who had hold of her, stopped next to Maman. He pried the knife from her hand.

Across the hall, a warrior knocked Josh's gun away, backing him against the wall. With one swipe of his staff, he angled the blade across Josh's throat.

The skin split and a bib of crimson poured down Josh's chest, spurting over the warrior. Josh sank to the floor, his eyes dimming.

She whimpered, "No."

"These humans with their toys are no match for vladset warriors," Maman huffed. "They can't even put up a decent fight." She motioned to the wounded guard. "Bring her."

What a fucking shit-show. Donovan managed to get around to one of the hallways leading to Astor's office, but everyone else was engaged. A never-ending supply of Blue Helmets seemed to ooze out of the hallways. He needed to get to Astor. He needed him to call off his guard dogs.

"This is Reese, going for the prize."

"Ten-four. Mason, here. Not far behind."

Donovan hauled ass around the corner, and down the hall. Heart pumping in his chest. The voices of his men chattering in his helmet. Adrenaline pounding through his veins.

There'd be Blue Helmets guarding the office.

Still, he didn't stop, he turned the blind corner, weapon raised. Bam. Bam. Both Blue Helmets slumped to the ground, tendrils of smoke snaking up from the front of their helmets.

Donovan kicked in the door to the conference room and strode inside. His gaze searched the faces huddled against the far windows and locked on Larkin Astor. "Call off the Blue Helmets."

They'd all die if they couldn't stop the seemingly never-ending flood of opposition. "Now." He lifted his weapon. "Move."

Astor didn't move. Didn't speak. Something was wrong.

At least fifteen men and women stared back at him from where they cowered. Their eyes kept jerking to the right.

Damn. Someone was behind him.

He turned.

A blast caught him in the arm, throwing him back. Pain lanced through his shoulder. A second shot hit his thigh. When a third shockwave wracked him, it took him a minute to realize that was him hitting the wall, not another shot.

Shit. He'd dropped his weapon. He still had his sidearm. Problem was it was holstered on his right hip and his right arm didn't seem to want to work.

He struggled to a sitting position and froze, his gaze locking onto the business end of a blaster before sliding to the person holding it. "Salcedo."

She swaggered forward. "Should've stayed out of this, Reese."

His arm wouldn't move. Blood was running down his sleeve, dripping on to the floor. He tried to get his leg under him, but . . .*fuck!*

"Everything would've been fine if you'd stayed away from Troon." She shook her head. "If you'd just brought the marks to me, you'd have gotten paid. I'd have made sure they disappeared before Prax could question them. But no, you and Macie always seem to be where you shouldn't be."

He blinked, trying to remain conscious. Shit, he'd had everything backward.

"Don't." She motioned to one of the suits, but kept her weapon trained on him. "Astor, get on the computer and download the frequencies."

For a few seconds, everything around him faded.

When he regained consciousness, they were arguing, Salcedo and Astor. Donovan breathed deep, trying to bring everything into focus. This was not the time to check out.

He couldn't believe she'd do this. No wonder she'd told him the CorTech contracts were "off the books." Why she'd gotten so nervous when Prax butted into their conversation. She hadn't been worried he'd been "compromised," she'd been trying to see if Vessa had sold out her and her buddies at CorTech.

"You'll do as I say." Salcedo's voice edged up.

Astor shook his head. "This wasn't part of the deal. Vessa—"

"She's no longer important. *Download the frequencies.*"

A blast echoed in the room. A woman dropped to the floor. Crying. Clutching her leg. Jesus. Salcedo shot a civvy.

"The frequencies. Now, Astor."

Astor folded his arms over his chest. "You can't do this."

She winged him. Blood bloomed through the arm of his gray suit.

Astor staggered back, grabbing his arm. His eyes wide. "You're crazy."

"I'm impatient." She motioned with her weapon. "The frequencies, *now.*"

Astor went to the terminal at his desk.

Donovan's vision blurred. Maybe from blood loss or shock. He dug his thumb into the wound on his thigh and everything came back into focus. "Frequencies?"

"Light frequencies." She gave a tight smile. "The vladset queen made the discovery of the century and our CorTech friends were thinking of keeping the sempisim all for themselves."

Everything was coming together now. "Sempisim?"

She nodded. "It's beautiful. Depending on the amount of heat and what you mix it with, you can use sempisim for anything from porcelain to steel."

He remembered the yellow light. "And if you shine the right light frequency at it . . . ."

She grinned. "Boom."

"Why?"

Salcedo snorted. "Come on, Reese. You know better than anyone that doing the right thing is a wasted exercise. I work for me now. For my benefit." She glanced at the executive, but kept the gun trained on Donovan. "Almost done?"

Astor nodded. "Almost."

He needed to keep her talking, distracted. "You don't think Vessa will come after you?"

"I'm not worried about her. Not anymore." She shrugged. "She'd never find me, anyway." She motioned toward Astor. "How much—"

Donovan shifted to lift his gun.

Her gaze narrowed. "Hey." She frowned. "Don't move. I'd hate to end our friendship by having to kill you."

He held up a hand in surrender. "I was convinced Prax was the traitor since he had access to the vladsets." He snorted. Salcedo was Earth's ambassador. "How much did CorTech pay you for your silence?"

Salcedo grinned. "Enough to retire far, far from here. But then I thought, why stop there, when I can have so much more?"

Christ, she'd double-crossed the IgA and now she was double-crossing Astor. She wasn't giving Donovan any opportunities to attack. Nor had she allowed him to bind his wounds. He was bleeding out, right here on the goddamned floor. He was getting weaker and Salcedo was getting more anxious with every delay. Astor still stood at the terminal, taking his sweet-ass time transferring the frequencies.

"Done."

Finally.

Larkin Astor met his gaze and grinned. Oh, dear God, what had he done?

"Give it here." Salcedo held out her hand palm up.

"There's nothing for you." Astor folded his arms over his chest. "I sent the frequencies to Vessa, cc'd the IgA, and erased the files."

Holy. Shit.

"Bullshit." Salcedo edged closer to Astor, shaking her weapon. "You better be lying or I'll kill every last one of you."

Astor shrugged. "You backed me into a corner, Salcedo. I've gotta protect the company."

Did he have a death wish? Salcedo stormed across the room, grabbing the wounded woman by the hair and dragging her up to her knees. Donovan reached across his body, wincing at the sharp pain in his shoulder. He eased the blaster out of his holster.

"I'll blow her brains all over the room." She shoved the muzzle against the woman's temple. Shit. He didn't want to kill Salcedo. The IgA would want her for questioning. She might have partners. They'd need her testimony to go after Vessa.

The door burst open.

Salcedo whirled around, releasing the woman and aimed at the door.

"Whoa! Hey." Macie's hands went up.

Donovan aimed for the shoulder of her outstretched arm and fired.

Her weapon dropped to the floor as her body jerked.

Macie leveled his weapon at Salcedo. "Uh-uh-uh. Don't make me kill you." His gaze flitted to Donovan before returning to her. "You all right there, Reese?"

"Peachy." He got to his feet and the room spun. He motioned to Salcedo, while he fought the dizziness. "Cuff her, will you?"

"On the floor." Macie pushed her down. "Hands behind your back."

She only lifted one hand behind her back. Macie squatted down, one knee to her back and wrestled her other arm behind her to cuff her. She cussed through the whole thing. "Damn, Salcedo. You got quite the vocabulary." Once she was cuffed, Macie straightened and looked at Donovan. "What'd I miss?"

— · —

32

After having so much freedom, stepping into the glass cage was disheartening. Maman had wanted her dead. She must have. She'd blown up the *Red Slag* thinking she was on it. So why have a change of heart now?

"You'll tell me why you're doing this after you fought so hard to be rid of me."

"I'll be rid of you again soon enough. Permanently."

"You'll explain! Why did you blow up our ship?"

"That wasn't me. Granted, I had some sempisim bolted to the belly of the *Red Slag*, but it was one of CorTech's allies that destroyed the ship. I sent Quimet to bring you home."

"Why?"

"That doesn't matter now. What matters is that your sister has become troublesome. You'll ensure Mujara remembers her place and behaves. I shouldn't have allowed either of you to live. That was a mistake. One I'm ready to remedy. Now, dress appropriately." She waved her hand to the corner of the cage.

Cooling cloths.

I'm beautiful and comfortable in my own skin.

Celeka backed away. Bad enough to be stuck in this cage away from her chief. She wasn't putting those back on. "No."

Maman gasped. She'd never dared to tell Maman no before. Always she thought through the consequences and came to the decision rebellion wasn't wise. Her mouth watered and her belly roiled. She swallowed and lifted her chin. Maman could fuck off.

Her lips curved at the fact she'd adopted one of her husband's sayings.

My opinion matters even if others don't agree with me.

For several moments, Maman stared, taking in her expression and posture, no doubt searching for a weakness. "Your time with the chief has changed you."

"Yes."

"I came here to demand the humans give me what I paid for. I expected a fight. Oddly enough, even though I didn't get to speak to Larkin Astor, he downloaded the frequencies to the ship." Maman whirled around to speak into the ship's com. "Hover over CorTech main building and drop one crate."

The ship shifted and Celeka braced her hand against the glass wall of her cage. "What are you doing?" Inwardly, she cringed. She needed to sound more vladset while speaking to Maman.

"You'll wear those cooling cloths and cover your weak form or I will level that building."

Donovan was in there. Macie. Their clan. She could face Maman's punishments herself but couldn't allow others to be punished for her. She undressed, removing the borrowed body armor, letting each piece fall to the floor until she wore nothing but her v-bands.

Maman hissed.

Still, she hesitated. The cloths wouldn't harm her. There was no reason not to put them on. It was a small sacrifice to save those she loved.

Slowly, she leaned down and picked up the cooling cloths.

She wound the bands around her limbs and torso, the rough fabric chaffing her skin. Her hands shook. Her breathing became uneven. Her heart pounded. With each limb covered, it was like being buried alive. There was a new veil at the bottom of the pile. She attached it to the cloths around her head and lowered the fabric over her wrapped face. "Let's leave, Maman. I'm covered now."

"Test the frequency."

"No!" She slammed her fist against the glass.

On the vid-screen, several humans had come up to the roof to investigate. Zeros—what was left of Team Three—not Blue Helmets. They crept closer to the broken crate. The yellow laser shot down from the ship and a blinding light filled the screen. The ship rocked from the explosion. Flaming bodies flew through the air. Brick and mortar caved inward, leaving the skeletal remains of twisted support beams.

The plume of black smoke began to disperse in the wind, revealing a massive hole in the roof. The flames prevented her from seeing how deep it went. More of the building collapsed.

She waited, breathless, for the flare of fire within her that would signal her mate's demise, but it didn't come. Donovan was safe. But the others . . . .

The screen went dark as the ship began its ascent and Celeka slid down the wall of her cage and pulled her knees to her chest. Tears streamed down her face beneath the cooling cloths.

She understood now, the guilt Donovan suffered. She hadn't killed those men, in all likelihood Maman would've done this no matter what, but they'd died trying to help her. She rubbed her hand over her heart. She underestimated Maman, thinking she'd leave the humans alone. And she gave Maman too much credit, that she'd keep her word and leave them alone if she complied.

Maman came close to the cage, her lips curved into a smug smile. "No more disobedience. Your chief is gone."

Beneath the wraps and veil, a slow smile spread on her face. Maman thought she mourned her mate? Good. Maman thought she'd broken her? Perfect.

She wouldn't underestimate Maman again.

She wouldn't give Maman credit where none was due.

Nor would she fail her chief a second time.

Like the rattlesnakes of Earth, she curled up and waited.

Donovan leaned against the wall while Wrecker and Acosta cuffed the board members. They'd have to explain how the hell all this came about to the IgA. CorTech would be disbanded, which would leave the citizens of Glendale in a lurch with no company to protect them . . . but that wasn't his problem. DCZ could deal with it.

"Where's Sorcha?"

Macie shook his head. "Don't know. Haven't heard her online in a while."

Panic clawed inside him. Everything urged him to tear the place down searching for her. "Wrecker, Acosta—take these people out and hold them. No one leaves." He needed to find Sorcha now.

A shock wave roared through the building, making his ears ring and his heart stutter. Parts of the ceiling caved in, dropping around them as flames roared down the outside of the building past the windows. The glass cracked and shuddered.

"Down!" Donovan dove for cover under the conference table as the windows imploded. Razor-sharp shrapnel tore through the room. He landed hard, pain spiking from Salcedo's shots. Smoke and debris filled the air, making him cough, which sent agony through his wounds. He pulled his visor down. He caught sight of Macie at the other end of the table. He had Salcedo. The other civilians huddled under the table with Wrecker and Acosta. Mouths open. Cuffed hands raised to protect their heads. Cuts and scrapes bleeding freely on their debris-streaked faces.

Jesus. He closed his eyes to avoid the terror on their faces. Images of the past, of bodies, burnt and twisted and sprawled over the wasteland of what was once Luke AFB flashed through his mind. People he'd known, worked with, reaching for help with limbs that had no skin.

"Reese!"

His eyes opened and fixed on Macie. His mouth was moving but he couldn't hear anything. No, that wasn't true. His ears had stopped ringing. He could hear the civvies screaming. The building moaning.

Focus. He slammed his hand against his helmet. The com sputtered and then Macie's voice came through.

"Breathe, man. Your vitals are freaking out."

Right. He sucked in a breath and tried to calm his racing heart.

The building swayed, making the steel beams in the walls scream and plaster crumble. He sucked in a hard breath and for heart-stopping seconds, he was sure the whole damn thing would collapse around them. Something heavy rammed into the table above them hard enough to splinter the underside of the table between him and Macie.

Finally, the building went silent. He waited, meeting Macie's gaze. There might be a secondary blast. The building might settle and then fall. He shifted his gaze to where the civvies huddled. "Shut up!"

Silence.

For a few heartbeats, there was no sound except for the shuddering whisper of a nearby fire. A roof tile dropped to the floor. "What do you think?"

Macie had his eyes closed, listening. "If we're gonna go, we go now." He opened his eyes. "No stopping. No searching."

Sorcha.

His chest tightened. "Everybody up!" He needed to get them to the bottom so he could come back. "Hustle. Use your shirts to cover your nose and mouth and follow him."

No one argued. They wanted to stay alive. They wanted someone to follow.

He crawled out from under the table, used it to pull himself up and leaned against it. He was dizzy, weak from blood loss.

Wrecker hauled the wounded woman over his shoulder and walked past, the others following.

Come on, focus. Get them out and come back for Sorcha. He forced himself upright. He could do this.

He took one step and pitched forward as darkness descended. He tried to fight it. Tried to hold onto consciousness.

"Reese?" Macie's voice wavered through the com. "Shit."

Everything went quiet.

33

"Chief Reese?"

Donovan stretched and forced his eyes open. He was groggy as hell. He didn't recognize the blurred figure hovering over him. "Who're you?"

"Naal Amari. I'm a med-tech with DCZ."

He sat up, fully awake. The explosion. Sorcha. "My wife. Did they find her?"

Naal's lips pressed together. "You'll be fine. We healed the two blaster wounds. We did have to do a blood transfusion, which—"

"Where's my wife?"

"I'm sorry, Chief Reese." Naal looked down at his hands and when he met his gaze again, the sympathy there struck the air from Donovan's lungs. "They were unable to find her. A third of the building collapsed. We have cadaver dogs out there. They're still finding bodies but the ones we're pulling out . . . ."

He understood. "They're dead." . . . But he didn't. The words made sense. He comprehended them. But he couldn't *accept* them.

Naal nodded.

Donovan spied a stack of clothes on a chair. "Those for me?"

"Yes, Mr. Mason dropped them off. He should be here soon to take you home."

Fuck waiting. He stood, pulling off the flimsy hospital gown, and grabbed the pants.

"Chief Reese, I must insist you wait. After the transfusion, it's imperative you rest the next few days. Some of the test results were . . . unusual, and—"

She could've been trapped, if he hadn't passed out, he could've gotten to her before the building came down. "I'm going. Now." With his pants on, he shoved his bare feet into boots he didn't bother lacing and strode out of the room and down the hall. The doctor followed him, buzzing around him like a pesky mosquito. He didn't listen. He walked out the front doors and into the quad—barely pausing long enough to grab a beer out of the cooler, ignoring the stares of his runners—not stopping until he got to his rundown piece-of-shit trailer. He never should've brought her here. He dropped the clothes he hadn't bothered putting on and opened his beer, staring at the couch.

His lips curved. Last time he stood here like this, his little warrior had slapped his beer right out of his hand.

He rubbed his chest. Ah, God. That hurt. That one tiny memory. The couch blurred the same as when the beer had covered his face, only this time it was tears.

He'd lost his wife.

Took him thirty-five years to find her, wasn't even married a fucking month, and he'd lost her. Donovan drained the beer, dropped the bottle on his pile of clothes, and pressed the heels of his hands to his aching eyes.

She was right. They shouldn't have come to Earth. He lost two weeks traveling here and spent one day fighting with her. Fifteen days he could've spent making love to her. Teasing her. Making her love him.

God, he was a first-class fuck up.

The door opened and Macie walked in. "They told me you checked out of the infirmary against orders. You look like shit, Reese."

Donovan glared.

"We, uh, ran a full scan during treatment."

He didn't care. He headed back to his room. Maybe to get dressed. Maybe to lock Macie out. He couldn't decide.

"Your DNA is changing."

She was gone.

"The scanner actually diagnosed you with early-stage blood cancer of all things." Macie followed him through the trailer, right on his heels so he couldn't close the door. "We stopped the machine before it attacked the new cells."

Great, he was babbling the same rubbish as the doctor. "What are you saying?"

"You're carrying cells like hers. They're altering your DNA. The doctors need some time to figure out exactly what they're doing, but they don't seem to be harming you. Actually—"

Donovan stepped over the mattress and dragged a shirt off one of the hangers in his closet. "What?"

"Your body registers as three years younger than at your last scan. The new cells seem to be repairing damage caused by age." A smile ghosted over his lips. "Guess she was right."

My flame will keep yours youthful and through you, mine will gain experience.

Now that was cruel. "What good is that?" Great. An extra fucking few years to miss her. To mourn her.

"You were trying to chase her off yesterday."

Donovan turned to stare at the callus prick. "What the fuck are—"

"Way I see it, we're all even now."

Even?

"You led the rebellion, which you have punished yourself for, for the last three goddamn years and as a result you lost your wife. Karma came calling. Now that you finally got that out of your system we can all start off fresh."

"You bastard. I lost my wife and you . . . you . . . ." He couldn't even get the words out. Wasn't he even sad about Sorcha?

Macie leaned his shoulder on the wall. "If you had it to do all over again, what would you change?"

"I . . . ." He motioned around him. "I wouldn't have come back here. I shouldn't have made her suffer for my mistakes."

"You'd quit punishing yourself?"

"Wouldn't be about me. I'd focus on taking care of her. Making a life with her."

"Even if she insisted on facing Vessa?"

"Anything." He lowered himself into the rickety chair in the corner. "I'd fucking do anything to have her back."

Macie nodded. "Good. Let's go get your wife."

Donovan stood. And when his knees gave out he sat. "What?"

"We got into the security feeds in Building C. Sorcha wasn't inside when it blew."

Relief swamped him, making him lightheaded and anxious all at once. "Where is she?"

Macie drew in a deep breath. "Don't freak."

He stood. "Where is she?"

"With the vladsets. Vessa was at CorTech. Sorcha and Josh ran into Vessa and a contingent of vladset guards. She's alive."

Plans raced through his head. He wasn't sure how long he was out for, how much of a head start Vessa had. They'd have to breach security on Troon, which seemed impossible but— "We need a ship. Maybe two. Men. Weapons."

"It's sorted." Macie pulled out his sidearm, pointing it at him.

Donovan frowned. "What the hell are you doing?"

He smiled. "God, I've waited a long time for this."

Macie fired.

— • —

34

Donovan's whole body went painfully rigid, and he toppled onto the bed. Holy hell, Macie shot him.

"Notice how I did that so you fell on a nice soft mattress?" He grumbled something, maneuvering around the bed.

If Donovan could've moved, he would've glared. If he could've spoken, he'd tell Macie to fuck off.

Was this revenge for all the times he'd drugged Macie to get him in a life-pod or were his motivations more nefarious? Did this mean Sorcha wasn't alive? No. No. He'd known Macie for years. They were damned near brothers. Had each saved the other's life. Had always backed each other up.

Something rattled. Hangers clanged against the metal rod in the closet. What the fuck was he doing?

Macie squatted down next to the bed, tipping his face so Donovan could see him. He had Donovan's duffle bag. "Bet right about now, you're questioning my motives. Wondering if I've finally snapped and intend to hurt you. You're probably reminding yourself we go way back. That I'd never. But you're wondering and that sucks, doesn't it?"

Paybacks. Yeah, they were a bitch.

He stood, maneuvered Donovan into position and slung him over his shoulder in a fireman's carry.

Big as Macie was, his bony-ass shoulder dug into Donovan's gut with every step.

"Yeah, I've waited a long damned time." He headed toward the ship. "For once, *I* have the great Chief Master Donovan Reese at *my* mercy."

He carried him out into the early morning sunlight.

"You know one of the things I always liked about you, Reese?"

Liked? Past tense?

"You're predictable. After the UN fell, you were more so. But now . . . ."

But now, what? Macie walked in silence, nothing but broken asphalt crunching under his boots. "You being unpredictable is making me unpredictable because I can't tell if your pattern has changed, or, hell, maybe mine have." He chuckled. "Or maybe the pattern is getting longer, you know, like the design on a nautilus shell gets longer closer to the edge. Thing is, for the first time in my life, I'm hoping the pattern *has* changed . . . because if it's not, if it's just getting longer, bad shit is coming for us and that's making me . . . crazy." He cussed. "You probably have no fucking idea what I'm talking about, do you?"

Not really. Macie talked about patterns and chaos and fate when he was drunk or gambling and he'd never made much sense.

"I know what you do, asshole. You left out that book on subliminal affirmation once. Read the whole thing." Macie snorted. "Bastard. Every fucking time I sit down to play cards, I hear your goddamned voice in my head. 'I don't need to gamble.'" He pitched his voice in a falsetto.

Christ, he didn't sound like that.

"'I have control over my life.' Blah, blah, blah."

"Everything's ready, Mason." Wrecker's voice. "We'll meet you there." SOB didn't even ask why Macie had him slung over his shoulder like a bag of potatoes.

"Thanks." Macie staggered, paused, jostled Donovan to adjust his position. "So now it's my turn, Reese."

Donovan stared, he couldn't do anything else. Just watch the cracked asphalt pass by the backs of Macie's legs.

"Hm, what ideas should I plant in your brain? 'I want to give Macie all my money?'" Macie strode up a docking ramp with a CorTech logo. "How about, 'Every time there's a pretty girl around, I want to tell them how great Macie is?' He turned down a corridor. "Nah, can't do that. Maybe on account of I have some asshole's voice rattling around in my head telling me I'm better than that."

Yeah, Macie was pissed. Even though he'd had the best of intentions, maybe trying to plant thoughts in Macie's head was a bit of a dick move. He hated seeing Macie fuck-up over and over. Every time the guy started doing well, he sabotaged himself and

Donovan couldn't stand watching the destruction. It was his fault so he figured it was up to him to fix it.

Macie dumped him into the life-pod and leaned over. "But you're wondering now, right? What's good ol' Macie gonna do? I bet . . . ." He grinned. "Yeah, I *bet* you're shitting yourself over what ideas I might plant." He nodded. "Notice I didn't even flinch over the gambling reference."

The affirmations didn't last forever and he'd been too busy with Sorcha on this last jump to refresh Macie's.

"What about, I, Donovan Reese, only like to wear women's thong panties. Backward."

That didn't paint a pretty picture.

With quick, efficient motions he stripped Donovan down to his skivvies. He lifted a syringe of neurotropic drug and chuckled. "Every time you hear a voice in your head, you're gonna wonder if it's mine." He put his hand to the corner of his mouth. 'Oh, was that my idea, or Macie's?'" He shrugged. "Guess we'll never know, Chief."

Macie would never hurt him, but he had no doubt the son of a bitch would embarrass him given half the chance.

Macie's eyes narrowed. "Huh. Weird. Your eye's twitching." He winked. "Must be pissed." He waggled his brows. "Am I right? Guess I know the first command— 'I will never hurt Macie.'" He disappeared but his voice echoed, bouncing from one part of his brain to another, repeating until it faded.

"How you feeling? You starting to get all warm and fuzzy? Is my voice echoing?"

When he woke up, he was going to flatten the SOB.

He nudged Donovan to his side and started placing the electrodes on his muscles. After a moment or two, he spoke again. "My wife loves me." That one sentence rebounded from one side of his brain to the other, repeating in softer and softer frequencies until disappearing altogether.

Jesus. At least he'd always waited until Macie was asleep and unaware.

He rolled Donovan onto his back and got right up in his face. "Did you hear me? She does. My wife loves me. Is it echoing? It will be by the time I'm done with you, you stubborn ass."

"My wife loves me just the way I am." Macie placed more electrodes along his legs, while his words bounced around Donovan's mind. But did she? He wasn't always loveable. He was stubborn.

"She loves my honor marks."

He couldn't argue. She'd fixated on his scars from day one.

"I will not hurt my wife's feelings by allowing my stupid guilt to get in the way."

No. He wouldn't. Not anymore. When it was just him . . . no one got hurt, but he refused to subject his wife to that again.

"I will keep the money I earn to support me and my wife and our future children. I can live and work from any planet I want."

Panic started to well up inside. He'd already said he would. But should he? The ghosts of the men and women who'd died because of his orders or deeds crept into his mind. What would they think if he lived out a blessed life while their loved ones suffered alone?

Macie came back into view. "I, Donovan Reese, will live not only for myself, I'll live for those I lost. I will *live* for them."

His throat wanted to close tight. He couldn't move, couldn't open his mouth. He was suffocating.

"Stop it. Breathe." Macie lowered the oxygen mask over his face and air rushed into his lungs whether he wanted it there or not.

Macie leaned down, bracing his arms on either side of the life-pod. "I, Donovan Reese, am worthy of my wife."

Jesus. Stop! His eyes burned and his whole body shuddered.

There was no give in Macie's eyes, though. He wasn't done. "I am worthy of a thriving business. I am worthy of living a full life and working toward seeing all my ambitions fulfilled. I will get my wife back and we will be happy together because I deserve happiness. I deserve joy and friends and wealth and good health." The suggestions came so fast they blurred together, bouncing around in his head.

A tear slid down his temple. He couldn't hide it. Couldn't turn away. Couldn't close his eyes.

Macie wiped the moisture away. "I won't be embarrassed because Macie's my goddamned brother and will never admit this to anyone." He started to turn away, but paused. "Oh, and by the way. You don't have to be sorry about me being captured back when I was spying. I forgave you before you even knew to apologize, dickhead."

Tears slipped unchecked down his temples. Even as his eyes grew heavy. Even as the sound of Macie's voice grew dimmer.

"I am worthy."

— • —

35

Donovan sat up with a start, heart pounding in his chest, ears ringing, skin pebbled over with gooseflesh. He shivered. Blinked. The room came into focus.

He pulled the oxygen mask off. Ah, God. He was hungry. Groggy. His throat was dry as the Sonoran.

Macie thrust a cup into his hand. "Sips. I'm not cleaning up your puke."

Several sips later, he eyed Macie from his peripheral. "Uh, listen—"

"Don't." Macie tossed his clothes onto the life-pod. "I never bring it up. You're not allowed to, either."

Shit. He hadn't thought Macie ever remembered. Fine. He'd respect his wishes. "Where are we?"

"Vladset airspace. Oddly enough, no one's come to check us out yet. This ship is a newer model, so unless the vladsets had a major jump in tech, we should've arrived before Vessa."

Donovan nodded. "IgA?"

"En route."

"You updated them?"

"Yeah. We've got six ships full of armed Zeros." He grinned. "Vladsets don't like taking on old, scarred warriors. So we're fighting with a bunch of old, scarred warriors."

He found his first smile. "Wonder who Vessa left in charge."

"Someone who's not watching their airspace." Macie shrugged. "I was thinking things over and the question that kept coming to my mind was, what does Vessa need Sorcha for? At this point, killing her would've been easier. At first, I thought maybe she intended to hand her over to the IgA, but then I remembered something I read when researching Sorcha—by all public accounts, Vessa has never left Troon."

Donovan pressed his fingers to his eyes. This was important. He needed to concentrate. "She wanted her alive when we were on Asteria. She wanted Sorcha to go to CorTech—probably to get the frequencies."

"Vessa took care of that, so why not kill her? I couldn't figure it out, so I called Prax. Guess what? Troon has a new queen."

We always protected each other.

"Mujara." Donovan stood. "Sorcha said they put Mujara in the arena. They were trying to punish her to get Sorcha's cooperation. Right before the Saph-link blew, she saw vladsets flooding into the arena toward Mujara. She thought they were attacking. They must've helped her stage a coup, instead."

Macie nodded. "Vessa needs Sorcha to control Mujara."

"Get the com up and hail Troon."

Four guards met them at the airpad. He glanced at Macie. "Stay back and stay on the com. If we get the okay, coordinate our teams."

"You got it."

Donovan allowed the guards to search him and take his weapon. "Don't lose that."

One of the guards, a half-breed with no spikes grinned and slipped it into an empty holster at his hip. "Queen Mujara allowed you to land. That doesn't mean she'll allow you to leave."

Right. The guards pushed him into motion, leading him to the throne room. They weren't nice, but they didn't rough him up, either.

He slowed when they entered the throne room. Mujara. Her skin tone was different from Sorcha's, a rich sienna. She had no spikes and she was taller and curvier than her sister. But she had that same thick, white hair and her eyes were the same circular rainbows of color. "My Queen."

"Am I—" Her voice broke and she started again. "You'll tell me if I am truly *your* queen."

Something was off about her. "You're Sorch—" She wouldn't recognize the name Sorcha. "You're Celeka's queen and Celeka is mine."

Her gaze shifted, locking onto the half-breed holding onto his weapon before returning. "You'll tell me if Celeka wishes to be yours."

This was Mujara. Her first concern was for her sister. He smiled. "I think she could do better than an old war-dog like me, but she keeps telling me I'm hers."

Her lips pressed together as she repressed a smile. "You'll tell me if my sister is well. Is she with you?"

Interesting. She slipped, asking instead of telling. His gaze shifted to the half-breed. His speech pattern had been more human-like, too. He returned his attention to Mujara. "Your maman stole her from me. I'm here to get her back."

Though she sat straight and tall, she gripped her hands together so tight her knuckles paled. "You'll tell me why I should grant you such a boon, when by all appearances you didn't protect her."

"I'll never make that mistake again." When she continued to regard him with no expression, his patience expired. "I'm taking my wife back from Vessa. I could give a shit how many vladsets I have to kill to see that happen, which includes you, though I'd prefer not to hurt you because my wife would get upset."

Mujara's lips curved at one corner. "You'll tell me if upsetting Celeka would truly bother you."

"An angry wife is not a pleasant experience."

A shiver ran through her, so slight, he'd have missed it if he hadn't been watching. "Maman is exiled."

"I think she plans to return. To use Sorcha—Celeka—to earn your compliance."

The half-breed strode forward, speaking rapidly in vladset before switching to English. Donovan's gaze narrowed. Standard he'd expect, but not English. "My queen, even if what he says is true, if any of them kill Vessa. . . ." Whoever killed Vessa would rule.

"I want my wife. My wife wants me. That's all. I can assure your reign is recognized by the IgA. No one will kill Vessa. We'll capture her."

The two glanced at each other. They were softening to the idea of their help.

"Sorcha and I are soul-mated. I won't leave without her."

"That's twice." Mujara stood and came down the stairs of the dais. She matched him for height, she had to be a solid six-foot-three of gorgeous woman, except she was baring her teeth and he didn't think it was meant as a smile. "You'll tell me why you call my sister by another's name."

The threat in her gaze was implicit. He swallowed. "She told me her vladset name meant Wretched. My wife is beautiful. Kind. Everything to me. I refuse to dishonor her by her old name. Her name is Sorcha now, which means 'brightness.' She's my brightness. My little flame."

Her lips parted. She started to walk away and then glanced back, giving him an unreadable look. "Jaqmori, you'll give the chief his weapon. He'll need it." She turned her back and returned to her throne. Only then did he noticed the small puckers of skin running down the center of her back, like the way the skin puckered around a spike or a nub—only there was nothing there. She did carry scars, though. Small and round, evenly spaced about an inch apart.

"Do you fear my sister, Chief?"

"No." He was still trying to figure out what those puckers were when she turned and sat, her gaze eye-level with his. "Should I fear you, my Queen?"

The corner of her lips curved. Trembled. "Only if you hurt my sister."

Jaqmori put a hand to his ear, listening. "My Queen, Vessa is hailing you." He motioned to the vid-screen hanging near the dais.

Donovan backed away. "Where can I stand so I'll be out of the shot?"

She pointed to a pillar near the wall where the vid-screen was located. "Stay back there. Don't speak."

"Say whatever you have to say to get them here." He went to the alcove and waited. He hoped to hell Mujara was on his side. She could've killed them. Could've imprisoned them. There were far more vladsets on this planet than humans. So far, she seemed okay. Still, something was off about her. While her tone and posture signaled she was in command, she had the same habit as Sorcha of gripping her hands in front of her when nervous.

The vid-screen clicked on.

They exchanged no pleasantries. "I have your other half, Mujara." Vessa waved her hand to the side where Sorcha stood in a small glass box. "I'll give you one hour to place your guards in cells and to return to your cell. You may leave one guard free who will take the holo-projector and record the cells to prove to me you are all well and truly contained."

Mujara's gaze slid to his briefly.

He nodded. *Do it. Get them to land.*

"You'll tell me what you'll do if I refuse."

"I'll destroy her."

In the background, Sorcha shook her head, her voice hollow from behind the glass. "Don't listen, Jara!"

The screen went dark.

Slowly, he came out from where he hid.

Mujara continued to stare at the blank screen. "I'll have your word you'll not harm my people."

"You have it."

"And you'll swear to me you'll not allow Cele—Sorcha to be harmed."

"Never."

She nodded. "You know how to work a holo-projector?"

"Nah, but I'm sure someone in my crew does."

"How do you plan to defeat Maman?"

He smiled. "I don't."

36

Sorcha stared out of her glass cage, hands spread flat on the clear walls for balance. Had Mujara truly given up so easily? Maman would punish Mujara and anyone who helped her attempt to take the throne.

The guards pushed her cage down the corridor on a hover-lift. Aside from the contingent of warriors with Maman, no one was around. "I want to see Mujara."

Maman didn't turn around. "You forgot the rules, Celeka. You'll tell me if you require a reminder."

She wasn't to speak to Maman. Not directly. If she kept forgetting herself, their punishment would be unbearable. "No, Maman."

The warriors pushed her cage around a corner and down the corridor leading to the throne room. Ahead, she caught a glimpse of a shadow behind one of the pillars. Her heart leapt in her chest. It was too soon for her chief to have arrived, but perhaps Mujara hadn't given in as easily as it seemed. She held her breath, waiting for Mujara's guards to jump into the corridor, surrounding Maman and her warriors.

Maman ordered ten guards to remain in the corridor.

The rest of them entered the throne room without incident. They pushed her cage to the center of the room and lowered it to the floor.

Maman walked straight up the stairs of the dais and reclined on her thrown. She waved a hand to the guard on Sorcha's right. "Oolock will interpret for us."

Her gaze shifted to the warrior. She recognized the name. Oolock was Mujara's betrothed, but he was loyal to Maman. In fact, before she'd heard his name, she'd thought he was Maman's consort. She couldn't imagine what Maman could've promised him to gain his favor over Mujara's. He had scars down his chest and arms. His gaze was direct if a bit arrogant.

Maman shifted on her throne, getting comfortable. "You'll tell me, Celeka, what the IgA knows."

Oolock repeated the question.

Sorcha opened her mouth to answer, but movement caught her gaze. She turned.

Her chief. Her heart stuttered in her chest. She pressed herself to the glass closest to him as if drawn by his presence.

Around her, the warriors drew their weapons.

He wore his battle armor, his weapons hanging from the belt on his hips, but he also held a vladset war staff.

He gave her a wink before stepping farther into the room and turning his attention to Maman. "You don't speak to my wife. You're not good enough."

Maman stood. "You'll tell me how—? You'll tell me where Mujara is?"

He remained silent. Pulled his gun.

"You can't think to fight us all." She nodded to the warriors in the room.

"I don't intend to fight *you* at all."

Other humans came out from behind the pillars, surrounding the warriors. All were armed with both blasters and vladset war staffs.

The Zeros. She grinned. Her heroes.

Donovan frowned and motioned to her. "Are you wearing those because you want to?"

Her heart thumped in her chest. She pulled at the cooling cloths, eager to have them gone. When she stood in nothing but her ribbons, Donovan's gaze raked over her before he nodded. "I don't ever want to see those again."

"Yes, my Chief."

Maman stormed to the edge of the dais. "You'll tell me why you dishonor her by putting her on display?"

"My wife is gorgeous."

The queen hissed, "Do you see my marks, Chief?" She stroked her hand over her bare arm, showing off the self-inflicted scars. "These are all the souls I've consumed. Each has made me stronger. Fiercer." She sneered. "You had best hope your weapon can shoot fast enough. It'll take far more than one blast to stop me from crushing you."

Donovan grinned. "I only need one."

One shot? What was he thinking? "My Chief—"

He met her gaze. Shook his head.

"One shot couldn't take out a vladset child."

"One." He nodded. Certain. Confident.

He was mad.

"You think so?" Maman's eyes narrowed.

"I know so because I'm not fighting you." He lifted his weapon, aiming to the side, and with one shot, shattered the lock holding her glass prison closed. "She is."

One shot. For her. He did trust her.

The only problem was that her fire was gone.

Maman's eyes widened and she stepped back, glancing over her shoulder.

Sorcha pushed the door open on silent hinges, her gaze flickering to the walls on either side of Maman's dais where the instruments of her past victories hung. War staffs. Battle sabers. Combat pikes. Spiked ravagers. Her gaze slid back to Maman. "I don't fear you."

"You should." Maman waved her hand at the room at large. "Kill them."

Battle erupted behind her—gun blasts peppered the scrape of metal sliding against metal and the smack of wood on wood. Sorcha paused. Should she—?

She shook her head. Donovan and the Zeros would fight well, she needed to focus on Maman. "Why should I fear you?" She strode closer to the weapons. Closer to Maman. "You are old. Tired. You can't rule in truth so you use lies and manipulations to control. You have no honor and so imprison Mujara and me while you hide in the palace from the people." She climbed the stairs to the dais.

"You're brazen to say such things." Maman backed away. She was almost to the far wall where weapons hung. "You don't look like a vladset, nor act like one. The gods are obviously so ashamed of you they've even taken your fire."

If she had her fire, Maman would be running in fear, like she'd run from Mujara.

"You *are* a wretched thing. Weak." Maman whirled toward the weapons.

Sorcha ran for the opposite wall, her hands grabbing the first weapon she could reach—a saber. She turned, raising her weapon.

Maman's war staff slammed down on the curved blade of the saber. Her red eyes bored into Sorcha's. For what felt like an eternity, they stood there, struggling to force the other back. Sorcha braced one foot on the wall behind her. She launched herself forward, pushing Maman back. Not much. Not enough for her efforts to feel like a victory, but enough to free her blade.

She raised her weapon. "I am not weak."

37

Donovan braced himself as a big son of a bitch strode toward him. He holstered his blaster and gripped the war staff with both hands.

He made sure all the Zeros had vladset weapons to fight with. This was risky, fighting with weapons they hadn't trained with. But he'd be damned if they stood there shooting inefficient weapons while the vladsets mowed them down.

He glanced back toward the doors. Macie was stuck out there in the hallway with ten warriors standing between him and the doors. He hoped to hell he was holding his own.

While the warrior was still a full ten feet away, he swung his war staff, the curved blade at the end swooped out, whipping past Donovan's nose, so close he felt a breeze.

He retreated a step.

Lesson One: Use the full range of the weapon.

He swung the staff like a baseball bat and when the vladset blocked, the clash reverberated down his arms. The vladset put pressure on the far end of his staff, forcing Donovan's to the side and down, trapping his blade against the floor with his own.

Shit.

Donovan jumped, using the staff to maneuver his weight into a two-legged kick that sent the vladset stumbling back and freeing his blade.

Something flashed across the vladset's face . . . maybe the first twinges of respect. He raised his staff for a new attack. At the same time one of the Zeros shot him in the chest. The vladset glanced down at the blackened smudge on his left pec. The warrior's gaze narrowed on Donovan.

He shrugged. "We may be small, but we travel in packs." He lunged forward as another blast hit the vladset in the same spot.

This time the guard visibly flinched. Donovan swung his staff. The vladset was too slow in blocking and the blade swept down his arm, shaving off a thin slice of skin.

Hell, yeah. First blood.

No sooner had Sorcha blocked the blow than Maman swung again. Fierce. Vengeful. Intimidating. She gave no quarter, giving Sorcha no time to recover from one bone-jarring clash before delivering another.

Sorcha was in full retreat, backing away with every blow, only managing to block. Unable to get ahead of Maman's blows long enough to make an offensive strike. Her arms burned with effort. Her shoulders ached. Sweat beaded on her skin, trickled down her back. She gripped her weapon so tightly, the metal handle of her weapon was giving beneath her hand.

No, that wasn't possible. She was melting it.

Her fire was back!

Sorcha grinned, blocking Maman's next blow. Maman might be bigger. Stronger. Meaner. But Sorcha's fire burned brighter. She allowed her flame to take over. Thought of heat and smoke and flames.

Her hair lifted around her as if a breeze blew up from the floor. The long white strands twirled around her face.

Maman's blow faltered, glancing off her saber.

The air around her shimmered with heat, giving Maman a watery, smudged appearance.

Maman backed away, her eyes widening.

Flames licked over her skin, at first as soft as a whisper on a hot afternoon and steadily increasing until a thousand butterfly wings beat against her skin. Flames flickered over her skin, giving everything an orange-red tint. The vortex caused by the heat lifted her, allowing her to hover over the stone floor. "You told me once a fight is only honorable if all opponents use their every advantage. If you wish to fight for your throne, it will be an honorable fight."

Behind her, a human screamed, his voice raw with pain. *Please don't let that be Donovan.*

She rounded on Maman, leaving her nowhere to flee but down the dais stairs. Behind her, the Zeros outnumbered the remaining vladsets. Sorcha's grin widened. "Do you remember when I burned you, Maman? Do you remember the smell of your flesh melting from my fire? I could've soul-devoured you then. Had I put my hand on your face and forced you to inhale my flame, you'd have gone to our ancestors with no soul, with my mark upon your face, like Quimet."

Maman backed away, then lunged forward, swinging her pike.

Sorcha dodged the blow and grabbed hold of the pike. The wooden handle ignited under her grip, edging up the long hilt toward Maman.

"You can't do this, Sorcha. The people will never follow you."

No. They wouldn't. She looked nothing like the vladsets and while they might appreciate her for freeing them from Maman, they'd grow to resent her and rise to revolt. Mujara could be like them. They'd follow her. "I'll rule with honor, Maman, something the people haven't known in years. They'll follow me."

"They won't. You're not like us." Maman swung the pike a few times, trying to put out the flames and when they flared brighter instead, she threw the weapon at Sorcha.

She knocked it aside. No. She was like herself. "You have shamed our people." She floated down the stairs. "Lying. Colluding behind the IgA's back. Murdering the humans you had a secret alliance with."

Maman backed away. "You know nothing. I couldn't stand idle while the IgA sanctioned us to the point of starvation."

"Had you followed the IgA's laws, there'd be no sanctions. Because of you, Troon faces exile from the IgA which will be far worse than the paltry sanctions we've faced in the past."

"We have the sempisim now; we can own the IgA." Maman stumbled. Righted herself. Glanced around for escape. "We don't have to bow to them. We can rule together."

Sorcha shook her head, edging forward. "It's not about bowing. The IgA is about cooperation. The IgA is about a larger community. For trading and protecting each other."

"Celeka, if you harm me—"

"I become queen." Her voice snapped, echoing through the throne room. She lifted her hands and lunged.

Maman truly looked afraid now. She darted into the glass cell, tripping and sprawling on the floor.

Sorcha slammed the door and melted it to the frame, sealing Maman inside. "Unlike you, I don't wish to be queen. I have everything I need. Everything I ever wanted. You and your throne can go to Dedia for all I care."

Now for the remainder of the guards.

Donovan may have drawn first blood, but the warrior had drawn second, third, and fourth blood. The noise in the room had diminished. Whether his team was winning, or lying on the floor bleeding out, he couldn't say. The asshole wouldn't give him a moment's respite and he was starting to think it a miracle he'd survived this long.

He swung wide, leading the vladset to swing out to block him. Instead of following through with the wide arc, Donovan pulled back on the staff, drawing it to him, out of the way of the warrior's before thrusting straight out. The blade sank an inch into the vladset's thick hide.

The warrior grabbed Donovan's staff, pulled it from his body and shoved him away, causing him to stumble over a body on the floor. He stepped wide, trying to avoid other bodies and remain on his feet. He turned and barely blocked what would've been a lethal blow. Still, the force threw him back, right into someone.

They fell together, tangled in a mass of limbs and . . . flames.

Holy Hell. He jerked away at the same time Sorcha doused her flames. "Dedia, no!"

There was no time to check himself for injury. He scrambled to his feet, preparing to fight the warrior racing toward them, grabbing Sorcha and pulling her behind him. Even as he braced for attack, she patted him down, stifling the spots on his clothing that had ignited.

Shit. His weapon. Where was—?

Blasts fired all around them, making the warrior slow down. He jerked a few times and slumped to the ground.

Jesus.

He put his hand to his chest as if he could slow his heart manually.

Jesus.

He braced his hands on his knees, closing his eyes. He didn't want to see what the damage was. He knew she hadn't burned him on purpose . . . .

"My Chief?" Her hand stroked over his back, his neck. Hot. She'd been aflame, she should be burning the shit out of him, but . . . .

He opened his eyes. His clothing was singed. Blackened in places. But his arms . . . he'd had his arms around her for a few seconds . . . and his skin only showed the palest pink irritation. He straightened and turned.

Sorcha threw herself into his arms, wrapping herself around his body. Smoke rose from her skin . . . she was so hot she was steaming. "You didn't burn. I was so scared I think my heart stopped."

Hot. She was hot, but no less so than when he pulled her from the burning room on Asteria. And yet steam rose from her skin.

It's changing your DNA.

Holy hell. He drew in a deep breath and exhaled. "We're okay, little flame."

"I thought . . . I thought . . . ."

"Shush. I know. I did, too."

"How did you get to Troon so fast?"

He smiled and kissed her hair. There was only one answer. "You left me. So I followed."

— • —

38

"Where's Macie?"

His gaze tripped away from hers, scanning over the bodies of vladset warriors and humans littering the palace floor. Shit. "He got caught outside with some warriors who stayed in the hall." He turned his com on. "Macie?"

"Here." Macie ran into the room with Wrecker, his gaze scanning the wreckage.

"You look like hell." His weapon was missing and he was covered in blood. He wasn't moving like he was hurt, though. "What the hell happened to you?"

He jerked his thumb over his shoulder, opened his mouth, and then shook his head. "Prax just landed. He's on his way in."

Sorcha stiffened.

"Relax, little flame. He's coming for her." He pointed to Vessa. "Not you."

Her gaze flashed back to Donovan's, then dropped. "I'm sorry I failed you in our battle on Earth."

"There's nothing for you to be sorry about. I'm sorry I wasn't with you. That *she* got to you."

"We didn't even know she was there." She lowered her face. "My flame didn't work on Earth. I didn't tell you. I think the heat on your world was too strong, but I didn't say anything because I didn't want you to think me weak."

"You're the strongest person I know. We're going to have words about your lack of faith in me later."

She tipped her chin up. "Words?"

He winked. "You know what I mean."

Heat flashed in her eyes before she glanced away. "I've caused much trouble."

"You're worth it."

She frowned. "Because I'm beautiful? Because I can succeed in whatever I put my mind to? Because my opinions matter?"

She knew. His face grew warm. "I'm sorry. I shouldn't have. I wanted you to see yourself as I see you. If it makes you feel better, Macie got me back."

A small smile curved her lips.

Maybe he wasn't in too much trouble. "I love you, Sorcha."

When her gaze flicked to his, moisture pooled in her eyes. "Truly? Even though I've made you do everything you never wanted to do?"

He tipped her chin up. "You were right to push for this. Mujara will make a good queen. We're safe from Vessa. The IgA knows what happened. We're safe because you wanted to fight. And you did so brilliantly, capturing her instead of killing her."

"Yes, Princess. You did well."

They both looked to the side as Prax entered. He paused and bowed.

Sorcha pulled away long enough to return the gesture.

Prax gave Donovan what he hoped was a *mock* glower. "I hear you almost had me in league with Vessa."

Donovan shrugged. "I couldn't figure out why you were so insistent I kiss my wife."

Prax smiled. "I've been liaison for Troon for ten years. I like to think I've learned a thing or two about vladset culture and history. For example, prior to Vessa's reign, soul-merging was a peaceful ceremony for married couples who were love matches. However, Vessa was frustrated by what she saw as a lessening of full-blooded warriors. She thought mating for love instead of bloodlines weakened the race, so she banned it, convincing the population soul-merging was a precursor to soul-devouring. You two, though, you were a love match."

Sorcha smiled. "How did you know?"

"Chief Reese was concerned with your happiness right from the start, wanting to ensure you had a choice as to whether you stayed married. He stood in front of you, shielded you from us like an over-protective mate. And then you came forward and tried to smooth things over, not wanting him to get in trouble. You protected each other. On my home planet, that is the surest sign of a love match." He clapped his webbed hands together. "Now, where is your sister?"

They both looked at Donovan.

Christ, he'd forgotten about Mujara. "Um, she's down in one of the cells."

Sorcha gasped.

"It was part of the ruse. She's fine."

Macie walked over in time to hear the exchange. "I'll grab her." One of the warriors lying prone on the ground grabbed his leg. Macie grabbed a staff sticking up from a body and stabbed until the arm dropped to the floor. "Fuck's sake." He stumbled back. "I thought they were all dead."

"You okay?"

"Yeah." He motioned over his shoulder. "I'll get Mujara."

Donovan turned back to his wife to see her staring at the dead warrior. "Did you know him?"

She swallowed. "He was Mujara's betrothed."

"Oh." Macie had damned near hacked the warrior in half. "Did she love him?"

"I doubt it. He was loyal to Maman."

"Then what—?"

Prax chuckled. "Don't worry, Princess. One way or another, the IgA would've insisted your sister marry someone loyal to us."

Donovan's gaze bounced back and forth between the two. "What am I missing?"

Sorcha shrugged. "Macie has inherited everything Oolock owned, including Mujara's betrothal contract."

Donovan closed his eyes. Macie was going to shit himself. A low rumble of laughter started low in his belly before breaking free. Oh, he'd enjoy the hell out of watching this.

Sorcha slapped his chest. "This isn't funny. If Macie hurts Mujara's feelings, I'll have to punish him."

Donovan pulled her close. "If anyone can tame Mason, it'd be someone like you." He pressed his lips to hers and she sagged against him.

"You think she could?"

"You tamed me."

"That's because I love you, my Chief, so I had to tame you to claim you for my own."

"You love me?"

"Oh, yes."

Prax grinned. "I knew you were a love match. Macie and Mujara will work out as well. They'll have the two of you to help them find their way."

Donovan grinned. "I know exactly what advice to give him."

Sorcha raised her brow. "What's that?"

"The same advice he gave me. Show no weakness and take whatever the queen is willing to give."

It was good advice. The best advice he'd ever taken.

Acknowledgments

A huge thank you to Mike Schneider who works in an applied physics laboratory and is absolutely brilliant. He spent quite a bit of time (probably more than he wished) chatting with me about piloting, what futuristic planetary re-entry might look like, tidal locking, and how physics relates to gambling (the last two for the next book). I can't express how grateful I am for his patience and willingness to share his knowledge. I have no doubt that when he reads Wretched, he'll have a hearty laugh when he realizes that after all those discussions and shared articles, I still took some creative license. Thank you, Mike.

ABOUT THE AUTHOR

Cara Crescent currently lives in the Pacific Northwest with her children and three overly dramatic ferrets. When she's not writing, you can usually find her curled up with a book, engrossed in a movie, or playing video games with her best friend.

Please visit her on the web at www.caracrescent.com

ALSO BY

The Original's Trilogy

The Beacon

The Shadow

The Knight

Sating Ember Moon

The Last Hero Novels

The Last Marine

Wretched

Don't Let Me Forget You

www.ingramcontent.com/pod-product-compliance
Lightning Source LLC
Chambersburg PA
CBHW031933110726
47902CB00001B/166